CONMAN

CONMAN

RICHARD ASPLIN

NO EXIT PRESS

First published in 2009 by No Exit Press,
P.O. Box 394, Harpenden, Herts, AL5 1XJ
www.noexit.co.uk

A CIP catalogue record for this book is available
from the British Library.

ISBN 978-1-84243-294-5

2 4 6 8 10 9 7 5 3

Typeset by Ellipsis Books Limited, Glasgow

Printed and bound in the UK by JF Print Ltd., Sparkford, Somerset

For Neal, who'll enjoy this one
and
Luthfa, without whom nobody would be reading this.
Love to you both.

part one

now

"Wait, is this a *con*? Is *that* what this is? Are you . . . are you trying the old switcheroo with me? Trying to pull wool over my leg? . . . You *swear*? Because let me tell you right now Mr Cheng, I've had exactly my legal limit of swindlers, marks, mitt fitters, cacklebladders and cold pokes. Up to the brim, you understand? Enough to last my family and me a long time. To last us the twenty years I'm going to have to spend in prison if I don't get the thing back, in fact . . . Yes, *prison* Mr Cheng. Big grey building? Nestling among ten acres of beautiful rolling concrete? Conveniently situated for group showers and buggery, ideal for the first time offender . . . ? Well it's where they put husbands like me. Idiot husbands who . . . Look, look forget it, just give me a price to have it back. A proper price. And don't try and jerk the fleece behind my back. How *much*?"

Look, I'm sorry. I didn't mean to come back in here disturbing you. It's just the police said . . . and it's a bad line and it's . . . Sheesh, bad day, bad line. Bad from the beginning. From forever. I won't be long. I'll get out of your hair. You get back to your drink. Ignore me. Really, I'm sorry.

"What? But you only paid . . . No *way*? Redford *and* Newman? *Nobody* gets Newman. The guy's a hundred and sixty years old, wired up to an intravenous bottle of spaghetti sauce in Beverly Hills . . . *Swear*? . . . Lord. Okay okay, but c'mon Mr Cheng, *please*. You gotta do me a better price. My daughter . . . there'll be lawyers. *Lawyers*. They'll say I . . . God. C'mon, it's *me*, Mr Cheng. *Please*?"

Woahh, sorry, sorry. Oh look, I spilt your drink all over – let me – barman? – let me get you another. Sorry. It's just this guy on the phone, he's got my life in his hands and the police told me to . . . oh it's too complicated to explain. *Barman?* Whatever my friend here is having.

"Look Cheng, haven't you been *listening?* I don't *have* that kind of money . . . Well, I–I'm suggesting you *lend* the thing to me. Just for a day or so. An *hour* even. The police said I needed . . . Yes, the *police*. Where do think I've *been* for the last . . . Well when's your buyer *coming?* . . . Oh for Chrissakes, three hours? . . . No, I keep telling you, I can't, I don't have it. Look I beg you, *promise* me you won't sell it . . . Earl's Court, I'm in Earl's Court. A pub. The World or The Map or something . . ."

Huh? *Atlas?* Oh, oh thanks. Thanks my friend. How's your drink? Look, I'm sorry about the yelling. It's just . . . well as you can see from the suit, it's been quite a day. This? I dunno. Corn syrup I think. I know, I know, it stinks. Hell, I didn't get any on your . . . ? Okay. Again, I apologise.

"Cheng? My friend here says it's The Atlas. Earl's Court . . . No, round the corner from there. Look, give me three hours. I'll come up with something. I *have* to. Jane's dad is saying she'll . . . *God*, just *promise* me you'll stall your . . . Fine. Three hours."

God. What am I going to do? *Three* hours. So that's . . .
   Right. Of course. *Great.*
   Excuse me? Hi, sorry to bother you again. My watch is . . . well it's . . . long story. Do you know what time it is?
   Already?
   Okay okay. Right. Calm. Don't panic. That gives me . . .
   Christ.
   Do you know if there's a bank or anything around here? Pawn shop maybe? Somewhere I can sell . . . I don't know, a lung or something? What's a lung worth? You want to buy a lung? A kidney? How are you for kidneys?
   Hn? Sorry, I know, I'm in a bit of a . . . I've had a . . .
   Oh no, no I couldn't, I don't want to intrude on your –
   Oh that's kind, you're very kind, thank you. You don't have a tissue, do you? My nose is beginning to . . .

Thanks.

Man. What time did you say – ?

God. Where's that phone. Let me . . . let me try her again. Sorry. I'll just be . . . I need to make a . . .

"Hello Jane, I – ? Edward *please*. I need to talk to . . . Because I'm her *husband* and I *love* her and I need to explain. We're a family, I would *never* . . . I *can*, I can *prove* I didn't . . . well no, but – in a few hours. I'm trying to . . . *Please* Edward, tell her . . ."

Christ.

"Tell her she . . . she is everything to me. *Everything*. You understand? She's why I get up in the morning. She's the whole point. Her and Lana. They're the whole point. They're all I have. Forget the rest. Forget the shop. That's not who I am. *They* are who I am. My family is who I *am*. You take them away from me and I have nothing. *Nothing*. And . . . and tell her if she goes and she takes our daughter I might as well be guilty of everything they say I've done because then I'm in prison for life anyway. You tell her that. Edward? Edward, are you – ? Edward?"

Great.

I'm sorry. You don't have to –

Well thank you. Thank you, that's very kind.

God look at my shirt, this syrup's getting all over the place. I'm gonna take my jacket off, put it on the . . . oh God it's everywhere. Gaah, my lighter's all sticky. My cigarettes. All my pockets . . . God it's all over the letters, damn. Sorry, can you hold . . . thanks.

How? Oh you don't want to know. No really, enjoy your drink. I'll just . . .

Man. Man oh *man*.

And look at *this* place. *Look* at it. It's like nothing *ever* happened. The bar, the tables. Like they were never here.

Hell, maybe they *were* never here? Maybe it's me? Maybe I'm losing –

Letters? Oh. You're still . . . Thanks, sorry, my mind's all . . .

From? What *these?* Ha. *From* indeed. Her name's . . . God she was right, they even *smell* like her. Go on, sniff the . . . *see?* Clever touch. And look, even the postmarks – oh you can't see, they're covered in this damned syrup. God it's everywhere. My matches, my notebook . . . Anyway, trust me. Postmarks. Six months ago. Four months ago. Here, this one? Three weeks ago? Clever clever clever.

In fact, you want clever? Let me read you . . . No I insist, here we go, you listen to this. You won't believe it.

"*. . . and the more I think about your words Neil . . .*"

Oh, that's me. Neil Martin. How do you . . . oh, sorry. It's just syrup, it'll scrub off. Sorry.

Anyway –

"*. . . the more I think about your words Neil, the more I feel the same. Just thinking of you gives me a sick ache inside. A painful teenage ache. Because that's how it feels when we're apart, Neil. Painful because I imagine you with her and I know I have to wait so long until I can see you again . . .*"

And so it goes on. Pages and pages.

Oh you don't want to know. Just hope you never meet her. Don't meet her or anyone like her. And don't . . . don't lie to the only person you ever truly loved, either. Don't ever do that.

I'm rambling. I know, I'm sorry. I'm a bit . . .

Just tell them the truth. I mean it. Tell them *everything.* Tell them you *love* them. *Show* them you love them. Every day. Don't let it . . . don't let it in. Don't let it *start.* Do the right thing. Do the good thing.

Oh, and balance your chequebook every month.

I know, I know, it sounds . . .

But I mean it. Every month. Cheques and balances. Keep on top of it. And plumbing too. Hell, don't neglect your plumbing.

That's how it can start.

Or at least, that's how it all started for me.

All . . . all *this.*

Plumbing. And a cheque. Writing a very small cheque.

Or rather, wishing I had.

God, I *really* wish I had.

then

one

With a deep breath, I flipped back through the stubs, reading out loud to the room like a teacher at registration.

"Okay okay. Let's not . . . let's not *panic*. C'mon now. Visa bill. Next bill. Road Tax . . ."

Dionne Warwick warbled from the stereo, goading me to take it easy on myself. Fat chance.

". . . vet bill, Mastercard, Jane's Visa. If you have not yet received a new cheque book . . ."

I flapped it shut and a little more panic squirted into my stomach.

It wasn't there.

Not that I really expected it to be there. It wasn't the cheque-book for the business account and it hadn't been there the first six times I'd checked it. But it was my last hope. A clutched straw at the bottom of an over-scraped barrel on the beach at Last Resort.

Throat tight, I chewed the inside of my cheek, trying to keep my gaze from the corner of the desk. From catching the eyes of the two beautiful female faces smiling from behind the glass of a silver photo frame.

Shit, I thought.

The cat wandered into the lounge idly across the Easiklip flooring and sat on the rug, looking up at me. I swivelled around in my creaky chair to look at him straight.

"Did you pay it?" I asked. "Please. Tell me *you* paid it?"

Streaky remained silent, but his look said he would have paid it if he'd been asked to. Because he wasn't the sort of forgetful cretin who'd put his whole family and future at risk. He started washing his bottom.

Trying to keep a lid on the fear, I swallowed hard, turned the photo-frame face down and began to wade purposefully through the paperwork on the desk for the hundredth time. Letters from the bank, from solicitors, trade fairs. It would be here. I must have paid. I must have. I'm not an idiot.

But what started as a purposeful wade collapsed quickly into a despairing yowl as an unquestionable fact arrived, dropped two leaden suitcases and took up permanent residence in my bowels.

I was an idiot. I hadn't paid it.

I got up itchily and clicked off Dionne because I don't know about you, but I like to choose a CD to fit a mood, and Bacharach just isn't panicking sort of music. I let the small flat sit in a brooding silence for a long while. Of course, the cat might have called it a peaceful silence, or a tranquil silence.

But then the cat didn't know what *I* knew.

Loose knees shaky, I wobbled into the kitchen to distract myself with tea. Blu-tacked to the kettle's smudgy surface was a small pink cardboard star with '£2' printed on it. I blinked and it vanished.

Easy there, Neil. *Easy.*

I jumped at the sound of the phone in the lounge. Our nice phone. White bakelite. Heavy, with a proper circular dial and a real *ringggg* to it.

I stood listening to the real *ringggg* for a moment. Hating it. I'd gone off the phone recently. I preferred letters.

Letters I could ignore more easily.

Ringggg.

I moved back into the lounge, past the couch that had a blue cardboard star on its arm, proclaiming "£50 o.n.o." and hauled up the receiver.

Bedlam. A party. Laughter. Music.

"Hello?" I said. More music and laughter. Some people clearly not doing their accounts. Or at least, not doing mine. "*Hello?*"

"*Heyyy, is Franny there? Francesca?*" Laugh, shout, thud.

"No. No there's no-one here of that name. I think you have the wrong —"

"*Is that Mike?*" Thuddy guffaw shout.

"No. There's no Mike and no Francesca. You have the wrong —"

He hung up, so I did too.

I blinked a few times. The small '£5' sticker on the telephone dial didn't move. I blinked harder. That got it.

I sat on the £50 couch and dragged worried eyes about the lounge.

This mental car-boot pricing, working out what I was going to end up selling everything for, had begun recently. Ever since the firm of Boatman, Beevers and Boatman, EC3 had written to me asking about the cheque. Their first letters I'd ignored. The next few I'd fobbed off. Brief responses about 'pending payments' and 'full recompense in due course'.

But they kept coming. Each one leaning a little harder, pressing a little further, like an escalating bar-room threat. ". . . Dear Mr Martin, please be informed that unless contact is made with this office by Friday, November 6th, we will have no choice but to take legal action . . . "

Yeah?

Yeahhhhh.

I was halfway back to my kettle, mentally breaking down the next ten days into a workable rota of self-loathing and deceit when there was a scream.

But a real *scream*. A terrifying, throat-tearing scream.

Palms cold, I bounded over the cat and back into the lounge. There was a rev of un-tuned engine and squeal of tread-less tyres. I whipped open the curtain.

She was on her knees, face in shadow, bathed in the UFO glow of the yellow street lamp, a crunch of broken glass lying like spilt diamonds about her. The light from my window must have caught her eye because she turned to face me, face torn with anger.

"The *police!*" she bellowed. "Get the *police!*"

Heart thundering, I heaved up the bakelite, whirring the nines and clamping it under my ear. As I was connected, I craned a look back out onto the dark street. She was stumbling to her feet, one shoe off, leaning on our wall for support, whirling her bag like a slingshot and yelling into the night.

"Go on! Take it! *Take it!* Kill yourselves, you dickless fuckers! Wrap it round a postbox. Very rock and roll. Very *in the hood!*"

"*Police emergency*," the phone crackled.

"Hi yes yes, a woman has been attacked, or carjacked I think."

"Two killed!" the woman bellowed up the street, kicking and whirling. "Two killed in nine-year-old Honda Civic on the *Upper Richmond Road!* Oh very *Tupac.* Very P fucking *Diddy!*"

The policeman took the details and said officers would be there soon, so I hung up and hurried down into the cold blast of the street. Lights were clicking on in the Georgian mansion block opposite, nets twitching as local residents felt the tremor of their property values dropping. The woman was slumped against my wheelie bin with her bag at her feet, breathing deep, shaking.

"I've called the police. They're on their way. You all right?" I jittered, heart thumping.

Gathering her thoughts and cigarettes, she eventually eased herself up. She had a nasty graze on her temple and three thick waterfalls of dark red hair had come unclipped from an evening-out arrangement, tumbling lazily over her face and shoulders. Her dark cocktail dress was now sequinned with pavement grit. She pushed her hair aside, revealing a striking pair of dark brown eyes.

"Bastards," she sighed eventually. "You got a light?"

"Uhmm, I-I've got tea?"

"Any vodka you can stick in that?"

"Er y-yes I should be able to find some. Come on in. God, you all right? What happened?"

"Put a lot of vodka in," she said, leading the way up the scruffy steps. It really was a very short cocktail dress. "Don't worry if the tea won't fit in there with it. And grab my other shoe could you?"

Head tumbling, I watched her disappear inside the flat and then scurried about on the pavement for a moment, eventually retrieving a dark brown velvet stiletto from the kerb and hurrying in after her.

"Groovy place. What do you do, collect this stuff?"

Her name was Laura. She sat on the couch, breathing deep. Nervous chit-chat, calming herself down. Her other shoe was off now, painted stockinged toes curling anxiously on the edges of the rug. The first vodka I'd fetched hadn't even touched the sides so I'd fixed her another. I drank tea and the cat watched her from the footstool as she lit up a shaky cigarette, taking long and slow draws, peering about the room.

"I guess so," I said, handing her a chipped saucer as a makeshift ashtray. "It's my job."

Laura peered about the geek-chic walls. The posters, prints and props.

"Superman, huh?" she said. Understandably I suppose, as the Man of Steel's iconic, brick-chinned visage was present a little too often in frames and figurines about the room. Not to mention his proud, hands-on-hips stance on my t-shirt. Laura exhaled a cloud of blue smoke and blinked at me from behind her hair. "This a gay thing?"

I coughed a little into my tea, getting it up my nose a bit while Laura took another shaky suck on her Lucky Strike and apologised, licking her lips.

"Sorry," she said. "Nervous. Stupid. I'm a bit rattled. After . . ." and she motioned at the window. "Forgive me, I didn't . . ."

"No of course, fine fine," I repaired. "You're not the first. I suppose it's all a little camp. But no. It's a . . . father-figure thing. Rather a clumsy one at that."

"Father figure?"

"Long story. It's turned into a sort of hobby anyway. Just the rarer stuff," I said, trying to sound as heterosexual and un-geeky as I possibly could from within a fitted tee and beneath a cheap framed print of Christopher Reeve. "How are you feeling though? Anyone you want to call?"

"I'll use your bathroom I think," she said and wobbled to her feet, hoisting her bag. I led her down the hall, through the narrow gallery of comic book covers and clip-framed movie stills and fetched her a towel.

The police arrived while she cleaned herself up. Two huge guys – one young Manc constable and one old Scottish Sergeant – thudding up the stairs, waterproof jackets rustling. I sat them down and made more tea, leaving them to worry the cat and sniff at all my Clark Kents.

Moments later, carrying a tea tray through, I met a fresh-faced Laura coming down the hall, zipping up her bag and coughing a lungful of acrid cosmetic tang.

"Knocked off a bottle of something in your bathroom," her voice said through the stinging cloud. "Bit of a stink I'm afraid."

I not-to-worry-ed, blinking back the stinging tears and gave her to Scot and Manc for their questions. The officers were clearly taken with her, that much was obvious, both talking at the same time, interrupting each other, trying the old 'sexy cop – sexy cop' routine.

I meanwhile fussed with spoons and coasters like a Jewish mother, dropping enough eaves to pick up a bit of background. Laura was thirty-four years old. She worked in a sandwich bar on Old Compton Street in Soho. She lived alone. She'd been heading out to a party. Yes, it was her car. A Honda. Yes, it was insured. No, she didn't get much of a look at her attackers. Yes she was shaken but not hurt. An ambulance wouldn't be necessary. No, she'd never met me before and yes, black with no sugar would be fine.

She took a mug from me and mouthed a silent thank you from her dark painted lips and I suddenly found myself momentarily joining the policemen in the gut-sucking-in.

Hell, not that I want you to get the wrong idea about my marriage. Jane and I are –

Were –

Well Jane and I. It's a happy marriage. Hand on heart. Other women, one-nighters, whatever. It's never really been on my radar. I'm a family man. Have been since always. A beautiful wife and the cutest baby daughter. Enough woman for me.

My gut-suck act was something else. A symptom. A defence. I'm a blusher, you see. A stutterer. With women. Talk too much, don't talk enough. Hopeless, always have been.

Luckily, Jane rescued me from a lifetime of bachelor bumbling by taking the lead at University. She brought me out of my sappy self one common-room afternoon, interrupting my reading with a drunken rant about how Batman wasn't a proper superhero. Bashful or not, this was home turf so I wasn't about to have that and we went toe-to-toe over strength vs powers for the better part of the evening. She knew her stuff and I knew mine and the rest sort of just fell into place.

She still won't have a picture of Batman in the house, so I have to keep my – numerous – Dark Knights in the shop office.

Now you can get all Freudy on my ass if you wish. We can tire the moon with whether I've ended up surrounding myself with a houseful of macho superheroes in body-stockings and scarlet cod-pieces *because* I'm no good around women. Or we can go the other way and say that I'm no good around women due to spending all day selling comic and movie junk and developing no conversational skills beyond *eBay* and *Kryptonite*.

I'll take either of those bets, no problem. A bit of both I expect.

What I *do* know is that if Jane hadn't stepped up and thrown down a beer-fuelled Bat-Gauntlet and my best friend Andrew Benjamin hadn't sat me down and given me a good talking to I'd be a lot worse than I am now. A woman like Laura would have had me snapping into a foetal position and dribbling. Fortunately for my gut, she didn't stay much longer. The cops gave her a crime number and they left. She waived a lift home, which left her sitting on the edge of my £50 couch staring into an empty mug.

"So," I began, easing myself into the armchair opposite. "Old Compton Street, you said? Just round the corner from me. Brigstock Place. *Heroes Incorporated*?"

Laura reached into her bag and started up another cigarette, her face glowing in the flickering match light.

"Missed that one," she said.

"Most people do," I sighed. "Not that it'll be there much longer . . ."

"No?"

"It's in a little trouble. A lot of trouble." I glanced over at the desktop of paperwork, my stomach tumbling. "Sorry, you've been through enough. I don't know why I'm –"

"Because you helped me out. C'mon, fair's fair." I looked back at her. Laura had sat back and crossed her legs, arching a stockinged foot. "Go on, get it off your chest. Trouble?"

My eyes lingered on her legs for an idle moment, before snapping back to my teacup.

"Well, there's a convention coming up next month. Earl's Court?" I got up and fetched a slithery flyer from the desk and handed it to her. "Mostly trade. I'm meant to have a stall. Me and this other guy, Maurice. Posters, autographs . . ."

Of course, Laura's eyes began to glaze over, much like yours are now.

Really, it's fine. It's not your problem and not that interesting. So I took the hint and took her cup and she got her coat. She gave me a thank-you kiss that, either accidentally or on purpose, landed a little too near my right ear.

And then she left.

I offered her a cab or a lift but she wasn't interested. Said she'd stick out a thumb. I went to the window and cracked it open to clear the stale cigarette smoke. I watched her sashay down the steps into the October night, light a cigarette and walk away up the street, heels clicking to the metronome of her hips until the trees took her from view.

I shut the curtains.

"We're baa-ack!" Jane called up half an hour later with a slam of the door. She began to thud up the stairs with bags and squeaky toys and, I presumed, our precious daughter somewhere about her person. "There's glass all over the pavement out there."

"Tell me about it," I called down, quickly creeping back to the lounge to shove letters into a box file, bury statements in my satchel and return silver frames on desks to the upright position. "What news from your dad?"

"Ooh big," she said. There was the static crackle as she peeled off her jacket and the tinkle of hangers in the hall cupboard. "You won't believe what he's done. Where are you?"

"In here," I said, heart thudding. I buckled my bag and slid it discreetly under the desk, stepping back quickly to view the crime scene.

"Dad has an accountant at Chandler Dufford . . . God what's that *smell*? Is that *cigarettes*? Has someone . . . ? Wait, and *perfume*?"

"Daddy had a stinky drama while you two were out. Didn't he? Didn't he? Yes he did."

Jane and I kissed softly in a cloud of warm milk baby smell, Lana strapped to her chest, her wide blue eyes swimming in and out of focus, watching her parents. I held them both for a moment, my family, swallowing hard, trying to bury the nagging stir in my stomach. Jane's soft blonde bob, shampooey and clean and familiar against my cheek made my head swim. A deep breath and I broke painfully away.

"Drama?"

I gave Jane the bullet points, following her like a puppy as she unpacked, unhooking Lana and unrolling the blankie out on the floor. Jane was in clumpy Timberland boots, her favourite faded Levis and my dark blue fleece. She rolled the sleeves revealing her smooth pale arms and I watched as she set our tiny daughter down, blowing raspberries on her soft tummy.

"Upshot is, she broke a bottle of your perfume in the bathroom? A Chanel one I think?"

"Didn't know I had any Chanel," Jane said, getting up and curling into an armchair. "But she got away all right? She wasn't hurt? The police gave her a lift did they?"

"She said she was fine. I offered her a cab, but she just left."

"You just let her leave?" Jane said. "She was probably in shock."

"What was I going to do? Restrain her? She wanted to go, I let her go."

Jane conceded with a shrug. I moved everything along and asked about her father's news.

"He wants to start a trust fund for Lana. For her education. I had lunch with Catherine and she said Jack's father had done the same for them when they had little Oscar." Jane's eyes shone.

"Trust – ?"

"An investment. I don't know the details. He wants to pay for her school. Someone from his accountants is going to come and see us to explain it all. What do you think?"

The room went noticeably quiet. I waited for Jane to look up at me.

"*Pay* for her school?" I said.

"Oh Neil, let's not –"

"Why does it need *paying* for?"

"Neil, *I* was a boarder from the age of eight," Jane said. "I turned out all –"

"This is another of his ways of saying I can't provide for my family, of course."

"No, this is a gift. It's what daddies do."

"It's not what my *daddy* does."

"Well your . . ." Jane let that one trail off. The usual awkwardness descended for a moment. Jane pushed on to cover it. "Okay, it's what daddies do where *I* came from," she said. "And where *I* come from is part of who Lana is. Grampsy did it for me, great grampsy did it for mummy −"

And off she went down the bloodline, from stately home to stately home like a hyperactive National Trust guide.

Jane has the oddest relationship to her heritage. Most of the time she finds it hugely embarrassing and covers it all with dropped aitches, Doc Martens and faded Tank Girl t-shirts. But once in a while − which I rarely tire of teasing her about − it all boils over and she goes completely St Trinians. Times like now.

I tried not to listen, trying to concentrate instead on the focus of all this debate − Lana's gummy wet smile and tiny jerking fists, podgy limbs like plump haggis in brushed cotton skins. I didn't last very long. Certain phrases have a knack of jerking one back to attention.

"Sorry?" I interrupted, catching my fear and swallowing it hard.

"The shop too," Jane said again. "Next week some time. We have to call and make an appointment. He'll bring all the spread-sheets and such. Greg somebody," and she rose, moving to her bag. "Dad gave me his card."

"The shop *too*?" I wobbled. My world, so I suppose to one extent or another, *the* world, lurched to a stop. My mouth dried up, eyes flicking guiltily to my satchel. "He's not going to want to spend all evening trawling through the *shop* stuff as *well*?"

"Well, dad said it couldn't hurt to show him the lot. Apparently there are tax write-offs for the shop dad doesn't think you're taking advantage of. It would help this chap to know the whole . . . ah, here we go," and Jane handed me a thick business card. *Chandler Dufford Lebrecht − Wealth Management,* followed by some city address. Jane lifted Lana from her blankie and curled themselves into the couch. "Did your Chanel woman stop you getting your accounts done?"

The sweet perfume sting was still hanging about the flat like a drunk guest.

"Huh? Oh I got a good chunk sorted. And what do you mean, *my* woman? She was in trouble. What was I meant to −"

"And your letter? Did you finish . . . y'know?"

The room fell quiet.

"To *my* dad?" I said, a little loudly. "You can *say it* you know. He isn't Macbeth."

"Sorry," Jane said. "I know. It's just . . ." and she fussed with Lana's babygro. "And I'm sorry before, about −"

"It's fine, it's fine," I waved. "And no, another page or so. I'll post it tomorrow."

"And have you − *oof! Who's a big girl?* − Have you written back to that solicitors yet?" Jane added, holding the baby aloft, nose to nose. "Boaters or whatever they're called? Told them you've sent a cheque? Aww, ooze a dribbly one den? Eh? Ooze a dribble?"

"Cheque? Oh yes yes, that's . . . that's all sorted."

"Would you love me if we were poor?" I asked quietly.

I was propped up in the yellow glow of our bedside lamp, listening to the pages of Jane's Terry Pratchett turn slowly and the clicky milk breath of Lana between us.

"Poor? What do you mean?"

"If something happened?"

"Like what?"

"Forget it," I said. "It doesn't matter. Go back to your book, I'm being . . . forget it."

I sighed and stared at the ceiling some more. There was a beige half-moon of damp along the cornicing. A water tank leak that never really got sorted properly. Thoughts wobbled and worried like loose teeth.

"Oh, before I forget," Jane said, making me jump a little. "Dad's popping down to Brighton for a charity something or other next week. I said you'd pick him up from Victoria? *Neil?*"

"I mean, I know this place isn't what your father wants for you." "Neil?"

"Hn? Yes yes, fine. And I know how he feels about me and the shop and everything."

"We've been *over* this," Jane whispered, shifting over towards me, snaking a scented, moisturised hand up to my cheek and giving me a long kiss. She broke away slowly with a smile. "You're providing for your family. Putting a roof over our heads. He respects that. Just do what I do and ignore all that other stuff. That's just daddy being daddy."

"Not easy to ignore when he's coughing up school fees."

"Oh let him do it," Jane soothed gently, giving my hand a squeeze. "He'll write a cheque and it'll be off his mind."

The world lurched.

I stopped breathing. I waited. Swallowed hard. An idea barged in-between us, all fat arse and elbows.

I waited some more. The idea jabbed me in the kidneys and coughed.

"How er . . . much?" I said, too loudly and too quickly. I fussed with Lana and the duvet a bit to cover my eagerness.

"The fees? Fifty thousand pounds," Jane said. "Greg thingy will bring a banker's draft or something with him tomorrow I expect. Oh and while I remember, Catherine and Jack are coming over for dinner next Thursday."

"Fifty? I-I mean, sorry, *Thursday*?"

"*Next* Thursday. Guy Fawkes. I'll do a Nigel Slater or something. We can watch the fireworks from the window." Jane turned and noticed the open book in my lap. "What're you looking up there?"

"Looking? Oh er nothing, nothing. Just work." On the duvet lay a greasily thumbed and well-worn comic-book price guide. *Robert Overstreet's*. 35th edition, cracked open near the front as casually as I could manage, considering it had 900 pages and weighed more than I did.

"What's it worth?" Jane asked.

"What?"

"C'mon. It must be in there. Has it gone up?"

"Oh," I faked. "Same as ever I expect."

"Dad thinks you've forgotten about it. His bank said you haven't been to see it for ages."

"Keeping tabs on me now is he?" I said.

I kissed Lana on the upper arm, kissed Jane softly on her tooth-pasty lips and then tugged the duvet about my chin and had a good long stare at the damp patch on the ceiling.

I thought about the box file above the desk. The contents of my battered satchel.

"Does he *have* to come over this week?" I said after a moment. "This Greg guy? Can't he just send us the money to put away?"

"Dad said it's more complicated than that. Plus he's having a look at the shop accounts too, don't forget? Free expert advice? You'll have to bring the books home. I thought you'd be keen."

"Mnn," I said.

After a thoughtful moment I clicked on the bedside light again, shimmied up the bed and hauled *Overstreet* from the bedside cabinet. I flipped back open to the Golden Age comic listings.

1938 to 1945.

I chewed my lip. I thought about Jane's father. I chewed my lip some more.

"Hey." An elbow in the ribs. Jane.

"Sorry?" She'd said something. I'd been miles away.

"I said we'd love you no matter what," Jane repeated, stroking Lana's arm. "You take care of us."

"Right," I said, taking one last yearning look before slapping the book closed and returning it to the bedside. I clicked off the light once again.

An hour later, Jane and Lana both breathing beside me in the dark, I must have finally fallen asleep because I remember the dream. The Man of Steel™, in handcuffs, heaving a huge, brown velvet chequebook over his head in glorious technicolour, the planet Krypton exploding above, taking his family away.

Forever.

Freud or not, I was in deep shit.

two

Now.

You might be wondering how my beloved wife came to know about Messrs Boatman Beevers and Boatman, what with all my deskbound subterfuge and satchel stealth? Or you may alternatively be asking yourself why I bothered with all the subterfuge and stealth when my wife already appeared to be up to speed with all things solicitor-like?

Well we'll get to that. We'll get to a fortnight ago's surprise second post. The heavy paper, watermark and the City of London address. The letter that should have arrived safely at the shop where I could have disguised it among the other, shall we say, less immediate daily post:

"*Dear Hero Incorporation, I picked up a Donatello Mutant Turtle Ninja at a boot sale for sixty pee. He's got one hand, made in Korea on his foot (claw?) and his shell has got* you are a gaylord *written on it in face paints. My mates think it could be worth a hundred quid.*"

It was the next day, Wednesday, 28 October, the day after the car-jacking, just after ten a.m. by the shop clock – a cracked plastic thing with Elvis Presley's sneery mush on it. Sneery in the way that we'd all be I suppose if we had a layer of dust on our face and two clock hands stuck to our nose.

I had a *Best of John Williams* on the dusty stereo, the theme from *Star Wars* rupputy-pumping tinnily from one working speaker, soggy trouser bottoms and the rest of the post worrying me on the cluttered desk.

I'd had one customer already, a regular. He popped in most Wednesdays to tell me yes, he'd have a coffee if I was having one, sniff through any new posters that'd come in, do a crossword clue in my *Empire* magazine and challenge me to a game from the shelf. *Downfall*, *Kerplunk*, maybe a quick buzz at *Operation*. I kept a few faded dusty ones around to kill time with my few more intense regulars. It meant I had to sit uncomfortably close to them of course, smelling their lozenge breath and listening to their phlegm rattle, but on the plus side it meant I got a half hour's silence without them whittering obsessively on about Bruces Banner, Lee, Wayne and Willis.

The day would pick up of course. As the hands of the clock swept Presley's quiff from his eyes, Mr Cheng would come and press his nose against the glass as always. But until then, I had just the post to worry me, which it was doing a very good job of.

I filed the Teenage Mutant Ninja Timewaster in the bin along with the other three or four handwritten missives, mostly requests from private collectors for me to either take dusty rubbish off their hands or supply more dusty rubbish for them to annoy their wives with. Of the three ominous A4 envelopes, one turned out to be from the Earl's Court Exhibition Centre: my contract, a detailed map pointing out Stall 116, Loading Bay C, set-ups times and so on, which I filed away for next month.

The other two – both solemn-looking buff things addressed to Mr Martin, c/o *Heroes Inc* – had me nauseous with nerves, an apprehension not entirely helped by the sick smell of rotten pulp floating up the cellar steps and John Williams who, having ra-pah-pah-pummed through *Star Wars*, was now sawing away ominously at the theme from *Jaws*.

I was just thinking that I might let the envelopes wait a while and go and have another coffee when, with a ting of the bell and a *well hey there*, one unexpectedly arrived.

"And what's *that* monstrosity worth?" she said, motioning at the wall behind the desk.

"Monstrosity? That, I'll have you know, is the first original poster I ever owned. UK quad, cost me fifteen pounds. Had it on my wall at college. An absolute *classic.*"

"Never seen it," Laura shrugged, unloading her tray of coffee and a shiny bag of buns and croissants.

Thankfully for my nerves, she was out of the cocktail dress and into work gear, but even that she managed to carry off with a moll's worth of 40s' vintage sass. She had a thin, flowery top on, low cut in a sheer material, her small white brassiere just visible through the fabric. A thick red belt with a large buckle beneath and a thin black pencil skirt. The heels were gone, replaced by small school plimsolls, the whole thing wrapped in one of those huge dark green coats with the furry hoods. She had her hair pulled back and piled high, but one thick glossy tousle fell across her face. The graze on her temple had faded to pink. Somehow, however, even decked out to distribute mochas to twitchy Soho-ites, she still had a disconcerting way about her. An old-fashioned thing. Hips, heels and cigarettes, all that stuff. You seen *Gilda*? No? 1946? Rita Hayworth, Glen Ford? Or what about *Only Angels Have Wings*? Hayworth and Cary Grant, 1939? Well, she looked like that. Like she'd have fluffy mules under her bed and a gun in her purse. Plus for someone who'd been hauled out of her car and dumped in the gutter by two ASBOs not twelve hours ago, she was holding it together.

"*You've never –*" I repeated back in a stupid high-pitched voice, spilling a little latte. "It's a *classic*. Redford? Shaw? Newman? Got that Joplin ragtime score?"

Laura peered over the yellowing poster, eyes finally settling on the bottom right of the frame.

"Six *hundred* pounds?" she yelped.

"I know I know. But I've had it signed by the artist Richard Amsel, here see? *And* Shaw *and* the director. There's another dealer who comes in for a drool over it almost daily. It should just be for display really but the way things are, I'm sort of hoping he'll –"

"And what's in these?" Laura said. She slid a bun from a greasy paper bag and moved on to one of a dozen or so fat files on the counter among the post and the remains of the morning's particularly heated *Buckaroo*.

"Posters. Well, photos of posters. The originals are in tubes downstairs."

"Like a nerd *Argos*," she said flapping past polaroids of *Heat*, *Heathers* and *Heaven's Gate*.

"Although, *that's* now ruined," I said, plucking *Hellraiser* out grimly. "And that. *And* that."

"Ruined?"

"Like me," I sighed. "Down here."

We moved behind the counter, through the arch and down ten rotten steps from the dull glare of the shop floor to the single-bulb gloom of the wet basement. There are in fact twelve rotten steps to the basement but as the concrete floor was still under nine inches of thick black water and Laura's plimsolls seemed less than aquatic, I thought it best we remained poolside.

"Ohmigod," Laura said, hand over her nose. "It stinks. This is what you meant yesterday by —"

"Quite."

"Where does that go?" She pointed across the dripping dungeon gloom to an iron door, purple with rust in the furthest wall.

"Into next door's basement. Antiquarian books. Fortunately for all his stock it's rusted over and water tight."

"Christ. And what's in all those boxes?"

"Now? Vintage fist-fulls of mushy pulp. Likewise the bottom two shelves all along that wall and everything in those bin bags."

"Urgh, God. And it all used to be —"

"Yep. Used to be."

There didn't seem much more to add. Laura said *it stinks* a couple more times and I agreed a couple more times and that was pretty much that. I snapped off the basement bulb and we ascended to ground level, the furry smell clinging to my sopping turn-ups. Laura started up a new cigarette to cover the black odour, I told her she couldn't smoke in the shop and she held up her cigarette to demonstrate that she could, look, when Mr Cheng arrived for his daily drool.

"You be oh eBay?" Cheng said, door jingling, pulling his spectacles from his brown suit pocket and cleaning them on a pale brown hanky.

"Not yet," I said.

"Ny Ac Com nuh fouh. Oh prih buh noh bah."

Mr Cheng never bothered to finish words once he'd started them. It had taken me a few months of conversation to be able to mentally fill in the blanks quickly enough to keep up.

"You shouh looh. Cheh ouh," he said, sliding on his specs.

"I will check it out. Thank you."

Laura perched on the edge of the desk and took it upon herself to open the rest of my mail. I asked her kindly not to, at which point she offered me a withering feminine look – which as I explained, I never know what to do with so I busied myself with Cheng. I watched him crane his neck over my poster for *The Sting*, peering over the signatures behind the glass. He stepped back once in a while to take in the full image, and stepped back in just as quickly to watch the ink, as if he'd spotted it slithering across the faded paper.

"Fye hundreh," he said, as he did every morning.

"Six hundred," I said, as I did every morning.

"My guy, he big colleck."

"Yes, so you keep saying."

"I geh hih thih, he buy loh moh. Buh he say whon pay moh thah fye."

I opened my mouth to administer the daily rebuttal but nothing came out. The words hovered apprehensively at the back of my tongue like stage-struck toddlers and for the first time, I allowed Cheng's offer to ruminate seriously. *Five hundred pounds.* More than I made in a day. More than I made in a *week.* I looked down at my soggy turn-ups and shiny wellies. Thought about the stacks of bin bags beneath me. The rows and rows of sopping boxes. I thought about a Freshers' Week fifteen long years ago, my hall-mate Andrew and I hanging the poster on the wall of my new room. Thought about what five hundred pounds would do.

"Let me think about it," I sighed finally.

Cheng blinked, removed his glasses and scuttled out.

"See yoh tomorr."

"I expect so," I said, and he closed the door behind him with a ting-a-ling.

"*Dear Mr Martin, in response to your letter of the fifteenth . . .*" Laura said suddenly. I looked over. She had her cigarette perched between her lips and was unclipping a photograph from the letter in her hand. "Blah blah blah, *without a viewing, we are unable to put an accurate valuation . . .*"

"*Sotheby's,*" I said, reaching out for it.

"*Although,*" she said, twisting around away from me, lifting the letter out of reach. "*In line with Overstreet's current price guide, we would estimate a value of –*"

"Can I take a —"

"Holy shit, Mr Heroes Inc. I think your problems are *over*. You *own* this?" and she held out the Polaroid. I nodded sadly.

"Don't get too excited. I can't sell it. It comes as part of the package when you have an honourable wife." I took the letter grimly and read it through, chewing the inside of my cheek.

"Honourable?"

"My wife. Jane. Despite her appearance and her love of Tank Girl and Terry Pratchett, her dad is Edward, the somethingth Earl of whassitshire," I explained. "Walsingham. No, Wakingham? Wakefordsham? One of those." I dumped the Sotheby's letter in my in-tray and picking up the final piece of ominous post, tore it open roughly. "Means he's got a draughty old house in Suffolk that's falling to pieces. Or is it Norfolk? One of the 'folks' anyway. A five-bedroomed whassit off the King's Road, complains about income tax, thinks I'm a scruffy pleb and drags Jane off in a frock to stand in a field staring at ponies every summer. He likes his extravagant wedding presents of course. They're designed to keep unworthy sons-in-law in his debt. To *keep* one *in one's* . . ."

My voice trailed off into a croak as I tugged out the flimsy yellow carbon paper from the final envelope, stomach rolling over and flopping out like a fat drunk on a guest bed.

Shit.

Laura was talking somewhere but her voice was thick and muted, like it was underwater. Like she was sunk. Sunk like me.

I blinked at the final demand and refocused. *Rod-o-Matic, Plumbing & Drainage*.

I recalled the man in overalls. The unpacking of gear. The pipes. The hours of juddering compressed air. The repacking of the gear. The apologies.

"What about insurance?" Laura asked, snapping me awake. She was stubbing out her cigarette and popping the top from a coffee. "Doesn't that cover burst —"

She stopped at the sudden shutter-shuddering slam of the door.

"You Hero? Hey, you?" a wide gentleman barked, barraging in, banging a brown evacuee suitcase against the displays. Draped in a ratty old coat, clearly tailor-made for someone else, a greasy wool hat pulled right down, his voice was muzzled by a spitty scarf.

"You Mr Hero? I've got shit to shift. Right up your alley." Waddling up the aisle, he heaved his battered case onto my photo files.

"Can I help you?" I said, clearing some space.

He flicked the case locks with grubby thumbs.

"It's me who's 'elping you mate. What'll you give me for this lot?"

I put the invoice aside and wiped croissanty fingers on my jeans. Glad of the temporary distraction, I spent the next five minutes rootling through the cluttered contents of the old man's musty suitcase. Despite everything – invoices and cellars and solicitors and intimidating café staff – I allowed my mood to momentarily lift, feeling the old hope tingle like warm electricity through my fingertips. I breathed it in: the fusty brown smell; the crackle of yellowing paper; the rustle of polythene and dull clink of thick porcelain. Boxes, bundles and bags, bulging with possibility.

Forgive me.

Long forgotten cases like these are the most enjoyable part of a dealer's life. More than a ringing till, more than that first cappuccino. Not due to any rookie pipe-dream of a mythical priceless trinket mind you. Those ideas are pummelled out in the first six months by the fat fists of experience. In almost a decade of running *Heroes Incorporated*, not one of the hundreds of identical cobwebby suitcases has yet to give up more than a tenner's worth of chipped pop-culture nick-nackery.

No. What these moments give is a return. A chance, for the briefest moment, to remember, *recapture*, the few precious seconds of boyhood when our strange fascinations first took hold. For a frozen moment business is forgotten and I am back in short trousers and school shoes, eyes wide, breathing in the smell of burnt popcorn. I am stroking the rough primary pages of a borrowed comic, bathing in the tinny glow of a Saturday cartoon or picking cold fingers among the trestle-table tat in a freezing church hall jumble sale, my father beside me, slipping me a heavy fifty pence, the air bubbling with women's voices, thick with the metal smell of orangey tea.

I was jerked from memory by a loud voice. I looked up from the worthless case of trinkets and tat. The owner was taking a vocal stroll about the shop, letting fly with his expert advice. *Ahhh, you wanna get rid of all this crap. This? This here? Worthless. These are on eBay for twenty pence. Market's flooded with 'em. Crap, crap, crap, whassis one? Crap.* On and on. Jolted by disbelief, I threw a look at Laura who dropped a matching jaw and threw the look back.

And then if this wasn't enough, the stranger, seemingly oblivious to buyer-seller etiquette, up-shifted a gear with a crunch and started getting personal. *Gor dear, fuckin' amateur hour this place. Got stuff worth more than this kickin' around in my loft. New to the game are you Hero?* He's calling me 'Hero' the whole time for some reason. *Hero, eh mate, new to this lark are ya? Bloody youngsters don't know what the fuck you're doing. Do ya. Hoy? Hero?*

Well I mean, really.

I was *this* close to slamming his ratty case and asking him to take his bric-a-brac, business and body-odour elsewhere when, at the bottom of the case, beneath a yellowing stack of *2000AD*s, my fingers curled around a thick roll of what felt like card. I tugged it loose.

Black and white photographs. Publicity stills. Cracked and faded most of them, corners bent and orangey. A quick crackle through revealed a veritable who's who of artists and writers from the thirties and forties – the Golden Age of the American comic book: Will Eisner, Bill Finger, Julio Raymond, each posed in shirt sleeves and fedoras, pipes in mouths, all sat chuckling around desks and easels. Shots commissioned no doubt by various publishers way back when. A quirky collection but nothing to get too excited over.

I was already warming up a thanks-but-no-thanks when two familiar faces at the bottom of the photo pile caught the words in my throat.

Could it . . . ?

Was it . . . ?

Holy.

Heirloom.

Batman.

I swallowed hard and looked up. The man had got his coat caught on a rack and was cursing and tugging at it, postcards and lobby sets swooping to the floor.

"Er, not really my sort of stuff to be honest," I said, attempting to keep the wobble from my voice. "I mean I'd give you a fiver just coz I like this *Dick Tracy* mug," and I waved a ceramic Warren Beatty. "But I'd be doing you a favour to be honest."

"Fuck off ya tosser, got some beauties in there," the man said, yanking his coat free, the postcards falling around. "Them *2000AD*s are mint. Hundred quid and it's all yours. C'mon ya tight fucker. You'll make double that."

"I'd be lucky to make half, to be honest. And would you mind controlling your language sir?"

"Then give me a fuckin' decent fuckin' price, ya fuckin' fairy. Seventy five," and he waved a grubby paw at the large MGM posters on the wall. "You'd only spend it on more Judy Garland shit for your boyfriend."

"For my *boyf* – ? Oh for heaven's sake." In the corner Laura was concealing a smirk behind her cigarette. I really was going to have to butch the place up a bit. But until then, I needed to close this deal sharpish. "Fifteen, and it's my final offer."

"Twenty."

"Fifteen."

"You . . . Give it then," he barked in a belch of boozy bitter, snapping his fingers. "An' I want a receipt."

I began jabbing through the laborious temperamental quirks of my Jurassic till, the man spitting *'urry ups* and *fackin'ell mates, in your own time why dontchas*. The till-drawer finally ground open, thin receipt chattering out noisily. I peeled off a couple of notes and handed them to him.

"'Bout time, ya fuckin' fruit," he mumbled, upending the case to let the comics, photographs and nick-nacks tumble to the counter and floor in a flurry. He staggered around and clomped mumbling down the shop, lurching clumsily onto Laura's toe. She yelled at him but with a thud and a clatter he was gone.

"Jesus. What an arsehole," Laura said.

"And thank the Lord," I said excitedly, riffling through the debris. "Otherwise I might have felt moved to give him the full market value for . . . where are you, where are you . . . here. Look at that!"

Laura ambled up the aisle and peered at the photograph through her cigarette smoke.

"And what *is* the market value," she shrugged, "for a signed snapshot of two Brylcreem boys with their underpants outside their trousers?"

"A great deal more than fifteen pounds," I said, heart lifting. Maybe this was a sign? Maybe it was like my dad used to tell me – that luck came in streaks? Run of bad, a run of good.

I caught a glimpse of the yellow plumber's invoice atop my in-tray. Further down the pile, two matching yellow demands and a Beevers & Boatman letterhead peeked out a little.

Christ, let my luck be changing.

"Fur-mur fob-mim *oof*," Jane said later that evening, to which I replied "Beg pardon?" for the obvious reason. "You *robbed* him?" she said, lifting her mouth up from the pillow a bit, and then added another small *oof* noise.

"*Robbed* – I didn't *rob* him," I said. "It's not like he – whoopsie – like he came in and I clunked him over the head with a cardboard Chewbacca and nicked his suitcase."

The *whoopsie* was because the essential oils I was massaging into Jane's shoulders had got a bit runny and began getting under my watch-strap. I warmed up a spot more liquid between my palms with a noisy rubbing motion and resumed the long broad strokes along Jane's pale shoulders. "I offered him fifteen pounds and he took it," I went on. "Fair and square."

"*Fair?*" Jane said, twisting to look up at me. I shushed her back into position. "Well then I hope *you* never get old and have to sell any of your –"

"Oh c'mon, shush shush, this is meant to be relaxing."

The lounge dropped into quiet once again, just Michael Nyman's score to *The Piano* tinkling softly from the (£10 o.n.o.) stereo. Lana was asleep in her cot next door, a chunky baby monitor propped up by Jane's pillow crackling murmurs and sighs. The flat smelled of our weekly date night. Baby poo smothered with oils, candles and clean towels. Propped up behind her, straddling the small of Jane's back, I rubbed and smoothed her soft bathtime skin and tried to enjoy the moment.

Jane shifted a little, brushing bath-wet hair from her face.

"*How* is it fair?" she said. "*Fair*, surely, would have been telling him what a picture like that was worth and offering him two hundred pounds? Or a hundred at least? That would have been *fair*. Do you know where he got it? Maybe they're his wife's collection."

"Wasn't very ladylike stuff."

"Right, we going to have *that* conversation again? When *we* met, I had more copies of *2000AD* than −"

"All right, shush shush, you −"

"Your team all cocky at the Freshers' Week quiz. Playing the *girls* . . ."

"You win, you win," and I gave her a soft kiss between her shoulder blades, inhaling her bathtime scent.

"All I'm saying is, maybe they were her pride and joy? Down a bit."

"Then why is he selling them door to door out of a suitcase? There?"

"Maybe she died? Right there."

"Yes *maybe*," I said. "But it looked more like he was about to spend the money on booze."

"Naturally. Drowning his − *ooh*, that's good, a bit more there," Jane said. "Drowning his sorrows. Married thirty years. She has a heart attack, he's left alone. Forced to sell her rare collections to meet the funeral expenses?"

"You wouldn't be saying this if you'd met him."

"Poor old chap."

I thumbed the dip beneath her left shoulder silently for a moment.

Did I want to tell her that I didn't have a hundred to give him? That apart from a listless *Kerplunk* and Cheng coming back in for another peer at Robert Redford at ten past four, I didn't have another customer and spent the rest of the day knee-deep in antique papier-mâché? No, I thought. Best not.

I moved across to Jane's right shoulder, gazing over the pale violin of her back. Swallowing hard I tried to concentrate. My wife. My perfect angel. But even there, hands kneading gently her velvet curves, guilt stared back. Plain guilt. The word stared up at me from her shoulders like Jane was a premier league football player and it was the tattooed name of her firstborn.

"But think about it hon. I do the *nice* thing, the *honest* thing," I jabbered, giving the word as naïve and foolish an inflection as I could. "Give the bloke two hundred and fifty quid, which is what a signed promo shot of Joe Shuster and Jerry Siegel is *worth* —

"Neil, you know that's not —"

"And then sell it on for two hundred and fifty, what's been the point of that? I'm trying to make a *living* here. For us. But if you'd rather I didn't . . ." I said, somewhat petulantly.

It was a strategic manoeuvre. It was only a matter of days before Jane discovered what I'd done. How much I'd screwed up. And I knew that when she did — when the smoke cleared and she was able to pick through the debris of what used to be her life — I was going to be on the wrong end of a very big row. A plate-hurling, parent-phoning, locks-changing, never-want-to-see-you-again scale bust-up. So I was pushing this point as preparation. Ground work. Something I could barter with later. *But hon, when I tried to make a little money to put things right you accused me of being unfair. Ow, ow that hurts, I'm sorry I'm sorry ow.*

Something like that.

Jane was laying quietly. She does this during disagreements. The silent thing. Implying I'm not worth listening to. Which makes me frustrated and shouty and incoherent and not worth listening to.

"All I meant was," she said, "you could have been nicer."

"So could he!" I spat. Streaky looked up from underneath the radiator. "He trod on Laura's toe and didn't apologise, he virtually pulled an entire display down, told me I was a tosser, *fuckin' amateur hour, don't know what the fuck you're —*"

"Who's Laura?"

"What?"

Jane lifted her head from the pillow a little.

"You said he trod on Laura's toe. Who's Laura?"

The room went quiet. The cat blinked.

"Oh. Uhmm the woman. The Chanel woman. Yesterday. With the car. Turns out she works nearby. Dropped in to say thank you. Brought me a coffee."

I didn't mention her buns.

"That was nice of her."

"Huh? Yes, yes. I s'pose. C'mere, let me move down a bit."

I edged down to the back of Jane's legs, adjusting my weight and began to smooth the oil into the base of her back. The conversation was over. Topic dropped. Died a natural death. We could leave it be, draw a veil, usher out the mourners without it being considered hurried or disrespectful.

Which I suppose, with less fear and beer inside me, is what I would have done.

"Your dad wouldn't have had a problem with it," I mumbled.

"Yours neither," Jane said back quickly.

Ooooh ref. Yellow card.

I stopped. Chin up, I wiped a hand on the towel and picked up my beer.

"Sorry," Jane said.

I sighed, easing myself to my feet.

"Neil?"

"S'all right," I pouted. "Just a bit of cramp," and I gave my thigh a half-hearted rub.

"I didn't mean −"

"It's fine," I said.

"Did you post your letter to him?" Jane said tentatively. She leant up a little, propping herself on an elbow. She was making peace. "You were going to send him those photos of Lana too. Neil?"

"Hn? No, no not yet." I sighed and sloshed back another mouthful of beer, fizzing about my gums, making my head swim. "I will. But . . ."

"What? What *is* it?"

"You have to admit it. Your dad would have slapped me on the back and bought me a drink. *Shrewd, young man, shrewwwwwd,*" I said in my best Edward voice. It's an easy one to do. You basically imagine Windsor Davies playing Shere Khan in a touring rep version of *The Jungle Book*.

"Dad never said you should −"

"He's told me I'm too nice to be a businessman. That I don't have the killer instinct. Never tires of asking me how the shop's going. *Made that first million yet young man?* You know he'd have preferred you to have got hitched to some −"

"Oh Neil, for heaven's sake, how many times. Dad doesn't —"

". . . some macho, six foot, alpha male provider. Like . . . thingy. Andrew."

"*Andrew?* Wait, where's *this* come from?" Jane sat up.

"Oh nowhere. Forget it. Forget it. I was just thinking about him today," I said. I perched myself on the chair by the desk. "That *Sting* poster he helped me hang when we shared halls. I've had an offer on it. Not much but . . ." I burped a stale beer burp, head thick and cloudy. "Andrew was much more your dad's idea of husband material though, don't you think?"

"Hairy Andrew, eco-warrior? With those chunky jumpers and wounded ducklings? Hardly Mr Wall Street, was he?"

"No, but he was a . . . provider. All that Viking, Nordic, outdoorsy hunter gatherer . . . stuff."

"*You're* a —"

"Big shoulders and that long flowy hair that all the girls tried to play with. Mr Sensitive New Man with the wounded soul. That bloody . . . Arran sweater and his save the seal cubs. You could have had him if you'd wanted him, y'know?"

"*Andrew Benjamin?*"

"If you'd wanted *him*. Instead. He had a crush on you."

"Andrew? He got *us* together. There was no . . . We were *friends*."

"Did you know about the poems?"

"Oh he didn't have —"

"Those red spiral notebooks he used to always carry. *I* shared a room with him."

"Then why didn't he . . . ?" Jane flapped and then stopped, shrugging the memories off, sweeping thoughts away. "Look, what's brought all this on suddenly?"

"Nothing, I . . . Nothing." I shook myself, chugging a little more beer over the sick ache in my stomach. "I'm being stupid."

"You are. He and I were friends. We all were. A team," Jane said. She suddenly remembered something. "Oh, talking of Dad, there's a letter from his accountant I think. On the desk there. Came this morning. And something from the bank it looks like."

"Bank?" I squeaked, covering it with a belchy cough. I spun the chair. There were two envelopes propped against the silver photo-frame.

"Shall I do your back?" Jane said, standing, waggling the jar of oil. "It'll help you relax."

"Uhm, no. No I'm . . . er fine. Should we look in on Lana?" I stood shruggily, edging around to block Jane's view of the desk, wiping my oily hands and ruining another towel in exactly the way Jane had told me not to.

She gathered the pillows and gave me a kiss. I smiled weakly and watched as she plucked the monitor from the floor and ambled in her loose tracksuit bottoms, cooing down the short hall to what was now either a study with a cot jammed in it or a nursery with a computer jammed in it.

Ignoring the pink cardboard '£15' star Blu-tacked to the desk, I lifted the bank envelope. Plain and business-like, my name peeked guiltily from the little window. Heart thudding, I tore it open and scanned through it, throat tight.

Oh Christ.

"Everything all right?" Jane said, appearing in the doorway, Lana on her hip.

"Oh, just a statement. Everything's fine," I lied, stuffing it in my jeans. "Everything's just fine."

Half an hour later, by the dim glow of a plastic caterpillar night-light, I was skulking in the nursery. Hunched over the rickety, flat-pack computer desk in the corner, another beer thudding about my temples, a freshly changed Lana dozed contentedly in her cot behind me. Fists closed, mouth open, her small room smelled of brushed cotton and nappies.

What the hell was I doing, dragging up old university memories to pummel Jane with? It was all getting out of hand. The fear, the worry. Knowing it was only a matter of days before our world was picked up, turned upside down and had everything we knew shaken out of it by men in overalls.

Pushing thoughts aside, I fetched the *Overstreet* guide from the bedroom, picking up my satchel from the hall on the way back. In the lounge I could hear Jane on the phone with her dad, promising we'd get his accountant guy over by the end of the week.

Returning to the sanctum of the nursery once again, I shut the door behind me and tugged out my paperwork.

Sotheby's, it turned out, were right. The valuations matched. I didn't know if this was what I wanted to hear or not. Whether it just made things more confusing, having *two* experts telling me I had an unboardable lifeboat out there. Pulling the buckled bank letter from my pocket, I took another long look at it. Volume four in a long line of statements, adding up all the bank charges and missed direct debits. You don't want to know how much it all came to.

I tore it up and buried it at the bottom of the bin under a scented nappy sack, concentrating instead on the stiff envelope containing the day's ill-gotten prize. Untacking the lip, I eased the faded photograph free and laid it on the computer keyboard, sliding the night-light a little nearer, shadows shifting.

Two men. Teenagers. Felt hats and shirt-sleeves, side by side in a boxy office. Smiling the guilty, awkward smiles of the suddenly famous. On the right, the artist, a pencil behind his ear and drawing pad clamped under his arm, no doubt at the behest of some unimaginative publicity hack. On the left, his partner, writer and occasional model sports a knotted tablecloth about his neck, a typewriter under his arm and – pulled over his suit trousers, causing them to ride and ruck – a huge pair of absurd underpants.

Best wishes – Jerry Siegel and Joe Shuster.

I eased the crumbling paper over carefully. A date on the reverse. 1933. Plus an inky stamp: image copyright Detective Comics Inc. 480 Lexington Ave NYC.

I set the photograph aside and booted up the computer.

Fifteen pounds I'd paid. A quick click and drag across a webful of collectors' sites moments later told me I should be slapping it on the *Heroes Inc* website for twenty times that amount. Did I feel guilty? Was Jane right?

Gor dear, fuckin' amateur hour this place. New to the game are you, ya fuckin' fairy?

Screw it. He'd had it coming.

As my old scanner whirred and stuttered, I tried to focus on the job in hand. Opening up a file, I spent a moment banging out a suitably gushy description – mint, must see, collector's item, perfect gift, offers in the region, bing bang bong, all that. The photo was taking a while to download so I took a quick surf across to eBay to check out Cheng's story.

Sure enough, there it was. *Action Comics,* issue 4. September 1938. Four thousand pounds. I didn't know the seller but it was getting a lot of attention, mostly from a collector in the US called Grayson, topping everyone's bid.

Me? Ha, what do *you* think.

No, I just sat there in the glow of a plastic caterpillar, watching the screen fill with tablecloths, underpants and fedoras, half listening to Jane next door on the phone with her dad.

They seemed to be discussing private schools.

Heart hammering, I was gripped suddenly with an urge to tell her. To come clean. Get up, march into the lounge, sit down, take her hand, look her in the eyes and just tell her. Blurt it out. Own up. The trouble I'd got us in. What was about to happen.

But −

Well I didn't. I couldn't. Her dad −

I just couldn't.

Instead I just sat there, not blinking, eyes on my screen. Feeling them getting sore. Worry, slithery and black, coiling about my gut. Tasting fear, coppery in my mouth. Praying, *praying*, silently, it would be okay.

That everything would *somehow* sort itself out.

Ha. Look at the state of me.

What do *you* think?

three

Oh by the way, before we go on – you got that, did you? Jane's little dig about Dad? The '*neither would yours*' thing?

Yes. It's . . . a little complicated.

Let's just say, so you know, I didn't quite enjoy the family life that Lady Jane did.

Not that my father and I weren't close, you understand. We were. In our own strange way. Closer than Jane and her father are even now in some respects. But it was a closeness that had nothing to do with annual trips to the Seychelles. Nothing to do with ponies, private school or party shoes.

Dad and I had what you might call a Saturday-afternoon closeness. A movie and a comic closeness. Through everything. Arguments. Hangovers. Casualty wards. Court appearances. Come Saturday afternoon, he was there.

Movie and a comic. Without fail.

Explains a lot, I suppose.

"*I'm afraid there isn't a lot you can do sir.*"

"Not a lot I can – ? That's *it*? *That's* your 24-hour help-line's helpful line? The bank are about to . . . I mean do you know how serious this is?"

"*I can put you through to a customer policy care supervisor.*"

"Isn't that you?"

"*Er, yes. I mean I could put you through to . . . another one.*"

"Who'll tell me something different?"

"*Uhmm, no.*"

"Right. Look . . . I just need to know if there's some chance that, well . . . that maybe you might pay it *this* time?"

"*Sir –*"

"And I-I increase my premiums, y'know, from now on?"

"*That's not how your policy works sir, I'm afraid. We do have a new*

Emergency 48 Hour Valuables Cover Plan that is along those lines though. Would you like me to put you through to sales sir?"

"Well that depends doesn't it?" I said through gritted teeth. "If your sales department is located within a worm-hole in the space-time continuum, enabling me to buy this policy three weeks ago when I needed it."

"I'll put you through to sales," she said and either Hank Marvin abruptly turned up at her call centre playing Handel's *Water Music* or she'd put me on hold.

Yes, it had been an unbelievably long shot, I admit. But when you've spent half a late-October Thursday morning crouched trembling and dripping in a pool of black gunk behind a water-damaged cardboard Chewbacca while a large, goateed, memorabilia-salesman called Maurice, with Judge Dredd on his lapel badge and spit dribbling down his pyjama top, kicks your shutters with steel-toed motorcycle boots, hollering both your name, how much of a 'feckin' faggot' you are and what his lawyers are going to do with you when they find you, lengthiness of shot often ceases to be of any relevance.

Hank moving on to a twangy version of *Moonlight Sonata*, I looked up at the sound of my bell tingling softly. A figure stood framed in the doorway.

"Good morning, sales?" the phone crackled. *"My colleague says you're concerned about worm-holes? Our Standard Homecare covers all damage to gardens, including lawns and fences."*

"I–I'm sorry, what?"

The figure began to wander up the shop towards me, unpeeling his ratty scarf.

"We do have a new Emergency 48 Hour Valuables Cover Plan which we're telling our customers about. This covers items in your care that you are not the owner of. For example, if you were looking after something for somebody else and it was accidentally –"

I hung up.

"Mr Cheng?" I hissed out of the side of my mouth. *"Mr Cheng, pssssst."*

Cheng, on his usual morning spot, peering and humming at Robert Redford through Perspex and pursed lips, turned.

"You rea to may a dea? You tay fye hundreh?"

"*What? Yes, yes all right, I'll take the five hundred. Just . . . just keep an eye on this guy. He was in yesterday. He might make some trouble.*"

The man got closer. His woollen hat was the same. As was the greasy coat. His shoes, however, were considerably smarter. Brown half brogues. Polished. Leather laces. They didn't go with the look at all.

"Truhb?" Cheng said far too loudly and turned to look at the visitor, now at the desk, peeling off his gloves. He had small, surprisingly clean, neat hands.

"Hello a-again," I said, flapping nervously about the desk.

"Indeed. Right, as it were, back at you," the man said. His voice was different. More clipped. Straight out of a Gieves & Hawkes display case. Maybe he'd got it as a free gift with his new shoes. I didn't know.

The three of us stood there for an awkward moment.

"I goh go," Cheng said finally, slipping off his spectacles and heading back out of the shop. "I come bah on Sundah wih the fye hundreh. You be heeh, yeh . . . ?"

"*Wait.*"

Cheng left, leaving the shop in an eerie silence.

"Ahh, but if you love him, set him free, Mr Martin," the man said, unbuttoning his coat and revealing a leather belt struggling with a pot belly. He whipped his scarf over his head. "Gahh, this wool gets in my throatlet. Would a glass of water be treading on the toes of your hospitality slippers?" The man placed his scarf on the desk and swept off his hat. A dark, oily fringe fell back over his face, which he tidied away expertly. He was younger than I'd first thought. Mid forties? His eyes, droopy and kind, had a wet twinkle to them. He was ruddy cheeked and chubby but something about him sparkled lightly like a panto finale.

With a *hmnn* on my lips and a *what-the-hell?* on my mind, I went and splashed water into the least grimy mug I could find.

"Ahhh, god bless you and your kin," he smiled and took a tiny sip, smacking his lips. "London tap. Sewage and mud. Still, nothing quite like it for infecting the blood. Now then, to beeswax," and he produced a pipe from inside his coat, a pouch of tobacco from his corduroy trousers and fixed me with those twinkly eyes of his. "Mr Martin. How are you fixed for tomorrow?" He was filling his pipe expertly with small delicate movements, a smile lurking somewhere beneath his expression.

"I'll be wading about in the basement all day I expect."

"Mnyess," the man said, wrinkling his nose a little. "I noticed that yesterday. A mite *pongy*."

"Is this about yesterday? The photographs you sold me? Because —"

"Fiffle. Fret ye not, young man," he smiled, a warm, crooked smile, showing half a mouth of neat teeth. He had the disconcerting way about him of an unsigned Valentine's card. "Would thou be willing to usher the baying hordes from your emporium for a hundred and twenty minutes? Say betwixt one and three? What do you say?"

Popping his unlit pipe into his mouth, he undid his overcoat and reached inside. I caught a glimpse of tweed, club tie and fine check as he produced a packet of Dunhill cigarettes, a silver Zippo, a box of matches and finally with a small "a-ha", the object of his search — a black Moleskin notebook. He slid a silver pencil from its elastic binding and held it poised over the page.

"I would very much like to stand you lunch," his pipe bobbed. "Shall we say Claridge's? They do the most scrumptiful chocolate cheesecake. Say you'll pull on your Friday shoes and join me?"

"Uhmm, can I ask, y'know . . . can I ask why?"

"A proposition, Mr Martin. Or dare I presume to be at the *Neil* stage?"

I gave a stilted nod.

"Splendiful. If it fails to interest, then we depart with tummies full of cheesecake and the warm glow of port and camaraderie. What do you say? Hmm? What do you say?"

"Business? You're what, a dealer?"

"Everybody is a dealer in something, Neil. Anyhap, I'm pencilling in one o'clock?" This done, he lit his pipe with matches and a soft sucking sound, sweet smoke beginning to plume into the shop and then extended a powder-dry hand. I shook it because it would have been odd not to.

"Until tomorrow then. *Affretando*," and with a bob of his pipe and a twinkle of the eye, he gathered his things, turned briskly and walked towards the door. As he did so, it gave a jangle and

Laura wandered in, cigarette in her lips, a cardboard tray of coffees in her hand and a bulge of a greasy paper bag in her apron pocket. "So sorry about your toe," the man said as he passed her. "Not too throbblesome I hope?"

Laura's mouth fell open, cigarette wobbling on her lip like the bus at the end of *The Italian Job*. The man reached the open door and then turned.

"Oh and Neil, I took the liberty of perusing that webular site of yours. The signed Siegel & Shuster snap you relieved me of yesterday? It's worth double what you're asking for it," he said with a wave. "Make yourself a tidy sum. Call it an advance. Toodle-oo."

Laura proceeded to unpack elevenses with a fuss of questions and lids and napkins and more questions as I hauled a sopping split black bag up the cellar steps and dumped it dripping by the bins out back. When I returned to the shop floor, she had undone her apron, tossed it onto a rack and was perching on the corner of the desk, crossing her legs and straightening the thick black seam of her stocking. She was in a sleeveless dress today. Grey wool it looked like. She had a single red flower in her hair and red ballet shoes.

"But you're not going to *have* lunch with him, right? The guy's clearly a fruitcake. I mean, what business? And what sort of businessman sets up meetings like that anyway?" She took a long draw on a fresh Lucky and held my look.

"Uhmm," I said, and pulled a handbrake on the world. *Was* I going? I didn't remember agreeing. But then I definitely didn't recall telling him to sod off either.

Laura was right, the guy was definitely a cake of the fruitiest variety. Toys in the attic, no question. And that voice? *Usher the baying hordes from my emporium?* Was he a vagrant pretending to be Little Lord Fauntleroy? Or some eccentric peer having topping larks posing as one of the plebs, fwarr fwarr, Rupert you're a *thcream!*

"I should listen to what he has to say at least," I said. "I'm not in any position to start turning away business, whatever it is."

"But he said *toodle-oo*. Who goes to lunch with people who say *toodle-oo?*"

Well, twenty-four hours later, *closed* sign swinging on my door, half out of bewilderment, half out of guilt and let's say a lot out of the fact it meant I would be out of the shop should a summons arrive, it turns out that *I* did.

Claridge's foyer is a huge light room, tall and pale. Embroidered chairs, chandeliers and dark wood tables set around a massive floral display. As I was escorted among the other well-to-do diners the following afternoon, I bowed my head a little, attempting to blend in with the carpet. But as the carpet was a dark flowery thing rather than a pattern of short, badly dressed men in misjudged ties, I didn't do as well as hoped.

My host was sitting at a corner table, back to the wall. Thankfully, he seemed to be out-cognito this time, sporting a pale pink shirt, paisley cravat and the glint of cufflink. A clear glass of something and an open newspaper sat at his elbow. He caught sight of me and bobbed his eyebrows, reaching up quickly to pop out two small Walkman earphones.

My jacket was taken and we were left to our introductions.

"My dear sir," the man said as I sat down, slipping his earphones into his pocket. "May I make so bold as to address you with some polite conversation? For although you are not in a condition of eminence, experience tells me you are a man of education, unhabituated to the beverage."

"I'm sorry, what?" I said. A blond, waistcoated waiter came and sighed at my order for a glass of house red, returning with a wine list. My lunch date hadn't stopped.

"I personally have always respected education, united with the feelings of the *heart* and am, if I may so inform you, a titular counsellor. Marmeladov, such is my name."

"Right," I said. There was an awkward pause. "Is that *Russian*?"

"Indeed, my dear Raskolnikov," he said with a twinkle, and then seemed to drop out of character smoothly. "I apologise. Silly habit. That the pop list?"

"Pop? Oh, uhh yes."

Marmaladov? *Pop list*?

The waistcoat was sent off for a ninety-nine Latour and some more water.

"Neato li'l diner they got here, huh?" my host said in a half decent New York drawl, throwing a look about the room.

"Yes," I nodded like a schoolboy. "Yes it's very swanky."

"Swankity swank chequebook and pen, I'd say. First time?"

I nodded.

"Me too. Your glamorous assistant keeping her beadies on the store for a mo is she?" he said, the waiter returning with the wine and water.

"Assistant? Oh Laura. No, she's just a-a . . . just someone I met recently. Works nearby. Popped in, that's all."

"Ahh. Someone you *met*," he said, and suddenly with a flap of elbows, his black moleskin book was open on the table and he was licking his silver pencil nib, jotting. "*Met* . . . I see."

Seemingly happy with his notes, the man nodded to himself with a tiny *harump* noise and sat back, his chair giving an antique creak. He sipped his water and smiled.

"So. Neil Derek Martin. Oh do tuck in by the way," and he pushed a plate of exotic breads at me. "Let's have it lad. Curriculum vitae. Births, deaths, marriages?"

"Me?"

"A name I call myself. Fa, a long, long way to hop. Tell me all."

"Er, look sorry," I said. If he was just some inbred gent who liked to wine shop assistants who took his fancy, then I thought it was best we got that out in the open. "You said you had some business for me, is that right? Is that what this is about?"

He looked at me. He seemed to be deciding something, one way or the other, tossing a mental coin. With a little nod, it clearly landed Neil side up as he put down his bread and wiped his fingers on his serviette.

"Indeed. Does Ecclesiastes 3:17 not tell us there is a time for every activity, a time for every deed? And more importantly, was it not Douglas Adams who stressed that time was an illusion and lunchtime doubly so? So in that spirit, I will allay your fears at the outset. I am in need, Mr Martin, of a consultant. An expert. Somebody who knows their, as it were, *onions*, and many in your field assured me *Heroes Incorporated* was the emporium to frequent and you, its welcoming proprietor, a man whose brains were pick-worthy. Hence my interest in your credentials. All very straightforward." He licked

his lips, eyes shining. "So. Are they to be trusted, these peers of
yours?"

"*Consultant?*" I said. Behind my eyes little men in green visors
began to set mental abacuses a-clacking with fat commission
percentages. "Well . . ." and I sat up, cleared my throat, and
proceeded to persuade him exactly how spot-on my peers had
been.

The blond waiter arrived back during my school days, and I had
lobster salad with mango and lime ordered for me. My host chewed
bread through my university years, nodding with the occasional *I
see,* the odd *righty-ho* and at one point a frankly upsetting *indeedy-
dumplings.* The waiter returned to top up my wine glass as I was
leaving university killing time at Brigstock Place.

"Owned by a Mr Taylor back then I understand," my host interrupted.

"Y-yes that's right. Do you . . . ?"

"Your part-time became full time eight years ago and when
Taylor retired, you borrowed a hefty deposit from a certain Earl-
in-law and bought him out. Which was . . . forgive me," and he
was back flipping through his notebook. Every page was full to
the edges with tiny blue handwriting. ". . . three years ago."

"Right," I said, a little disconcerted. "Sorry, how do you know
. . . ?" But he didn't look up from the book. Just stuck his tongue
out a little, flipping the pages back and forth.

"Jointly run stall at Earl's Court every year with another dealer.
One Maurice Bennett. Fairly reliable mail order. Clunky website
that could do with updating. Stock-wise, perhaps an over-reliance
on Golden Age comic books and *Superman* memorabilia they tell
me, but otherwise, pretty much exactly what I'm looking for."

"Right. Good," I bounced. "I-I mean, I'm glad I come recommended."

The lobster arrived in its dressing and we spent a silent minute
or so deciding exactly how to wrest its secrets from its shell. My
host expertly dissected it like a graceful surgeon. I plumped for
the all-out overhead attack, shrapnel flying, hundreds wounded.

"Can I ask at this point," I said, "who *you* are?"

"Who indeed," he said, in exactly the cryptically playful manner

I was hoping he wouldn't. "Well how shall we begin this, Neil? Shall we perhaps say I'm *two people*? Or is that tricksy and playful and liable to have you opening my throat with your butter knife?"

"Tuesday's character with the suitcase being your *other* self?"

"Quite," he smiled. "My grumpy seller routine. I sometimes wonder if the hat's a bit much. Let's call *that* rather rude man . . . Rudy, shall we?"

"*Rudy*?"

"And we'll call *this* me . . . Mr Whittington."

"And that's your name? Whittington?"

"Good heavens, no. I'm merely riffing, as I believe old jazzers used to say, on a mayoral theme. But Rudy and Whittington, for the time being, are who I are. Anyhap, pleased to break shellfish with you, Neil. Here's to swimming with bow-legged women," and he held out a glass to clink. I clunked it obediently.

"But you're not *actually* Mr Whittington," I said, head beginning to thud a little.

"Well it would seem I *am*. Thanks to *you*, dear fellow. The moment you deigned to pick out a tie and polish your shoes, in fact, *you* cast me as Whittington. You've treated me politely. You let me order your food, choose your wine without complaint. For all the room to see," and he wafted a knife at the other mumbling tables, "we are two well-brought-up gentlemen enjoying a well-brought-up lobster. Mr Martin and Mr Whittington."

He wiped his mouth and lifted his glass with a small smile.

"I know I cannot be *Rudy* today, Mr Martin," he said. "This is not how Rudy is treated. *Rudy* is used to receiving sighs, eye-rolls, tuts and threats. He is used to being ejected from shops, not joined at lunch tables."

"Right. Right, I see what you're —"

"He is used to being cheated, Mr Martin. Usually, mentioning no names *just* yet, by unscrupulous dealers who are shrewd enough to spot a half-buried Siegel & Shuster autograph in a case full of junk."

"Yessssss," I said slowly, putting down my knife and fork. I felt the lights were beginning to dim for the main feature. "Yes. Look I'm sorry about that. I don't know —"

"If I was Rudy *today*, Mr Martin, you would by now have

presumably asked our preposterously blond waiter to rifle through my jacket while you distracted my attention? So you could meet him in the lavatory and cut up the score. You *haven't* done this, so I presume today I'm Whittington."

I felt my face colour, my underarms prickle.

"Sorry," I began. "I don't know why I did that exactly –"

"Some unseen force guiding your hand perhaps? Your female friend working you with wires? A spectral –"

"No, I mean . . . I don't *normally* do that sort of thing."

"Ah. *Out of character.*"

"Right, exactly."

"Hmn. In my experience Neil, we are never 'out of character'. It is a contradiction. The fact one has *done* a thing means it's surely part of one's character to do it. Your character simply hadn't got round to it yet. *Your* character it turns out, is one who, when the right opportunity arises, likes to make a *dishonest* buck fleecing rude and smelly fellows out of their heirlooms. That's who you are, Neil. And try as one may, one can't *escape* who one is."

Shit, I thought. The whole damned lunch was a set-up. He was no dealer, no collector looking for expert evaluations. Just a bored aristo, whiling away his yawning afternoons by egging harried shop staff into impropriety, only to enjoy ticking them off about it in fancy hotels at a later date. I crumpled my serviette and tossed it to the table.

"You feeling guilty now, Neil?"

"I don't know," I said. Which was true. I didn't. Not at that point. I was too cross.

No fat consultancy fees. No two per cent commission. No lifeboat.

Shit.

"Or do you just feel caught?"

I sighed. Whittington was topping up my wine glass.

"You really want to know?" I said.

"Even more than I want to know where you got that rather fabulous tie from."

So I thought about it for a silent minute, the restaurant around us fading to quiet, and then really told him.

If you're wondering why I bothered, why I didn't just tell the mad old fool to get stuffed, head back to the shop and begin nailing *out-of-business* signs over the windows, then I'll tell you. And I can be sure of this because I've spent a great deal of time recently asking myself that very question.

It was because . . . hell, because the truth was I *didn't* feel guilty. I knew I should. But I didn't. Even with him sitting there in front of me. I mean he'd come into *my* shop, yelling, shoving, shouting the odds. Criticising this, pointing at that, knocking over displays. And despite her protests during our massage, I had Jane to support. A young family to think of.

Frankly, it had served him right.

"Of *course* it served him right," and my host gave a shiver of disgust. "I'm surprised you went as easy on him as you did. Most people just hide the Siegel & Shuster under their desk and throw me out."

"*Most people?*"

"Whereas *Whittington*? You wouldn't dream of swindling *him*, correct? You, Neil Martin, like most, have decided to treat the world depending on how it treats you first. With either contempt or courtesy depending on whether it's a Rudy or a Whittington. Good, good," and with a smile and a twinkle and a little nod, that seemed to be that. He clicked his finger to beckon over our waiter, whom I watched as he bowed smartly and wafted off for the sweet trolley. When my eyes fell back on the table, a stiff brown envelope had appeared between us.

"To beeswax then," Whittington said. "I require, as I mentioned at the outset, your help. If you will, a *hand*. I have in my posses-sion —" and he paused, weighing the words, placing two flat palms on the envelope, "an item of interest."

I licked my lips.

"Valuable?"

"Bahh, schmaluable. The trick, poppet, is *not* in finding an item of value. But in finding a customer who values your item. But if this satisfies your curiosity, a short correspondence with a friendly gavel-wielder has fenced off a sterling ballpark of *high six figures*. But only if —"

And he stopped mid flow, the waiter approaching the table, gliding a silver trolley across the rug. We sat in silence while he talked us through the spread in a clipped public school brogue, Whittington pointing at the cheesecake, which was sliced and served. The waiter wheeled off and Whittington resumed.

". . . if waved about in a room full of the right people, of course. Mmmn, dig in dear fellow."

"Can I ask what it is?" I munched.

"What it *is,* old chum, is *for sale.* Which is where I'm hoping Neil Martin and his Brigstock Place *emporia de retrograde* might come in. Mmmn! Didn't I tell you? This cheesecake is to die for. I shouldn't really," Whittington said, licking his lips and delving in again, "but I had to. A man called Grayson – dealer like you – told me if I was ever here I was to try it."

"You want me to display this thing in my shop?"

Whittington continued to munch.

"Where I *guarantee* it will be snapped up within *hours.* Now, naturally I wouldn't . . . mmn this biscuit, dreamy. Naturally I wouldn't expect you to do this for nothing, little chum. So what do you say? What's fair?"

My heart began to thud, hope rising in my chest. I concentrated on my fork, slippy in a clammy grip.

"Shall we say, what? Twenty per cent of whatever you can get for it? How's your dessert by the way? Isn't it *divine?*"

Well I *mean.* The dessert might have been divine. Or it might have been turds and biscuits. At that point, my head was suddenly, and rather understandably, elsewhere. It took all my self-control, in fact, not to snatch his little silver pen and that little black book of his, jump onto the table-top and dance around in a circle doing the maths right then and there. My father had been right. A lucky turn, a lucky streak, call it what you like. Things were on the up.

Whittington continued to witter on about having happily ascertained my character as a professional and whatnot, but I tell you, I wasn't taking it in. Twenty per cent of a high six-figure sum. We were talking a *hundred grand.* A hundred grand, *minimum!* For hanging whatever the hell it was in my window. *A hundred grand*?! My feet were dancing, my face trying to control a big goofy grin, maths running through in my head — pay off the solicitors, pay back the bank, get the basement cleaned up. I could hear music playing suddenly.

The theme to *The Archers*, as a matter of fact.

Yep, you heard me. Deet da-deet-da tum-ti-tum. The bloody *Archers*.

Whittington put down his fork and reached under his newspaper, sliding out a book of matches, an oily Zippo lighter, a small penknife, a fountain pen and finally a small silver mobile phone. The tinny theme was louder suddenly. I felt other diners glancing our way.

"Apologies apologies," he said, thumbing it open. "*A-hoy hoy?*" A frown scuttled across his brow. "Hmn, where should we . . . let's see," and Whittington flipped to the back of his notebook where a list was written in a neat blue hand. "*The Clarendon* I did yesterday," and he crossed out a name. "*Claridge's* I'm at as we speak, so it's . . . yes. There's a little Italian place on Brewer Street. *Con Panna*. I find public places more private. What time shall we say?"

I thought this a good time to excuse myself and go to the bathroom. I needed to splash myself with cold water. To walk, to dance. Needed the opportunity to drop to my knees and scream worshipful thanks to the patron saint of lucky escapes. St Jammy of Dodger, or whoever.

I left Whittington to his call.

Stood among the glistening tile and gleaming brass of Claridge's gents, I breathed long and slow, releasing the best part of a half bottle of ninety-nine Latour against the porcelain.

A hundred grand.

My stupid face grinned back at me in the pale reflection of the polished wall. And well it should. The disaster was averted, the crisis passed.

If I'm honest about it, in the huge tide of relief that sunny afternoon, the biggest and most refreshing waves were those washing in from Chelsea. Specifically, from a large five-bedroomed house off the King's Road.

See, I knew what Jane's father thought of me. Unsurprisingly I suppose, as he made almost no effort whatsoever to hide it. When

Jane fell pregnant for example. He'd exploded in a spray of cigars and tankards, which Edward's type always does. The *family line* and all that.

However, when the dreaded 'daughter' word was eventually wheeled into his Chelsea Park Gardens study? Oh the glare. The blame. Me and my plebby working-class sperm. All probably on strike or at the dog track the day they were called up for action.

I had received the lecture. Me sat in one of his fat leather chairs, nursing a peaty scotch, Edward pacing under an oiled ancestor. I wasn't to hesitate to come to him. Whatever his granddaughter needed, day or night, she's not to go without, best of everything. On and on.

But all the time I knew. I *knew*. And he knew I knew. I don't know why he didn't just say it. *Son, you can't support my daughter. So let's speak man-to-man shall we? Well, man-to-scruffy-Nancy boy at any rate.*

No honestly, that's his voice. I'm telling you, Windsor Davies playing Shere Khan.

I'm well aware of your upbringing. Who your father was. What he did. So let's not pretend shall we? I'll help you buy your tatty shop. You do what you can with your posters and nick-nackery, but I'll provide for Jane, as you probably expected me to anyway, eh? I've seen how your eyes prowl over this house. Now finish your drink and get out.

So for the past month, well you can imagine can't you? The fear of Jane's *dearest daddy* finding out? It would have proved, in his whisky-addled mind at least, that he was right all along. And he would have been *thrilled* to hear about my fuck up. Not in front of Jane of course. No no, in front of Jane it would have been hand holding and chin-upping and there-there-ing. But afterwards? He'd have dined out on it for the rest of his life. Golf club, functions, board meetings. My idiot son-in-law, *fwahh fwahh fwahh*.

But hell, that was the past. That afternoon, I was grinning. Heart light, bursting, floating like the last day of term. Because I knew I wasn't going to have to hear it. I was going to return to the table, coffee and mints, sign a contract for twenty per cent commission, hang whatever this eccentric guy wanted hung in the window and be in the clear.

In the clear.

The only thing that did worry me slightly, as I zipped up and rinsed my hands in the bath-sized basin, was that my new business partner had yet to get around to giving me his real name.

"Whittington? Oh, I see. No, no poppet, we must start as we mean to go on," my host said, plucking a white card from his breast pocket and sliding it across the linen.

"*This* is you?" I picked the card up. "J Peckard Scott? *Motivational speaker?*"

"Less or more," he said. "My vating is that of the motor-driven variety, yes. Geeing up, confidence boosts. I slap backs. Tell people what they want to hear. What's interesting about the whole procedure of course," he said, glugging my wine glass up another inch, "what your *Watchdog*s and your *Daily Mail*s don't realise is that *innocent* parties are never involved. Oh they like to *suggest* those we catch out are poor *victims*. Guilty only of being in the wrong place at the right time. But it's drivel, of course. Imagine the logistics of picking marks at random. Poppycock. We'd spend all of our time laying out the game, telling the tale, putting him on the send, setting up the whole damned store, only to find he didn't have any money, or he was too savvy, or too stupid. Nonsense, nonsense," and he shook his head sadly. "It's a myth. The likelihood of a hopscotching grifter just pouncing on a hapless innocent and fleecing him for his life savings are zero."

"Did you say *grifter*?" I didn't much like the sound of where this monologue was going. Principally because it didn't appear to be going anywhere we'd agreed on. In fact the whole lunch so far had something of the unlicensed minicab about it.

I tried to get a handbrake on this conversation before he veered us both into a lamp post.

"You said you have something you want me to sell . . ."

"I need your help, Neil, that much is certain. This memorabilia lark isn't what you'd call my field. Not my crop, not my farm. I'm on very muddy ground in fact and these aren't even my wellies."

"You being a motivational speaker," I said, to which Scott made a disconcerting *nyeeahhh* noise.

"Let's say I level the playing field Neil. I even things out. Assist the intelligent, the hardworking. Give them a step up. Which means, thanks to Newton, the lazy and stupid take a step down. But that's fair isn't it? I mean isn't that what we all *really* want?"

"Well I s'pose," I said.

"Anyhap, enough of that. We still on, what do you say? Still like to earn yourself an easy hundred grand or so?" and he picked up the envelope once again. "Of course you would. Because you *deserve* it, correct? You're a hard workin' man, tired of just *getting by*, I expect. Getting by while crooks and scroungers get to swank about in Essex mansions bedecked with sovereign rings. Hardly fair now is it? Which is why it's only right, what you and I do. Evening out the score. Rewarding the hard-working, intelligent and gracious," Scott turned the envelope in his small hands. "Punishing the lazy, rude and spoilt."

"What *I* do?"

"In your little shop. The Siegel & Shuster photograph? No bidders yet I notice. I'd check your emails if I were you. Bound to have someone offering cash for a quick sale."

"Wait," I said firmly, hand held up.

"But don't fret over it, sweetkins. After all, to some extent *everyone* acts as judge and jury on every soul they meet. Usually on nothing more than fleeting circumstantial evidence. Their shirt, their shoes. We at least –"

"*You.*"

"*We* give our defendants an opportunity to display their grace. A chance to state their case before we dish out a suitable sentence."

At which point I stopped him. I'd had just about enough of this. I can't recall exactly what I said, being a little drunk at the time. Something like, *stop, I've had just about enough of this* I expect. I do recall I held a hand up like a traffic policeman which was unusually assertive of me. But frankly I wanted some answers. What was all this *about*?

Scott waited. He took a swig of water. He waited some more. *About?* he said. Then, looking over my shoulder briefly, he fixed me with both eyes and told me. Quite calmly.

Justice, dear boy.

I blinked back at him. The restaurant paid neither his motive nor my blinking much attention.

He said it again, something fluttering like a shadow across his demeanour.

"Justice?" I queried, head thudding, "Sorry, I'm not sure I —"

"*Justice*. Man's to mete out and man's alone. Who else will even the eternal score? *God?*" and he barked an angry laugh. "No no. There lies a long, cold, wormy wait for those hoping for judgement day, young Neil. No retribution is coming, no bearded magistrate waits in the wings to bang the almighty gavel."

"Justice for *what?*" I said. "You've been ripped off?"

"Ripped off, ripped apart, ripped to pieces," Scott said. The mood seemed to have shifted. "We all have been at some time. Ravaged, raped and ruined. Dreams crushed, guts torn out by a harsh, unfeeling world." Scott's jaw ground, bitter muscles bulging in his cheek. "Posit love, for example."

"You what?"

"You love someone and they don't love you back. Happens all the time. Your whole world for three aching lonely years. It's destroying. Agreed? Observe the sentencing though. *You* are destroyed, *they* are not. *You* are dejected, *they* are not. Is that fair? Is that *justice*? Look at the crimes. *My* act is to see beauty in another and worship unconditionally. *Their* act is to reject this worship. To ignore, to pity and to condescend. But it is *I* who am sentenced to spend the rest of my days alone. While the one I love goes on, brushing the speckled lint of her guilt away with a laugh and a gesture."

I sat and listened.

"The world we have created," Scott said, sitting back a bit, chin up, "has scales tipped crazily off kilter. Good folk weep alone, sobbing at kitchen tables, heads full of their love's face, the lonely night stretching out forever. And the *selfish* objects of their innocent desire?" He spat the word, spittle glistening on his lip. "Those who think they are *better*, are out laughing and drinking, sparing no one a thought but *themselves*. Now, Neil. In a world *this* crazy, *someone* must even out the score, don't you think?"

The table went quiet. I wiped clammy palms on my trousers, dizzied by the open wound of his confession.

"*And*," I said, my voice cracking. "S-Sorry. And this . . . this is why you do . . . whatever you *do*? Because of . . . a *woman*?"

Eyes wet and weary, Scott looked at me solemnly for a beat.

And then his face sagged, cracking a goofy grin.

"*Naaahh,* not really," he laughed loudly. "Ha! I do it for fun. Shits and giggles. No more than that."

"What? But – ?"

"Tut-tut, Neil. Too many *movies* dear," he smiled, leaning over and tapping me one-two-three on my forehead with a firm index finger. "That's your problem. Things aren't always *about* things, Neil. There's no convenient back-story to people. And why should there be?"

"You –"

"I mean bally jove, nobody goes looking for a *shark's* back-story, do they? To find out what went on in *his* childhood that made him a killing machine."

"We're not sharks," I said, angry, confused and not a little bit drunk.

"Ahh, but do you know why, though? The only reason I am not a shark is that my mummy and daddy weren't sharks. That's all. The only reason *you* aren't a shark is that Mr & Mrs Martin happened not to be sharks. Now, you going to let that itsy bitsy teeny weeny yellow polka dot quirk of fate cost you your business? Your home? Cost you . . ." and he paused. He looked at me. "Your *family*?"

The whole sumptuous room seemed to lurch slightly, like it was trying to pull out at a busy junction. Scott began twiddling the envelope in front of him. My better judgement nudged my back bumper, tooting.

But I stayed where I was.

"What do you know about my family?"

"Well Zilch McGrew, as a matter of fact," Scott shrugged, "but I know something about *people*. I know, for example Neil, that young men with thriving businesses, savings tucked away and a bank manager they play golf with, tend not, by and large, to go to lunch with peculiar-acting men. That's more the behaviour of the desperate, wouldn't you say?"

I blinked at him, keeping him focused.

He went on, as I rather feared he might, turning the envelope slowly.

"More the behaviour of a man in need of a quick fix. A one-off, chance of a lifetime deal, that'll get him out of whatever unfortunate hole he's stumbled into. Coffee?"

four

I should have left. I don't know why I didn't. But I should have.

Though actually –

Actually no, I know *exactly* why I didn't. It's because – and I'm aware of how stupid this sounds – it's because I hadn't seen inside the envelope yet.

It was there, inches away, and it had something in it of value otherwise what was all this about? And hell, it's not like we'd done anything wrong. We were just two guys. Just two guys talking. So I let him order coffee. And I told myself, a coffee, a look in the envelope then go.

Just for curiosity's sake.

Coffee, envelope, go.

"Picture this if you might," Scott said, fine crockery now between us. "You're out walking one lunchtime and you spot something valuable in the street." He had sat back and was turning the envelope in his fingers. "Say . . . a gold watch. Like this one," and from the side of the table, Scott's foot slid out quickly. Lifting his brown brogue, he revealed beneath it a heavy-looking gold watch. He returned his foot to under the table. The watch remained where it was, curled on the carpet.

"Naturally," Scott said, "you bend to pick it up."

I looked at the watch, lying there. I looked up at Scott.

"Well, go on then," he said.

Hesitantly, feeling this was the first in what might turn out to be a long line of regrettable moves, I leant over to retrieve the watch from the floor, when Scott suddenly lunged for it gruffly, the table clattering. He grabbed it up with a snarl of *Mine!*

Startled, I looked up and Rudy's greasy hat was back, along with his character it seemed.

"Now I'm a fuckin' tramp, arn' I," Scott drawled, face low

among the wine glasses and coffee cups. "Didn' see me lurkin' in
a doorway did ya? See, I spotted this watch too. Juss as you did.
An' I wanna pawn it, sharpish. Get m'self a few beers wiv' dis li'l
beauty I bet. Look at it shoine," and he curled it in the lamplight.
"Rolex an' all. Heavy. Bet we could get two 'undred nicker for
it, eh? Whaddya say mate?"

I wasn't sure what my line was here. I was toying with 'uhmm',
or possible 'goodbye' when Scott kicked me, helpfully, under the
table.

"Ow! Uhmm, maybe. Okay, yes," I said. "Look, what is – ?"

"You better do the deal though mate," Scott interrupted, handing
the watch over. He was right. It was made by the nice people at
Rolex and had the easy weight of a housebrick. "No bloke's gonna
truss' me are they. Fink I 'arf inched it or summink. Nahh, you're
the *gent*. Best you try an' flog it. See if you can get two 'undred.
Then we'll split it."

The table went quiet. I glanced about for a prompt.

"Well go on then, man," Scott said brightly, dropping out of
character for a second. "Off you pop. You're the salesman. See if
you can shift it. Try our dessert waiter. He could do with a bit of
reliable timekeeping. "

So up I got. Was it his charm? His smile? The fact I'd got outside
the better part of a bottle of wine and the envelope was now on
my side of the table? I don't know.

But up I got.

I was halfway around the room, wandering woozily among the
tables when our waiter naturally approached. Did I need something? I figured, in for a penny, and I offered him the watch. Well,
you've got to have a go, haven't you? But bang, just like that, he
asked me how much.

So I said make me an offer and he looked at it, umming and
ahhing. And he said *three-fifty*.

Three-fifty? I said back, just out of surprise, to which he said
'all right, *four*.'

So eager to bring a halt to this bizarre charade and get back to
my table where I could work quietly on my headache, I agreed. He
said he hadn't got the cash on him, he'd have to get an advance from
the head waiter, but he'd bring it over to the table with the bill.

Job done, I returned to the table, thinking hell, maybe this has proved . . . whatever the hell it was meant to prove.

"Aah ja' get on then mate?" Scott asked with a theatrical burp.

"Done. I'm guessing this is what, some sort of −"

"Got me' share 'ave ya? I need that 'undred."

"Not yet. A few minutes. The guy's bringing it over with the bill."

"I ain't got toime to 'ang about 'ere wiv you. Where's me 'undred. C'mon, I ain't gettin' shafted. 'Arf the money's mine by rights an' you know it. C'mon, 'undred nicker. C'mon."

Our waiter appeared at the table shifting nervously within his waistcoat, eyes darting.

"*Boss has cleared it*," he hissed. "*I'll be back with it in five minutes*," and he scuttled away to the kitchen.

"'Undred. Now," Scott said. "Or I'm takin' this for m'self," and he picked up the watch from the table.

"Okay okay," I said, sliding my wallet out and flipping woozily through most of the shop's remaining petty cash. "Here," I said, counting out five twenties.

"Cheers guv, gawd bless ya," Scott said, slipping the twenties away in his top pocket and pulling off his hat. He sat up with a small smile.

"Now what?" I said.

"How do you mean?"

"Now what happens?"

"That's it."

"That's *it*?" I frowned. I craned around and saw the waiter in conversation with an older major domo looking chap in stripey trousers. He was handing him a white envelope. "You give me a watch and I sell it? I don't understand. Is this meant to represent something? The shop? My selling skills?"

Scott just smiled.

The waiter appeared at our table as expected, but then as very much not expected, unbuttoned his waistcoat, yanked off his tie and tossed it to the table, pulling up a spare chair and glugging out the last inch of wine into a new glass. I looked him over. He was tanned in a gap-year sort of way, about my age, but weathered by sunshine and outdoorsyness. His blond hair was patchy and bleached and he had a healthy Colgate smile.

"Neil?" Scott said. "I'd like you to meet Henry David."

"Pleasure mate," Henry said in a brand spanking new Australian accent. "You wanna top up?"

I looked at him. I looked at Scott.

"Goes back to the forties," Scott said. "As most confidence tricks do. The tat, the poke, the gold watch. These were a grifter's bread and butter."

"Confidence – ? But, wait," and I looked to and fro at Scott and Henry again, click clack back and forth for a day or so. As I did, Henry opened his white envelope and slid out a small sheet of grey paper.

"My P45," he said.

"And the watch?"

"For insurance purposes," Scott pursed like an antiques dealer, "our experts would recommend a value in the region of about four of your Earth pounds. Keep it though. A souvenir."

"And my hundred quid?" I said.

Scott smiled.

He gave me my money back eventually. Said *the first lesson is always free my boy, the first lesson is always free.*

Scott continued, laying out the finer details of the short con while I *righty-ho*-ed as convincingly as I could. But truth was, this was all getting about as wrongty-ho as things got. What had happened to coffee, envelope and go? What was I still doing here?

"No," I interrupted after a deep breath, sliding my coffee away. "Sorry, but whatever it is, the answer's no. You're going to play this gold-watch trick, right? On some helpless guy? Using whatever's in here," and I picked up the middle one of the three woozy envelopes beside me, "to con him out of his money?"

The two men looked at me.

"But you can't do it without *me*, right? That's what this lunch is all about?"

"Regrettably the man we are targeting is not interested in fake gold watches. Nor diamonds, art, antiques or dead-cert greyhounds. He's a buff. Buffer than that envelope you're holding in your hand

in fact. Memorabilia. And a real expert. Not the sort to be taken
in just by Henry and I slipping Spider-Man into the conversation
and wearing Albert Hitchcock T-shirts."

"Al*fred*."

"Well exactly. The grift is all about trust, Neil. If we're going
to skin this fellow – and frankly we'd be raspberry fools not to –
we have to first convince him we're his kind of people. *Your* kind
of people. Dealers. Experts."

"Nerds," Henry added helpfully.

"Right," I said. "And that's okay because . . . ?"

Scott and Henry exchanged bemused looks.

"I mean, it's all right for you to skin this man out of his money
because what? He's stupid?"

"And greedy," Henry said.

"*Terribly.*"

"No," I said again.

"*No?*"

"No. No, I'm sorry. I can't help you. My father? Now *he's*
someone you should talk to."

"Father!" Scott cried, hands leaping. "That reminds me. Thank
you old chap," and he began to flap about in the bag next to him.
Henry and I watched for a moment.

"But I'm not like him," I said slowly. "I'm not like my father.
If that's where you've got this idea from? I'm . . ."

"*Honest?*" Henry suggested. Scott emerged with a jiffy bag.

"Yes. Honest. If you like."

"Hmn. Quite a *liar* for an honest man, aren't we Neil?" Scott said.
He upended the jiffy bag and slid out a glittery greetings card, adorned
with kittens and bows. He signed his card quickly with a flurry of
kisses, peeling out a fat wad of five-pound notes from his wallet. He
tucked them in the card and tried unsuccessfully to close it. "Sorry.
For my parents. Wedding anni . . . oh this isn't going to shut, it's too
. . . Have you got change, Neil?" and he held out the wad of fives.

"Wait, what do you mean, liar?"

"Hmn? Oh, all that stuff a moment ago? When you agreed that
the intelligent and hardworking deserve a step up? And that the
lazy and stupid should take a step down. You said that was what
you wanted."

"But I didn't mean –"

"*Excuse me?*" Scott clicked his fingers, the head waiter wafting over. "My dear chap, would you be a bless dumpling and shove the bill on that?" and he handed him a credit card. The waiter glided off. Scott turned back to me. "It was the rationalisation you comforted yourself with, Neil, when you happily offered a mere tenner for Mr Rudy's photograph."

"Look," I said, trying to focus. "Look that was –"

"And if you're an *honest* man, Mr Martin, wouldn't you have offered my Rudy two hundred pounds for the watch just now? We *both* found the watch on the floor. You agreed to split it fifty-fifty with the tramp . . ."

". . . But I offered you *four* hundred," Henry said.

"Didn't see your honesty leap forth into the – ah, *marvellous*," Scott beamed, the waiter gliding back. He signed the credit card slip briskly.

"I'm off to the dunny," Henry drawled, sliding his chair out with a scrape. "Back in a bit," and he mooched off.

"I wonder if you'd mind," Scott was saying to the head waiter. "I have to send two hundred pounds to my parents but the bank could only give me these fives. Could you see if you have some twenties you could change for me? I can't get the card closed," and he waved the kittens at him. "Oh and my jacket?"

The waiter backed away with a bow.

"Look, dear fellow. All of this is spectacular in its beside-the-point-ness," Scott said, "because we're not involving you in anything dishonest. Henry and I will be the ones playing the game. We're just cutting you in on your share of the score."

"A high six-figure sum," I said, my eyes flicking involuntarily to the envelope on the table once more. My life seemed to be governed by envelopes these days. Thin ones from banks, fat ones from solicitors.

This one in front of me.

"Absolutely. Twenty per cent, as we agreed. Now where's that Henry got to? I could do with the loo myself," Scott said, glancing about the room.

"Sir," the waiter said, presenting a small plate. Ten purple notes lay there in two neat fans.

"Ah, my good man, god bless you," and Scott handed the waiter his pile of fives, scooping up the twenties. The waiter began to count the notes out into the dish as I watched Scott slip the twenties into his card.

"That's better, excellent, excellent," he said. He closed the card and slipped it into the envelope, sliding the whole lot into the stamped jiffy bag and sealing it tight. With a lick of his pencil he started to write his parent's address on the front.

"One eight five, one ninety," the waiter finished up. "One ninety five . . . No no, sir, you are short by five pounds."

"Hn?" Scott said, the envelope licked and sealed. "Oh that blasted bank, I didn't even check it. Sorry, may I?" and he took the notes, counting them out himself. ". . . one ninety, one ninety five . . . You're right. Damn and I've sealed – Neil, be a bless poppet. You don't have five pounds you can give this – no. No, wait. Henry owes me five. Let me get it from him."

Scott stood up.

"You'd better have your twenties back, dear chap," he said, handing the sealed, stamped jiffy-bag to the waiter. "I'll see where Henry's got to. Two ticks," and Scott wandered off towards the bathroom, humming a tune.

It's called the Flue.

The thing, the trick. It's called the Flue. They explained later. After I'd sat there with this stern head waiter for ten minutes of course. Fidgeting, rearranging the coffee cups. Waiting for Scott and Henry to come back. Which, of course they didn't.

Another waiter came and flanked the table, a clean and manicured hand on my shoulder. The head waiter cracked open the jiffy bag and opened the card.

I don't know how Scott did it. Secreted them, palmed them, whatever you want to call it. Anyway, he'd walked off with his fives and the waiter's twenties leaving me to put things right, so that was the last I saw of my petty cash. The waiter let me keep the greetings card though. It was addressed to me after all.

Dear Neil, he'd put, *like I say, only the first lesson is free. I'll be in touch – Christopher.*

Christopher Laurie. AKA Rudy, AKA Whittington, AKA J Peckard Scott, AKA Lord knows who.

And when I say 'they explained what the trick was called *later*,' you understand me right.

Later. When I saw them again.

Which I'd absolutely no *intention* of doing, you understand?

God, growing up in my family had taught me that if nothing else. I was well out of it.

It was just that . . .

See, when my headache and I got back to the shop, Laura was waiting for me.

She said I'd had a *visitor*.

five

"Some hairy fellah. Making a real scene. Rattling your shutters, kicking the door. He was pretty pissed off. Wanted to know where you were. Where *were* you? You've been closed for hours."

"Sorry. Were you . . . ? I mean was there something I . . . ?"

"Just wanted to say hi," Laura said. "Brought you a bun."

She looked at me, not blinking. In a way women don't tend to look at me. Ever. I felt the usual spidery heat creep up around my ears. I apologised with a shruggy cough, hauling up the cold clattering shutters. *Saying hi*? This woman needed a hobby. Or her coffee shop needed a marketing drive.

"And this hairy fellah," I probed. "Forty-ish? Beard? *Red Dwarf* T-shirt under a pyjama top?"

"*Star Trek*. Or *Star Wars*. One of those."

"Figures," I sighed.

We moved into the chilly shop. Two dozen notes pushed under the door from eager collectors offering me top dollar for my entire stock, plus a bunch of flowers from the offices of Boatman Beevers and Boatman apologising for their miscalculation were all notable by their absence.

"That smell's not getting any better," Laura said. "Still under-water down there?"

"For the time being," I said. She was right. The fleshy stench of death and rot was seeping into every page, every poster, every print, even up here on dry land. It wouldn't be long until my life's work was all just skip filler.

Moving out the back, I snapped on the blinking lights, the filthy kettle and my Disney tape, *The Jungle Book's* 'Trussst In Meee' slithering about the shelving, spreading unease. I promptly snapped it off again, my unease levels being dangerously high as it was.

"So who's the hairy fellah?"

"The *fellah* is Maurice. Freelance dealer," I said, booting up the laptop in the office with a clickety-click. "Also a *Connect Four* grandmaster and the one man I don't want to see. It clearly isn't enough for him that his solicitors are lurking in my letterbox every morning."

"Solici – ? He's *the guy*? Shit." Laura had perched herself against a packing crate full of poster tubes and was gesturing at me with a Lucky Strike. "And you've been out avoiding him?"

"Not quite. Remember Wednesday? That chap in the hat with the photographs?"

"Your lunch date?"

"He wants my help," I said, rattling in my password and leaving my web-page to drag itself into life, "and he's willing to pay well for it." The kettle clicked off loudly so, leaving the computer whirring, I clambered over tubes and cardboard in the kitchen to throw coffee granules all over the lino. "Did Maurice say he'd be coming back?"

"Not to me. Wants help doing *what*?"

"Oh you don't want to know. One of these?" and I waggled the Nescafé.

"Quick one," she nodded, so I found another mug, wiped living things from it and splashed some hot water about. I heard her edge into the small kitchen behind me.

"Really. I want to know," she said.

"Nnnyyeaa*hhaayyy*!" I said, which isn't much of a segue, I'll grant you. But Laura had chosen this moment to slide her hands onto my shoulders.

Not *place*, you understand. *Slide*. This with the addition of fifteen extra aitches in every word. *Whhhhant to knhhhouw*, like she was blowing out birthday candles in my ears.

Anyway, me being me, the spoon went one way, the milk went another, my body spasming like an epileptic marionette on the end of a cattle prod, barking my leg on the cupboard with a yelp. Elbows clucking, I spun around, pinned twitchily against the now-granulated counter top, chins doubling. Laura stepped away a little, palms and eyebrows raised.

"S-sorry," I said, blushing, waving a spoon feebly, "and ow." My knee began to throb.

"Not a lot of room in here, is there," she said. "That mine?"

and she reached for a coffee mug, waving off the awkwardness
like it was a drowsy wasp. I stood blinking, slack-jawed. Should I
say anything? What *was* that? An *advance*? Or was she ridding me
of dandruff like she was my mother?

With an awkward half-smile and a feeble "eh-heh", noise, I
blushed and bumbled out of the kitchen, returning to my laptop,
punching in my password and trying to think about other things.

Had I ever been comfortable around women? *Truly* comfortable? Their casual tactility, their teasing squeezing? It had certainly
taken a while with Jane. Two and half long university years in fact,
trying to work out what was flirting and what was friendliness.
Through candle-lit comedy quarrels over Tolkien and *Time Bandits*.
Over *Thunderbirds*, *Thunder-Cats* and *Blue Thunder*. And even by
the end – *after* I'd proposed, *after* Jane had accepted – one freezing
Christmas-Ball night, flushed with wine, wriggling in a too-tight
tuxedo, only *then* was I certain Jane's hand jammed down my
rented trousers in the front seat of her Fiat Uno wasn't just *having
a harmless laugh*.

Laura slunk from the kitchen so I attempted to move it all along.

"Do *you-uu*," my voice squeaked. "Ahem, sorry. Do you think
it was dishonest?" I said. "Only giving him a tenner for the signed
Siegel & Shuster pic?"

"The frhhhuitcake?" Laura said breathily. "If he wanted to be
treated fhhhhairly, he should have been more pohhhhlite. Is that
what he said then? That you were dishhhonest?"

"He said a lot of things."

I focused on the screen, my page advertising the Siegel & Shuster.
There they stood proudly, typewriter under arm, pants over trouser.
Christopher had been right. Not a single click of interest. And
right about my email account too. There among the usual spammy
drivel from *facebook.com*, three cheeky chancers – dealers no doubt
– offering fivers in cash to *take the photo off your hands*.

"A lot of things about what?" Laura pressed.

"About . . ." I looked up at her. Her eyes widened. Or I was
falling towards them. I didn't know which. I did know, however,
that I needed to tell someone about my meeting. *Anyone*. Get it
out there, out of my head, off my chest, into the real world.

J Peckard Scott, Christopher Laurie, Henry David, a brown envelope and how they were planning to put the *con* into 'massive *con*sultancy fee'.

"Hell, I'd do it," Laura said, coffee cups drained, a long-story-shortened later. "Who wouldn't? Mixing with grifters? Learning the tricks, all the switcheroos and double bluffs?"

"I don't know," I said, knees loose. "I . . . I don't *know*. They said I'd be doing nothing *technically* illegal. But . . ."

"You'd be ripping-off this comic buff, whoever he is."

"Well, helping Chris and Henry rip him off. Y'know. *Technically*."

I could feel myself slipping, my insides writhing like angry snakes. A hundred grand. A hundred *grand*. Just for helping. Maybe I wouldn't even have to *be* there? And maybe he *did* deserve it, whoever he was? Maybe he deserved it more than I deserved to let bad plumbing take my family and livelihood? Take my life?

Christ.

I gave myself a shake and moved out of the office, into the dull glare of the empty shop, over to the basement archway. The thick dead stench of damp and waste clung about the wooden steps, about the peeling walls.

"What does your wife think about all this?" Laura asked. "The solicitors? Going under?"

A guilty pain leaned on my kidneys.

"I haven't told her," I said.

"*You haven't* – ?"

"No. Not . . . Not yet. Not everything. She knows there was a *leak*. But the rest? She doesn't . . ." I chewed my lip angrily. "She doesn't need the worry."

"You're coming home with solicitors' threats, stinking of rotten cardboard. And you haven't –"

"I promised," I said. I swallowed hard. I thought about my wife. Her father. "When Jane fell pregnant. I promised I would take care of them. Both." I shut the basement door, fat, swollen wood sticking, bulging in the frame. "Y'know I'm the *only* person she's ever met that hasn't cared about her title. Who wanted to talk to her about *her* interests. Who didn't think dressing as Wonder Woman and playing Lois Lane at primary

school wasn't *unsuitable for someone with her heritage*. She loves
me for that. And I love her because she doesn't care who she
is. She likes a summer blockbuster, popcorn, can name everyone
who's ever drawn *Judge Dredd* and doesn't mind who knows it.
She's . . . I *love* her."

The shop fell quiet. I let my eyes drag around it. For the last
time? It seemed that way.

"Do you think you'll be able to keep your flat? I mean, legal
fees? They can really . . ."

The pain in my side leaned a little harder.

"I don't know."

"Maybe it's time you told your wife. In case?"

"Not yet," I said. "I've got a few . . ." I sighed. "Not yet."

Laura was pulling on her coat.

"And you're sure she hasn't figured it out?"

"Jane? Never," I said. "I've been careful."

"Hey there," I hollered a few hours later. I had nursed a lonely
pint in the pub near work for a while, scoring numbers onto
napkins with a chewed biro but it was no good. I had to get home
to my family. Thumping through the door, I wrinkled at the perfume
that still clung about the thin walls of the flat, twisted with baby
poo and warm milk. "Hello-oo?"

No answer.

"J?" I said, climbing the stairs.

Nothing.

There is a sixth sense thing. A shiver. An uneasy vibration of
atmosphere that tells one somehow when something isn't right.

Regretfully it turns out, I don't have it.

Which is why I slapped a chirpy grin on my mush, dropped
my satchel to the hall floor next to the pushchair and Jane's overnight
bag and wandered into the lounge. Jane sat on the tatty couch
watching television. Lana was on her lap dozing.

Overnight bag?

"Hey sweetheart," I said, leaning in for the kiss. Jane didn't
reciprocate. Didn't respond. Didn't move. Hovering an inch from
her awkwardly, I slowly retracted again. This wasn't right. I looked
over at the television. It was awfully dark. Awfully dark and awfully

quiet and awfully off. Off, as in *not on*. In fact, not on, in the same way going through all my box files and digging out all the secret paperwork and laying it all on the carpet in a huge incriminating fan is *not on*.

Overnight bag.

Shit.

"Were you going to tell me?" Jane said. The cat, clearly hogging all the sixth sense, squeezed out from beneath the couch and darted into the hall for cover.

"What?" I said, my voice squeakily high. The wrong thing to say. "What have you —"

"Found out?" Her voice was firm. Level. Practised. She'd had this conversation already without me. Jane cradled Lana gently, laying her on a blanket next to her and got up.

"Look, Jane, look —"

"Look at what? Hn? Look at what?" she said. Not shouting, exactly. But not happy.

Oh God. Oh God she knows. She knows. Oh God. Keep calm. Calm.

Shit.

"Take . . . take it easy, it's not as bad —"

"Look at what? All the solicitors' letters you've been hiding? Look at the bank statements you've stuffed at the bottom of your files? Final demands from *plumbers*? *Drain clearers*? *Skip hire*?"

"Jane . . ."

"Dad phoned. Said his financial chap would be able to put together some portfolios before we scheduled the meeting."

"Jane —"

"But he'd need some idea of our status. So he asked me to look up some figures. The savings, the shop . . ."

Daddy knew. *Daddy* knew. Oh *Christ*.

"Did . . . did you tell him . . . ?"

"About what? About *WHAT*?! Where would I fucking *start*?!" she yelled suddenly, writhing, fists clenched. "The *two* missed *mort-gage payments*?! Is that right? How have we missed *two payments*?! *Where's the money?!*"

"I was going to —"

"They'll take the *flat*, Neil!"

"They won't take the *flat*."

"They'll take the *flat*! That's what happens! You don't pay? They *take the flat*!" She scooped Lana up, cradling her, protecting her in her shoulders. Crouching unsteadily, she rootled through the carpet of paperwork. Through letters I'd thought I'd hidden. Letters *I had* hidden. God knows how she'd found them.

"Who the fuck are *Rod-o-Matic*? Is this *right*? Three *thousand pounds* you've paid them?" She stood, brandishing an invoice. "A *little leak* you said?"

"I said —"

"You *said*," and her eyes blazed, "a *little leak*. You stood by my hospital bed. Six weeks ago. In the maternity ward. I *asked* you and you *said* a 'little' leak."

"I . . . I didn't. I was . . ."

"And *THIS*?!" she screamed, moving to the mantelpiece, snatching up a letter. My Siegel & Shuster photograph and a ceramic Lex Luthor were sent tumbling.

"Easy —"

"What the *fuck* is *THIS*?!"

From my spot by the door I recognised the letterhead. Boatman, Beevers and Boatman.

"*Thirty-six thousand pounds*?!" she yelled, waving the heavy legal stationery at me. "Why do we owe this Maurice man *thirty-six thousand pounds*?!"

"It's all right," I said, moving towards the mantelpiece for repairs, stomach tumbling. "I-I mean I'm sorting something out . . ." The photo was okay, a little bent at the —

"Leave that. *Leave it!* Who is he? What have you *done*?"

Lana began to hiccup and wake in her arms.

"Earl's Court," I whispered. "We were splitting the cost. Shhhhh"

"Don't *shush me!*"

"Lana —"

"*Tell me!*"

"Maurice . . . shit. Maurice brought me all his gear. Boxes. For the fair. I didn't know what was in them. I stored them in the shop cellar. You were in hospital. Then . . . I don't know, a pipe burst . . ."

"*Oh!* So it's a *burst* now? What happened to *leak*?" Jane began to vibrate. Almost imperceptibly. Hands, teeth. Eyes wide and white. Lana gurgled, shifting in her arms.

"I thought . . . I thought I'd sorted it. But . . ."

"*But?*"

"Overnight. I don't know what happened. Frost or something?" I suggested feebly.

"What happened?"

"I-I was going to tell you –"

"*Neil!*" she bellowed. Lana began her keening siren, little fists tight.

"I didn't . . . You weren't in a state to –"

"Oh so it's *my* fault!"

"No! –"

"You idiot. *Idiot!*" and she pushed past me with a sharp elbow, storming down the hall. I scuttled after her, hands in my hair.

"I came in one morning and it was everywhere. The pipe was spraying this black . . . The boxes, all over the shelves. Maurice's stock, everything I was storing. Pulped. Beyond salvaging. I lost half *my* stuff as well," I pleaded. As if this made it all right somehow.

"What about the insurance?"

"Well usually, but *Maurice's* stuff. Extra coverage, I . . ."

"You said you'd sent a cheque," Jane said. She was standing by the worktop in our freezing kitchen, shushing Lana's tears, jigging her in her arms. "When that letter first came and I asked you. You said not to worry. Said you'd sent a cheque to the insurance. Neil?"

"I know. I *know*. I was *meant* to. I guess –"

"*Meant* to? Great. *Grrreat.*"

I looked at her beautiful face, torn, twisted and bent with rage. I was empty. Spent. I had nothing to give.

"So how are you going to pay it?" she said flatly.

Not *we*, you notice.

"C'mon? How? Where are you going to get the mortgage money and thirty-six –" She was pale. Trembling. I was going to get a smack in the face or tears. I was bracing myself hopefully for a smack in the face. "*Tell me!*"

I opened my mouth and a little croak came out. I was breaking her heart and all I could offer her were frog noises.

"*God!* This, *this* is why you were looking at that *stupid* price book isn't it," she blazed. "That night? Seeing if you could bail yourself out. Isn't it? With Dad's present. Sell it. Isn't it? Tell me. *Tell me!*" Jane shrieked, eyes glistening. The plush, embroidered, imported rug I had built her life upon had been tugged, with one sharp yank and her life was falling about around her.

"It's all right, it's all right," I lied, moving gingerly forward.

"*It's not all right!*"

I tried to hold them, but she turned her shoulder, writhing with rage. I stepped back, arms loose and shruggy, able only to watch as Jane strode out of the kitchen. I stood breathing deep, kicked in the gut, alone in the kitchen among the £2 car-boot kettle and the £25 'o.n.o.' washing machine. I could hear Jane putting Lana to bed in the nursery next door, cheap blinds clattering, drawers slamming.

Deep breath. I moved out into the hall where I met Jane emerging, eyes red and raw.

"It's all right," I said. All I could say.

"How?" she said. Quietly, steadying herself on the banister. "How is it all right?"

"They're old letters. I've sorted it out. Please, *trust* me. Let me *explain*, it's okay shhhhhh, it's okay . . ." and I folded myself around her shaking body. "It's all going to be okay . . ."

Lies.

Of course lies.

But she was crying. *Crying.* I've never learned what to do with tears. I didn't have teenage summers full of making-out and breaking up. I had teenage summers full of visiting my dad and watching *Batman*, *Backdraft* and *Beetlejuice*. I can't deal with tears. Shouting and fighting I can cope with. I had a million comic-book pages full of instructions. But tears? There's no response. What do you do with tears but hug and lie? Whatever words will stem the flow. Verbal duck-tape – *easy, it's okay, don't worry, trust me*.

They say you should never trust a man who says trust me, I know. But what else could I give her?

The truth? Ha.

Jane didn't want the truth. I mean, people don't, do they? Oh they *think* they do. They *tell* themselves they do. But they don't. Jane didn't. She wanted to hear that everything was going to be all right. That her husband hadn't lied when he had promised to take care of her. That her father had been wrong when he'd said I was a scruffy waster. That I'd spoken to the insurance people. That they would cover the damage. Valued customer, twenty-eight-day-flood cover, emergency call-out, blah-blah-blah.

That was my role for the next few hours. To be the man she thought she'd married. The man I'd promised to be. Strong and soothing, using lies like Bonjela, cooling the ulcer of her anxiety. *There there, easy now, don't worry.*

I guess Jane must have bought it. It calmed her down, anyway.

I made tea. Cleared up the paperwork. Rubbed her feet, made soothy noises. While all the time of course, through all the lies, I was –

Well. Shitting my pants, obviously.

"You . . . you should write to them."

"Write . . . ?"

"To everyone," Jane sniffed, looking for a dry corner of her kitchen towel. "The solicitors, the bank, the skip-people. Let them know the situation's taken care of. That they'll get their money. Five *working* days, is it, this emergency cover?"

"Hn? Oh. Oh yes. Yes. I-I will," I said, absently enough so I could claim to not remember.

Jane was curled in the chair, cushion hugged tight on her lap, feet tucked beneath her. The television (one owner, £25 o.n.o.) burbled the Channel 4 news. I was at the mantelpiece, surveying the damage. Lex Luthor had a little paint missing from his elbow and there was a white crease running across Joe Shuster's shoe, but it didn't seem to have worried him. He still stood, hands on hips, feet apart. Proud, strong, invincible. Pretty damned confident for a man in a trilby hat with his underpants over his suit.

"I can't believe you didn't *tell* me."

"I know," I said softly, swallowing the guilt, keeping it low. "I know, but we had a deal. You've got enough on your plate with the little one. It's about time for her feed, isn't it?"

"Just about. We should . . . what's that? Is that new?"

Jane was staring at my tacky wristwatch. I waggled it and laughed and made some comment about a customer giving it to me. Chunky. Fake. Ha-ha, anything in the freezer?

Fortunately for me at this point, we were interrupted by a toot-toot from the street and a buzz on the intercom. Jane and I exchanged shrugs. Sniffing and wiping, Jane moved to the intercom in the hall. I went to the window.

A dull green Bedford van was at the kerb among the remains of Laura's broken glass. First thoughts were another robbery. Same characters targeting the same street. But the bonnet was up, back doors open and a fluorescent Halfords repair kit was visible on the pavement. A figure sat in the passenger seat. An awfully formal car-jacking if it was one.

Jane wandered back in.

"A guy just needs some water for his radiator or something. Do you want to take him down a jug? I'll see what we've got for tea."

"Evenin' mate," Henry said from the doorstep, his Antipodean smile failing to reflect my rather British panic. Despite the chill, Henry was in a bright surf-wear T-shirt and denim jeans cut off at his calves. "Thanks for that," and he took the jug and shuffled down the steps in his flip-flops to the van.

"*What . . . ? Wh-what the hell do you want? How did you get this address?*" I hissed, jumpy, pulling the door to and following him onto the cold street. Under a black October sky, early Hallowe'en fireworks whizzed and whistled, bursting and banging brightly. "What are you *doing* here? Jesus . . ." I shivered, throwing anxious looks up at the soft light in the window above me. The television was flickering.

"Forgive the interruption old fruit," Christopher said, pumping down the passenger window, letting a sweet plume of pipe smoke escape into the night. He sat, comfy in a dark tweed jacket and striped club tie. "Knocking up the ole homestead and such. But my grandfather's clock, while too tall for the shelf and standing ninety years on the tufted Wilton, is whizzing around like a gumshoe's desk fan."

"*Gumshoe?* What do you *want?*"

"Tick tock tick tock," his pipe bobbed. "What's it to be?"

My heart slammed hard, fingers cold against the edge of the van door.

"Consider the lilies of the field, Neil," Christopher said, sucking on his pipe. "They do not sow or reap."

"Yes, yes and they don't rip each other off at three-card monte either. What's your point?" I could feel panic spreading about my chest. My throat was closing, fat and tight.

"My point Neil, as I suspect you are aware, is that this planet of ours, this island earth, is divided into the strong and the weak. The hunters and the hunted. The circle of life, as Elton John revoltingly put it. Every mouse knows it is food for cats, every antelope that it is food for lions. Nature has designed us to freely exploit one another for our own good. It's her plan."

I jumped at the loud splash beside me. Henry poured the water into the kerbside drain.

Christopher was still talking.

"Now in the savannah, in the forest, these roles are irreversible. Antelopes cannot *choose* to be the hunters. Creatures are born *into* their roles and they do their best to survive. In *our* species, however," and Christopher's eyes flashed, "the playing field is more or less level. We can choose to be lions or we can choose to be antelopes. Everyone makes that decision for themselves. Now, you think that in a world thick with lions, those who *choose* to be antelopes are, what? Saints? Salts of the earth?"

A car hissed past us, headlights bright. A dog barked in the distance somewhere. A firework banged, lighting up the street in pink neon. The world dropped into silence again.

"No. These people are *fools*, Neil. Saps. Dunderheads. Boobies. Antelopes queuing up to put their heads into the lion's mouth – too gutless to go hunting themselves."

From the warmth of his passenger seat and the comfort of his logic, Christopher looked at me, eyes glinting. He plumed a little pipe smoke once more.

"Oh they'll pretend it's because they are 'good guys'. Because they are fine upstanding citizens. Nice, honest fellows who don't think that way. And I suppose as the lions gnaw at their throats, tearing them to bloody bits, they can lie back with a clear heart.

But the truth is that it's because they're fools. Fools who can't grasp the rules of the game. But hell, good luck to them," and he raised his pipe in a mock toast. "We are born screaming onto a cold and lonely planet, Neil. Three score years and ten and then we are food for worms. If you want to spend that time being poor, polite and picked-on like a martyr, go ahead. You'll get a big turn out at your funeral, I expect."

"But then so did Reggie Kray," Henry drawled, handing me back my empty jug. He began to pile the repair kit back into the back of the van.

"Our mark is a fool. Simple as that. A greedy, dishonest –"

"*Dishonest?*" I said, hauling the sarcasm on with a truck. "Well mercy me, what next?"

"Lions hunting lions is at least a fair fight, Neil," Christopher said without missing a beat. "You would prefer we targeted you? Your lovely wife?"

I swallowed hard. I turned and looked back up at the window, winter wind ruffling my collar, prickling my neck. The nets twitched and Jane was there, bathed in a cosy indoor glow, Lana bobbing on her hip. She tilted her head to one side. My wife. My family. My home.

Five working days, is it, this emergency cover?

Hn? Oh. Oh yes. Yes.

"Look," I whispered, a sick claw gripping my gut. "I need . . ." My stomach wriggled free and gave an uncoordinated back-flip, a feeble 3.2 from the judges. "I-I need *assurances*. It's just a consultancy job. *You* didn't tell me why you needed the information, *I* didn't ask, right? I mean . . . Christ, I mean it's not *dangerous*, right?"

"*At last when he was out on the street, he exclaimed 'Oh God, how loathsome this is!*" Christopher warbled camply. "*Could I really? No, it's nonsensical! It's absurd. Could I really ever have contemplated such a monstrous act? It shows what filth my head is capable of though. Filthy. Mean. Vile. VILE!*"

"Chris?" Henry said, slamming the back doors. "You want to lay off the Dostoyevsky?"

"Forgive me Neil darling. The most dangerous part of your role my dear fellow, will be taking a crisp cheque for a hundred thousand smackerooni's up to the poppet at your bank next Wednesday and handing it over without peeing your pants with excitement."

"Wednesday?"

"November fourth. Five days Neil. That's all it'll take."

Five days.

My heart thudded. A cold London wind flicked grit and ash about my face. Somewhere distantly the dog barked again. A siren whooped. Policemen. Out catching bad men.

"It sounds risky . . ."

"*But what had he said about risk?*" Henry said, shutting the bonnet with a clunk and twirling his keys on a finger.

"Thank you Henry," Christopher bobbed. "*Risks were what made the whole thing fun.*"

I looked at him.

"Ripley. Certainly more fun than a court appearance. More fun than selling the sorry, sopping remains of your shop for a pittance."

"All right, all right. You don't have to —"

"Disappointing your wife. Your father-in-law. Certainly more fun than spending cold nights like this kicking around in a freezing bedsit, eating Pot Noodle and wondering if you'll ever see your daughter again."

Henry climbed into the van cab and started the engine.

"It'd really be helping us out mate," he said. "Trust me."

"Trust you?"

"*Trust* me," Christopher smiled, pipe bobbing. "Come on, old chap. What do you say, eh? What do you say? You onboard? *What do you say?*"

"Mr Martin?"

I jumped. And I mean jumped. Copyright *Scooby Doo* 1975 Hanna-Barbera All Rights Reserved. Limbs shot out, keys dropped, feet left the floor. I might even have made an involuntary *mnye-hhha* noise.

All understandable of course. From the moment Christopher and Henry had left me on Friday night, taking their pipe smoke, Halfords kit and a large chunk of my soul with them, I had been on the jumpy side: checking out of windows, drumming my fingers, fidgeting through *Have I Got News For You*.

"Mr Neil Martin?"

I turned. A tall, broad black man with cropped hair and a dark voice stepped out from the doorway across the street, squinting into the grey morning light.

Policeman. Everything about him said policeman. Late thirties, waxy barbour, dark khaki slacks, the black, thick-soled shoes, the rolling, world-weary nowwhatavewe'ere gait. He had a coffee in his large hand and a rolled-up tabloid under his arm. He moved slowly towards me across the icy cobbles.

Oh God. Oh God.

Hands jittery, knees loose, I twittered with my keys. This was it. Accomplice. Accessory. It was all over. I turned to resume unlocking the shutters, trying to act naturally. Fumbling, hands numb, I dropped the keys again with a heavy clink. Shit. Shit, come *on*. From behind the grille, inside the shop, a row of faded faces watched, damp cardboard edges fluffed and bent: Clint Eastwood; Edward G Robinson; Mae West. They sighed a collective, cardboard sigh. *Some villain you turned out to be.*

In the greasy reflection, I could see the policeman still approaching. Not smiling. Either he was one of those men who couldn't do two things at once or I was in trouble.

"DI Thomas," he said in his dark voice, winter breath swirling around the steaming coffee. I turned slowly. He had stopped a cuffing's distance from me. Big frown. Big trouble. "You've been speaking to my colleagues I understand?" he said.

"Uhm, your *colleagues*?" The world slowed down a little. I thought back to the last time I had had policemen in my life. Indeed, in my lounge. "Er . . . you mean from Monday? Laura's car?"

"*Car*?" DI Thomas looked at me, easing his head forward an inch, peering hard into my eyes.

He had a big face. Big and broad. A wide slab of forehead and a close cropped afro. His eyes, white and wide, scoured mine.

We stayed locked like that for an awkward moment, cold wind biting our faces, until eventually the policeman broke the stare, broke a smile, stepped away and waved his newspaper in the air like he was signalling a taxi.

"Just being careful mate," he said, grinning. "I understand you're our store man?"

"Store – ?"

"Good *morning*, Master Martin," another voice said, and suddenly I was surrounded. Christopher was at my side, a take-out tray in one gloved hand, pipe in the other, *Financial Times* under his elbow, Walkman headphones looped about his neck. He smelled of leather and aftershave and his tray smelled of breakfast.

"He's clean," the policeman said, sucking on his coffee.

A third gentleman was flanking my left. Younger, late twenties or thereabouts. Dark, sunken eyed, he had olive, Mediterranean skin, a wiry, angular way about him and was topped with an unruly thatch of long dark curly hair. He looked dazed and tired, mouth hung open like its catch was broken. He blinked dully at me, Walkman hissing away in his ears. He sucked hard on a stubby cigarette, stale and musty, like a Goth's laundry bag.

"Happy Hallowe'en," Christopher smiled. "Introductions over croissants I think," and he waggled the cardboard tray, eyebrows bouncing towards the shutters. "Shall we?"

It was Saturday, it was ten past eight and it had begun.

"Don't worry about Pete. Come come, have a pastry," Christopher wafted, slapping down his newspaper and setting up the breakfast things on the counter as the phoney copper moved swiftly through the cold shop, snapping on surgeon's gloves and heading through to the back office.

Julio, he of the olive skin and unruly hair, had dumped a large purple Reebok sports bag to the filthy floor and was now sending his eyes scurrying about the shop's ceiling, floorboards and windows like a timid child looking for loft spiders. He curled an unimpressed lip before tugging out another set of surgical gloves, snapping them on in a cloud of talc.

"What that fackin' stink?" he said in a slow, Portuguese accent.

"Sorry," I shrugged. "Downstairs, there's been a —"

"An' you some gaysexual?" He peered and sneered about the walls.

"God, why does everyone think I'm some kind of — ?"

"Back door?" the black policeman said, appearing in the shop again.

"What?"

"Back door. Where does it go?"

"Uh, nowhere. Just out to the alley. It's an old fire escape. What do you — ?"

"And who are your neighbours?"

"*Neigh* — ?"

"Next door, gaylord," Julio sighed. "Left right. Who got we?"

"God. Uhm, right is a design studio. Empty most of the time. Left is a guy called Schwartz. Rare books. Wouldn't worry about him. Memory like a sieve. If I've asked him to clear up his rubbish once, I've —"

"That come down?" and Pete pointed a business-like finger at the wall where Garland and Astaire clinched in faded technicolour.

"The *Easter Parade*? Well, I-I suppose —"

"And that the basement?" he thumbed at the peeling doorway. "Show me."

"Chop chop gentlemen," Christopher said, popping his pipe into his mouth and rummaging in his overcoat pocket. "Shutters up, thirty-eight minutes," and he retrieved a kitchen timer. Pale blue plastic, its front cracked and greasy, he gave it a wind and set it down purring amongst the cups.

Dizzied with the activity, I led Pete to the bulging, buckled doorway and heaved it open.

"Christ," Pete scowled, gloved hand over his face. "You got sewage down there?" and he reached in, twanging on the bulb. The black water had risen, now covering the bottom three steps. A deflated bin bag drifted past on the oily tide like driftwood.

"What remains of my livelihood," I said.

There was a loud, rusty scrape from the back office, followed by an even louder tutting.

"Oh no no no," Christopher twittered, emerging. "You've a back door that sounds like a Melbourne housewife, Neil." He had his black notebook out and was jotting with his silver pencil, pipe bobbing in his mouth. "First job, sort out those hinges. Pete? Oil. I want that door smoother than Guinness. Than Guinness spilt on cashmere, in fact."

Julio tugged a can of *3 in 1* oil from his purple bag and tossed it to Pete who snatched it from the air and disappeared out the back. From the bag then came a small Roberts radio which Julio clicked on to a mumbling news programme and propped on a rack. This was followed by a copy of *USA Today* and a *Daily Mail,* both of which joined the other papers on the counter. The cover stories were streaked and striped with coloured highlighters.

"Hey," Julio sighed, standing up within a cloud of foul smoke. His accent was tired, thick and phlegmy. "Laptop. Pet or partner?"

"Sorry? Pet or . . . ?"

"*Your password, dear chap?*" Christopher whispered, leaning in a little.

"Oh. Uhmm, pet. Streaky," I said, spelling it out. The man rolled his eyes and disappeared into the back office. "Aren't we . . . aren't we missing someone?" I asked.

"Humn? Oh, young Henry might be with us a little later with any luck," Christopher said, flipping through the *Daily Mail.* Occasional stories were rung with the same highlighter colours. "He should be picking up our MacMuffin, as Julio dear likes to put it."

"Fack-you," a voice snapped from the office.

"Tick tock tick tock," Christopher said, popping the top from his latte and licking the frothy lid. "Nerd-watching 101 begins in thirty-eight minutes and we've still the papers to get through. Neil, we'll keep to your office back there if we may? Base of ops, so to speak," and he moved over to the radio, turning up the volume.

"MacMuff – ? *McGuffin*, right?" I said.

"*The key element in any suspense story.* Very good dear boy, very good. You know your Hitchcock. Although," Christopher said, checking his Mickey Mouse watch. "Twenty past eight? Hmm. It's possible Henry's now deep in conversation with the desk sergeant at Paddington nick, buying his freedom and selling us all down the Swanee Vestas. Now then Neil-i-kins, we're going to need a full set of keys, my poppety-poo. Each, I'm afraid. And a handful of air fresheners while you're about it."

"Wait, did y-you say *desk sergeant*?"

"Hmn? Well it's possible of course. If Henry's been picked up pulling some short-con for a little beer money, dropping us lot in it would be the natural thing to do. Now then, these keys . . ."

"But," I jittered, glancing about the shop. Christopher was rootling through his pockets, wrinkling his nose, humming absently to himself. Pete and Julio rattled about in the back office. None of them seemed remotely bothered that, apparently, the police were swooping and whooping down Wardour Street towards us at that very moment.

Feeling that someone should probably do something, I scuttled a panicky scuttle up the shop, sliding home the bolts on the front door.

"Shouldn't we . . . ?" I began, having not the faintest idea what it was we should or shouldn't. "I mean . . . Henry?"

"Or on the other hand, he might just be running a bit late," Christopher shrugged. "Who's to say? Nobody knows anybody, Neil."

"There no honour among thief," Julio said, emerging from the office doorway, clicking off his Walkman, hoisting it from his belt. "Trust no one. Absolute no one. You think I trust Pete boy? Or Mr Cheesy Big here? Not for second."

"Me neither," Pete added, behind him. "Hinges sorted. Guinness on cashmere on Leslie Philips."

"But you must . . ." My head span. "I mean, you all work together?"

"Insurance," Christopher said, peeling off his Rupert-check

scarf to reveal a paisley cravat. "We are each other's '*Get Out Of Jail Free*' cards. Any of us, if caught, could buy our freedom by naming everyone else. That's why we have each other around."

The three men fell silent. From the radio, the news burbled to itself.

"Holy crap," I said, dizzily. What the hell had I got myself into?

"Now Neil, be an utter love pot and cut us four sets of keys." He had flipped to the back of his notebook and peeled out a fifty-pound note. "Wardour Street should have somewhere. Neil? Neil, you still with us dear chap?"

"Me? Uh-uh, no way. I'm not leaving you here by yourselves."

They looked at me, a frozen tableau. Three nations: Pete and Julio in the doorway, Christopher by the radio, clutching his coffee. Apart from their hands, sheathed eerily in white surgical gloves, all tall, rather plain, rather forgettable men.

"No offence," I said, trying and failing to assert some sort of authority. "But . . . I don't know if I trust you. Not yet."

"Yes. Terribly wise, dear fellow, terribly wise," Christopher sang. "You don't want to be too trusting young Neil. Places you in grave danger."

"From who?"

"People like me, as it happens. Now then, Pete? Make a list. You're going shopping."

Julio, Christopher and I spent the next hour clearing the back office, hauling dripping, stinking bin bags out to the back alley in an atmosphere of clinical detachment. At one point I attempted to lighten the mood and enquired as to how long they had all been friends.

Julio promptly snorted, lit a foul cigarette and turned up the volume on his Walkman.

"*Friends, dear boy,*" Christopher wafted, patting down his pockets for his tobacco, "*is an American televisual programme. Friends are merely enemies who haven't found you out yet. In life, as in diarrhoea, we are alone.*"

And it certainly appeared that way. There was no chummy banter, no small talk. Words that were exchanged were about the job and the job alone. Escape routes, doorways, timetables, costumes.

Julio, Pete and Henry were just men in Christopher's line of work. Men bound by mistrust, suspicion and paranoia. Never relaxed, never at ease, never off guard. Circling each other. Backs to the wall. Twitchy at the doorbell. Jumpy at the phone.

Almost as jumpy as me, in fact.

"I'm *not* stalling, Maurice, I'm not. You will *get* the rest of your money. I've agreed to accept Cheng's five hundred for my *Sting*, so . . . I *know*, but he assured me that sale would open the doors to his other contacts. Plus my insurance company are . . . Well I've told your solicitors, they're well aware . . . I'm just saying, you'll get it. Just a few more days. There's no need to come round kicking my shutters and . . . *Fine*, fine, you *do* that. See how far it gets you. Hello? He-hello?"

Shit. I hung up the phone, clammy hands all a tremble.

"Problem Neil?" Christopher piped up.

"Huh? Uhmm, m-maybe. Look . . . you're sure about this hundred grand right?"

"In good time, poppet. You were telling us? The Golden Age . . . ?"

"Oh, er yes. Right. Basically all collectable comics fall . . . It's just this guy, his solicitors? I've got to pay him. In a week's time they'll start handing out summonses."

"Fall − ?"

"Sorry. Fall into ages. Golden Age, Post-Golden, Pre-Silver, Silver and Post-Silver."

I breathed deep, trying to steady myself, push worry aside. The three men sat in the chilly office among the remains of take-away breakfast, below the dangling, piney tang of a dozen Magic Trees sellotaped to the strip lights and scribbled their shorthand obediently.

"And people speak this way, they do?" Julio piped up at the back through a cloud of cigarette smoke − his six or seven hundredth query of the morning. "Would say, *come this way sir, I have for you some fine Pre-Silver comic for sale?*"

"Oh no no. It's a technical term. Collectors' guides, pricing guides, that sort of thing. People will ask for characters more often than not. *Got any Captain America pal?*"

Julio nodded and continued with his notes.

"Earlier the better. Golden is naturally worth more than Post-Golden," I went on, pacing anxiously, trying to shake off my jumpy nerves. "Pre-Silver more than Silver, you know. Popular characters, your Supermans and Spider-Mans – that's hyphenated –"

"Uh, *Neil* sweetums?" Christopher interrupted.

"God. Sorry. Sorry." I clenched my brain, thinking for a moment. "Okay, something like '*Yeah, Conway's Post-Silver could have kicked Stan Lee's Silver Spider-Man's arse.*'"

"Got it . . ." Pete jotted. ". . . *arse*. Right."

This was proving to be the main problem in my hastily ill-prepared lecture. Christopher and his team had no interest in *actual* knowledge. None at all. Only the *appearance* of knowledge. The names to drop, the attitudes to adopt. It was almost eleven o'clock and I'd pretty much wasted the first two hours droning on about paper manufacture, insisting they all remove their gloves to feel my beloved *Sting* poster – the linen-backed surface, how the autograph ink had taken to the cloth.

"In fact, to be honest, if in doubt about anything," I said, "just pick something pre-forties and make sneery noises about everything else. Pretend you work at HMV and someone's asked if you've got any Celine Dion."

The room nodded and jotted.

"And what pray can you tell us," Christopher said. He placed his pipe to one side, licking his lips, fountain pen poised. "Of original *pieces*?"

"*Pieces* . . . ?"

"Mnm. Collectables. The one-offs. Micheal Keaton's Batman codpiece p'raps? A typewriter belonging to this, this . . ." and he riffled back through his Moleskin. "This Stan Lee chappie?"

"That he actually *used*? God, I don't know. I mean if there was proof he'd written, like, the first X-Men story on it or something, then, gee . . ." and my eyes widened at the thought. "Something rare like that could be big bucks. But –"

"*Big*?" Pete and Julio said together, looking up quickly.

"Sure. Could be. I mean like anything else there's an element of fashion to the market. Maybe if an artist dies, or it's a fiftieth anniversary. '78 was a good year for *Superman* gear, what with the movie.

But he's perennial. Most of your Golden-Age-ers are. Any memorabilia for the biggies: Captain Marvel, Batman, Doc Savage . . ."

I realised the three men were staring at me. Unblinking, mouths ajar.

"Am I . . . what? Am I missing something?"

Pete and Julio looked across at Christopher.

He opened his mouth to speak, hesitated, and then changed his mind, pronouncing it would be a good time for a break.

"How you feeling dear boy? Quite a morning. All hunky-dory? You're doing terribly well."

Leaving Pete and Julio slapping their notebooks shut and stretching their backs, Christopher slipped an arm about my shoulders, steering me from the damp cramp of the cluttered office, out into the quiet of the shop. Grey winter light peered through the greasy windows, illuminating the faded cardboard and dust. Despite the straining scented trees, the place still smelled of death.

"Me? Oh, fine," I said, trying to cover the fat knot of nerves jammed somewhere deep in my intestines. This wasn't right. Helping these men. Getting involved. Having them here. This *wasn't right*. I needed to say something. To stop them. To –

"Splendiful. Splendifully wondellent in fact." Christopher wound his kitchen timer around fifteen minutes, setting it purring away once more. "We are but clay on your wheel and you mould us like a young Demi Moore." He slid his droopy eyes over the still terrain. "Bit slow today?"

"Today. Yesterday. Tomorrow. Look . . . Look Christopher, I'm not sure I –"

"*Thousands of sales people are pounding the pavements,*" Christopher interrupted in what I now was recognising as his 'quote' voice. "*Tired, discouraged and underpaid. Why?*"

I looked at him. He looked back at me, eyes shining.

"*Because they are always only thinking of what* they *want. They don't realise that neither you or I want to buy anything. If we did, we would go out and buy it. If salespeople can show us how their services or merchandise will help us solve our problems, they won't need to sell us. We'll buy.*"

I was about to ask him the origin of this particularly fatuous nugget when his two cohorts appeared from the office. Christopher grabbed Pete's arm.

"Pete. Your shopping list. Add a bible for our Mr Chips here."

Pete gave a nod, jotted a note in his book and, zipping up his Barbour, headed out into the freezing street, leaving Julio rustling about with his shoes.

"Julio, dear?" Christopher said.

"I check basement," Julio muttered, elastic-banding two Selfridges carrier bags about his battered walking boots like wellies. "Security in this place is joke." He shot me a sneery look, spitty dog-end hanging from his lips and he barged past, clamping headphones back over his hair.

"Then I'll give our Henry a call I think," Christopher smiled. "He should be on his way. Best to check we're not all about to get pinched don't you think? Yes. Yes, best to be sure. Hmn. Righty-ho," and he fumbled for his mobile phone and tum-ti-tummed back into the office.

Thus I found myself alone with just a sickening gutful of dread and the post. I decided to get the post out of the way so I could concentrate fully on the sickening dread.

There was the usual from Earl's Court. Parking and unloading facilities. All stalls to be opened by 9am on the thirteenth of November for Health & Safety inspection. Although from the view from the top of my cellar steps, it was looking more and more like I'd have no choice but to cancel completely. Five sopping bin bags, a signed Siegel & Shuster and a cracked Elvis clock weren't going to make much of a stand.

Two letters were from green biro obsessives, one of them wanting anything connected to Corey Feldman, *pre-Goonies only*, underlined four times.

The bank had written too, of course. As always. I tore it in half and binned it, unopened. Same with the Beevers and Boatman. I couldn't think about them, my head was too full of Christopher and Jane. Terrified she was going to walk in.

In fact, I was in no state to worry about basements or bailiffs so I just started tidying up. Filing letters, the Earl's Court stuff. Keeping distracted, keeping busy.

Which was why I found it.

I picked it up, listening for sounds. Nothing. Just the purr of the kitchen timer, Christopher's mumble and the rustle of Julio splashing below me, cursing in Portuguese. Prising it open carefully, it gave a crackle, half a dozen loose pages slipping from the flimsy spine. It was cheap. Moleskin-looking, but fake. Rymans or WHSmith, two quid tops. The only person I had ever known to carry a notebook like this had been my old university pal Benno. He had favoured the red spiral-bound type and filled it with moony poems about a girl named only as 'J-' that had caused something of an awkward evening when I found it slipped inside a Bob Dylan LP. Christopher it appeared was more of the stream-of-consciousness type. Filling almost every page, in his painfully neat nib, a torrential flood of ideas. In no order, with no system. Just on and on and on.

Friendsreunited. Maurer & Fitzgerald Ltd. Insurance & Valuation. Aldersgate EC1. O'Shea. Breath mints. Matches. Zippo. Bic. Less sleep. Less sleep. Less sleep. Bloomsbury? Revenge. Gold watch. Hamp', Warwick', Hertford'? Peter Simons/Simon Peters?

I flicked an anxious look over my shoulder before turning to another random page.

'People rarely succeed at anything unless they have fun doing it.' D. Carnegie. EBAY 5PM. Pigeon Drop. Jump the fence. 'They were at least agonisingly aware of the easy money in the vicinity, and convinced it was theirs for –'

". . . a few words in the right key," Christopher completed behind me, making me drop the book with a start. "*The Great Gatsby*. May I?" he said, holding out a gloved hand.

"I . . ."

"Not a problem Neil darling, not a problem at –"

There was a honk from the street and the rumbling bubble of an idling taxi.

"A-ha! That's our boy," Christopher said.

"He late," Julio called out, thudding up the rickety stairwell.

"Let us lend a bicep shall we? Come come, *animato, animato*," and he pushed me up the shop, through the jangling door to the street.

It was freezing. The cobbles twinkled, frost dusting them like powdered glass, wind biting noses and chins. The surrounding streets honked with muffled traffic, sirens, delivery vans, restaurateurs and the distant throb of disco from the lunchtime bars.

A few yards up the street a black cab squatted, grumbling. The passenger door was open, Henry clambering out, peeling the requisite Walkman from his blond thatch. Again, despite the weather, Henry was all big feet and biceps in thin shorts and a lime-coloured singlet. The cabbie was at the swing-down boot, hefting out a large cardboard box. About two feet square and a fist's width deep.

"Henry m'boy!" Christopher said, jigging beside me excitedly. "How do they look? Convincing?"

"Real beauties, mate," Henry grinned. "Just like the real thing."

"Well we'd better let our expert be the judge of that. Bring them through, bring them through. Pete's shopping, just left. We were enjoying the last fleeting moments of an interlude."

Henry paid the cabbie and lifted the box to his shoulder, shooing us in ahead of him. We shuffled inside, Julio twanging out of his carrier-bag galoshes and clearing poster files and newspapers from the counter to make some space.

"Turn the radio up. That today's *Mail*?" Henry asked, laying the box down carefully. "Anything of note?"

"I've marked basics," Julio said. "Open this up. Let us see what we pay for."

"You guys expecting to make headlines?" I asked.

"Not at all, not at all, " Christopher said. "One never knows what a mark will wish to discuss, dear boy." His eyes shone with excitement as he ran gloved hands over the heavy packing cardboard. "One must be in a position to keep a conversation up. One's *opinions* on the state of the nation are going to be whatever the mark's opinions are of course, but you can't get caught out on the details. Awkward silence gives people time to think. Have the facts at your fingerbobs." He held out a palm like a surgeon. "Scissors?"

I scuttled into the back office, rattling about in a Yoda pen tidy, tugging out a Hello Kitty pair and handing them to Christopher. After a moment's dramatic pause, the three men exchanging nervous smiles, he promptly slashed at the corner staples with a swift one-two. Scissors down, Julio held the box firm and Henry reached in, sliding a large bubble-wrapped display case out onto the desk.

"Come on, come on!" Christopher jittered and all three dove to the wrap, clawing and tearing at it with Christmas morning giddiness until the tattered plastic fell away.

"Sweet and lo and behold," Christopher said, gloved hands over his mouth, eyes shining. Julio and Henry flanked him, hands on hips, nodding coolly at the treasures laid bare.

"Y'think our guy'll go for 'em?" Henry said.

"Neil?" Christopher said.

I looked, blinking, at what lay within, heart hammering. My mouth was dry, cold lips unpeeling slowly. I swallowed, leaning in a little, fingertips squeaking, smudging the Perspex.

No. They . . . they *couldn't* be. I bent further, nose inches from the plastic. *Surely* . . .

"Well?" somebody said. It could have been Christopher. Or Henry. Or the cast of *It Ain't Half Hot Mum*. It really didn't matter. My mind was full of the treasure.

"Are these . . . I-I mean, these are . . ." My eyes ran over the thinning, salmon pink cotton, pinned to the white velvet backboard. The traces of the original red dye were visible at the edges, where the main fabric met the elastic. And what elastic it was. Shaky and withered, it bunched and rippled like the underside of old fish, a pale watery yellow, ribboned at the waist and leg. I squinted at the faded label at the back, washed and bleached by biting detergent and a half-century of all-American sunshine: *King Jockie of Mississippi*. You'd have to be a geek to know what these were. What these represented. What these *meant*.

"Wow," I said, dizzily. I gripped the wooden edges of the box and stood slowly. "These . . . I-I mean, these are what I *think* they are, right?" I squeaked.

"Well it seems from your ghostly pallor young Neil that they *appear* to be. Which for our purposes, is what matters."

"They're *fake*?" I said, head thudding. This was too much. The world was tipping. First one way, now another. I looked again at the box.

"Very," Christopher said. "Courtesy of an unscrupulous tailor just south of Paris. Working only from photographs of course, but he assures me the materials at least are genuine. From the frayed waistband to the hand-soiled gusset."

"God ..." and I bent down, peering closer, reading the label again, hungry fingers splayed, breath fogging the view. "Th-they ... they ... I mean, they look ... God they ..."

What I was trying to say, of course, was that even flat mounted and displayed like this, without Joe Shuster's groin inside them, without the matching tablecloth cape, they still looked exactly as they did in the cracked photograph on my mantelpiece.

seven

The rest of the day passed quickly. Fake vintage underpants were slid back into their box, Pete duly returned from his shopping trip and Christopher mapped out the con. How it was going to work. Each man's role. Step by step.

We were only bothered three times. Two customers – tourists who said whatever the Hungarian was for "this shop stinks" half a dozen times and left – and a phone-call from Jane which sent me scurrying out of the office, hunched over the handset. She was apologising for the night before and checking I'd posted the letters to the bank and solicitor. I whispered it was fine, yes it was all sorted and I hung up, beginning to worry. A little bit about the lying to Jane, but a great deal *more* about how these lies were the least of my worries.

My head consequently started to hurt, a situation not remedied by the disagreement going on in the back office.

"*Mnyesss*," Christopher said, slowly, stretching the word like a trombone note. "Yes, agreed. The blow off is still patchy. The timing's . . ."

"The blow off is no good," Julio sighed through the stale fug of his cigarette smoke. "I been saying for weeks."

"Have I missed something?" I said, sitting down. "Blow off?"

"Step nine. We take his roll – now we ask mark to get up and walk," Julio said. "Not go run to police, not pull gun, no swear revenge. Just happily tip hat, thank-you madam and take stroll into sunscreen."

"Why would someone do that?"

"Because dear fellow," Christopher bobbed, "if the play is right, the mark never discovers he was conned. He walks away having lost his money, but convinced it was just bad luck. Or that it was his own fault somehow."

"Or in this case," Pete said, "convinced he's made a –"

Pete stopped at the sound of the door tingling.

The room went quiet, breath held, the only movement being wide white eyes clacking to-and-fro like desk toy marbles. Teeth clenched, I slid from my seat and moved to the office doorway.

"There you are, skulking out the back. You want leftovers? I've got cold burnt cheese and tomato or cold burnt cheese and ham?" Laura said, tugging a greasy paper-bag from her apron. She was wandering up the shop, little red ballet shoes squeaking, peeling off her green coat to reveal a dark cotton print dress in the 1950s style: full skirt, belted waist and a little red cardigan pulled tight across her chest.

"Wait. Shit," I said, moving quickly to meet her halfway. "You can't stay."

"What?"

"You can't . . . It's . . . I'm kind of in the middle of –"

"What have you got back . . . Ohmigod!" she said, hand flying to her mouth. "The man! The trick! You *agreed*! Is that . . . ?" Laura leant in conspiratorially, whispering. "Is that *them*?"

"No," I lied. Apparently not very successfully.

"Ohmigod, let me say hello," and Laura began to push past.

"Shit, no no no," and I found myself with my hands on her squirming shoulders.

"C'mon, just a peek . . ."

"*No!*" I barked. She wriggled in my grip. "I *mean it*. These guys aren't mucking around. Laura, please just, *Laura!*"

She stepped back suddenly, the shop falling into quiet.

"Sorry," I repaired, stomach twisting. "Sorry but . . . look, this is serious stuff. You can't *be* here."

"Spoil sport," Laura said with a childish pout. "You want the ham?" and she handed me a greasy bag.

"Sorry. I-I mean thank you," I said and Laura turned to go. "You don't have to . . . I mean, it's *nice*. The sandwiches. The coffee," I said. "Having you pop in . . ."

Laura looked at me, blinking, expressionless.

". . . but you shouldn't feel . . . that you *have* to, I mean. Because of me helping out. There's no . . ."

I was waiting for Laura to leap in. Say something. Smile, laugh, shrug. Make some gesture to help me out of this hole.

She continued to stare. She continued to blink.

"What I mean is, the debt is repaid. Thank you," and I rattled the sandwich bag.

Laura blinked one more time and then sent her hand into her apron for her cigarettes, lifting them out and removing one, all without breaking her stare.

"Your new friends don't want me around?" she said finally, clinking her Zippo shut and pouting a curl of syrupy smoke from her lips. "Or *you* don't?"

I shrugged like an adolescent, feeling the familiar prickly anxiousness about my neck.

Laura held my look until I was forced to examine the floor and find invisible dust on my sleeve to pick at. When I looked up again at the tingle of the door, she was gone.

"Who hell that?" Julio said as I squeezed back into the cramped office.

"Nobody."

"This nobody, she know about us?"

"No."

"*Lying*," Julio, Henry and Pete said together.

"Fine," I said and reminded Christopher of Rudy's clumsy rendezvous with Laura's plimsolls a few short days ago.

"Where she work?" Julio asked, flipping his notebook, pen poised. "We should watch her."

"Tch, we haven't the time or manpower, young Julioworth and well you know it." Christopher turned to me. "You trust her?"

"*Trust* her?"

"Have you seen her naked?"

"What? *No*. God *no*. I'm married, I wouldn't . . ." The men stared at me blankly. Apparently in their circles, being married didn't mean what it meant in my circles. "No. I hardly know her. She just works around the corner," and I held up the greasy bag. "Sandwiches."

The four men looked at each other, making little humming noises, passing a thought about the room telepathically until Julio finally spoke.

"It no matter either way because blow off is going to get us all pinched."

"God, Julio, please —"

"We sit here, mark will land tomorrow. You *hope* . . ."

"Julio —"

"He have not bought the comic. You have made no approach. We have second-rate McMuffin —"

"*Maguffin*. I told you. And in a few moments we'll know if he's —"

"And the blow off is joke. We all going down, I tell you, we all going —"

Julio stopped complaining suddenly and everyone else stopped pretending to listen.

Because on the desk, the kitchen timer was ringing.

"Ahhh, that's all we have time for ladies and gentlemen. Julio?" Christopher said, and with a sigh, Julio obediently rose, moved to my laptop and began to flurry his gloved fingers over the keys. The machine whirred and blipped as it dialled its signal. Christopher moved to a chair, flexing his latex hands squeakily like a concert pianist.

"What's . . . ?" I began.

"Five o'clock," Pete said, stretching his back, reaching for a cigarette.

Five o'clock? A vague memory from Christopher's notebook passed through my head without stopping. *Five o'clock* . . . Christopher tapped the keyboard with light fingers. Clicking and dragging, the screen slowly stuttered open to a brightly coloured web page.

"Well look at that," he smiled. "*My my my, said the spider to the fly.*"

The other men gathered about his shoulders silently, seriously, breath held, eyes on the glowing screen. I scampered over and peered through the scrum.

eBay. The comic-book collectables page. Item? The 1938 edition of *Action Comics*. Issue #4. The very one Cheng had mentioned. And the winning bid? £5,400. Bidder. *GraysonUSA*.

"*Fly*?" I asked nobody in particular. "You don't mean . . . Shit, do you mean . . . ?"

"Oh well done Holmes," Christopher smiled. "Yes. The bait is

ours. We have sprinkled it onto the virtual lawn, the grassy lay-by
of the information-splendid highway as food to tempt Mr Grayson
to the surface."

"So there's no *real* comic?"

"Regretfully no. However, real or not, Mr Grayson has now
won the thing – therefore forcing he and I to meet. Absolutely by
chance of course."

"But . . . but what if one of these other guys," and I flicked a
finger at the scroll of other bidders. "What if they'd pipped him
to the prize? Bidded higher? This guy. Whittington? Or Peckard
Scott or . . . oh. Right."

And that, my friend, is how they do it.

The team have got about forty phoney items for auction up at
a time, watching for the same bidders' names reappearing. Plus
Christopher is watching the genuine auctions too. Anyone buying
rare albums, vintage clothes, antique ceramics.

As he began to type his congratulatory email to Grayson, I
asked him straight out: did he *really* expect this American to buy
a pair of forged underpants?

Christopher didn't stop typing. He just smiled.

Nobody was going to buy anything, he said.

It was cleverer than that.

A whole lot cleverer than that.

"Hey?" Jane said, sizzling some veg and beansprouts about the wok
in a hissing plume of smoke a few hours later. I was at the
cupboard, Lana bouncing on my hip, one hand hunting gingerly
for the cleanest wine glasses, the portable on the dining table
burbling *Holby City*.

"Sorry, what?"

"I asked if business was picking up? You sounded busy today,"
Jane said. "Can you get some bowls out."

I clattered through crockery and murmured something about
hmm-yes, on-and-off or up-and-down or knees-bend-arm-stretch-
rah-rah-rah, my head a hundred light years away.

What if . . . God, what if this Grayson changed his mind? It
could happen.

We'd all watched apprehensively as Christopher had shared a brief live email exchange with him regarding his successful bid. And sure, Grayson had *appeared* keen enough in his messages – pleased to have won the item, insisting the transaction was in dollars, asking all the right questions about paper quality and cover condition, how they might arrange a viewing – but you could never tell.

What if –

"Oh I'll do it myself," Jane snapped. "What's the *matter* with you this evening?"

"Hn? What? Oh s-sorry, let me . . ."

"Don't worry," she said, clattering out two bowls and attempting to tip the wok and scrape the hissing meal out cack-handedly. "Just take Lana through. Oh and grab the soy sauce."

I picked up my wine glass and ooze-a-good-girl-den-ed into the lounge.

A news bulletin was chattering away to itself on television. I stood and watched for a moment. A be-capped police chief stood beside the revolving Scotland Yard sign, talking sternly about something or other.

What if what if what if?

In his email, Christopher had claimed to be a small-time dealer based up in Blidworth, near Nottingham. Yes, he'd typed, he was sure Grayson's *Memorabilia Museum* was wonderful but no, he sadly had no plans to visit Kansas in the near future. His only scheduled jaunt was a train down to London this coming Monday for a private viewing of the lots that were to be auctioned at Sotheby's. The exchange would have to be done some other –

What? Hadn't Grayson *heard*? Sotheby's? Golden Age Originals? Actual items owned by Stan Lee, Bob Kane, Siegel, Shuster and the rest. Surely as a collector he'd received a catalogue? No? Some sort of oversight, it had to be . . .

By now of course we were all watching with shredded nerves, teeth chomping on latex-wrapped fingernails as Grayson's eager emails pinged back almost immediately. Where? When? Private viewings? London? Where in London?

"Here you go. You might want to put Lana down first. Did you bring the soy sauce?"

"Uhh, sorry," I said. Jane eased herself onto the couch with a shake of the head. I settled the little one beside her and mooched back into the kitchen to rootle around the cupboards, stomach churning. I could hardly eat, appetite swallowed by hollow nerves.

As quietly as I could, I pedalled open the smeary kitchen bin (£2, nearly new) and scooped a heavy tangle of dinner on top of the tea bags and potato peelings.

Christ, what if Grayson changed his mind? Didn't come? Or worse, did some investigating first? Or was an undercover cop? What if he'd made his fortune through twenty-five years in the American underpant industry and could spot a re-sown label and a hand-frayed waistband at 100 yards?

"It's in the cupboard," Jane called through.

"Okay," I croaked feebly.

Leaning against the worktop, bent over, I took slow, deep breaths, trying to shoo the fear and anguish from gnawing at the raw bone of my insides.

I felt sick. I felt scared. I felt panicky.

I felt . . .

Well, I felt about twelve years old.

You see, all this worry? The waiting? The *what if*? The constant click-clack click-clack, back and forth, back and forth, yes-no yes-no? It was how I grew up. Hell, it's how most children grow up in a household financed by gambling. The ups, downs and mood swings. A home at turns *The Cosby Show* – laughs and hugs and chunky sweaters – only to become *The Amityville Horror* at the turn of a betting slip.

I had probably spent my entire conscious childhood, from wide-eyed toddler to shuffling adolescent, in this state of constant anxious balance. Never quite settled, never quite calm. On my hands and knees, crashing Matchbox cars along the patterns in the carpet, one ear out, listening for the sound of Dad's tread. His key, his greeting. The gifts. The grief. Or later, sprawled out with a young Jane, Andrew 'Benno' Benjamin and a scrabble board in an echoing University corridor, stomach tight, waiting for a call. Just a loan. Just a few bob.

My dad was one of *those men*, y'see. Every family has one I suppose. You probably do yourself. Some distant uncle that always has a roll-up on the go, a deal to be made and a guy he has to pop out and see about something, never you mind, *nudge nudge*. The sort who leaves loudly halfway through a family wedding, the church echoing to a cheap mobile ring-tone version of the *Only Fools and Horses* theme.

Three anxious hours and barely half a bowlful of thai noodles later I was brushing my teeth, Streaky was scoffing his tea, Jane changing Lana in the nursery.

I stared at my frothy face in the mirror. A new face. The face of a criminal.

Jane appeared behind me, Lana in her arms.

"Don't be long," Jane said, snaking a hand around my waist and kissing me between the shoulder blades. Her reflection in the soap-spattered mirror smiled sleepily, then left, snapping off the hall light and carrying our daughter to the warm lamp-glow of the bedroom.

Jane and I had been each other's escape I suppose. Jane had taken me away from my father, his deals and his schemes. Given me a shot at normal, honest life. While I had grounded Jane and shown her happiness without pony-trials and garden parties, let her be who she wanted to be.

Was I about to find myself back with my father?

Would I send Jane scuttling to the bosom of her bloodline?

I spat and sloshed and unravelled some floss, looking at it closely.

Did you get floss in prison? Could you hang yourself with it? Dad would know.

See, money won is twice as sweet as money earned, young man, Dad would say. Or, *if hard work never killed anybody, who's that clogging up the cemetery?* That was another favourite. All these delivered in a chuckle of cheap scotch and peanuts. See, Dad had no time for the working man. The nine-to-fiver. The commuter. *Tch, there they go*, he'd say, every morning. And I mean *every* morning. In his vest, pale ropey arms stretched over the sports pages, roll-up perched in a stolen pub ashtray, slurping sweet builder's tea from a *World's Greatest Mum* mug. I'd be munching Frosties, head in a *Superman* comic, he'd be staring out through the net curtains in the sitting room, out at the suits and briefcases and umbrellas, hurrying to the station. *Tch. There they go. What are they son?*

Mugs Dad, I always had to say. *S'right,* he'd chuckle back. *Teacups the lot of 'em.*

A job. Nine to five. These things were for mugs. A regular income. A car. Holidays. Birthday presents. Shoes.

Ahhh, give over. Those'll do 'im another year. Anyway, I'm off out. Fellah I have to pop out and see.

Heh-heh, never you mind, *nudge nudge.*

Twanging off the light, I fetched a book from my satchel and trudged into the bedroom. Jane was sitting up with her Terry Pratchett, stroking a restless Lana on the arm softly with hushing noises.

"Dad's pretty pissed off at you stalling his accountant," Jane said idly. "Says you haven't called him yet?"

"Stalling? Who's stalling? I'm not stalling. I'm just . . . busy. The basement, Earl's Court. It's just a bad time. I'll call him next week."

"That's what I told him, but you know what he's like. Wants to know what you're trying to hide."

"Hide?" I clambered in, sliding under the duvet to stop the cold air getting in.

"Ignore him. What's that you're reading there?"

"Huh? Oh, nothing," I said, flapping the paperback. "Just uh, I thought I'd give it a —"

"Dale Carnegie. *How to . . .* what is it — ? *How to Win Friends and Influence People?*" Jane laughed.

"I know. Someone bought me a copy."

"Who?"

"Hmm? No one. Just a —"

I stopped.

I listened.

"Hear that?" I said.

Shoving the book to the bedside, I got up quickly and scuttled out of the room, Jane calling behind me. I went to the lounge, to the window. Streaky curled about my ankles. I picked him up and cradled him, pushing the curtains aside and peering out into the orange street.

A siren. Somewhere.

My heart thudded hard, my breath held. I could hear the cat purring, vibrating against my body.

A siren. Approaching?

I waited.

What had Christopher said as we'd closed up? *Confidence tricksters don't carry guns or knives. Nobody but the wealthy get fleeced and all they really lose is their pride. Our investigations into Mr Grayson tell us he's unscrupulous. A crook and a bully and it was only a matter of time before his double-dealing caught up with him. Just desserts, that's all this is. The police have more urgent things to investigate than people like us.*

People like *you,* I had corrected him.

People like *us.*

I listened. The siren was getting more distant.

I let the cat jump to the floor, shushed the curtain closed and moved over to the mantelpiece where, from fifty years away, behind cracked glass, two young men beamed into the camera lens. Boxy suits, brillantined partings, the pose was awkward. The typewriter shoved under an arm, the paintbrush popped into a top pocket.

The rough household tablecloth around the neck.

The clean cotton underpants.

"What was it?" Jane said.

"Nothing," I replied, moving back to the bedroom.

"*Nothing*? You're in such a funny mood tonight. Isn't he Laney? Hmm? Ooze in a funny mood den? Daddy? Yes he is," and she jiggled Lana in her arms.

"I thought I heard . . . s'all right," and I climbed back into bed, changing the subject as best I could. "I'll have a go at that bathroom tomorrow. There's still a yellow stain on the lino from that broken perfume bottle. I'll get some disinfectant after work."

"*Work*? On a Sunday?" Jane said. She put her book away, snapping off her light and snuggling down with the baby.

"Yeahhhh," I said, overloading it with a tired irritability. "I know. It's just I've got all this Earl's Court stuff to go through, seeing if I've got enough gear that's dry enough to make the stall worth doing this year. Shouldn't take too long."

"Is it finally dried out down there?"

"Not really," I sighed. "And the fumes are twice as bad, so don't
. . . y'know, don't bring Lana by for a surprise visit tomorrow or
anything," I added as casually as I could. "It won't be good for
her. I'll only be a couple of hours, tops."

"Mnnf," Jane said, duvet bunched about her shoulders.

"J?"

She turned over, mumbling sleepily.

Ignoring my book, I stroked Lana's head for a while in the
darkness, wishing there was someone to stroke mine.

A couple of hours, tops.

Tomorrow. Sunday. 9am.

Day two.

I thought about this for a moment. I thought about a *Star Trek*
fan called Maurice. A waterlogged cellar. A summons due in six
days. I thought about a pair of pale, aging underpants. A pale, aging
in-law. A wife. A daughter. A father.

A promise.

I rolled softly out of bed, trudged to the bathroom in the dark,
knelt down on a yellow lino stain and threw up a glass of wine
and half a bowl of thai noodles.

eight

"I've got it mate," Henry's voice floated out from the back office. "No no, just shot it. Say half hour? . . . Bonza."

"Bonza?" I queried. "What's bonza?"

"Henry's getting us a Sotheby's catalogue mocked-up," Pete explained, peering at my creaky till, face scrunched like a half-chewed toffee.

It was a crisp Sunday morning. Numb fingers buzzed around Starbucks paper cups, breath fogged in the damp shop air and the counter wore a pile of fat Sunday papers like loft lagging. The fire-escape was wedged open to to try get rid of the funny smell, traffic honks and the hum of shoppers floating in on the freezing wind. All in all, a Sunday morning for breakfast in bed, full strength radiators, fluffy dressing-gowns and quiet thanks for not being brought up Roman Catholic. But here I was, surrounded by strangers in a damp, dusty shop, shivering under the warmth of a faulty strip-light.

"We've got a helpful printer dropping our item into a genuine . . . ah-ha!" and the till drawer sprang open with an antique *ching*, ". . . brochure."

Leaving Pete to master the till-roll, I moved shivering into the back office cum storeroom cum base-of-operations cum, it appeared, photographic studio. Chairs and boxes had been pushed to one side and on a flashy looking tripod a tiny digital camera perched, peering down at the underpants on their velvet back-board.

Henry was on his mobile phone, leaning on the work-surface, all sun-washed denim and leather bangles. Christopher paced briskly, brogues squeaking, eyes bright, clapping gloved hands together for warmth. By the chilly fire exit, Julio stood smoking angrily, and by way of no change whatsoever, appeared to have just rolled out of bed. Or more accurately, out of a cardboard box under Westminster

Bridge. He had sleep and saliva crusting about his face, his thick hair bunching up on one side, greasy grey combat trousers and hiking boots.

"Half an hour then," Henry said and snapped his phone shut.

"Now don't forget you're giving the Bloomsbury room a thrice over at ten," Christopher said. He paused to pluck a tobacco pouch from his tweed jacket pocket and peer thoughtfully over a half-played game of *Kerplunk* on an upturned box. "The agent's the usual teenage barrow-boy – all hair-wax and St George cufflinks – but I've had him swear on his Burberry braces this place is what we're after. Give it your professional opinion. If you think it's hunky-dory, tell him I'll sign for the keys this afternoon."

"And it better be ready for us by Wednesday," Julio said pointedly. "We cannot foul up blow off."

"Gotcha," Henry nodded, sliding the tiny memory card from the back of the camera and slipping it into his trousers.

"Oh and while you're at our printer," Christopher said, clicking his gloved finger with a squeaky snap. "Be a poppet and get a discreet quote for a ream of Fitzgeralds. We're running low. Pete?" he called.

"One second . . ."

"Grab Henry the *Maurer & Fitzgerald* letters. They're in the purple bag."

"Sure, I'll – oh for Chrissakes. *Neil!* This bloody till?"

We moved back out into the shop where Pete was cursing, poking at the sub-total key, trying to tug his trapped *Watchmen* T-shirt from the drawer. Henry dumped the revolting sports holdall onto the counter, removed a plastic wallet and slid out a sheet of headed paper.

"And make sure the printer's clear," Christopher called out as he left. "We need our page dropped in, bound and sitting on this counter when Grayson walks in here tomorrow morning, on pain of . . . well, death isn't my style. On pain of a great deal of pain. Tell him that. Now off you pop."

"You think he'll definitely be here?" I asked, reaching past Pete and stabbing the sub-total to no avail. "Tomorrow?"

"I have every confidence he is over the Atlantic as we speak,"

Christopher said. "American Airlines Flight 609 from Kansas to Heathrow."

"And what happens if the catalogue isn't ready? Any chance Grayson will buy your auction story without it?"

"By which I presume, despite constant references to the contrary Neil, you mean *our* auction story?"

I attempted a swallow, only to find my Adam's apple had swollen to the size and consistency of a cue ball.

"It is unlikely. A convincing blute is key to this sort of game." Christopher patted himself down like a suspect, eventually drawing his pipe from his trousers. "Otherwise it's just a bunch of guys yakking. Never forget the persuasive power of print, Neil. Talk is one thing of course, but to give a mark something solid? Proof, that he can hold, smell, touch. There in black and white − or in our case four-colour offset litho. Works wonders. Just ask yourself why Catholics travel thousands of miles to glimpse the Shroud of −"

Christopher stopped at the jangling commotion of Henry clattering back through the door, breathlessly. Everyone tensed, eyes wide.

"Just so as you know, there's someone lookin' like he's headed here." Henry panted. "Late sixties. Brogues, driving gloves. On a mobile phone. Mentioned Neil's name."

"Doesn't sound like Windsor Davies does he?" I winced.

"More like that tiger from *The Jungle Book* . . ."

"Aww *crap*."

The place promptly exploded in a frenzy of elbows and cursing. Henry was out of the door and down the street. Christopher shuffled Julio and himself out of sight quickly with a *move move!* just as the door jingled with the aroma of tight tweed and cigars.

"Neil? Made that first million yet young man? Jane said I'd find you . . . oh. Hullo there."

Pete, trapped behind the counter − smiley cartoon shirt still gripped in the till's teeth − took a deep breath and looked up. He gave his wide smile.

"Good morning sir," he said.

"Edward," I squeezed, mind thudding with panic. "Gosh. Uhmm . . ."

The shop went quiet, until Edward's crashing upper-class duffery forced him forward, hand extended.

"And who's this? Weekend staff is it? Hn? Hn? Weekend staff?"

Fortunately where Edward came from, all black men were good only as manual labour so having my own carrier-bag wallah appealed to his bigoted in-bred idiocy.

Edward pumped Pete's hand violently. "Edward Spencer. This layabout's in-law. Well? Saints preserve us Neil, some common courtesy wouldn't go amiss."

"S-Sorry. Sorry, this is, uhh −"

"Ted," Pete said. "Everyone calls me Ted. Friend of Neil's. I'm giving him a hand with the exhibition."

"*Ted*," Edward said, eyebrows bouncing. "Good man, good man. Heaven's Neil, what's that frightful stench? Law, it's no wonder you can't close a sale."

"Just some . . . some plumbing problems," I said quickly. "Nothing uhm . . . wh-what brings you . . . ?"

"I'm meeting some friends at the club for Sunday lunch. Janey mentioned you'd abandoned them. And what's this she's telling me about you giving my accountant the runaround? This is my granddaughter's future Neil."

"I wasn't giving anyone −"

"Don't make me regret this, young man," Edward juddered crossly, chins wobbling over his collar. "Get him over. Get that money *working* for you. It's in your hands now. Janey's given me your sort code and whatnot −"

"*Whatnot?*" I blurted, knees a-buckle.

"For the transfer. Close of business tomorrow it'll be all yours. I'm leaving for the coast for a couple of nights and I want to see a draft portfolio of whatever my man thinks is for the best by the time I'm back in London. It's not just sitting there to look pretty."

"Absolutely," Pete interrupted, causing Edward to turn, his shuddering jowls following behind with a wet clapping sound. "Sorry," Pete said. "It's just I have a wise father-in-law myself. Financially shrewd, y'know. Knows a thing or two."

"That right?" Edward dissembled. "*Shrewwwwd?* Good man, good man." Pete was warming him like a vintage port. Edward began to pace the store slowly, silk hanky over his nose, dragging disapproving eyes about the wares with the odd tut or two. I took the opportunity to throw panicked looks at Pete, but he tossed back some reassuring nods.

"I mean look at this. *Six hundred pounds?*" Edward spat, getting dribbles of his upper-class genetic code all over Robert Redford's glass. "Good God man, no one's going to wander in off the street and pay that sort of money for something they could get in Tesco."

"That's what *I* keep saying sir," Pete piped up. The *sir* was a beautiful touch. Edward's chest ballooned out like a bullfrog after a Sunday roast. "We should be focusing more on ... well ... " and he let the sentence trail off, reading accurately Edward's unstoppable desire to finish everyone else's −

"Exactly!" Edward said. "It's all tourists around here. You want to have a few souvenirs in the window. Ceramic bits and doo-dahhs. They're moving them by the handful not a hundred yards from here. You've had that bloody eyesore up there since you bought this place."

"I had an offer on it just last week in fact," I said. "An offer which will open up a whole new raft of contacts, so −"

"Then what the bally hell is it still doing *up there*? Apart from making the place look untidy?"

"Well I'm considering −"

"Tcha! And while you *are*, he's on the interweb getting it for half price from Tesco dot com. What have I told you Neil? Time and time again."

"Close the −"

"*Close. The. Sale,*" Edward punctuated firmly. He began to button his overcoat, tugging back his shoulders, shifting his portly frame under the cashmere. "For goodness sake man, this is Book One stuff. Tell him, Ted."

"Book One stuff," Pete said with a barely concealed smirk.

"Good man. Tell Janey I'll call her this evening. And *you?*" he said, fixing me with a podgy index finger. "I won't be able to concentrate on my trip with the thought of little Lana's future sitting dead in some *easy saver* account," and he curled his lip. "So best we get this sorted before I go I think. Be in my study this afternoon. We'll say five o'clock."

"*This afternoon?*"

"Cab and back with your paperwork. Won't kill you. I'll have my Chandler Dufford chap there to take a look. Five o'clock. Bring your bookkeeping. No excuses," and with that, Edward harrumphed out of the door into the street and away.

After a beat, I exhaled, Christopher and Julio emerging from the office.

"Flattery," Pete smiled, pre-empting my strike, "is telling the other person precisely what he thinks of himself. Now how the hell does this – a-ha!" The till drawer slid open petulantly.

"*And all of us,*" Christopher said, popping his pipe in his mouth and lighting up. "*Be we workers in a factory, clerks in an office or even a king upon his throne. All of us –*"

"*– like people who admire us,*" I finished. Christopher's face took a turn lighting up.

"Our bible. Mr Carnegie. You read it."

"Bits and pieces."

"Good man, good *man*. We'll make a grifter of you yet. Now, where shall we hang these pants?"

Come four-thirty that afternoon, true to my promise to Edward, I was in a black cab heading west. Sliding left and right on the rear vinyl seat, listening to the light London rain rattle on the window, the Euston Road rolled along outside, grey and dusty, punctuated once in a while by a bright flash as a crocodile of anoraks slithered by, tourists presumably somewhere snug inside.

Heart thudding and throat fat, I sat forward, tugging the all-important paperwork from my inside pocket. I crackled it open on my lap for the fifth time, reading it over again, stomach anxious and squirty.

Nothing had changed.

Of course, nothing had changed.

With a sigh, I sat back, head lolling on the seat, feeling the engine's vibration bubble the vinyl. I couldn't relax. I was too jittery, too twitchy. I flipped the paper over and slid a black, Darth Vadar biro from my denim jacket, clicking the helmet at the top in and out, in and out.

I began to scribble, mind furrowing, mumbling a mantra.

"I've been trying to call. I'm stuck in traffic . . ."

£100,000. Minus £39,000 = £61,000.

"I've been trying to call. I'm stuck in traffic . . ."

Minus mortgage payments × 2 . . .

"I've been trying to call. I'm stuck in traffic . . ."

Minus Rod-o-matic, minus skip-hire . . . minus replacement plumbing, replacement heating . . .

I checked the figures again.

If all went according to plan, in three days' time I'd have enough left over to refit the shop. Enough to take Jane and Lana away for a week.

I sat back, rattling Darth Vadar between my teeth anxiously.

If all went according to plan.

"I've been trying to call. I'm stuck in traffic . . ."

Relax. It'll be okay. *Relax.*

Pushing the paper aside, I pulled my paperback from a carrier bag, flipping open the page to where it was folded and tried to focus, to keep my mind distracted. Dale Carnegie was banging on about the Battle of Waterloo.

Napoleon apparently invented his own names and ranks: Marshals of France; Legions of Honour; Chief High Whatnots of Oohja – and handed them out to thousands of troops to bolster their confidence. He was criticised of course for giving out these 'toys' to war-hardened veterans, but had simply replied '*men are ruled by toys.*'

An uneasy thought struck me and I lowered the book.

Inventing cosmetic roles just to beef up self-esteem?

I looked around the cab.

Sending underlings on pointless errands to make them feel involved, make them feel part of the gang?

My mobile began to purr. Edward, no doubt. Calling to check I was on my way. Tossing Dale Carnegie aside, I dug around in my jacket, hauled out the phone and thumbed it open.

"I've been trying to call. I'm stuck in . . . oh, it's you. Yes, yes fine," I said, chewing the inside of my cheek anxiously. "Got it all here."

I looked nervously over the paperwork beside me on the seat, lifting the top sheet and staring at it.

"Yes, I know where I'm going," I said.

Terminal three arrivals. American Airlines. 609 from Kansas SLN.

"Are you sure you need me to do this?"

"*Of course dear chap*," Christopher crackled. "*Nearly there?*"

I took a look out through the rain-dimpled windows. The cab skooshed beneath a large green road sign.

Hammersmith. Hounslow. *Heathrow*.

"Arriving at London LHR at 5.10pm?" I'd said, flapping the print-out exactly one hour ago. "From *Kansas*? What am I supposed to do with this?"

"We think you gotta go meet Grayson," Henry said, looking up at me.

"Meet him? When? What are you talking about?"

"At the airport," Pete said. He checked his watch. "Ten past five."

"*Me?*"

A morally flexible printer now busy inserting Jerry's jockies somewhere in a Sotheby's catalogue between Batman's bat-boots and Wonder Woman's wonder-bra, Henry had returned and we had gone through the game again slowly, walking through the store, acting it out, looking for snags, problems and potential give-aways. We now sat, camped out around the salty remains of our McSundayLunch in the back office. On the radio, *Gardeners' Question Time* was drawing to its usual nail-biting conclusion. Christopher was out front with what appeared to be an eight-year-old in a Fisher-Price *My Little Estate Agent* costume complete with a fat Burberry knot and swing-along Audi key fob.

"The tale needs more," Julio said, wiping grease from the tip of his gloves and lighting one of his foul Lambert & Butt-cracks. "A push. Convincer. Must be you."

"No," I said. I said it again. "No way. I'm not getting involved in this. I've got to . . ." and I flapped my hands about the shop. "I'm meeting my father-in-law at five. I don't *get* involved. That was the deal."

"You just take hundred thousand for sitting on arse," Julio said. "Make coffee and lending us your four walls, eh?" The dynamic in the room seemed to shift. I was cornered suddenly, looking down three barrels.

"Look, I'm not . . . that wasn't the agreement, that's all I'm saying."

"Splendillously excellerful," Christopher said, appearing in the doorway. "Bloomsbury's signed and sealed. What news of our convincer?"

"And as if by magic, the shopkeeper bottled it," Pete said.

"Bottled – ? I see," Christopher said. But he didn't say it right.

When people genuinely see, you'll notice that they say "I see," with a sort of dah-dum. High-low. *I* see. Like that. What you have to worry about is the reverse. What Christopher did. The low-high. The dum-dahhh.

I *seeee.*

"It's a very straightforward play," Pete said. "You meet him off the plane in a couple of hours, follow him to –"

"Wait!" I yelled. "That wasn't the plan."

"Plans must be flexible, Neil."

I looked over the room, my throat tightening.

"I knew it," I snarled, more at my own stupid self than at the group. "I fucking knew it. Shit," and with locked teeth and angry knuckles I slammed out of the office into the shop, where the bell was tinkling and Mr Cheng was pushing through the door.

"G'afternoo –"

"Closed!" I yelled, Cheng slipping off the step and backing into the street, handkerchief flapping.

"Neil, Neil, Neil, sweetheart . . ."

"Fuck. Fuck!" I spat, slamming the door, lashing out, flailing, kicking at displays and racks, head thudding. "Forget it. Forget it. It's off, it's over. Just – fuck it."

I stood, breathing deep, surrounded by fading memorabilia.

Why? My head thudded. *Why?* Why did I *ever* think it would be simple? That I'd be able to keep my hands clean? Hadn't my father taught me anything?

Christopher stood by the desk. He examined the bowl of his pipe for a long minute, finally reaching into his jacket and removing his notebook, penknife, Zippo and fountain pen, stacking them on the desk before finally locating a book of matches. He sparked one with a flare and lit his pipe, filling the room with sweet blue smoke.

"You're a good-looking fellow, Neil. You aware of that? Your wife, Jane is it? Jane. Buys you lotions and creams I bet. Moisturisers, antiseptic sticks. I expect it's why everyone assumes you're a homosexual."

I looked at him. He smiled gently.

"Of course all the camp kitsch and homo-eroticism won't be helping," and he waggled his pipe at the four walls. "Bulging biceps, sculptured abs. Gargantuan groins straining away in tight lyrca. It's all a little Freudy don't you think?"

"For the hundredth time, I'm a happily married –"

"Shush shush, of course you are, of *course* you are," he patted, shaking his head. "I just mean you look after yourself. Your appearance. Jane likes you to look nice. And who can blame her."

"Look, I'm not doing it. Whatever this is designed to do, butter me up, whatever –"

"You use a shaving foam or a cream Neil? Or one of these frightful fluorescent gel whathaveyous?"

"I have a father-in-law who not only loathes me but trusts me about as far as he could throw a well-paid divorce lawyer's annual bonus. Which isn't far. If I don't go and see him and spin him some story about lost accounting books, my marriage and my life are all over. *I'm* going to do that, *you* are going to sort this. We had an agreement."

"And so we did, Neil. And so we did," Christopher puffed calmly, sending his brogues on a tour of the store. "I have an old-fashioned folding razor myself. My father taught me to use it. Can't abide these new ones. Two blades. Three blades. Four blades. It's like the old days of the bi-plane. We'll have razors the size of Venetian blinds soon enough. Progress I believe it's called."

"You see this?" I said, suddenly rather cross, striding up the shop and clattering out through the door to the freezing street. I pointed up at the fading shop sign. "It says *Heroes Incorporated*. It doesn't say, and here's maybe where you're getting confused, *Boots the Chemist*."

Christopher smiled a little, his pipe bobbing.

I stomped back in, slamming the door with a crash.

Christopher didn't even blink.

"Now then. My father always told me the secret of a good shave was to be generous with my lather. Take time with it. Remember why it's there. To soften the beard. Warm it and wet it, loosen its hold. Help the razor do its job."

The shop sat quietly. On the wall, Elvis said five past three. There were no sounds from the office, save the distant lazy murmur of the Sunday radio.

"Neil?" Christopher said. He was waiting for me to look at him. I held on for a moment, just to show this was still my territory. And then looked at him.

His face seemed to have softened slightly, like he'd been overdoing the lather himself.

"We don't think Grayson is ready to be shaved yet," he said, removing his pipe. "Oh we've got his face wet. Perhaps even a little warm. But this particular shave is going to be very close and very quick. In the chair, one swipe, and then he's back on the street."

The other three men began to emerge from the office through a cloud of cigarette smoke. Tonight Matthew, I'm going to be a threatening mob.

"If we sit him down and he isn't ready? That's it. Nothing we can do. We just wind up with a load of blood on our towels."

I swallowed, tasting green and sick about my mouth.

"Someone has to apply the final lather."

Grayson looked just like his picture. As I expected he would.

Through the stark flat echo of Arrivals, through the clatter and chatter of tourists, students and wintering families he appeared, waddling and puffing.

The hat was in attendance – one of those plasticy trucker baseball caps. A mesh back and a foamy front, this one blue, emblazoned with the red and yellow Superman insignia. He was in a crumpled cotton jacket, polyester-looking slacks and the obligatory box-white trainers.

Weebling and weaving sweatily through the slalom of holdalls, skis and suitcases, tiny eyes blinking, he fished into his bag for what looked like a ticket wallet. His bag was the tourist type, not quite a handbag, not quite a satchel. It was black leather with gold clasps and buckles, about the size of a hardback book, slung on a twisted leather strap over his shoulder so it sat high between his flabby breasts.

From my position, skulking behind Dale Carnegie, secreted between the scrum of awaiting families and the bored sighs of taxi-drivers, I stepped back slowly, edging towards a pillar until he passed me with a whiff of aeroplane sweat, not six feet away, paying me no attention, pulling his wheelie case behind him and wobbling off towards the exit.

Heart thundering, mind racing a mile-a-minute, I waited. Grayson was receding slowly, couples and crowds milling between us. The clock above the exit read 17:27. I had a brief image of Edward's furious features in his Chelsea study. Apologising to his accountant. Phoning Jane in a rage.

No time for that now.

I took a deep breath and set off, watching Grayson's blue mesh cap bob away across the echoing concourse. I had no idea if I was following him correctly, of course. Do you hang back? Stay close? Who knows? My only frame of reference being mid-period Hitchcock, I was tempted to buy a felt fedora and a large newspaper with eyeholes cut in it. But for a short greedy fat man, Grayson was waddling at some pace so there was little time for that sort of thing.

Knickerbox. WHSmith. Scotts of Stow. Past Times.

I hung back gingerly as Grayson bumbled and window shopped, coming to a suspiciously abrupt halt every time he paused to catch his breath, wipe his forehead or rummage again in his little black holdall. At the end of the wide arcade, approaching the sickly yellow EXIT sign, he tottered left, around a corner out of sight. Mindful of Christopher's instructions I put a mincey spurt on – a fine manoeuvre, as long as your target hasn't decided to stop suddenly.

Shit.

The floor was slippery. Arms jittering, mind flashing, I dodged past, inches from his crumpled shoulders, with no choice but to keep going, moving past him, away towards the sliding doors.

Shit shit shit.

I came to as leisurely a stop as I could without actually skidding, Keystone style. Panicky and ill-informed regarding stealth procedure, I was forced to fall back on the old favourite of checking-the-watch-irritably, a transparent move but the choice of embarrassed train-missers and bus-chasers all over the country. I chewed my lip theatrically and tried to say "hmmm, now where *did* I leave something important?" with my eyebrows to the passing crowd, and turned slowly, keeping an eye out for a blue cap.

Gone. Nowhere.

Exits? Absolutely. Trolleys? No question. Tensile barriers, Sock Shops, Ceramic Beefeater Marts? Lord yes. But no fat Kansas memorabilia collectors.

No.

Oh no no no.

I kept turning.

Blonde hair, brown hair, black hair. Green caps, yellow caps, red caps. Umbrellas, bobble hats, Union Jack deely boppers.

Shit.

Swallowing hard, legs shooting out one way, body another, elbows flapping in neither direction, I was slowly squeezed by panic.

I'd lost him. He'd gone. I'd fucked it up. I'd have to tell Christopher and the others. They'd make me pay. Half a million pounds. I don't have half a million pounds. I don't have anything. Shit. I was in deep –

There.

Fifty yards away, among the throng, the flash of blue millinery.

"S'cuse me, sorry, s'cuse me, coming through," I began to hurry after him, tripping on holdalls and trolleys. He had swung back on himself. A low illuminated yellow sign said *bureau de change*. He turned right and waddled over to a large desk, where some mascara was waiting to swap up his dollars.

Stomach rolling, I slowed, coming to a halt by the higgledy-piggledy pin board of currency prices. In the dark glass, I watched the reflection of Grayson among the little crooked flags and equally crooked exchange-rates. He was peeling a frightening quantity of dollars from his black handbag, counting them out onto the desk.

The woman behind the desk insisted on counting it too, which seemed to piss him off. He started jabbing at his wristwatch and barking in a southern twang about *service* and *profes-sionalism* and the *customer always being right*, which naturally, this being London, made her smile thinly and count it all over again more slowly.

I took the opportunity to check my new timepiece, which for a clumsy fake, was proving surprisingly reliable. 5.32pm. Henry had told me he'd be ready to take the call about now. He'd be sitting in the shop with the others, circled about the phone, Julio probably muttering about how it had *gone to shit* and how I was *trust to be notted*.

Irritably, Grayson tutted over his currency, scooping up the ster-ling, folding it into his handbag and spun on his heel with a weeble wobble.

Oopsie. Off again.

I followed, keeping too far, too close, too far, my pace scuttling and lunging crazily, until we were out through the hissing doors into the hissing rain. It was cold, wind washing filthy sheets in gritty grey gusts. Grayson was moving, as hoped, over to the bleak concrete of the taxi rank where pale, crinkled, weather-worn men were stewarding cabs about with ruthless inefficiency.

My mobile phone began to buzz in my pocket. Henry. Shit shit shit.

Other terminal doors were hissing and thudding, families and couples stumbling through with bags, pointing at the taxi queue. I let one or two in ahead of me with a wet smile so as not to be too near before taking my place in the queue.

Breathing out, wiping clammy palms on my jeans, I sent my eyes on quick reconnaissance. There were about a dozen people in the queue in front of him, one by one, two by two, clambering into the passing cabs that barely stopped.

Grayson was glancing around. Bored. Checking his watch, pulling out a mobile phone of his own from his little handbag and dialling with a fat thumb. As the queue shortened, he shoved his wheelie-case forward roughly with his trainers.

With a deep breath, I fished out my buzzing phone and thumbed open the line.

This was it.

"*Neil, where are you? Dad's furious? He's waiting for you at the house. His accountant's there, he's got a train —*"

"Shit. Jane, Jane —"

"*Where are you now? Are you nearly there? It's half past five. He can't wait much —*"

"I-I've . . . shit, I've been trying to call," I whispered, "I-I'm stuck in traffic. We'll have to reschedule. Apologise for me can you? I'll get the cab to turn around, head back —"

"Oh Neil, for heaven's sake —"

"*I know, I know.*"

I could feel Jane's fury crackling down the line. Another shell loaded into her father's arsenal to pummel her with at their next lunch.

"*I'll have to tell him to just go,*" she sighed. "*You're still on for picking him up from Victoria when he gets back next Tuesday though? I can tell him that? I said eleven-thirty by the newsstand outside. You'd bring the car and drop him back here?*"

I looked up. Grayson was still drawling away on his phone, kicking his bag forward. Cabs rolling up, rolling off.

"Oh, yes yes. Look Jane, the er, the cab driver's trying to talk to me, I'd better —"

"Catherine and Jack have confirmed dinner on Thursday, okay?"

The family in front scuttled forward three feet.

"Fine, fine, whatever," I said, voice wobbly. "Call your dad. Apologise. Look, I-I have to go. Love you. Love you lots."

"*Call us later.*"

I thumbed the line closed, breathing out hard, heart thudding. Rain drummed on the plastic awning above. Around us, cabs were rolling in squeakily, dropping off, yellow lights snapping on, then sliding over, splashing black surf against soggy socks. Grayson was three groups away from the front of the line, still on the phone. Slippy fingers and thumbs, I dialled the shop, clearing my throat. The phone was snatched up on the first ring.

"*Heroes Incorporated,*" an Australian voice crackled.

"It's me," I whispered. "Sorry, Jane w-was —"

"*Yes and no answers mate,*" Henry interrupted brusquely. "*Can you see him? He should be on a phone. Christopher's on the other line confirming tomorrow's buy with him.*"

I looked over. Grayson was nodding, fat fingers peeling the pages of an *A-Z*.

"I see him."

"*Within fifteen feet?*"

"Yes."

"*Quickly. Turn your back on him. Don't look. Now complain about the line. Bad line. Apologise. Speak up, shout.*"

"Uhmm, hello?" I said. "Hello?" A little louder. The family facing me stared back. I mouthed an apology. "Where are you, I can't hear? Hello? Can you hear me?"

"*Good. Keep the voice loud. Not shouting. But he has to hear you. More, keep going. But keep your back to him.*"

"You're breaking up a bit . . . can you hear me now?"

Henry continued to prompt me. I stood, one finger in my ear like an idiot, shuffling backwards along the queue, speaking at an obnoxious volume.

"Pardon? . . . Yes, yes I heard about it. That's why I'm here . . ."

I swallowed hard, heart slamming.

"No, not according to *Sotheby's* website . . . what? . . . No, Joe Shuster's . . ."

At which point, despite all of Christopher's warnings, I turned around.

I couldn't help it.

I turned around.

Grayson was staring at me. Not blinking. Eyes fixed on mine.

nine

"Mr Grayson?" Christopher cooed. "Mr Grayson, it's Christopher Laurie. We spoke yesterday. How is your hotel? . . . My sincerest apologies, truly. I . . . Yes, yes I understand, but my train was terribly delayed leaving Blidworth and there were signal problems at Daventry . . ."

The next day. Monday morning, Christopher's clipped gentry tone might still have been in attendance but his clipped gentry tweeds were spending the day back in the closet. He was attired in ugly loafers, cheap shiny-bummed suit trousers and had his chubby pot-belly inside white polyester shirt-sleeves, rolled roughly above his elbows. His sweaty frame oozed petrol station-pies and cheap salesmen's hotels. Perched behind my till, chattering into his tiny phone, he peered into a small shaving mirror balanced on top of a silver attaché case on the counter, dabbing tentatively at a painful-looking gash on his forehead, blood shining on his finger-tips.

"I know we arranged the buy for ten o'clock but I'm running about forty minutes behind . . . Hmn . . . Yes yes of course, I have it here with me now," and Christopher ran a palm over the silver case. " . . . Uh-huh . . . And you have the agreed fifty-four hundred – ? . . . And where are you now? Well then what I'm thinking, save you sitting around waiting, is if you wouldn't mind, maybe meeting me a little north of there? . . . No, just a short stroll, I promise you. I have a viewing appointment with the owner of a shop on Brigstock Place. He's holding some items for the auction I mentioned and I'm keen to . . . well it's just off Beak Street . . ."

I had my breath held and my fingers crossed. Which, while making me feel a little better, made holding a step-ladder as Julio clambered up to unscrew Judy Garland from the wall rather difficult.

"My train's due in at Charing Cross in a few minutes. I'll join you there as soon as I . . . Again I *do* apologise . . . That's marvellous. Until then," and Christopher hung up.

"Well?" Julio said, handing me the *Easter Parade*, but Christopher raised a blood-smeared finger, requesting silence. His phone began to rumpty-tumpty-tumpty-tum again but barely got a chance to deet-dee-deet-dee-deeee-dee before he clicked it open.

"Henry? . . . Good. Keep with him. He'll probably go along Piccadilly and cut north . . ."

I hefted up to Julio the display case containing the aging underpants.

". . . Righty-ho. Keep him in sight and let us know when he's ten minutes away," and Christopher thumbed the line closed. "Grayson is on his way. Uniform looks very natty Julio dear."

Julio too was out of his usual garb of combats and walking boots, squirming up the ladder in a crackly polyester security-guard outfit, all epaulets, shiny peaks and the great smell of dry-cleaning.

"Now, it's three-quarters of a mile," Christopher said, lifting the mirror and pouting at his scar thoughtfully. "We've timed a steady walk at just under twenty minutes. That's if you don't stop and you know where you're going. Grayson's heavy and new in town. Chances are he'll get a little lost and do a little browsing. Which gives Pete," and Christopher checked his kitchen timer, "about a half hour to get back from the printer. Shouldn't be any problem at all. Excellent. Splendid. *Bon.*"

The Archers were calling again.

"Ah, that'll be him. Hopefully just around the corner." Christopher opened it up. "Dear fellow! How close are . . . Arses. When . . . ? Are you . . . ? Daww, frolicking fuckbusters," and he snapped his phone closed, jaw grinding. "That was Henry again. Grayson's in a cab. Two minutes away."

"Cab? Aww fack . . ."

"B-but the brochure . . . ?" I flapped. Oh God.

"*Check the back!*" Christopher hollered. "*Go, go!*"

With a panicky jitter, I left the team spitting, cursing and wobbling up ladders, slapping back through the office and out of the fire escape into the cold alley. Wading among the split bin-bags and next door's soggy book-boxes, I moved quickly, my All-Stars splashing through piss and litter, bouncing off the damp walls. Up ahead, where the alley opened onto the street, traffic slid slowly past. White vans pulled in and pulled out, couriers blurred past with a yell until a cab finally squeaked to a halt, the back door flying open.

"*Pete!*" I bellowed.

He looked up, eyes wide. He was dressed just as I'd suggested – the traditional shopkeeper's garb of black denim, tatty Converse and an unironed *Green Lantern* T-shirt. Just as I was in fact.

The only key difference between us being the glossy brochure tucked under an arm.

"Hey," a muffled American voice said. "Hey, you open?" The door rattled hard.

"*Down!*" Christopher whispered, backing away quickly in a low hunch. Julio sprung from atop the step-ladder in a blur of braiding and Air-Ware sole, wiping a shiny forehead and pulling down the peak of his cap.

"Wait wait," Pete hissed behind the till, breathing deep. Flustered fingers hovered over the keys. "Sub-total twice, right? Then total?" He lifted the empty telephone receiver to his ear and licked his lips.

The door rattled again.

"*Let's go ladies,*" Christopher hissed, grabbing the mirror and case from the counter and bustling me out to the kitchen in the back. "*Keep it tight.*"

I fell stumbling against the wall in the dusty darkness, heart rattling like the shutters. Christopher stood close, the warm pipe-smoke smell of his clothes deep in my lungs. I could feel his breath on my face, hot and fast. He smiled, placing a shiny finger to his lips.

We listened.

Footsteps. Julio. Those heavy security-guard boots. The crack of the lock and the jingle of the door. Traffic. Loud. The wind rattling the steel grid over the window.

"*Wish I could, pal, but I can't.*" Pete's voice. Firm. "*Huh? Speak up, this line . . . Well you can call Los Angeles but they'll tell you the*

same thing I'm telling you . . . Japan? No I don't. It's all by strict appoint-
ment only. I just get a list from the Sotheby's people."

We could hear Julio muttering, giving the visitor the once over.
Who are you, what do you want, appointment only – the whole Securicor
bit.

Pete continued down the empty phone.

"*They're running the same closed system in LA, I'd add a nought to*
that if you want to be taken seriously." Glossy pages flapped. "*No, if*
you haven't received a catalogue I wouldn't expect an invitation to LA
or London sir."

Christopher looked at me in the darkness, wet eyes full of
excitement.

"*Gotta go, I've a customer."*

I held my breath.

Pete hung up.

"Mister . . . sorry, Mister Laurie?" he said. "You my ten o'clock?"

"Grayson. Bob Grayson. Call me Bob. Pleased to meet you
fellahs. Phee-yew! Gotcha self a stink in here ain'tcha?"

"Mr Grayson, I'm sorry, it's by appointment only. Could you
show Mr Grayson the way –"

"Now juss' hold yur horses fellahs. S'okay, ah'm a fellow collector.
Perhaps you heard o' my museum in Kansas? Here ya go, my card."

"That's very nice Mr Grayson but I'm afraid –"

"Bob. Call me Bob. Over for a few days. Juss' agreed to buy a
pretty piece on eBay. Right up yur street. Meant to be meetin'
your Laurie fellah here for the exchange. Said he's runnin' a li'l
late."

"Look sir, there are strict instructions regarding pre-bid viewings for this auction. Mr Laurie had no business arranging –"

"Auctions auctions eh? Everywhere ah'm goin' that's all ah'm
hearin'. Howzabout ah give you first gander at mah new purchase
when Laurie shows up, an' you let me take a peek at whatever's
causin' all this fuss, huh? Now, what we got up here?"

"You step back a little please, case is alarm. Thank you."

"Now then, now then, what's awl this? *King Jockie* of Mississippi?
Holy . . . These wouldn't be . . . Jeez, these cotton fellahs what ah
think they are boy? Mah gawd . . ."

"Sir, I must ask, step *away* from case."

"Whell ah' never did . . . That the catalogue yew got there boy? Lemme take a lookie at that."

"Mr Grayson –"

"Shush now. Here we are. Manufactured by *King Jockie*. Bought from *Glenville Tailoring* in Cleveland in 1932. Wh'ell ahll be . . ."

In the darkness of the kitchen, Christopher winked and turned quietly, moving silently on tiptoeing loafers through the office to the fire escape. Stopping to check his scar in the mirror one last time, he heaved open the door silently. An icy breeze scuttled through, fluttering the office papers inquisitively and he was gone.

Swallowing hard, I concentrated on the play out front. Grayson seemed to be reading aloud.

". . . *still facing rejection from, among others, National Allied Publishing and the United Features Syndicate, artist Joe Shuster feared it was the amateur quality of the artwork that was holding them back. In 1937 –*"

"Mr Grayson –"

"Ah said a-hush now, this is history here. *In 1937 he hired Joanne Carter as a female model and began to rely further on the poses of Jerry for those of his most famous creation. Usin' a red cotton tablecloth and these men's briefs, pictured, the very first infamous poses of –*"

"Sir, please, alarm is very sensitive . . ."

"Easy now boy. Customer's ahlways right, don't they teach you that in this country? No one's touchin' nuthin. Ahm juss' tryin' to get a lookie –"

The door gave a jangle.

Christopher.

Then a voice. Not Christopher's. Not Christopher's at all.

"What's all this?"

No. Oh no no *no*.

"Well g'mornin' miss," Grayson said. Not a line anyone was expecting to hear. Not a line anyone wanted to hear.

I stood in the dark, grabbing the counter top, knees buckling.

"Neil about?" Laura said. There was a soft clicking. Heels moving up the shop towards the counter. A shuffle. Men moving. The kick stool being shoved to one side.

"*Laura?*" Pete said.

There was a beat. A silence. The script was slipping. I could feel everyone flipping desperately for the right page, stage-hands panicking, the director gesturing in silent fury.

"Hey," Laura said.

What was she doing? I'd *told* her we were . . . What the hell was she *doing*?

"Ain't you gonna introduce us to this lovely young thing?" Grayson said with an oily voice. Even hiding in the kitchen in the dark, I could sense his wet eyes widening. "Bob Grayson. Pleasure, miss. A pleasure."

Laura giggled. In the way you might when a randy old bastard kisses your hand.

"Well, Neil said he was having important viewers this morning," Laura cooed. "He didn't tell me how *distinguished* they'd be. A pleasure to meet you."

Oh for Christ's *sake*?

Julio and Pete had gone uncomfortably quiet. Unlike my bottom, which was beginning to register its discomfort at the situation. I looked at my chunky watch. Christopher was due any −

"Jesus H Christ!" Grayson yelled, the door jangling and clattering. "My . . . Jesus buddy, you all right?"

"Ow, ahhh." It was Christopher's voice. He sounded in trouble. "Bastards, those damn . . . ahh, shit."

"You okay buddy? Your head looks . . ."

"Just a knock I think. Oww, shit."

"Siddown, siddown."

There was a bang and shuffle of the chair being heaved out to the aisle of the shop. Everyone seemed to be cooing and oo-ing.

"They took the fuckin' . . . ow. You got . . . you got some water? Any water?"

"Of course."

I braced myself in the dark as hurried footsteps approached. Pete entered the kitchen, pushing past me in angry silence. He ran the tap noisily.

"*What's happening*?" I hissed. "*Pete*?"

"*Happening? Your girlfriend's fucking the whole game!*" Pete spat. "*What's she doing here*?!"

"*I-I swear, I don't know! I told her . . .*"

"*Get out of the way. Out of sight. Christ, extras cluttering up every corner,"* Pete muttered. *"You out here, her out there. Julio is right. Goddamn amateur hour, this whole damned play."* He shut the tap off and stared at me. *"Go on! Move it. What are you waiting for?!"* he hissed.

Dumbstruck, I backed away in the darkness, through the narrow door of the staff toilet, back of my knees bumping against the cold bowl. Pete tutted and left, pushing back into the glare of the shop clutching a mug of water.

I breathed out as quietly as I could, heart thumping.

I could hear voices. Muffled now.

Teeth tight, I edged back out a few feet towards the doorway, ears aching for sounds.

"Thank you. Christ. Are any of you Grayson? I'm meant to be meeting a Bob Grayson —"

"Mr Laurie?"

"That's *you*? God, you're here. Thanks so much for . . . look I'm sorry . . ."

"What the hell happened boy?"

"Kids," Christopher croaked. "Fuckin' . . . Daventry train got into Charing Cross late. I was heading over here. Hurrying. Up whassit. Had my case with me. Silver case. Your comic."

"Had it?"

"Got just up here. Soho. These two kids. Couldn't have been more than fifteen? Yelling. I turn, spinning around. Then *whack."*

"Jesus."

"Wait. They got *mah* comicbook?"

"Took the whole case. Left me on the pavement. Is it cut? It feels like it's cut . . ."

"You look right. Need cleaning up though. How you feel?"

"They got mah book?" Grayson said again. "Ah come all this way? Five an a half grand's worth of comic book, you let 'em just *take* it from you?"

"Five and a half *grand*?" Laura said.

The room went eerily quiet for a second too long.

"Ah was meant to be buyin'. *eBay*. We had a deal," Grayson said. He wasn't happy.

"Shouldn't someone call the police?" Laura suggested.

The shop fell quiet again. What was she *doing* here?

"I call now," Julio said, impatience in his voice. "Let them sort out." Louder.

Shit.

I scuttled quickly back into the tiny toilet. Locking the door, I sat down, knees bouncing. Heart thudding in the dark, I tried to focus, tried to concentrate. Shuffling. Footsteps in the office. Voices were mumbling in the shop.

Grayson. More mumbling.

Laura. The scuff of a chair.

The door jingling. Traffic. The door closing.

A long silence.

I listened to my heart beat for a moment, blinking hard.

Still nothing.

Then the soft trill of a mobile phone. Rumpty-tumpty-tumpty-tum. Christopher's low voice.

"*Neil!*" Pete yelled. "Get *out* here."

Slowly, I edged out of the dark cubicle, through the office, blinking like a rabbit into the white glare of the strip lights. Christopher was on his mobile. Julio – cap off, tie unclipped, hair miraculously back to its ruffled state – stood, arms folded, on the left of a sheepish-looking Laura. Pete flanked her right.

"Hey there," she said with a small apologetic smile.

"Enough from you," Julio growled.

Incongruously for a Monday morning, Laura was back in evening wear. Hair up, long pale neck exposed, soft shoulders peeping from her short black cocktail dress, stockinged legs in red velvet heels. Some of her swagger, however, was noticeably absent.

Christopher clicked his phone closed, causing everyone to turn his way.

"Henry's got him. He's jinked west onto Regent Street and is heading south. Probably back to the hotel to calm down. Henry will call again when he's settled."

Pete and Julio relaxed a little, rolling their shoulders.

"Which brings us to you, miss," Christopher said pointedly, all eyes falling dubiously upon Laura. "You mind telling us quel le *fuck* you are doing here? This some twist is it? Neil?" and he looked at me. "Getting your girlfriend involved? You trying to get clever on us? Hn?"

"Wait," I protested. "I didn't —"

"A wrong note. *One* wrong note, that's all it takes," Christopher said. He tugged his handkerchief from his pocket and began wiping the fleshy putty and dripping scarlet corn syrup from his forehead, examining the stained cotton once or twice. "Our mark picks up the *tiniest* sensation, the most minute *ruffle* that things are not absolutely perfect, he'll walk. No explanations, no goodbyes. Bang. Back on the plane. And we're half a million down."

"He had nothing to do with this," Laura said. Her voice cracked a little. "I just stopped by. I wanted . . . I just wanted to see what you guys were like."

"What we *like*?" Julio snarled. He looked at Christopher contemptuously. "We should walk. There no way he went for it. I got a pony say he's take his money and he's back at the airport. Or he calling the cops. Smelling fish. We bloody walk."

"Pete?" Christopher asked.

Pete looked at me, breathing deep. He turned to Christopher. "I don't know. He appeared pretty impressed with the pants."

"He bloody walk, I fuck tell you. He out of here."

"And on the plus side," Pete added, "he did seem to like the broad."

"This whole thing is fuck," Julio said. "I out of this, I out of this," and he shook his head, pushing off towards the office.

"Julio, wait —"

"I was just curious," Laura went on, looking about the group. "Neil said you guys were professionals. Thought it'd be a kick, y'know?"

"*Julio?!*" Christopher hollered again.

"Your *kick* has probably just cost us five hundred thousand pounds, little lady," Pete said, "which I myself am in no mood to just to write off."

"Look," I said, voice wobbling a little like a schoolboy's. "Christopher, look —"

"I'm thinking," he said, bottom lip protruding like the prow of a tiny ship. "His fancy did appear taken, that's true . . ."

The shop fell silent.

"If Grayson walks now," Pete said, lighting a cigarette with the snap of a Zippo, "he'd miss his opportunity for a date."

"*Date* – ?" Laura yelped.

"Hmn, indeedy," Christopher said slowly, his great mind rolling it over. "Julio?" he called again.

Julio appeared in the office doorway, security guard uniform off, back in combats and boots and a heavy coat, purple Reebok bag on his shoulder, thunder across his face.

"I go out of here," he said.

"You stay where you are," Christopher said. He checked his watch, hmmmm-ing to himself again, at which point, on cue, his mobile began to rumpty-tump. He flipped it open, raising a finger for Julio to wait.

"Henry? What's the position? . . . Uh-huh, right . . ."

We all glanced about each other.

"Fine. And no calls, no cabs? . . . Good. Stay where you are and wait for my word."

Christopher snapped his phone closed.

"Grayson's back at the hotel. Ordered lunch from the front desk and gone straight to his room. No cabs. No airports. Seems pissed off but not going anywhere. The plan holds."

"Then you fuck crazy," Julio said.

"You," Christopher said, pointing a finger at Laura. "You will do exactly as we tell you over the next seventy-two hours, you understand me?"

Laura's eyes flicked over to me quickly, then back to Christopher.

"Take Grayson's card, call his hotel and make yourself available for dinner."

"Dinner?" Laura said, eyebrows aloft, chin burying into her neck. "Ha, I don't think so mate. I've seen everything I came to see and now I'm off. You like him so much? You take him to –"

CRACK! – Christopher slapped her a stinging swipe across the cheek, flat palmed and loud.

Laura spun, hand to her face, white with shock.

I stumbled, knees loose, diving at Christopher spastically but Pete shoved his broad body between us, chest out, chin up, forcing me backwards.

Blinking, breathing deep, Laura stood, regaining her cool, flicking hair from her face. Christopher pointed the business end of his mobile phone at her.

"This is *your* doing, honey. You sashayed in here with a wiggle in your walk and a giggle in your talk. It's ten minutes past too damned late to start backing out now. You have half a million pounds you want to donate to the Save the Trickster Fund?"

Laura just blinked back at him, shaken.

"Thought not. Then, young mademoiselle, I regret you're involved right up to your pretty little earlobes. You will be *available for dinner,*" Christopher reiterated, bristling, like wind over a cornfield. I got the impression that enough was beginning to be enough. "You are thrilled to be asked, you've never seen a place like it, he's such a gentleman, etcetera etcetera. Pearls, furs, the lot. Laugh at his jokes, pick fluff off his collar, get him to impress you. But don't fuck him."

"!" Laura said, eyes wide, jaw dropping.

"You think that's wise?" Pete said, stroking his chin. "We gotta keep him sweet . . ."

"No," Christopher said. "He gets her on the king-size wearing her ankles as earrings on the first date, he's got less of a reason to stick around." He turned to Laura, who had shifted her weight onto one hip and hoisted one eyebrow up within the flickering fluorescents attempting to assert herself a little. "Let him know it's on the menu —"

"*Believe,*" Laura corrected, voice shaky. "You mean let him *believe* it's on the menu."

"Potato, potah-to," Christopher said. "Keep him keen. Think you can manage that?"

Laura looked at Christopher. Then around the room.

Julio slid his bag from his shoulder and dropped it to the floor with a thud.

"Okay, it's ten past eleven. Henry will call Grayson this afternoon. Four o'clock. He agrees to the meet, we're back here tomorrow for scene two. Julio?"

"This is mistake," Julio said.

"Julio, you're checking the case and getting it to our man at the Windmill. Pete?"

"Installing the alarm," Pete nodded.

"That's it," Christopher said smartly. "Let's go munchkins. Choppity chop."

Pete stuck around wiring the alarm dutifully while Christopher addressed another in a long line of jiffy bags, changed ninety-five pounds into fivers and he and Julio set off to prove once again there *was* such a thing as a free lunch. I made Laura a nervous coffee, managing to shake most of the granules onto the kitchen floor.

I took her drink over to the counter and placed it down on the back of an envelope.

"I'm sorry," I said.

"Forget it," she said.

"These . . . these are serious men. This is a serious business. I . . ."

Laura lifted her coffee, the envelope tacking to the bottom of the mug. She peeled it off and handed it to me. It was the letter to my father, still unfinished. I balanced it atop the final demands in my in-tray.

"He was out of order," I said, looking at her. "That was . . ." My hands were still a little shaky. I swallowed hard. "But it shows . . . well, believe me, they're not going to have their money taken away from them just because you want to play Jessica Rabbit."

Laura laughed at this, which was a relief in some ways, if not rather irritating in a dozen others. She jabbed a thumb at a yellowing poster of Humphrey Bogart Blu-tacked to one damp wall, pistol in his hand, hat over his eyes.

"That's who you remind me of," she said. "*Don't get involved shweetheart, dis is a man's racket, y'hear? You don't wanna get yourself bruised, toots.*"

"This is serious," I said. "It may be a bit of fun for you but if . . . ? I don't like the idea of you alone with this American."

"I can handle –"

"*Handle y'self*, I know I know. You . . . you've got some sass, that much is true."

Laura raised a finely plucked eyebrow.

"But a hip-wiggle when you go to the powder room is fine for a Saturday night up west. It isn't going to save you if this man smells a rat. I . . ." I looked at her. "I don't want you involved."

"Awww. That's sweet."

"I mean it. You stumbled into this and that's my fault. I should get you out of this. We don't know anything about this Grayson guy."

"Apart from he's a comic book geek. And a very wealthy one at that." Laura slipped off the edge of the counter and handed me her coffee mug. "Hell, I've done a lot worse."

"Christ, this isn't a *date*."

"Well until I can find myself a wealthy comic book geek of my own," and she was suddenly snaking her hand around my ear, pulling me forwards a little, "he'll have to do."

She leaned in quickly, closing her eyes, at which point the world was suddenly wrenched in half by a head thudding shriek. I slipped off the desk, coffee splashing, Laura backing away hands flying to her ears.

"Jesus Christ!" I yelled, the words thick and muddy through the blurring wail.

Abruptly, the alarm stopped, leaving the room swaying and throbbing in a high-pitched silence.

"Sorry," Pete said, appearing in the office doorway with his pliers. "Alarm's set. Better keep your hands off the pants from now on."

"I'll try," Laura said.

I looked at her. Had she . . . ? I felt my cheeks beginning their familiar adolescent glow.

"I . . ." my voice croaked.

"Quite," Laura said. "And I'd better get off to work. Are you . . . ?"

"I'd better give Jane a call," I said quickly, nodding and fidgeting.

"Then wish me luck," she said, flapping the Kansas business-card and I watched her wander, heels clicking up the shop, through the door with a jangle, and click off up the cobbled street.

I stared into space for a few minutes and then gave Jane a call to tell her I loved her very very very very much.

ten

"*Kissed* her?"

"Kissed her."

"Where?"

"Left cheek."

"Thank you Desmond Morris. I mean *where*?"

"Oh." Julio flicked through his pocket book irritably. "At Oxo Tower. Before dessert. Then they cab to Garrick Street. A club. Private members. A bar. Dancing."

"Did Laura behave?"

I felt Christopher, Pete and Julio all not turning to look over at me.

"Grayson all over her some more and she flirt a little back. He mostly talk up his background. Kansas. What he got, what he getting, how much he worth. Trying to impress. Told her he had contacts. That there would be no way he would not get to this auction. He was a major player."

"And after Garrick Street?"

"Cab back to hotel. He offer her drink in his room, she say *another time maybe.*"

"*Another time.* Good girl," Christopher nodded. "Hmn, this may yet turn out to be not quite the fiasco we imagined." Whipping out his telephone, he thumbed down the address book. "And the case is in place, Julio?"

"Drop it off on way here."

"Test the bottom?"

"Of course."

Christopher checked the kitchen timer as his mobile dialled out.

It was Tuesday morning. Elvis had the big hand on his preposterous collar and the little hand in his right eyebrow and I had my hands round my second take-out latte. Was it wrong of me to be feeling . . . not friendship. Not friendship at all in fact.

But camaraderie? A sense of teamwork?

While at university, I had thrived on the chumminess. Relied on it, I suppose. Jane, Andrew and I, biffing about together. Leaning on each other. Lending revision notes and kindly ears – depending on what was required obviously. But since then . . . ? Well shop life can be a lonely business, failing-shop life even more so. It had only been four days since we'd met, but I was getting used to having these guys around. Still didn't trust them as far as my cardboard Chewbacca could throw them of course.

But for better or worse, camaraderie was what I felt.

Monday had been another painful evening at home. Our weekly classical-music, candles and massage night had been spoilt by my fidgety nerves. Nerves which I successfully managed to transmit, through the magical powers of pummelling and oils, into Jane's bare spine, causing her to develop a blinding headache and a bad back. Candles out, lights on, music off, Lana was changed grumpily while I clattered crockery in the kitchen and fretted.

As we had dressed for bed, flossing and splashing, Jane had tried to get me to concentrate on the plans for Thursday's dinner with her old school friends Catherine and Jack.

Thursday, I'd thought. By then it would all be over. God, it couldn't come quick enough.

Jane, noting my distance, then tried to get me involved in some stress-relieving sex instead; however, it turned out that Thursday wasn't the only thing that couldn't come quick enough so there was some rolling off and reaching for books, leaving me staring at the damp on the ceiling and worrying.

"Henry, it's me," Christopher said, getting up for a bit of a pace among the postcards and posters. "We're set here. You ready to make the call? Where's our mark . . . ? She's with him? *Now?*"

Christopher threw a look at me, which I gave a baffled twist before batting back.

"No. No time, we'll have to play it with her in tow. Dammit. Look, make the call. I'll hold on. And remember, you're a fifteen-year-old rapscallion with a stolen attaché case under your arm, quick cash on your mind and heroin up your nose. Go."

The shop fell quiet, save the usual soft burble of the midmorning radio news. Everyone stared at the floor, waiting, waiting. Everyone but Christopher, naturally, who, popping the phone under his chin, began to flap with a pouch of tobacco, tumpty-tumming idly before being jerked back onto the line.

"Well . . . ? Splendiful, good man. He heading off now? . . . Well a hackney carriage from South Molton to Windmill Street should bring him to our door in fifteen minutes. Stay with him," and he snapped the phone closed. "Marvellous."

"Shit," Julio added.

"No, no Julio, chin up now," Christopher jollied. "He's taken the bait as we knew he would. The young lady's attendance might in fact work to our advantage. If Grayson —"

"No, I mean *shit.*"

We all looked at him but he didn't look back. He was staring over Christopher's shoulder. At the front door.

It rattled hard.

"Heh? Heh? Ne?" Cheng hollered, peering through cupped hands, breath fogging the wire glass. "You ohp?"

"Christ," I said, pushing past, hurrying up the shop to the door. The three men shuffled towards the office, backs turned. "I'm . . . we're not open yet," I shouted. "Later, can you come back later?"

"Noh," Cheng said urgently. "Mus be now. I goh. Fligh to US. One o'cloh. I ha the fye hundreh," and he began pointing behind me to Redford and Newman on the back wall.

"What's he want?" Julio called out.

"Shit," I said, teeth gritted. "He wants to buy *The Sting*. He's got a flight at one."

The door rattled again, Cheng fanning twenty pound notes like a Geisha.

"*Send him away,*" Christopher hissed. "*Grayson could be here any moment. Get rid of him.*"

"My buy veh keen to buil relationshih," Cheng insisted. "I tahe pohst now, he order big lahte."

"Neil!"

"I . . . shit, I can't," I said. "He's got contacts. If I sell him this, I can sell him others. I'm . . . I'm sorry, I need the business. I'm letting him in," I said and began to flick the latches. "I'll be quick."

Cheng bustled in, flapping his money, a large bag over his shoulder, the men disappearing deeper into the office.

"Can we do this quickly, Mr Cheng? I'm in a bit of a hurry." I scurried down the shop, grabbing up the kick stool, moving behind the desk and clambering up.

"Ease, ease," Cheng said, hands held out. "I dohn whan damage."

I lifted the huge frame from the wall slowly, stepping back down, turning and laying it face down onto the untidy desk while Cheng busied himself in his bag, tugging out a large plastic poster tube.

In the back office, Christopher's mobile phone gave a muffled chirrup.

"Whas thih?" Cheng said. He was peering into the new display case, sweet breath fogging the Perspex. "Holy . . . thih reeh? When you geh thih? You seh thih?"

"They're not for sale," I said, flipping the clips on the back hurriedly, releasing the back-board from the frame. With finger tips, I wafted the delicate poster out, holding it up for Cheng to see.

"Jesuh, you hah the tablecloh too? Thih worth thousan. Jesuh . . . How muh you whah? My collec' he gih you ten thouhsah?"

"Mr Cheng?"

"Grayson's on his way," Pete said behind me, making me start. "Henry just called. Get rid of your customer. Now."

"Sure, sure, no problem. Mr Cheng? Mr Cheng? I'm going to have to hurry you. I'm sorry . . ."

Cheng was slowly and methodically measuring his plastic tube against the short edge of the poster, nose inches from the paper, peering closely, blowing away invisible dust.

"Let's pick up pace shall we?" Julio said, shouldering me aside. He was pulling on his security guard's uniform, shiny peak pulled down hard over his eyes. He grabbed up the poster in two rough fists, scrabbling it into a roll quickly.

"Whey! Whey! Bubbuh wrap, you bubbuh wrap!"

"He's a minute away," Christopher called out suddenly, appearing in the office doorway, mobile phone held to his chest. "Pete, take the counter. Get rid of this guy as fast as you can. Julio, watch the door. Neil, get in the kitchen. Let Pete take over. Mr Cheng is it? Mr Cheng?"

Cheng looked up.

"Neil's *assistant* is going to help you now. Thank you for your business. I hope you make your flight. C'mon people. Focus." He was back on the phone. "Okay Henry, we're set. ETA? . . . Good. Wait for the call," and he snapped the phone shut, pushing me out of sight, a hand on my shoulder. We moved hurriedly through the office into the tiny kitchen once again, pulling the door ajar.

Hearts thudding, we stood and listened to each other breathe in the darkness. The sounds in the shop. The snap, crackle and pop of bubble-wrap, the rustle of paper, Cheng complaining in staccato yelps.

"Reciep?"

"Yes, one second," Pete said. The till chattered.

"Get *rid of him*," Christopher hissed to himself, checking his Mickey Mouse watch.

Grayson would be here any minute.

"Reciep?" Cheng said again.

Any second.

"Come on!"

The door jingled.

"Well g'mornin', g'mornin'," Grayson hollered cheerily. A cold wind rustled through the shop. "Come on in honey, come on in, putcha bags down here. Ah jus' wanna show these gennermen our little good fortune here." We listened to the door close. "A g'mornin' sir, you got yur heart set on these briefs too, huh?"

"Whah? Noh, I need reciep. I hah plane to cah," Cheng said. He was beginning to sound irritated.

"Allow me," we heard Laura say, followed by a click click and a chatter and the sound of the drawer springing open.

"Beautiful *and* handy," Grayson chuckled horribly.

"Ne?" Cheng called loudly. "Ne? He ouh the bah there? Ne?"

Christopher looked up with an angry, accusatory glare, eyes white and wide in the half-light.

"Mr Cheng," Pete soothed. "Why don't we —"

"*Ne?!*"

"Wha's the fellah shoutin' about? Someone back there? Huh?"

I held my breath, hard and tight in my chest. Christopher's eyes narrowed slowly.

"Remember your plane?" Pete was saying. "I think it's time you were heading off, don't you? I have to deal with Mr Grayson now, I –"

"Hey boy, what kind'a salesman are you anyhow? Shovin' yur customers out? Let the man take his time. He knows when his plane is. Jeez this country. Ah tell ya miss, the service in this place . . ." and thankfully Grayson was off, lecturing Laura on how to treat customers, superior American till technology and tight-assed limey bitches at the Bureau de Change. Somewhere within all this we made out the clatter of Pete chivvying Cheng out onto the street.

Christopher stared at me in silence for an age.

"I . . . I'm sorry," I whispered. "He's a big customer, I-I . . ."

Christopher put a gloved finger to my lips. I smelled the synthetic rubber, tasted the acid battery tang.

"Step away from case sir," Julio was saying. "I not tell you again."

"Okay boy, ahm juss' showin' mah gal here. You see this sweetheart? Look at them. The definin' image of the definitive hero of the twenny-eth century. Universally understood. And these. *These.* The very pair, the *inspiration.* Sketched, painted, rendered a thousand times. A cultural mahl-stone . . ."

While Grayson gosh-gollied and goddarned it, in the kitchen Christopher, one finger still pressed against my lips, was silently fishing out his mobile and thumbing through the address book, face glowing in the faint green light of the display screen. Breath held, heart slamming, there was a pause and then the phone on the shop desk jangled into life.

"That'll be *Sotheby's* in LA," Pete said loudly.

"*LA?*"

"Hello? *Heroes Incoporated?*"

"*Relax,*" Christopher whispered into his little phone, inches from me. "*It's all going fine.*"

"Yes hi, I thought it would be you. What time is it there . . . ?"

"*Remember the delay on the line. Lots of pauses. Make sure Grayson can hear you. And talk insurance.*"

"What? Are you there . . . ? *Insurance?* No, I've had all that covered. You told me to . . . revalued? What do you mean? The *tablecloth?*"

Outside, the shop went quiet.

"Oh my God. Are you serious?! When? When was this?"

There was the squeak of Pete dropping into the chair.

"Everythin' all right boy? Your boss don't look so good."

"I don't know," I heard Julio saying. "LA have matching table-cloth going up for auction simultaneous. Maybe they had offers in?"

"Then, God, I don't know," Pete went on. "Maybe . . . maybe you should have it collected or something? . . . Well like you said, I've just got the one guard and the alarm . . . Yes, but who's going to pay for that . . . ?"

"What was the reserve for the cape, kid?"

"I no can tell you sir. It a private auction by invite only."

"I thought you were going to bid," Laura said. She sounded grumpy, a little spoilt.

"An' that I am li'l lady. Hey bud, what's it gonna take to get me into that auction room?" and there was the sound of a zip.

In the darkened kitchen, Christopher cocked his head a little to listen. I pointed at my chest.

"*Round his neck*," I whispered. "*Wallet?*"

"Christ," Pete said, hanging up noisily.

"Problem?"

"Lock the door. Double lock it. And double check the fire escapes." There was a clink as Pete tossed Julio the keys. "Damn. I knew I should have let *Forbidden Planet* . . . LA want armed bloody guards."

"Armed?"

"They've had a load of early bids in for the tablecloth. Reserve has tripled. They think the pants are likely to go likewise. We should have them moved. Sir? Sorry sir, I'm going to have to ask you to vacate the store? Sir?"

"Ahll right, ahll right. One second. Ah juss came by to give you a promised peep at this l'il baby. Lookie here." There was a shuffle and a thud and two loud metallic clicks. "You remember yur fellah yesterday? Mr Laurie?"

"With the cut head? Is . . . is that it? You got his case back?"

"Ha-haa, come here my beauty. Look at that. Careful now . . . We were shopping. Ah was buyin' this lovely lady somethin' pretty. When some guy calls me up. Juss a few minutes ago. Young kid he sounds like. Says he's got a case in his possession. Nuthin' in it but a comic book, train ticket to Blidworth and my name and number. Little tyke says if I want it back, it'll cost me two hundred bucks. Ha!" Grayson barked. "Kid obviously ain't a collector! Two hundred. Boy, talk about the deal of a lifetime! Told me I could pick it up at some strip joint just down the street there. Two hundred! Your fellah had me payin' over five grand."

"Are you going to call him?" Laura asked.

"Shit, sweetheart!" Grayson laughed. "Why the goddamn hell would I wanna do *that*?! Finders keepers is what it is. Ain't no more complicated than that!"

"*And there we have it, dear boy,*" Christopher whispered in the darkness, eyes wide. A smile slid across his face. "*You can't say we didn't give him a chance. I now pronounce our mark guilty and will have great pleasure in administering his sentence.*"

"This isn't real."

"Huh? Say what?"

Pete's voice.

"This train ticket. It's just a photocopy. And it's two years old. Look."

We listened, breath held, as the shop fell quiet.

"Odd," Julio said. "Let see the case? Was there anything else in there?"

"Nuthin'. Inside's a li'l frayed here at the edge of the . . . shit, what's this?"

"You got something?"

"The bottom here. At the edge. I can get mah finger in this . . ."

Which is how Grayson, as planned, came to find eleven other forged copies of *Action Comic* #4 that Christopher had planted. All identical. Hidden rather clumsily in the suspiciously frayed and patently obvious false bottom of the case.

Grayson, understandably, went rather nuts. And I mean nuts. Even in that cramped kitchen it was loud. Yelling, swearing. "*Forgeries? That bastard selling forgeries? That limey fuckin' son of a bitch. You wait till I get mah hands on that guy. You just wait!*" Christopher and I held our breath and gripped the formica while he swore and slammed and swore some more. Julio must have been trying to calm him down at one point because it was suddenly all *get your fuckin' gloves off'a me buddy!* and *you think 'cause ah'm an old man I won't slap your mouth?*

I, meanwhile, among the crashing and thrashing, was frankly terrified.

Doubly so when Christopher leaned in and said *brace yourself.*

"*Brace* – ?" I whispered. "*What do you – Jesus!*" I screamed, which I was almost certain I wasn't meant to.

Fortunately, there was no way Grayson or indeed anyone in the back office could have heard me, such was the deafening, room-shaking blast of the alarm.

Outside, over the teeth-loosening din, we could just make out the shop erupting into bedlam – chairs falling over, people yelling, shouting, Laura's screams. We made out the scuffle of everyone barging into the back office, a click and light suddenly spilt underneath the kitchen door. Shouting, arguing. Then a crash. Loud. Like splintering wood. Among this, the shouts continued, the alarm continued, throbbing the kitchen, throbbing the world, fading up and down, tone adjusting in sweeps for what felt like an age before it suddenly stopped with a whimper.

Leaving silence. Breathing.

And then the yelling.

Pete bellowed at Julio. Julio bellowed at Pete and Grayson. Grayson bellowed at Julio and Pete. Laura shouted *everybody shut-up!* over and over again.

Pete was blaming Julio for moving off his post and not locking the door. Julio was blaming Pete for making him look after angry Americans when he should have been on his post and locking the door. Grayson was still yelling about coming all the way to London to be swindled, tearing out Christopher's throat, giving him a horse-whipping, Kansas style (whatever the hell that was).

Then Pete's yelling dissolved into panic. He began to wail *a million dollars! A million dollars!* Over and over, which made everybody else stop for a moment and pay attention.

"A *million*?" Grayson shouted.

"Yes!" Pete yelled. "That's what the tablecloth . . . Aww shit."

"A million . . ."

"Everybody wants it. Museums, collectors. Jack Nicholson, Nicholas Cage, they're all bidding – dammit!"

"Jesus Christ," Julio said.

"Call the police! Don't just stand there cursing. This is your fucking fault! Check the street! Check the street! And call the fucking police! Awww *Christ*."

Footsteps. Up and down. Doors slamming. Car horns. Voices.

"Police please . . . Hello? Yes, there's been a robbery . . ."

All the while, Pete wailed. His insurance. Not covered. What'll he do? What'll he do?

By the time Julio had got off the phone, having explained all breathlessly to the speaking clock, the talk in the shop had got a little personal.

"Yes!" Pete was yelling. "Yes I *do* happen to think I'm in trouble! I'm sorry but I do!"

"Ah came five thousand miles to buy a comic book for mah museum, only to have some con artist try and swindle me with a fake! Ah think my problems are a little more –"

"I don't give a shit about your problems! So you spent two hundred quid on a bag of photocopies! I just had a three grand display case ripped off the wall and someone's walked off with a million dollars' worth of priceless pop-culture pants. My insurance only covers me for three hundred thousand US dollars! Where the fuck am I going to get the other *seven hundred grand*!"

"The police are on way," Julio said. "They want everyone stay here."

"Here?" we heard Laura pipe up. "I'm not staying here. This has nothing to do with me. I've gotta get back to work."

"Gimme the contact for this Christopher fellah. Conman thinks he can pull one over on me does he? Ah'll show him, the sonofabitch."

"You're waiting here, Bob?" Laura said. "For the police? Er, aren't they going to ask you what you're doing here? Where you got the case?"

"Case . . . ?"

"The comics, idiot," Pete said. "Forged or not *Bob*, that case is stolen goods buddy."

"Hmn. Maybe . . . maybe you're right. Sweetheart, maybe ah'll come with you. Drop you off at yur l'il café there . . ."

"No you wait," Julio protested. "I have tell the police −"

"C'mon honey, let me grab yur bags here," and there was a rustle as Grayson hauled up the shopping.

"Wait!" Pete said loudly. "*Conman?*" The shop fell into a sick, queasy quiet. "That's what you called him. This seller, this Christopher bloke. *Conman*. Right? Who just *happened* to tell you to meet him here yesterday?"

In the dark kitchen, Christopher and I looked up, hearts hammering. We listened.

"I don't like yur tone, fellah. Now you juss back off . . ."

"Made sure we *all* got his attention right, with his *convenient* mugging story? Right?"

"Just wait for police −"

"Giving *you* the opportunity to come back here today with your prize. Throw a tantrum? Trip the alarm? Keep us all busy out the back there?"

"Bob, Bob don't listen to him."

"Now you just wait one second buddy . . ."

"*Bob!*"

"Ah'm comin' sweetheart. This young fellah is lookin' for to learn his-self some manners."

"You're going nowhere. You're going to talk to −"

"Getcha hands off-a me, fellah. I didn' have nothin' to do with no robbery. Ah wanna talk to this Christopher guy as much as you do, believe me."

"Hey you aren't leaving, you come back here . . ."

The front door jangled roughly. Traffic. A cold breeze slid beneath the door, dancing about the kitchen, prickling my forearms.

"Get yur hands off me, boy. Miss, less go, c'mon, less go."

"Hey. *Hey!*" Pete hollered.

The door jangled again, closing firmly with a slam.

Christopher and I stood motionless. An age passed in the dark, inky silence.

"All clear!" Pete called.

Armpits soaking, face drenched, heart going a mile a minute, I squeezed out and followed a giddy Christopher into the shop.

God it was a state. Racks pulled over, glass cracked. Everyone saying okay? Okay? All right? Okay? I began tidying up, gathering pictures and postcards from the filthy floor as the team debriefed, when suddenly there was a knock on the fire escape.

We all stopped as Julio hurried through to the back office and swung the door open.

The visitor struggled in, through the office and into the shop.

"G'day fellahs," he said, a heavy, stolen display-box in his arms and a big Aussie grin on his face.

That night. Tuesday night.

I couldn't sleep.

I lay under the duvet in the chill, still blue light of the bedroom, blinking at the radio-alarm clock. It blinked back at me. 01:35. I rolled onto my back gently and eased myself up a bit, the aging mattress groaning, head hard against the greasy board. Sitting up for a while, listening to the dark creaks and clanks of the aging central heating, I got up silently and joined the cat in the kitchen. I put some milk on to boil as quietly as I could.

I took a silent tiptoe down the landing, beneath the silent black and white stares of Brandon Routh and George Reeves to the nursery, easing the door open and moving quietly in, teeth tight, shoulders hunched.

The *Where the Wild Things Are* curtains glowed with the orange streetlight gas, light spilling between them onto the cot where, lying on her podgy tummy, Lana lay. I crept in, pushing the door to and moved over to the washing-piled chair.

I sat. Lana lay still among the dead-eyed soft toys, shallow baby breath clicking and sucking, tiny wrinkled fingers curled, face lit by the soft green plastic glow of her caterpillar night-light.

I would stop lying to Jane soon. One more day. Money in the bank, solicitors off my back, everything back to normal. I planned on telling her, you see. When it was all over I mean. When all was well. After Lana's first birthday maybe.

Or second.

Definitely by her thirtieth birth*dayyeaahhrghh!*

Streaky yowled, scrabbling out of the room and I dashed through into the lounge where the white phone was *bringgging* shrilly, my teeth gritted in an attempt to stop Jane waking up. Like that ever works.

I snatched it up.

"Hello?" I whispered, heart thundering in the darkness. I tiptoed to the lounge door, sliding it closed. "Hello?"

There was a clatter and a chatter on the other end. A party?

"*Neil? Neil it's me.*"

"Laura? Are you all right? Christ, it's nearly two o'clock, where – ?"

"*I'm at some restaurant. Some club or something, I don't know. It's off Park Lane somewhere.*"

"With Grayson?"

"*He's scaring me. I mean it Neil, he's really scaring me. I don't think this is a good idea. He's shouting. Slamming his plate, throwing things. They've asked him to calm down like three times. He's drunk, swearing. I think whoever decided he was a good victim made a big mistake.*"

"You still with him?"

"*I said I was powdering my nose. He'll track Christopher down, have him killed. Saying he knows people, won't be made a fool of. Who the hell does that shopkeeper think he is, accusing him of being a crook. Ranting, rambling on. I don't like it.*"

"It's okay, it's okay. It's bluff, it's all *bluff*. He's a *nobody*, he doesn't know *anybody*. Christopher was saying he –"

"*I want you to get me out of here.*"

"What?"

"*Come and get me. I don't like it. I want to go home, I don't want to be involved anymore. It's dangerous.*"

"Look, Laura. Look, I can't come and –"

"*Please. I don't know what he's going to do. Please Neil.*"

"Can't you tell him . . . I dunno, tell him you don't feel well? That you want to go home?"

"*I tried that. He won't listen. You've got to get me –*"

"Neil?"

Jane called out softly from the bedroom. Shit.

"Neil?" The squeak and rustle. She was getting up. Shitty fuck arse.

"I've got to go, Laura. Hang in there."

"*I don't know if I can keep this up. He's threatening to –*"

"Try . . . just try and keep him happy," I hissed.

Jane was coming down the hall. Lana was crying.

"Jesus Christ!" she yelled. "*Neil!?*"

"Oh God. I've got to go. Just . . . just do what you can. Come round in the morning. No. Shit, Henry's taking me to Bloomsbury. Lunchtime. Come round lunchtime. But be careful, okay?"

"*Neil!?*" Jane shouted again.

I hung up and hurried back into the kitchen. Or rather, where I thought I'd left the kitchen. It now seemed to resemble a Dresden dairy after particularly heavy shelling. Steam and stench and hissing and dripping and burnt milk all over the hob.

"Jesus Christ, you want to burn the house down?" Jane scowled, bleary eyed, Lana on her hip bawling. She began to roll off great florets of kitchen towel.

"I-I, sorry, I . . . the phone . . ."

"Get the mop. Jesus, look it's everywhere. Who was calling?"

"Hn?"

"On the phone, who was it?"

"Oh uhmm, I dunno. They thought we were a cab firm. Couldn't work out what they were saying."

"Look it's all burnt in . . ."

"Sorry. Give me the towel, I'll do it." I hurried sleepily to the sink and began to skoosh the cold tap.

"Leave it now. Just leave it." Lana was tearful and irritable, Jane jigging and shushing her absently. "Forget about it now. I'll worry about it tomorrow. Did you pick up that cleaner for the bathroom floor?"

"Shit, sorry. It's on my list."

"We've got Jack and Catherine coming over Thursday don't forget."

"I know, I know. It'll be fine."

I dumped an armful of soggy paper into the swing top bin while Jane tramped off to the toilet, trying to placate Lana with a bit of *ooze-a-silly-daddy-den*. I threw the burnt pan into the sink, adding a squirt of Fairy and another skoosh of water to let it soak.

I went back to bed, mind reeling with thoughts of Laura and Grayson.

Knows people. Won't be made a fool of.

Bluffing. Surely bluffing?

"G'night," Jane said with a kiss, lowering the baby into the bed and snuggling back down, body squirming to track down the warm spot.

One more day.

"Sleep well."

Bluffing. Bluffing about having us killed.

Killed? Was that what she said?

I sat up and watched 02:13 become 07:00.

Ooze-a-silly-daddy-den.

eleven

"Is . . . is everything all right?" I yawned, wiping gunk from my face and licking the early oily film from my teeth. "You seem —"

"Move it, *aaairse-hole!*" Henry bellowed, slamming the horn down with a piercing blare and pulling the Bedford van sharply into the oncoming Wednesday morning traffic. Behind me, I heard boxes tumbling over, clanging against the rusty shell. "No," he spat, revving aggressively, the van lurching forward three angry feet at a time. "Everything's not *awlroit*. Everything's shot to — *aairse-hole! Getcha fuckin' pommie wreck outta my* — and the cabin vibrated again with the blare of the horn.

One clammy hand on vinyl seating, the other gripping the dash, I quickly decided to leave my I-Spy suggestion for another time and contented myself with a game of Hanging-On-For-Dear-Life.

"Bloomsbury's off," Henry said, pulling away at speed, throwing me back against the seat. More boxes tumbled behind us.

"What? *Off?* But — ?"

"Fuckin' estate agent screwed us. Got all his dates ass about face, the bloody idiot. We were meant to — *aairse-hole!* Learn to fuckin' *droive!* Meant to have delivered all this shit last night. Got there to find balloons on the door and a lounge full of students dancin' to Abba and painting their Doc fuckin' Martens. Said they had another month on the lease."

"A month — ? Shit, so what *happens* . . . God sorry, what happens now?" I yawned. Christ it was early. I pumped down the passenger window to get a little air between my ears.

"Well Julio is about ready to walk. Says the whole play's jinxed, what with your lady friend stickin' her oar in and — *move it!*" Henry pulled the van off the roundabout, grinding the gears, north onto Fulham Road, "and Christopher acting like some first year novice. This Kensington move of his is a bad idea. A baaaaad fuckin' idea."

"Kensington? What's Kensington?"

"A baaaaad fuckin' idea. Liable to get us all pinched."

"No, I mean what – ?"

"Christopher wants to use a Kensington pad for the final play. In place of Bloomsbury. That's where we're going now."

"And this new place is definitely empty?"

"Empty? HA! Not – *move it! C'mon! Shift yourself!* Not exactly empty, no. Hold tight."

A quarter of an hour later, the glass front of Imperial College flashed with the reflection of a tense young Australian face and a pale, terrified British one as the van whipped past and swung wide off Kensington Gore. We slowed, crawling through the quiet curling avenues behind the Royal Albert Hall.

Henry was right. This was a very bad idea.

"Here we go," Henry said, rolling to a halt with a squeak. "Through the purple door, first floor, flat six. I'll check the back. Go."

I clambered out into the chilly stillness, wind whipping between the cavernous mansion flats either side of the street, winter sunshine glinting off the high attic windows. Henry, his broad surfer's frame squirming in a revolting navy suit, heaved open the van rear doors and tugged out a battered burgundy briefcase.

"Go. C'mon, whatcha waiting for?"

What I was waiting for, in all honesty, was the squawk of megaphones, the whoop of sirens, the thump of overhead helicopters and the immediate arrival of a vanload of short-haired men with Kevlar on their chests and overtime on their minds. But I made do with just shrugging nervously and pushing through the purple door into the echoing tile of the ancient flats.

I slapped up the cold stairwell. The place had a hospital smell, a sick, stale antiseptic odour like bedpans and lino. Hands clammy, heart throbbing loud and fat in my ears, I reached the dark wood door of number six. The smell was stronger, sharp and yellow, biting my eyes. I knocked gingerly, the door swinging open with a creak. I held my breath and stepped through. I could hear a voice. Croaky. Sick.

"He-hello?" I said, moving inside slowly.

". . .Yes, I-I am afraid you have me banged to rights there m-my yankee friend. Sorry, excuse –"

A dry hacking cough spluttered from the room at the end of the bare hall.

"Urgh, God. I did indeed have an accomplice lift the garment from the store during the fracas and deliver it to me . . . If I could, Mr Grayson, I would . . ."

More groaning slithered out into the hall.

I peered around the first door. A bedroom. Average-sized, tidy. There was, however, something unplaceably not quite right about it. Feeling a frown settle between my eyebrows I pushed further on. On the right, a second door. I eased it open. Bathroom. I let my eyes drag over the glass and tile.

"You – *cough hack splutter* – sorry, you can check with who you like Mr Grayson . . ."

Chewing the inside of my cheek, I moved softly down the hall, mouth and eyes full of the tight antiseptic pong. It was horrible. The smell of death and cleaning. I confidently expected to turn the corner and find weeping widows, coffee machines and a gift shop selling lilies and throat sweets, but I didn't. What I did find, however, was a small through-lounge kitchen-diner arrangement and a pair of red underpants in a large Perspex box leant up against a sideboard.

Oh, and a Christopher, laid out wearily on a couch under a blanket. Unshaven, head bandaged, eyes closed, face pale, murmuring weakly into his mobile phone.

"You do that. I-I'll speak to you later . . ." he coughed, wiping his feet on death's doormat, exhausted at the effort. "Uhh–ntil then," and he closed the telephone, letting it drop to the carpet. Christopher breathed deep and slow, chest rising and falling.

"Hello?" I said softly. God, was he all right?

Christopher opened his eyes wearily, focusing about the room until he found me. He licked dry lips and smiled.

"What ho!" he said clearing his throat noisily. "Gahhh! Yuck," and he flung back the blanket and sprung lightly to his feet, snatching the phone from the floor. He was dressed in some natty red jim-jams and a plaid dressing-gown.

"You . . . you all right?" I asked.

"Righter than a ninepence worth of right-handed, right-wing, right-thinking rain dear fellow," he twinkled, slapping me on both shoulders. "Got to lie down. Affects the sound of the larynx. Henry not with you?"

"Here!" Henry yelled from the hallway, struggling in with a large cardboard box, his briefcase slung on top. "Cor, don't ya think you've overdone it with the bleach? You can smell it on the street."

"I'll open a window or two," Christopher said. "It should have faded just enough to be clinging by the time Grayson gets here."

"I'm gonna say it *again*," Henry sighed.

"Henry dear, it's the only –"

"This is a very, *very* bad idea. Won't you let me ask around, talk to – oof, give us a hand mate –" and I helped him stagger the box over to the kitchen worktop. "That's it. Let me talk to some people? Find an empty place?"

"Grayson is all ready on his way."

"You called him?"

"Just got off," Christopher said, waggling his phone.

"*Big* mistake," Henry muttered, brushing down his suit and heading off for another box.

Christopher and I unpacked the first one, piling starchy linen and rough grey towels onto the kitchen counter.

"*Very* surprised to hear from me was Mr Grayson. *Very* surprised. Crosser than Good Friday on Golgotha too, of course, but there we are."

"That's what Laura said. She called me last night. From some club."

"Upper Grosvenor Street. Our Henry was three tables away. Quite a temper our American friend's got."

"Said he was going to track you down? Have you killed?"

"I certainly hope so," Henry said, bustling in with another box, this one full of tubes and surgical tape.

"Henry's right. His anger is vital to the plan after all," Christopher smiled. "Henry dear, you bring the drip?"

Henry flapped out a tatty checklist and jogged back out, slamming down the staircase again.

"So what did he say when you called?" I asked.

"Well once I'd listened to him yell about *tearin' out mah eyebawls* and *fuckin' with the wrong cowboy mister* and other delightful family favourites, he calmed down long enough for me to explain my sorry situation. I admitted I was indeed a con artist, which of course he'd figured out already —"

"What with him getting his hands on your tricksy briefcase?"

"Quite," Christopher said. "He resumed with verse two of his *Tearin' out mah eyebawls* number for a bit, naturally. Anyhoo, I calmed him down, apologised for dragging him all the way from Kansas to buy a forgery. Explained it was nothing personal and what-not. And I admitted, somewhat reluctantly, that it had been I too who had been behind the underpant smash-and-grab yesterday."

"How did he feel about that?"

"Understandably irked," Christopher said. He began to break down the empty cardboard boxes, stacking them in the kitchen. "Especially as Pete did such a good job of pegging him as an accomplice. Anyway, I explained to him I'd been trying to kill two birds with one stone — meeting him at the shop for the exchange so I could take a gander at the security — but that I hadn't foreseen getting clunked about the head by two acne-pocked borstal cases on the way."

"Which I guess Grayson figured was no more than you deserved?"

"Quite-ola, dear chap. Here, let's move this onto the sideboard there," and we ferried the tubes and tape into the lounge.

"Henry said this is *your* flat?" I asked, peering about the . . . well, about the nothing very much really. Apart from a few starter pieces of Conran basics — couch, sideboard, bed, bin, broom — the place was bare. Not a single personal item to jazz it up a bit. No photos in the bedroom, no soapdish on the sink, no nick-nacks, bits or, for that matter, bobs. Minimalism schminimalism, this was perverse.

"I know, I know," Christopher said, sensing my bewilderment. "Home is a place to rest one's head. That is all. Once you start down the road of the thousand-pound couch and the two thousand pound hi-fi, you suddenly find you're a smug little so-and-so, up to his Banana Republic khakis in insurance and paranoia. Just the kind of chappie people like me like to take for their bankroll in fact."

"But it can't be wise, can it? Bringing Grayson *here*?"

"It's insane," Henry interrupted, appearing in the doorway with a long steel drip, trailing tubes and tape, a green first-aid box under his other arm. "Goes against a cardinal rule. *Never shit where you eat.*"

"Ahhh, too true my antipodean chum. But you are forgetting another valuable maxim – *don't let incompetent Bloomsbury estate agents screw you out of the opportunity to fleece greedy fat Yanks out of half a million pounds.* An oldie, but a goodie I feel. Now I explained to our man Grayson that I *had* every intention of taking delivery of the said underpants and selling them abroad – probably Japan. But poor me, if I hadn't collapsed late last night in a pool of blood. Tch. Those borstal boys and their heavy handed thuggery. Done my poor skull more harm than we thought. Ahh, which reminds me. Corn syrup?"

"Check," Henry said, tossing a heavy can from a box across the room to him.

"Splendid. This'll give Grayson the impression I'm at death's doorknob. Dripped up, croaky and dying. Stuck here with a fortune's worth of stolen underpants. Doped up to the eyes. Unable to travel. Private nurses bleeding me dry. It's no wonder I'm eager to halve the underpant's price for a quick –"

The Archers began to rumpty-tump from Christopher's dressing-gown pocket. He flipped out his phone while Henry and I fetched the last boxes from the van. We returned a sweaty minute later to find Christopher pacing and flapping in his gown.

"Henry, get your stuff together. Grayson's on the move."

"Now?"

"That was Julio at the Waldorf. Grayson's just booked a cab for Brigstock Place. Leaving in thirty minutes."

"Awww fuck it," Henry spat, dumping the box with a thud and grabbing up his briefcase. He flipped the catches and began to double-check a load of yellow papers. "What's his damned hurry?"

"Calm down, deep breaths. We're prepared for this. Grayson asked me to give him a few hours' grace to make a decision. He's obviously going over to the shop to talk to Pete, make peace, find out if there's any heat. Just earlier than expected is all."

"Sounds like an act three beginner's call for Mr Furious Insurance man," Henry said, slamming his case.

"Exactly. So go, go, go," Christopher flapped.

Henry went went went.

"And keep the van out of sight!" Christopher called down after him from the rusty window.

"Shouldn't I . . . ?"

"No no, I need you here young man," Christopher said, patting my arm in a fatherly manner. He led me back into the lounge where the garage-sale medical gear lay strewn about. "In about thirty-five minutes, if Henry does his job, Grayson will, ahem, *accidentally* overhear exactly how much our underpants are worth. He'll realise that I, on my sick bed, out of the loop, in my dying desperation, have vastly undervalued the item and he'll be over here like a shot to close the deal . . ."

"Before the nine o'clock news blabs about record-breaking Beverly Hills auctions . . ."

"And I double my price. Quite. Now give me a hand with these blood bags dear fellow."

The next half hour or so passed as anxiously as I suppose you'd imagine.

Between minute-by-minute telephone updates from Brigstock Place, Christopher and I dressed the flat with the bottles, bandages and bric-a-brac of the recently pulverised, splashing a bit more *Domestos X-tra Pungent* about the mansion stairwell for good measure, all in all giving the 'store', as I suppose I should put it, a convincing ambiance.

Whether it would be convincing enough to make Grayson believe a bed-ridden Christopher was a dying thief willing to part with his final touch at a knock-down price, we wouldn't know until it happened of course. We could but cross our drip-feeds and hope.

"Are the rest of the guys from London too?" I asked, tearing off a strip of surgical tape and holding it out. "Lots of wealth around I s'pose. A lot of thingys. Marks."

We were in the stark white glare of Christopher's bathroom, getting a convincing-looking drip attached to his arm.

"I'm the only city slicker amongst us," Christopher said, fiddling with a tricky tube. "More out of necessity than anything else. You saw those letterheads Henry ordered for me?"

"Letter – ? I heard you *mention* . . ."

Christopher clicked his fingers. "In the lounge."

I scuttled through and found a plastic wallet on the side table. That strange feeling of teamwork, of *camaraderie* returned, just for a minute. Was I beginning to *enjoy* this? Being part of a team, a gang once again? I brought it back into the bathroom where Christopher was fiddling with his taped-up arm.

"*Maurer & Fitzgerald Ltd,*" I read aloud. "Insurance?"

"A useful method of obtaining an introduction. Offer a valuation, free appraisal. Gets one's brogues in the door. The letterhead says Aldersgate as you see. I've found it gives it that little bit of credibility. But it does mean I need to be in town. As you are discovering, marks are a panicky breed. Always want a last-minute check, a last-minute review. Hence my need for this place. Cotton wool?"

I tugged off a handful of wispy fluff from the packet.

"Your big businesses are here of course, which is a plus. But then so is the *savvy*. Your city chappie is a clued-up fellow. Suspicious, switched on. Used to a little distrust. Makes things difficult. The home-counties, though? The major shires – Hamp', Warwick', Hertford'? That's where the *real* juice is. Your mock-Tudor double-garages with golf bags and phoney Agas. Portly chief executives, rolling chins in cashmere cardies. There we go. How's that?" and Christopher proffered a veiny left arm, plastic nozzle buried beneath cotton wool and tape.

"Very convincing."

We moved back down the acrid hall to the lounge, among the rough towels and bleachy bedpans.

It all *looked* very convincing.

"Spending their weekends laying down wine and laying down nannies while dried-up wifey makes jam for the parish. Last twenty years in charge of some office or other. Never had a problem they couldn't solve with the flick of a Duofold and a wave of a secretary."

Very, *very* convincing.

"I sit down next to them in their local pub. Top up their pewter tankard, help 'em with a crossword clue in the *Mail on Sunday* and bob's your uncle."

The pills, the pyjamas, the props?

Uncanny.

"I mean there's no way I can be smarter than *them*, right? No way I can be playing an angle *they* haven't thought of? With all their wisdom? Hmm? Neil? You all right young man?"

"Huh? Yes. Yes just . . . just thinking that's all," I said.

Utterly uncanny. Boy, when these guys wanted to make you believe something . . .

"It's okay old chap, just a few hours now. Pete should be calling *aaaa*ny minute."

But Christopher's voice was fading away. Becoming thick and muted. I could see his eyes shining and his mouth going two-dozen to the dozen, but I wasn't hearing him. I was trying to stop the room spinning. To stop my knees buckling. My mouth from drying up, my hands from trembling.

"I . . ." a voice croaked. It didn't sound like mine. But then I couldn't really hear properly, what with the panicked slam of my heartbeat and the blood roaring in my ears. "I . . . I should go."

"Go? No, no lad."

They were in the shop. Pete. Henry. Julio. They were in my shop. They had keys. My keys. My shop. On their own. Right now.

Christopher keeping me here. Away from them. Away from whatever they were doing.

"Probably best you stay here, there's a chap. Let the boys play their parts. Like I say, Pete should have spun Grayson his story. Bound to call *aaaaaa*ny minute now."

Boy, when these guys wanted to make you believe something . . .

"Neil? Neil, where are you − ? *Neil?*" Christopher's clipped voice hollered behind me as I took the concrete mansion steps three at a time.

"Okay mate?" the cabbie asked.

"What?" I said, palms cold and wet, sick stomach lurching as

he grumbled through the bustle of Knightsbridge. "Yes. No. Sorry."
I sat back on the farty seat, feet tapping, slapping out an anxious
rhythm on my knees.

Christ. What had I done? What had I *done*? Trusted these men?
Handed over my keys, my property, my *life*? They would be clearing
the shop. Clearing it all. How long had I let them alone with the
keys? Think, *think*.

The cab swung around Hyde Park and up Piccadilly.

Yesterday? Yesterday afternoon, after closing. Five o'clock. I checked
the cheap Rolex again. It was just after eleven. Eighteen hours. They
could have been in there for eighteen hours. Filling a van. Two vans.
A fleet. All hired under false names, all untraceable.

Step one, they'd said. Locate and investigate the mark.

*Stock wise, perhaps an over reliance on Golden Age comic books and
Superman memorabilia they tell me, but otherwise, pretty much exactly
what I'm looking for . . .*

Step two. Gain the mark's confidence.

*Shall we say Claridge's? They do the most scrumptiful chocolate cheese-
cake.*

I leant forward, cracking open the side window and letting a
blast of drizzly air onto my face, breathing deep, breathing slow.

Who could I call? Jane? No no. The police?

*Your character it turns out, Neil, is one who likes to fleece aged fellows
out of their heirlooms for a quick buck.*

Christ.

"Mate? Mate? I said I'll take you up Shaftesbury Avenue, awroit?"

"Uhh, yes. Yes fine. Just . . . just quickly."

Grayson. God, who was he? A genuine mark? I *had* been sent
to meet him off the plane.

Not that I'd actually *seen* him get *off* a plane.

Shit.

But.

But no, Henry said Grayson had a suite at the Waldorf.

Henry *said*.

The grift is all about trust, Neil. No guns, no brickbats, no threats.

Trust.

*We're going to need a full set of keys, my poppety-poo. Each, I'm
afraid.*

"How far you want me to go mate?" the cabbie called.

I looked up hastily, eyes scanning the street. Souvenir shops. Gielgud Theatre.

Near enough.

I pulled out a handful of coins, shoving them through the scratched partition, some clattering to the floor and pushed out onto the busy street to a blare of horns and a yell of cabbie, moving fast up Wardour Street.

And it's all right for you to skin this man out of his money because what? He's stupid?

No. No please no Lord. Whatever I've done, whatever punishment this is.

And greedy. Terribly greedy.

Soho was at a busy standstill, the coughing grime of white delivery vans idling at litter-strewn kerbs, pigeons flapping and strutting. A distant siren.

I swung left onto Brewer Street, eyes wet with the cold London grit, running, body jiving and jittery, past coffee-bar tables and fluttering strip joint ribbons.

I was sorry. I was sorry. Just please, please don't let it be me.

But why not? God replied silently, in that way of his. *Werenst thou happy to see thy neighbour taken to thy cleaners big time?*

He had me. Pinned me, like some celestial Paxman.

Jinking left, right and left again, I swung myself around a lamppost on the corner of Brigstock Place and slammed hard with a yelp into a black wallet.

A black wallet slung about the chest of a fat American.

"Jesus felluh!" Grayson barked. I stumbled backwards, hands raised. "You in some kind'a . . . Hey. Hey, wait a secun'."

I blinked up at him, mind reeling and spinning.

"Wait . . . wait, don't ah know you?" and he narrowed his tiny eyes, pulling his fat head back an inch. I backed away, mumbling, stumbling. "Sure. Sure, ah know you," and he clicked fat fingers. "Didn' ah . . . At the airport?" he nodded, jowls wobbling, pointing a podgy digit.

I could only mouth and flap helplessly like a dying fish on a wet deck.

"You wuz talkin' 'bout the auction, right? That why yur here too?" and he tossed a thumb over his shoulder at the shop front. "Well yur too late. Fellahs had 'umselves a robbery yesterday."

"Robbery?" I croaked, mouth dry.

"Guys had the very jockies worn bah one Jerry Siegel. Made in Cleveland. Ones he wore when he was posin' for his buddy. Ah saw 'em. Apparently matchin' tablecloth juss went in auction in LA three hours ago. *Two million dollars.*"

"Two mill – ?"

"Two *million*," Grayson whistled. "Some movie star bought 'em they say. Anyhow, ah wouldn't go in there if I wuhz you," and he began to straighten his shoulder bag, fat eyes glistening. "Owner guy has his insurance fellah there. Weeeooo-eee!" and he chuckled a dry chuckle. "Reckons the jockies would'a gone for near the same amount. All hell's broken loose."

"That so?"

"Anyhoo, ah got mahself somewhere ah need t'be. Hey, you know where . . ." and he began to fish awkwardly in his black bag, tugging out a greasy post-it. "You know where Beeth-nail Green is? That far? Cab take me there?"

"Beth – ? Uhm, sure, sure," I nodded. "It's a few miles north of here. Any cab."

And with a nod, Grayson waddled off around the corner and away.

I staggered across the empty cobbles. Empty specifically of vans, trolleys, stolen stock or double-crosses. Head thudding, jittery with nervous energy, I peered through the wirey glass of the shop door. Pete was behind the counter, Henry in front, waving his arms. A briefcase lay open on the desk. Voices raised.

"*Look, I had it, I don't have it anymore. Stick that on your liability form.*"

"*But in cases such as –*"

"*No no, we agreed. Way back when this was being organised. I spoke to Japan and they quoted –*"

"*Mr Martin –*"

"*They quoted three hundred thousand. Their figure.*"

I pushed in, the bell jingling softly. The familiar draughts of damp dust and decay filled my lungs.

"*It was made clear however, on page five of –*"

"No, no no no."

"On page *five*, in light of the circumstances in Los Angeles, the second auction, recommendations were made that –"

"Hold it. Neil?" Pete said, catching sight of me lurking by the postcard rack. "Shit, it's you. Christ. Grayson gone?"

"Just ran into him," I said. "He's looking for a cab."

"Phwooo, thank God," and the two men collapsed all over the desk.

Heroes Incorporated was just as I'd left it. Nothing stolen, nothing missing, nothing cleared out. No empty racks, no empty walls. Just two men high-fiving each other and saying 'good job' too much.

"He say anything to you?" Henry asked, closing his prop briefcase and tugging off his ugly tie.

"Uhmm, just that the Siegel pants are probably worth around two million dollars –"

"Ha," Pete grinned. "You should'a seen his face when I let it slip. You all right Neil?"

"Me? Uhh, yes." I looked about the shop once again. The shelves. The smiles. Humphrey Bogart on the wall. Elvis pouting down from above. "I just . . . It's fine." I gave myself a little shake.

"Grayson say he was heading Kensington way to meet Christopher?"

"Actually I think he said something about Bethnal –"

The phone interrupted us with a jangle from the counter. I lifted it gingerly.

"*Heroes Incorporated?*"

It was Christopher. Where had I run off to? What was the big hurry?

I coughed and bluffed and laughed it off, embarrassed. Made some noises about an appointment that I'm certain he didn't buy.

Upshot was he had good news and bad.

The three of us took a vote. Good news first.

Grayson had taken the bait. Now believing the stolen undies were worth four times what poor bed-ridden Christopher was asking for them, Grayson was absolutely clamouring to get his sweaty fat fingers on them and get out of the country.

So the deal had been agreed. Grayson would bring the money

in used dollar bills, to Christopher's Kensington flat on the way to the airport.

In the shop, this brought on a round of dancing, another round of high fives and us inevitably to the bad news.

Grayson had moved his departure flight back by a day.

What fives there were, were now considerably lower.

"Tomorrow?" Henry said. He stopped dancing. "Tomorrow? Why tomorrow?"

"Henry says why −"

"*I can hear him. Pop him on,*" Christopher said. I handed the receiver over and sat myself down behind the desk.

"That gives Grayson what?" I said anxiously. "24 hours to change his mind?"

"Or to figure out he's being played," Pete said. "Shit. He could call LA, start asking questions. Some comic book shop, some collector or other. Auction? What auction?"

"I'll get him to talk to her," Henry was saying. "No worries," and he hung up. "Christopher thinks we'd better get the dame involved again."

"Dame?" I wobbled.

"Your beloved Laura. To keep him busy. Off the net, away from the phone. Sounds like she's the reason he's stickin' around anyway. Quite taken his fancy has our little waitress."

"No. No way," I said. "We can't. You didn't hear her last night."

"We heard her," Pete said flatly. "This is a whole different situation."

"Right," Henry backed him up. "Last night Grayson was angry. He'd been conned. Made to look like a patsy. A five-thousand mile flight to buy a fake comic book? Of course he was angry. Jesus, who wouldn't be. But tonight?"

"Tonight, hell, he's a big shot again," Pete said. "He'll be all '*ahh showed him, that lahmey sonofabitch*'. Swaggering around. He's conning the conman. Getting his own back to the tune of one and a half million pounds. It'll be champagne and cocktails and dancing. Here's what you do −"

"No. No no no, she's not getting any more involved."

"She'll be *fine*, listen to what we're *saying*. Grayson's a hero. Mister success-story, Mister big swinging dick. He'll treat her like a princess. Dance her round, twirl her about, buying drinks, buying flowers. He won't be able to get the dumb gullible grin off his face."

"I . . . I don't know. She sounded . . . last night I mean, she –"

"Track her down. Track her down and just get her to *call* him. Tell him she misses him. Wants to see him tonight. Restaurant, club, casino, whatever it is. Anything to stop him sitting in his room watching cable, mulling it over in his head."

Lord. I checked my watch. Lunchtime. She'd be at the coffee shop, steaming milk and spreading tuna.

We were so *close*.

"Well . . . okay," I said, getting up. "Okay I'll go see if she's up for it. But I'm not sure she'll –"

"Er, hold your fuckin' horses, mate. You'll *see if she's up for it*?" Henry said, eyes widening. "Let me explain something to you pal," and he produced a long finger and proceeded to point the business end of it at me. "She's *part* of this now. Full time. Bang on. Paid up. This isn't a fuckin' reading group. She can't just phone ahead on the night and say she don't fancy it. Say she wants to stay home and pick her feet and watch *ER*, you get me? For the length of this game, she's on the team. That means she jumps when the team jumps, she sleeps when the team sleeps and she takes a shit when we say so."

I nodded to show I understood. Then nodded again. And then a third time. And a few more times. Pretty much until Henry and Pete let go of my throat.

"You gonna answer that?" Laura asked.

"In a second," I replied, ignoring the faint chirrup on the table beside me. "I need you to tell me you understand what I'm saying. You have to call Grayson. You have to call him. Now."

We were in a booth in the coffee shop. I'd arrived to find her skulking in there with the Metro crossword and a double espresso, on a short break. She had a plain, tight T-shirt on and a red scarf about her neck like an extra from *West Side Story*. Her red ballet shoes were off, small stockinged feet stretching and pointing under the table, red toenails done just-so.

"Could be important," Laura said, glancing at the phone. "Could be Maurice, telling you he's called off his lawyers? How long have you got before they dish out a summons? Friday isn't it? Maybe he's had a change of heart?"

"A change − ? Maurice is a pyjama-wearing Trekkie. If he doesn't change his shirt when he gets out of bed, how often do you think he changes his heart? Look, this is serious." The phone continued to deedle-deet. A few other diners glanced over.

"Could be your Mr Cheng? His collector might want to buy your whole stock. Gets you out of trouble. Won't need your new friends anymore. Won't need me. I can stay in and have a bath."

"*Laura* −"

"You want me to answer it?" and she reached forward.

"No, give it here. Christ." I checked the display. A sick weight leaned against my heart, insides rolling. Swallowing a fat throat of nerves, I sighed, thumbing off the phone.

"Ahhh, married life."

"*Yes*," I said, bottled anger suddenly spilling among the ketchups and sachets on the formica. "Yes, *married life*. That's what this, *all* this, is about. That's what I'm trying to protect. Trying to *save*. And *you* can help."

Laura rolled her eyes a little.

"Fine. Okay," and I sat back, petulantly. "Mock. Whatever. But it's all I've got. And I'm hanging on to it. I'm not letting burst pipes, bad plumbing, stuck-up in-laws or fucking insurance cheques take my family away from me. I found someone who loves me and I love her and I've fucked it up and I'm putting it right. I'm not losing her. Not because of this. Not because of you."

"*Me?*"

"We need you. *I* need you. Call Grayson, get him to taiii-iyyyyyeee −"

Laura smirked, removing her stockinged toes from my trouser leg.

"Laura, *please*. Get him to take you to −"

"A casino, a restaurant, karaoke, yeah yeah I get you," Laura said. "And your guys *guarantee* I'll be safe? I'm telling you, last night, I swear he was about to −"

"He'll be celebrating," I soothed. "As far as he's concerned he's about to buy Superman's *actual* underpants for practically nothing."

"Half a million pounds is practically nothing?"

"If you're Bob Grayson, yes. You've seen how he lives."

"Well I've seen how his credit card lives," Laura said. She looked at me and then checked the clock on the café wall. "I'm due back," she said, tugging a grimy apron from half under her bum. "I'll call him when I'm done here. Six-ish."

"Six – ? No no no. It has to be *now*". I tried my best to repeat Henry's speech, throwing in a *you wanna play the moll*, and a bit of *this ain't no fuckin' readin' group*. I might have even said, *lookie-here lady*. I can't be sure.

Either way, Laura took it on board in her own inimitable style.

"No, I'll take a shit when *I* feel like it," she said, standing up. "Your team of hoodlums don't tell me what to do. They might frighten you, but I've been slapped before and I can walk away any time I want."

"Okay, I'm sorry, I –"

"S'all right. I know I still owe you for helping me that night. You came to my rescue. I'll make the call," and she kissed me gently on the cheek. "Go home and try not to worry."

Good advice, I thought.

So, bearing that in mind, I went out to dinner and panicked.

twelve

"Promise me you won't get upset," Jane said.

I looked up from my dessert into her beautiful clear blue eyes, shining with candlelight and wine.

My wine, I mean. Not hers. Jane was on mineral water, what with the breastfeeding and everything. But I'd probably put away the better part of five glasses of red so everything – Jane's eyes, the restaurant flowers, the *Best of Clannad* wafting among the spotlights – all swum in a warm fuzzy buzz.

"Promise," I think I said, winey teeth and purple lips darkly reflected in the long stemmed glass.

It had been Jane on the phone in the café. Suggesting a late supper. Designed to clear air that frankly I'd had no idea I'd been fogging up. But apparently, it turned out over an overpriced main course, my late night phone calls, odd shop hours and distant demeanour had not gone entirely unnoticed. And what with Jack and Catherine due for dinner come Thursday night, Jane had thought it best to book babysitters and make sure all in Putney was rosy.

"I thought you might . . . I mean not now. But before. With everything," and she waved a slender hand loosely. "I thought you were having second thoughts. About us."

"What are you saying?" I said. "Thoughts? What on earth . . . ?"

"Thank you sir," the waiter said, suddenly at my shoulder, sliding a silver tray onto the table with a folded slip on it. I plucked it up, opened it and swallowed hard.

Jane continued to talk softly but I only picked up every fifth word, busy as my head was with some panicky mental calculations.

Pay bill, write cheque to VISA. Day's post. Three days to clear, add a nought, carry the one . . .

"Just, you know, recently. You seemed to get all withdrawn. I put it down to the leak. The worry, Earl's Court and what have you. But you're less and less involved with Lana. It's like it's dawning on you what you're getting into. Parenthood. And with *your* father as a role model . . ."

"Hn? Sorry. Yes. I-I mean no, no, don't be *silly* . . ."

. . . plus the APR. Plus fees. Plus starter, two bruschetta, a bottle of house red . . .

Fuck it, I thought with a rattle of my head, fished out my wallet, closed my eyes and flipped out the first bit of plastic I could find. The waiter coughed, so I removed my expired Blockbuster membership card, did a quick red-faced swap and downed another mouthful of wine.

The waiter wafted off.

It would be fine. I'd be shoving my share of Grayson's cash straight into my bank's branch on High Holborn come one o'clock tomorrow. A few more hours spent a little more overdrawn I could live with if the bank could.

I focused back on Jane. She had her head bowed, embarrassed, mumbling.

"Say again?"

"Forget it, it doesn't . . ." and she shook her head a little. "I just mean how you reacted to having Daddy's trust fund in our account. Not wanting to deal with it."

"That was —"

"And then all the talk about how I should have married *Andrew* at University . . ."

"Jane, I didn't —"

"*Yes*, yes you *were*. Making out I should be with some hairy, nurturing, alpha-male *provider* type. All chunky knits and Greenpeace stickers on his Land Rover. You were planting seeds in my head."

"I never meant you and Andrew —"

". . . and then coming home that night to a house full of someone else's perfume."

"God, Jane . . ."

"I *know*. It's girly and stupid and I'm ashamed of myself. But you were being so secretive. Phone calls in the study, keeping the finances under wraps. What was I meant to think?"

"You were meant to think I was fulfilling my promise. Looking after you. Letting you concentrate on yourself, on our little –"

"Sir?" the waiter interrupted. He was back again.

"On looking after Lana. Playing her more Mozart, reading her books," I said, pen poised. But there was no slip to sign. No PIN to punch. Just an awkward expression on top of a smart waistcoat.

"I do apologise. Your card has been . . . Well, the credit card people are on the telephone. If you'd walk this way, I'm sure we can –"

"*Rejected*?" Jane said, her expression hardening slightly about the edges.

"It's all right, it's all right," I said, scraping back the chair, smiling over the panic.

"That's the Visa. You said you'd *paid* the Visa," Jane pressed, loudly. Other diners looked over. "*Neil*? Have you written those cheques or not? That Maurice man phoned today. I told him you'd sorted it out. *Neil*?" The anxiety was creeping back into Jane's voice, skulking at the back of her throat like a vindictive warehouse packer, bending and manhandling the words before shoving them out.

"It'll be a mistake," I said, getting up. I bunched my napkin and tossed it to the table. "They'll have screwed up somehow, I'll sort it," and the waiter led me away, towards the back of the restaurant, giving me a few private seconds to shit my pants.

Rejected? Oh Christ. Christ, the bank. What was in all those letters I'd binned? More missed mortgage payments? More charges. Frozen accounts? Shit. Oh shit shit *shit*. My legs were cold, knees loose, throat tightening. What was I going to do? What was I going to *do*? I didn't have any cash on me. I had nothing.

I looked at the back of the waiter, bustling ahead of me. Was that a back you could reason with? Were those the buttocks of a reasonable man? A man who'd understand a discreet IOU between men? Or would there be embarrassment? A fuss? Police?

"Sir," the waiter said as we neared the swinging double doors at the rear. The air sizzled with plumes of garlic, the crash-clatter of steel pans and thick china. "Sir, forgive the subterfuge," and he handed me a credit card machine.

Two meals. Plus drinks. Plus service.

All present and correct.

"But this . . . ? You said − ?"

"The *gentlemen* said it was important."

"*Gentlemen?*" I said, bewildered, jabbing four relieved digits.

"Through here?" The sounds of the kitchen faded up in the mix. Shouts and bangs and thick smells. I looked up. The waiter had the kitchen door open.

"Where the *hell* is she, you sneaky son of a bitch?" Pete said, eyes blazing.

"Yes," Christopher oozed. "Hate to be a bore, intruding on your evening and such forth but as Pete so delicately put it, where the hell *is* she, you sneaky . . . what not? Hmmn?"

We were standing in a cloud of steam in the noisy kitchen. The air was wet and hot and I was getting that way myself. Men in grubby white cotton pushed past us, yelling, shoving. The doors swung wide and loose, cracking me on the back as trays and plates were waltzed in on high fingertips.

Pete and Christopher weren't happy. Weren't happy at all.

"You spoke to her? Explained what we needed?"

"What? Yes, yes of *course*," I hissed. God, I'd been gone a while. Jane was going to start − "*Hey!*"

"Worry about *us*," Pete said. He had my tie in his flat, dark hand, wrapped around his knuckles, pulling hard. I stared frightened into his wide eyes. "Listen. Julio followed Grayson to a pub in Bethnal Green. He stayed for an hour then headed back to pick the girl up from the café. Both back to his hotel then to a restaurant off Grosvenor Square. Four hours later, they were still in there. Julio goes in. Gone."

"Gone?"

"*Poof*," Christopher said camply. "Sorry, no offence duckie," and his eyes flicked up and down my sports coat and khakis. "I mean, *vanished*. No sign. Not out the back, not out the front. What's in Bethnal Green? Where are they? What have you two cooked up?"

"I d-don't − Ow, *ow!* You're pulling too −" I pleaded as best I could with a vintage silk garrotte pressed against my Adam's apple. "I don't *know!*"

"She was your call," Pete hissed, almost lifting me off my feet. My eyes stung, dazzled by the bright ceiling lights. I was sweating great wet LP-sized circles under my arms. The noise, the fear, the overwhelming garlic.

"Look, look *please*," I said, swallowing hard, arms flailing. "Maybe Julio went – *ow*! Maybe he went to the wrong restaurant?"

"Oh?" Christopher said. He sounded like he'd raised an eyebrow but as my neck was being forced backwards and I had little blood to the brain, I could have been mistaken. "Oh I see, so this is *our* fault?"

"Who the *fuck* do you think you are?!" Pete spat and suddenly I was shoved backwards, head cracking bang against the tiles, baking trays tumbling to the floor in a head-ringing clatter.

"Let him go," Christopher said. Pete opened his grip and I collapsed, slumping against the wall, head low, breathing deep. I tried to loosen the tight knot of my tie, swallowing huge lung-fuls of dry, boiled air.

Jane would be asking about me. On her feet. Asking for the waiter. Coming this way.

"The woman *you* brought into this is out there somewhere with half a million pounds' worth of our mark," Christopher was saying through the fug. I tried to stand up, chest wheezing and whistling. "Are you *promising* me, hand on wife, you have no idea, not one clue, as to where they are?"

"I haven't a clue where . . . *What*? What did you just – ?"

"So this isn't some misguided double-cross you and the girl have –"

"*Wife*?" I said, head banging with horror. "Hand on – ? What are you *saying*?"

"I am attempting to ascertain –"

"You *touch* her," I gnashed, finger pointing, barging forward. I didn't care, red mist of rage blurring my sight. "You come within a hundred *miles* of her, and you won't be faking a head wound, hear me?"

"Back OFF!" Pete bellowed, stepping up, elbowing us apart. I fell back, breathing hard against the sweaty tiles.

Christopher harrumphed for a moment, making a decision. He pulled back his shoulders smartly and straightened his blazer, fixing me with his clear grey eyes.

"Whether we need to speak to *Mrs* Neil about this is entirely up to *you* dear boy. Now pay attention. Grayson's flight is at ten past three tomorrow. He's going to Heathrow via Kensington. I'll be there, holed up in bed with bandages and tubes and priceless pants. Grayson will deliver nine hundred and twenty thousand dollars, in cash, at noon. *Noon*. Understand me?" He checked Mickey Mouse on his wrist. "Just under thirteen hours time. If he *doesn't* —"

I swallowed hard.

"If he fails to show. Then the responsibility falls to whoever had him last. I shall be holding your Laura answerable for the debt. Are we clear?"

"Laura? B–but I mean, she doesn't . . . I mean be *reasonable*, she can't *make* him —"

"Of course, of course," Christopher smiled. The mood was shifting, brightening. Somewhere, the sun was peeking nervously from behind a cloud. He clapped me on the upper arm chummily. "Reasonableness is my middle finger. *You* recommended her, *you* told us she was trustworthy, she is *your* responsibility. Naturally the debt will move to you. Payable in twenty-four hours."

Jane and I squabbled on the chilly pavement a few minutes later. *You said you'd sorted it all out*, she shouted. *It was just a misunderstanding*, I lied.

God, I wanted to tell her. More than ever. Just blurt it out. Explain, come clean, open up. But we were so *close*. Thirteen hours, Christopher said. Lunchtime tomorrow. I just needed the bank, Maurice, Jane, the world to hang on until then.

In thirteen hours *everything* would be all right.

I suggested a cab, to spoil Jane a little, repair some damage, but Jane wanted a walk.

Doesn't sound like we can afford a cab does it? Jesus.

She set off three paces ahead.

We were home and paying the babysitter in fifteen silent minutes. Jane went to look in on Lana, straightening blankets, stroking her cheek. I hung back in the kitchen meanwhile, biting my lip and mumbling. I know I should have been busying myself with the verbal wallpaper, covering the cracks, making good, keeping up

appearances. But my mind just wasn't up to it. It kept slipping
back to Laura. Where the hell *was* she? Had I given her the wrong
impression this afternoon? No. No, I had made it perfectly clear.
Get him to take you out. Dancing, eating, drinking, whatever.

God. Don't let her have screwed this up.

I heard Jane mumble into the hall, shutting Lana's door.

"Hey sweetheart," I offered gingerly, wandering out, to find the
bathroom door closing with a slam and a click. Which I mention
because I don't know what your circumstances are, but in *our*
house you see, that has a meaning.

Bathroom door left open, all is well. Wander in. Sit on the edge
of the bath. Pass me a magazine. Talk about the day. Scrub my
back. Everything rosy.

Door locked? Well that's that. It'll be grumpy bed-socks and
duvet hogging and pointed light-snapping-off.

I stared at the locked door for a second with a sigh. Jane was
making sink-running noises.

I should knock. Apologise. Hug. Nip this in the bud. Extend
the olive branch. I should knock.

I should.

I didn't.

Instead I moved into the lounge, chewing my cheek. The answer-
phone (£3 o.n.o. – adapter included) was blinking.

Beeeeep. *Neil? Maurice. Where the hell are ya? Huh? Oh you can
hide! You can hide but you can't run! Twenty-four hours you've got. I'm
getting what I'm owed even if I have to drag you through the courts.
And don't think I won't. Don't think this hiding is fooling anyone. Read
the letters. You've got one more day and then it's a summons. Thirty-six
grand or my solicitor will have you for fuckin' breakfast you irresponsible
little –*

I hit fast forward. Another beep. A hang-up.

A third beep. Breathing. Another hang-up.

I picked up the phone in a sweaty grip and 1471-ed it, one
ear out for gurgling plug-holes.

"*Oh two oh, seven seven three four . . .*" the polite machine intoned
with painful enunciation.

I spun a three gently to return the call and listened to it dial
and ring, sliding over to the door and pushing it to.

"*Yeah?*" a voice said. Loud. Confident.

American.

I slammed the receiver down and jumped away from the phone like it had spiders all over it.

It was him. It was *him*. Grayson. Seven three four. Where the hell was that? The shop was four three nine. Did that mean anything? Seven three –

The phone let out a bakelite *bringgg*.

He'd called back. Shit, he'd called back. He had my number. 1471-ed me. As I had sown, so had I whassit.

It was still ringing. A splash from the bathroom.

"*I got it!*" I screamed, fumbling it up. "Uhm h-hello?" I whispered.

"*Neil? Oh Jesus, thank the Lord it's you.*"

"Laura, fuck. Hang on," and I scuttled to the door, pushing it closed. I scuttled back, grabbing up the phone. "Where the *hell* are you?" I whispered. "Christopher and Pete are going *nuts.*"

"*I've only got a second. Grayson's in the shower.*"

"The shower?"

"*Shut up, listen to me,*" She sounded panicked. Scared. "*I called him. Like you said. Said we should go out. He turns up at the shop two hours later. Pulls me out of work.*"

"Pulls – ?"

"*Literally. By the wrist. The boss starts yelling. Grayson tells him I quit. I'm not coming back. He won't have me serving coffee any more. He takes me back to his hotel –*"

"Quit? Wait, what are you – ?"

"*He's got these dresses he's bought, all laid out on his bed. Thousands of pounds worth. He tells me he's split up with his wife.*"

"Split – ? What *today?*"

"*No no, like a few weeks ago. Says he wants to marry me.*"

"Oh Christ."

"*I know. Says I'm the most beautiful creature he's ever seen. About to do a deal for two million pounds. I can share everything with him.*"

"Share? Oh Laura, Jesus –"

I sat down. I stood up.

"*I have to come back to Kansas with him. A millionaire's wife. Marry me, marry me, over and over. What am I going to do?*"

"What did you tell him?"

"*I tried to stall him. Told him I was overwhelmed, flattered, y'know? He'd knocked a girl off her feet, all that. But then he – wait! Shit he's coming back –*"

Silence on the other end.

"Laura?" I hissed. "Laura?"

Nothing.

"Neil?" Jane called from the bathroom.

"S'all right!" I hollered back. "Don't worry. S'nothing."

"*Hello?*"

"I'm here. You'll have to be quick."

"*He wouldn't take no for an answer. Got violent.*"

"Jesus, has he hurt you?"

"*No, but he's scaring me. Shouting. I lavish you with gifts, treat you like a goddamn prom queen, on and on. So I agreed.*"

"You did?"

"*Well what the fuck was I meant to do?!*" Laura spat. "*You've got me in his room, telling me to keep him happy, at all costs keep him happy.*"

"Okay, okay. So what now, he's still in the shower?"

"*We went to dinner, now we're at some hotel casino place. He's on top of the world. Singing, twirling me about. I've made him the happiest man alive. He's told me to take a wad of money from his black bag.*"

"His bag?"

"*On the bed somewhere . . . here. Jesus Christ.*"

"What?"

"*There's gotta be . . . My God.*"

"And do what?"

"*Huh? Take it down to the casino.*"

"Which? Where are you?"

"*Berkeley Square somewhere. He said take it down to the roulette table and put it all on today's date. The fourth. Black four. Fourth of November. The day he got engaged to his princess. What shall I do?*"

"You've gotta do it."

"*I don't know. Neil I'm scared. What have you got me into here? I want to leave.*"

"No, no Jesus you can't leave. Look, look it's just a few more hours." The cat was watching me pacing, head wiping to and fro like a tennis spectator. "It's a few more hours. Go. Go downstairs, place the bet. A big wad. Four black. Whatever he says."

"*And then what? What then? Come back here? He's going to want to go to bed.*"

"Shit." I pictured them both. Laura's curvy frame, struggling, squirming, eyes tight shut beneath Grayson's white walrus blubber, pumping and sweating. "Shit, then keep him talking. Get him onto the casino floor. Get him drunk, wait for him to pass out, whatever it is."

"*But I — shit. He's turned the shower off. Fu —*"

"Laura? *Laura?!*"

Nothing.

I closed my eyes and hung up the phone, heart thudding in the silence.

"Who was it?"

I took a deep breath and turned. Jane stood in the doorway.

"Uhm . . . Maurice."

"Maurice?"

"Right," I nodded. I nodded some more. It felt good. I kept nodding, moving forward. I took Jane's tiny hands. "Leaving a message. Insurance came through. Everybody's happy. We're on for Earl's Court. Everything's fine."

Jane sagged, relaxed, relieved. She smiled and I folded her into my arms.

"Everything's okay now?" she asked, head against my chest.

I breathed deep, smelling toothpaste, cotton and her hair.

"Everything's perfect," I said.

I turned my wrist and looked at my chunky watch.

Twelve hours, thirty-two minutes.

thirteen

"What? The *time?*" I shouted over the static. I craned around and took an anxious look at Elvis on the wall. "Just after eight."

"*You go hoh sooh?*"

"Home? No no, eight in the morning. It's the morning here. Thursday."

"*Ahh, mornih,*" Cheng said. "*I in Los Ahngeh. Is midnih he. My buy verh pleeh wih hih post. Verh pleeh, Neih sir. Verh pleeh,*" he went on. Something like that, anyway. To be honest, I didn't care whether he was pleeh. Verh or otherwise. I yessed and really-ed and that's wonderfulled for a few anxious minutes before getting rid of him, hanging up and breathing out.

The shop was cold and still, Elvis backcombing his quiff minute by aching minute. Despite the stalactites of Magic Trees twisting and fluttering in the office, the place smelled somehow more rotten and damp than ever. A clammy, wet odour of must and fur crawling stale and dank like cobwebs, among which the portable heater whirred and clanked. The morning street was a chill blue, the winter wind catching the shutters and giving them a wake-up rattle.

Cheng's call had almost killed me. The phone shrilling out as I'd scuttled in, snapping on the lights. I'd wanted it to be Christopher. Or Laura. Pete, Henry, Julio, anyone. Someone just to fill me in, tell me what page we were on.

I moved into the curling lino darkness of the back office, filling the kettle in the kitchen. My hand was trembling about the handle. Only the slightest bit. But enough. I left it standing in the sink and returned to the shop, sifting through the usual post, trying to manhandle the morning into some sort of regular shape.

Something from Earl's Court I needed to sign and return. Something from the bank. *It is of utmost importance that contact is made with your branch manager at the earliest possible* and so on.

I put it to one side and took some slow, deep breaths. I would set everything straight when I called in on Holborn in the afternoon. Nice and friendly, terribly sorry, all my fault, here's a hundred grand, say no more about it, we really must play golf.

The last letter was a second response from Sotheby's. *Was I still interested in a valuation of my item? Our team of experts would be pleased to offer a comprehensive* yeah yeah yeah.

I tore it in two and dropped the pieces into the bin. God, I thought, dragging clammy palms over my face slowly. Imagine if I had done it. Put it up for auction. How would I have explained that to Jane. Or to Edward?

Jesus. Lucky break. Luck. Luck was turning.

I jumped at the sound of the door rattling. There was a recognisable silhouette visible through the mesh. A familiar shape of messy hair.

"You *spoke* to her? When you *speak* with her?"

"When? Last night. Midnight-ish. I got in from dinner and there was a —"

"And why fuck you not *tell* us?" Julio was tired as always, great blue rings beneath his eyes. He glugged a steaming take-out coffee, blinking crusts from his face, wiping gunk from his lips and smearing it on his heavy anorak pockets. He dumped his familiar purple Reebok bag to the floor and began to dial his mobile phone, checking his watch over and over. "Eh? *Eh*? Why you not *call*? Christopher panicking. We thought whole play was *fuck*."

"I couldn't," I explained. "It was late, my wife . . ."

"So what she say? He better still be on for noon."

"I-I think so."

"*Think*?"

"Sh-she said he was in a good mood. He proposed to her. What about you guys? Is everything still —"

"*Propose*? What propose? What she say?"

"She said yes. I-I think. Y'know, to keep him happy. They were gambling at some casino off Berkeley Square. He told her to take a big wad of cash from his —"

Julio shushed me, holding up his coffee in a gloved hand. He was on the phone.

"Is me. I'm with him now. He said he speak to her last night. Some casino."

The phone crackled loudly. Somebody, I was guessing Christopher, wasn't happy.

"Bag? *Angry*? I not know, hold on," and Julio put the phone to his chest and glared at me. "Grayson is back at Waldorf. Twenty minutes ago. He on his own and furious. Why so? What she done? She refuse to fuck him? Huh? She cross her legs like some high-school virgin? And what you know about bag? He say anything about bag?"

I shrugged dumbly. *Bag?*

"He know nothing," Julio told Christopher. He took some instructions, nodding, glugging some steaming coffee. "Got it," he said and hung up.

"So what's going on?" I asked, but Julio was pushing past me, into the back office. I followed him through, worry gnawing at my stomach. He was unrolling a pair of surgeon's gloves, pulling them on in a snap of latex and talc. He began to load up the Reebok bag. The blue plastic kitchen timer, the can of 3 in 1 oil, grabbing handfuls of Magic Trees from the overhead lights, his eyes scurrying about the floor and ceiling.

"Is it all still on?" I said in the doorway. "Tell me it's still going ahead?"

He was ignoring me, gathering up old newspapers.

"Look, I'm sorry I didn't call, okay. My wife suspects I'm −"

"It still on," Julio scowled. "As long as you and girlfriend haven't screwed. Christopher is at Kensington place. Pete getting him set."

"Henry − ?"

Julio pushed past me, shoving my post to one side and rolling up a set of headphones from the desk. He snatched Christopher's Rupert-check scarf from about the neck of my cardboard Chewbacca.

"Henry at hotel. Watching for Grayson to leave. We have three and a half hours."

"And Laura? Where do you think she −"

"Who the fuck know?" Julio spat. He dumped out four sets of shop keys with a crash and zipped up the bag smartly. "That it." He pulled the bag up and began to head for the door.

"Wait! Wait, what do I do? What if Laura calls? What if Grayson comes here?"

"He won't. You job is done."

"But what if −"

"*Done*," Julio barked. "Finished, over with. Relax. All back to normal for you."

"Relax? Sure. Sure, fine. When Grayson's on the plane and I've got my cut in the bank and − with all due respect − you and Christopher and the rest are all out of my life forever. Then, *then* I'll think about trying to relax."

"You wait for call to say buy has take place. Then Henry tail Grayson to airport. Moment plane is in air, it all over. You meet Christopher at flat. Then hey, we go out, have a few drink. Celebrate con well play, yes?" He opened the door with a jangle.

"O-Okay," I said. "Don't you . . . y'know. Don't leave me hanging here," I said.

Julio left.

I turned and leant against the door, letting it click shut behind me and sighing an anxious sigh when the phone began to ring.

Christopher.

Was Julio still there? How had Laura sounded? Was I holding up? Not long now.

I explained Julio had cleared everything out and gone. Stripped clean. It was as if they had never arrived. And me? I was ready. I just wanted it over.

Christopher told me not to worry. He and Pete were all set. The room was ready, the drip was in, the pants were wrapped and they were ready to go. Grayson had just called. He was still on for noon. The only loose cannon now was Laura. Did I have any clue where she was?

"Literally no ideaaarrgg*hhHH!*" I said, followed by a "Sorry. No no, not a clue."

The reason for this being that Laura suddenly stood in the doorway to my office, shaking her head, eyes wide, very much the worse for wear.

"I screwed up Neil. I-I screwed everything up." Her face began to collapse, bunching on the edge of tears and she fell into my arms, her slim body almost disappearing in my hug. Something flipped against my fingers. At her neck, a £2950 price tag still on the dress.

Everything that had first struck me about Laura the night the thieves had taken her car – the feistiness, the sway of her walk, the way she put her weight on one hip, the dip of her head – that was all gone now.

She looked eight years old. Maybe seven. Her hair was a tangled crackle, wisps falling out around the sides. The little make-up that remained had been stolen from mummy's dressing table and applied in haste. Mascara streaked down one eye like a bruise, lipstick thin, half rubbed away. Her dress was crumpled, torn a little at the neck. No tights. One shoe missing, her bare foot bobbing on its ball, cold against the peeling office lino. She was sniffing, trembling.

"I did . . . I did what you said," and she swallowed hard, wiping her eyes, mascara creating a feline swipe across her temple. "Last night. I did it. I went to his bag, his black bag, and took some money out."

"Four black."

"He . . . he was in the shower. He just said take a fat wad from th-the black bag. A hundred big ones he said. I – I . . ."

"Which you did. Then what? C'mon," I urged. "What happened then?"

"Well it was more than I thought, y'know? There were thousands in there. *Hundreds* of thousands. All wrapped up in fat bands, like from a bank, y'know? Hundred dollar bills. Piles of them. So I took a wad. Like he said. Like *you* said. A *wad*. Like you *told* me to."

She gave a messy sniff. I fetched her some loo roll from the toilet. She bunched it up and wiped her nose.

"The casino gave me a tray. These square chips. Four black." She was breathing deep, slowly now, recovering. "Well it lost. Red nine. So y'know, I went back to the room. What was I *supposed* to do?"

"It's all right," I soothed. "It's all right."

"I get out of the lift and he's in the corridor. He's yelling. Standing there in his pants. *You dumb bitch, where the hell's my goddamn money!* You *bitch* this, you *goddamn whore* that. People are coming out of their doors."

"But –"

"He grabs me, pulls me back to his room, throws me across the bed." Her hand instinctively reached up to her upper arm. There were the fat blue welts of a hard grip. "He had *two.*"

"Two?"

"*Two.* He had two. How was I to . . . ?"

"Two what? Laura? What are you – Lift your head, I can't hear your –"

"You *said.* You *told* me. Take a wad. Go to his bag . . ."

"I know. Slow down, Laura –"

"His bag. Black one. On the bed. Go to it. Take a wad. *You* never said. *He* never said . . ."

"Slow *down.* Relax. Tell me. Two . . . ?"

"*Bags. Fucking bags. Two fucking –*"

"Bags. He had two bags?"

"YES! Two stupid black bloody stupid *bags.*" She wriggled away from me. Angry. At herself, at the situation, at the world. "A stupid black girly thing. Like a –"

"Handbag," I said, swallowing hard. "Like a handbag."

"Right. *That's* what he meant."

"That's what he – ?"

"*THAT'S* what he meant! Take a wad from *there.* Not . . ."

"But you . . . Oh. Oh God, you . . ." I trailed off, sick cold fear creeping in around the edges. "What did he – ?

"A hundred pounds. He'd meant a hundred *pounds.* From his purse. A wad of fives. A hundred *pounds.* Not . . ."

"God, how much did – ? Laura? How . . . ?"

"It was dollars. Wrapped in bands. A hundred grand."

"A *hundred grand*?! But –"

"Then he starts. Whacking me. Hitting me. Hard. With the little bag, like a whip, over his head, round and round. It's got th-these clips, metal fasteners . . ."

"Oh Jesus, Laura . . ."

"And all the time he's shouting. I'm trying to stand up but he's shouting. *What have you done you dumb bitch, what have you done!*"

"So . . . wait, I don't understand. Where . . . ? You took a hundred thousand from – ?"

"His *bag*. A holdall thing. On the bed. He *said* on the bed. *You said* take it."

The room began to throb and spin. I held her tight, to keep her still, to keep everything still.

"Ow, *ow* Neil –"

"Shit, sorry, I-I'm sorry." My head thudded. "Okay so, he's angry . . ."

"He's slapping me. Over and over. I'm screaming, *praying* someone will hear. Knock on the door, call the police, *something*. Then he just stops. Just walks away. Slams the door. Disappears."

"Where . . . where did he –"

"I don't know," Laura said. She looked up at me with her bruised eyes, blinking and teary. "I . . . I lay on the floor for a while. It hurt, y'know? It hurt just to move. But eventually I got up and lay on the bed. I remember the light was on, the ceiling light. Bright. I could feel it against my eyes but I couldn't move. I couldn't get up to turn it off. So I just lay there."

"You want to go to hospital?" I said, backing away, looking her over. Her knees, her thighs, bruised with angry black flowers.

She shook her head.

"Let me . . . just let me sit down."

I led her to a chair, returned to the kitchen and boiled the kettle for tea. As it bubbled away, I went back to Laura. She hadn't moved. Head bowed, shaking, shivering, one bare blue foot curled around the toe of her remaining shoe.

"He –" she began, stalling over the word. Over the thought of the man who had done this. "He woke me up a few hours ago. Shaking me. Still angry. Worse. A sort of calmness about it. I thought he was going to kill me. He was talking."

I knelt and took Laura's hands. They were bony and freezing. I gently rubbed the knuckles, trying to wake them, to bring them to life, returning her to the ring. Round two.

"Said I'd ruined *everything*. On and on. I'd ruined *everything*. It was . . . I mean he wasn't making *sense*. Pacing about in his tuxedo, little silk socks. The fat –"

"It's all right, it's all right."

"He doesn't have any money," Laura said heavily. "It's . . . it's a pose, all a fake."

"A *con*?" The room swayed a little. I held on to Laura's hand for some ballast.

"No, no. Not like that. A *bluff*. Just *pretending*."

I heard the kettle click off but I left it.

"His wife *left* him. Months ago. Adultery. Cleaned him out. Lawyers took *everything*. The museum, his house, car, TV. He has a few thousand pounds, that's it. He's trying to get started again with it. Investments, you know? Collectables. That's why he was so angry. Before . . ."

"eBay. Action Comics number four," I nodded. It began to make sense. "The perfect start to a new collection. No wonder he travelled all this way."

"All this way just to get ripped off."

"God," I sighed. "But wait, the half million? The pants? Christopher. Noon today, the deal? If he's broke, how . . . ?"

"He borrowed it."

"*Borrowed* – ?"

"Said he made some calls a day or so ago. Went to some dodgy club off Bethnal Green Road. Above some shop. Explained the situation. He's borrowed the five hundred thousand pounds off some bookie for a week."

"Five hundred . . ." I stood up, Laura's hand squeezing mine, not wanting to let go. I began to put the maths together. "So he's short . . . Wait, you spent a hundred grand in *dollars*. That's about –"

"*I* spent!?" Laura said. "*You* told me to do what he said, take a fat wad, keep him happy, black four –"

"It's okay, it's okay –"

"It's *not*!" and she tore her hand away hard, glaring at me, eyes wide and wet. "It's all *off*. He's threatening to walk. To get on the plane and go home."

"*Home*? No. No wait wait, it's just, no wait." I put my hands down on the desk for support, breathing deep. "It's . . it's just a hundred grand. Sterling, about fifty-five thousand, give or take. He can go and see Christopher with four hundred and fifty grand."

"He *won't*. That's what I'm *saying*. He's frightened. *You* were right. *Christopher* was right. It's all just *bluff*. He's pathetic. *Scared*. He won't go in without the full amount."

"Okay. Okay," and I began to pace. I felt suddenly damp under the arms, short of breath. It was so near. Three hours. It was so *near*. "Okay," I said. "Okay so . . . so we call Christopher. Yes. Yes, we call Christopher. Now."

An idea was beginning to slot together.

"Call – ?"

"Christopher," I said quickly. "We call him. Tell him what's happened. He's lying on a hospital surplus bed in his flat as we speak, tubes sticking out of him all over, waiting for Grayson to show. We tell him there was a screw-up."

"He'll kill me. He'll *kill* me," Laura strained. "He'll think it's my fault. They said. That guy. *They're not in the mood to write off five hundred grand*. They'll pin this on me! I'll wind up in the boot of some car. Christ Neil. Neil what am I going to *do*?"

"It's . . . it's all right. Listen. Listen, Christopher, he's a *businessman* for God's sake. We tell him Grayson's come up short. Doesn't matter about the *details*. We'll say . . . we'll say *he* put the bet on . . ."

"He *did* put the bet on."

"Huh – ? Yes, yes I know, I know, I mean –"

"You think *I* screwed this up! I was just doing what I was told!"

"Shhhh, it's okay, it's –"

"*He* said put a bet on! *You* said put a bet on! If Christopher's going to kill me then my last dying words are going to be telling him *whose* orders I was following!"

"Okay okay, you're right, you're right, okay. Shit. Look, we'll tell Christopher to call Grayson –"

"From his death bed? He's meant to be sick you said?"

"To check, to confirm, to – whatever. Get him to sound urgent, like something's happened, like he really needs the sale. A bit desperate. Grayson will say he doesn't have it all and Christopher can say that it doesn't –"

"He *won't*," Laura shouted. "I tried this with him. That's the point. He *won't* tell him. He's petrified."

"Fuck," I spat. I kicked the desk, mind hammering. It didn't help. "*FUCK!* Then . . . well then why doesn't he . . . ? I don't understand, why doesn't he borrow more from the bookie? The guy's lending him *five*, what difference does *another* —"

"He said they don't know him," Laura said. "They don't trust him. The deal's been signed, shaken on, whatever it is. He said he can't go in and start changing things. They'll smell a rat."

I closed my eyes, teeth grinding hard and angry.

"So . . . so then I don't get it. I don't get it."

"What?"

"Christopher just called. Just now. Says he's spoken to him and he's all set. How is he all set? What's his . . . Wait. Why's he dropped you off here? *You* don't have the money. What have you . . . ?"

"I lied to him."

"Awww for Christ's —"

"I *had* to! I told him a friend might have it."

"*Me*?!"

"I didn't mention any —"

"ME?! You told him about *me*?!"

"*No*. No, I just said I could raise it among people I knew. Call in favours. My dad, my brother. I told him I could make calls. *Anything* to get me out of the cab. You don't know what he's like," and her hands traced the angry bruises on her arms.

"Awww fuck it. *Fuck it!*" I lashed out, spinning in the small office, sending jiffy bags and pen tidies scattering. What were we going to do? What were we going to *do*? Three hours. *Three* hours.

"Neil? You listening?"

"Hn?" I turned. Laura was looking at me. She'd dried the red squinty smudges that passed for her eyes. Her jaw was tight and fixed. Shoulders pulled back. I got a glimpse of old Laura. Just for a second.

"I said let's go. Run. Both of us."

"Run?"

"Together," and she stood up, stepping towards me, close. I felt her hands take mine, her breasts press up against my chest. Her breath was warm and sweet on my face. "Just . . . just leave. Run."

"*Run*? What are you talking about?"

I didn't get an immediate answer. Or maybe I did. I can't be sure, what with the kiss and everything.

It was hard, fast and urgent, her mouth on mine hungrily.

Surprised as I was, I opened my mouth in shock, which Laura took for complicity, her tongue lunging in, meeting mine, dancing and curling. My hands were on her shoulders, hers on mine, gripping, pinching, nails hard. I felt her knee push between mine, moving forward, her thigh —

"*Jesus!*" I said, pulling away hard.

"Neil," she said again, in a half moany collapse, moving in for another go. I straightened my arms, keeping her back, stepping away, bumping against the door frame.

"No, No, Laura, Jesus Christ, what — what are you doing?"

"I thought — ?"

"No," I said. My heart was slamming slamming slamming like it would pound the print off my shirt. "No, Laura. Fuck. This isn't . . . No, this isn't going to happen. Nobody's running."

"You don't want me?"

"What? What no, no it's not — Christ, that's . . . Jesus," and I turned, moving out into the shop, mind thudding. This wasn't right.

I heard Laura click out behind me in her one shoe, sniffing a little. I took a deep breath and turned to look at her.

"Laura, look, listen to me. I have a wife. I have a family. I love my family. I told you. That's what all this is about. I'm trying to protect them. Provide . . ." I shook my head. "I can't run. I don't *want* to run. Let's . . . look, let's just think about this."

"Then I'm going," she said, turning.

"Laura, wait, *wait!* Just hold on. There must be —"

"I'm out of a job, you don't want me, Christopher's going to kill me. I've got no car, I've got no shoe. I've got nothing. I'm going."

"Wait!" I yelled. "Just . . . Look, we can fix this." I checked my watch. "You've got Grayson's number? His mobile? Call him. Tell him . . . Shit. Tell him you've *got* the money."

"*Got it?*"

My mind was spinning, clicking, wheels turning, pieces dropping into place like the *Downfall* ball-bearings on my shelf of games. Doing the sums. Adding it up.

"Half of it. Tell him you've got *some* of it. *Most* of it. It's all you could raise. Tell him you got it from your brother, your mum, your boss. Something."

"But we *don't* have it. What happens when –"

"We can get . . ." I said with a determination I didn't recognise. I found myself at the desk, on the telephone. Almost of its own accord, my hand was reaching for my morning's post. "We can salvage . . ."

"Neil?"

"It's not too late. We can *get* most of it. It'll still . . . it'll *still* add up. Call him. Call him now . . ."

"What are you doing? *Most* – ? Who are you calling? *Neil?*"

part two

fourteen

"*Neil? Neil Martin?*"

The voice was hard to place immediately, like a brass band playing *Smells Like Teen Spirit*. My head crash-zoomed out of its thick mist and suddenly the pub, Thursday night, life, was clattering and ringing about me in surround sound. Yelling, belching, till drawers chunking, fruit machines bleeping.

Twisting around on my stool, a tanned face grinned down at me. I blinked three times, blowing dust from the mental yearbook.

"Christ," I said, his features pulling into focus. "*Benno?* Holy *shit!*"

"Heyyyyy!" Andrew said.

I stumbled to my feet, the room buckling and bending a little, falling into slaps and growls and gruff hugs.

"Good to *see* you mate," Andrew said, gripping my upper arms and giving me a manly shake. "Bloody hell. How long has it been? You all right? You on your tod?"

"Er . . . ?" I blinked back dizzily, checking about my soggy corner table for a large collection of close friends I might have forgotten about. "Yes, yes. Just me. God, what are you . . ." I stumbled. "We were talking about . . . I mean Jane and I . . . just a few . . . What-what are you . . . ?"

"Back in town. Bit of business," he said, jutting his chin out a little and tugging a hands-free wire from his ear with a pop, gathering up the thin cable. "Bit of *big* business." He noticed me giving his garb a quick scan, dressed as he was less for business, more for a night in with Pringles and *Robot Wars*. "Oh don't let this get-up fool you," he said, peeling off his denim jacket. "I'm Mr Madison Avenue these days. Hotel dry-cleaners buggered-up my – *hey!* Over *here!*" he broke off, beckoning across the busy scrum. "Mr O'Shea? I'd like you to meet a very, *very* old friend of mine. Mr O'Shea? Neil Martin."

O'Shea was a bullish, stocky Irishman. A whisky barrel in a suit. He pushed through the pub crowd and tore my shoulder off with his handshake, white eyebrows like two seagulls squabbling over a discarded ice-cream. He sat us down and got some drinks in.

"Bloody hell. What's it been? Eight years?" I said. "What are you − ?"

"I'm with Keatings. New York," Andrew went on, emptying his pockets of breath mints, matches, a Zippo and an old Bic before fishing out his mobile and wrapping it in its wire, laying it on the damp table. "Six years now. Just over for a fortnight to see our friend here," and he tipped a nod at the squat, brick-built frame by the bar. "Mr O'Shea is selling his Manhattan real estate and bringing his dollars to a big new development planned in Holborn. I'm just shepherding both sides through for him."

"Real estate? What happened to − ?"

"And what's *your* story, Mr Martin?" O'Shea asked with a twinkle, returning with the drinks. He had a surprisingly high voice with a waft of heather to it. A voice more suited to hollering gibberish at sheepdogs than at shareholders. "How do you come to know this shyster?"

"*Shyster*? Ha ha!" Andrew laughed. Far too loudly for far too long, eyes flashing with nerves, which told me that if my old pal was in big business, O'Shea had to be in *huge*.

"Uhmm, University," I said.

"We were down the hall from each other," Andrew gabbled, sipping his drink. "Hung out. Played chess on the stairs, you remember? When you weren't at the cinema. This man saw *everything*. Had a bloody great Robert Redford up on his wall for three years. Do you remember? Caused some rumours, I can tell you."

"Yeah," I sighed.

"Neil here was in the arts crowd. Drama types. That lot. They didn't really have much time for us environmentalists."

"*Environmental what now*?" O'Shea furrowed, shooting a quizzical look at Andrew.

"Oh a long time ago, a looong time ago," Andrew soothed with a grin. "But bloody hell, Neil Martin," and he shook his head. "My word. Good to see you, old man," and he raised his glass. The two men clinked so I joined in obediently. "So, spill the gen.

What you doing with yourself for eight years? Running an Odeon somewhere?"

"Uhm, no. No, not exactly. I've got a shop. *Had* a shop. Soho. Sorry, you've caught me a bit –"

"*Soho!* Ahhhh, loik *that* is it?" O'Shea smirked, his gull-brows taking flight in a fluster of feathers.

"N-no. Nothing – Memorabilia. Movie stuff, comics, y'know."

"Ahhh. Sure but Soho's not the same since they cleaned it all up," O'Shea said, drifting off. "Far too respectable these days. What happened with that little street I had Keatings look at not so long ago?" he said to Andrew, ticking him off a little. "Had my eye on that, I did. Going for a song it was. You should have been quicker with that, lad. Get me a valuation on what the square foot is going for now. What I would have made. Someone in your office is going to compensate for that."

"Consider it done," Andrew nodded, reaching into his khakis and tugging out a red spiral-bound notebook, sliding a pencil from the coils.

"I shouldn't be the one chasing you up on this stuff son," O'Shea said loudly, draining his glass. "Anyway now, big day tomorrow. I'm gonna leave you youngsters to it."

O'Shea stood and Andrew followed. I watched them pump each other's hands vigorously, shoulders jarring, exchanging nods and dates and figures and manly shoulder slaps, before O'Shea bid the pub farewell, pitching and yawing out onto the street.

Benno came back with more drinks, collapsing into his seat. The grin was now just a loose smile. More relaxed, like someone had taken the guy ropes out. He rolled his shoulders and rubbed his face. It appeared the jovial bonhomie he'd kept on the boil with his business partner was something he was having difficulty sustaining at length.

"You all right old mate?" I asked.

"Work. O'Shea's . . . forget it. Forget it. Boring. Heyyy, here's to *you*. How long's it been? God, Neil Martin . . ."

I sat and watched as he did this for a little while longer until eventually we toasted again.

Drinks downed, and with a little shudder, shaking the office pressure from his shoulders, Benno began to relax a little. He bullied me into tugging out my wallet and we compared pictures of wives and children.

A sudden, sick feeling struck me and I felt my palms drain cold. Had – ?

Had Benno somehow heard? About the shop flood? On some obscure estate-agent blog? Got wind I might be in trouble and be causing Jane to look elsewhere? Did he still – ?

I mean, Christ was it possible he'd taken the flight to the UK to try to muscle in on his high-school crush after all this time?

No. No, he couldn't.

Of course he fucking couldn't.

Idiot.

I shook myself and breathed out, trying to slow my heart. What the hell was happening to me?

I slapped my wallet shut and laid it aside, Benno still flipping me through his glamorous life. His wife, sitting lit by a low sun on some sort of tractor in a wheat field, college sweater and all American teeth like a GAP ad. The obligatory twins in matching mittens, all pink cheeks in Central Park snow. Ben and Sandy, his two collies, outside his Long Island country house. The whole bit.

I looked over my old friend with tired eyes, looking for traces of the beardy face from those nights in chilly halls a lifetime ago. He was barely recognisable. Gone was the shoulder length hair, the knotted leather wrist bands and beads. Gone was the sloga-neering T-shirt, the donkey jacket and battered walking boots, splashed with caked-in mud. Gone. Nowhere to be seen.

In the years since University, Benno had gone and become a man. Very clearly. He had not only reached that estate, but packed its boot with deck chairs and driven his family to the Hamptons in it.

Sitting there, listening to his stories, melancholy sidled up in that way it has and gave me a nudge, pointing out, quite rightly, that Benno appeared now to be everything Edward wanted *me* to be. Everything Edward wanted for Jane. Everything Jane *deserved*.

I flipped open my wallet again and blinked at the smiling faces, creased and buckled behind milky plastic. I promptly closed it again.

Benno continued. Here she is in Barbados. Here they are outside their new home.

He was a man. A *real* man. You only had to look at him. Man's hands, a man's voice and man's shoulders, on which he success-fully took the burden of a proud family. A family that he would never disappoint. Never let down.

Not like some.

". . . I mean there were bigger places up there, sure. But we thought five bedrooms would be enough. The dogs like the space, the twins have their own room. Pricey, but then if this damned Holborn deal comes off, which knowing O'Shea . . . Hey, you should come for Christmas," and Andrew closed his wallet and flipped his notebook open again.

"Still with the red notebooks eh?" I said, my voice cracking a little.

"God yeah of *course*. You remember. Old habits," he smiled, giving it a waggle. "Batteries can't fail on these." He flipped through pages of scribbles to a clean sheet. "Let us have your number. I'll get Veronica to sort out the details. Neil? . . . Neil? Hey hey hey, you all right old chap?"

"God," I sighed.

"Heyyy, what's up?"

"Sorry, nothing. It's . . . Nothing."

"Mate?"

"I just . . ." I began, but that one stalled straight off the grid. "I never meant . . ." but that one ploughed straight into the first one and the two were towed off in clouds of smoke. "You've caught me at a bad time," I said finally. "I've had something of an afternoon. Culminating with the two hours I just spent with the police."

"The police? Bloody hell, really?"

"Actually no," I said, my head thumping. "Not really."

The bank had kept me waiting in a variety of different-sized rooms, reading a variety of different-sized posters, a variety of different sized young women in polyester giving me slips to sign, exchange rates to confirm and my driving licence the once over.

I'd sat fidgeting on different-sized chairs throughout this drawn-out tour, shirt damp, knees bouncing, trying to focus on the last anxious hour.

Laura had cleaned herself up a little. Said she'd better go and hobble along to the coffee shop. Talk to her boss. Explain. Try and get, if not her job back, at least her plimsolls.

She'd called Grayson from my mobile while I'd been on the phone to the bank giving out mother's maiden name and date of birth. Even with the account supervisor chattering away in my ear, I'd made out Grayson's yelling. *A few grand down? He wasn't going in a few grand down!* This, punctuated by a smattering of 'dumb bitches.'

But he'd finally seen sense. Christopher, bed-ridden, wounded and dying, wasn't going to argue over stolen property for the sake of a few thousand pounds.

Finally, in the smallest of the bank's rooms, behind heavy glass and deep locks, I signed the last of the bank slips and watched as another member of staff counted out the bills onto the desk in front of me. I licked my dry mouth and took deep breaths, watching her slip the large pink notes into paper bands, stacking the piles just-so on the table.

Thank Christ I'd never listened to Edward. Thank *Christ*. If he'd had his way, Lana's money would now have been earning its keep in offshore funds, index-tracking unit trusts and all sorts of nonsense. Locked in and untouchable.

But as it was, by ten thirty-five, I was moving swiftly and conspicuously back across the squeaky bank floor, watched by a cluster of quizzical bank staff, a bulging Tesco carrier bag wrapped about my knuckles, out onto the chilly street.

The morning traffic was beeping and coughing. It didn't seem to be moving any faster than I could, but what with the bag of notes, I felt I would be safer in the back of a cab, so waved down, address given and seat taken, I slammed the door and collapsed with an anxious sigh.

Holborn to The Waldorf was south, straight down Kingsway. Ten minutes, fifteen tops. That'd still give Grayson an hour to get over to Kensington. Plenty of time.

Stomach churning, I watched the traffic for a while, mind 'else-where. It would be all right. The team would be angry of course.

A few grand short is likely to piss off the most generous of shyster. But it was this or nothing. And nothing would be noticeably worse.

And me? I did some mental calculations. *Fifty grand to Laura. She passes it to Grayson. Take into account the exchange rate, my twenty per cent . . .*

Ninety-five grand or so. Minus Lana's fifty back in the bank, I'd be forty-eight grand up. Maurice's solicitors, the bank? They'd be covered. *Just*, but they'd be covered.

In fact, all in all, I'd almost managed to relax by the time the cab wheeled to a halt in front of The Waldorf with a squeak of brake pad. Standing between a braided doorman and a large potted plant, Laura shifted from one tiny plimsolled foot to the other, bare arms wrapped around each other tightly, gazing out at the traffic. Her eyes widened with hope as she caught sight of me. She ran across the wide pavement to the kerb.

"Is it all right? Have you got it?" she said in a frightened voice.

I handed her the bag, the cab idling grumpily.

"How you doing?" I said. "You okay?"

She nodded little nods, blinking. Her face was washed, scrubbed clean, eyes pink and sore.

"And have you spoken to him?" I asked. "Grayson? Is he okay?"

"He's not happy," she sniffed, clutching the bag to her chest. "But I reasoned with him. Told him it was all I could get."

"And the team? Henry? Pete?"

"I spoke to the guy in the lobby. Black guy. Pete is it? I explained what had happened. That it would be short. They weren't best pleased."

"But it's all still going ahead right? We're still on?"

She nodded, blinking tearily.

"Then you'd better go," I said. "It's nearly eleven."

"When will I see you? Do you want to wait for me here? I'll be down in a second."

"No," I said. "No, I'd better get out of the way. Come back when you get the chance."

Then, after a hesitant beat, shifting on the pavement, she leant forward to kiss me, hand snaking up about my neck, pulling me towards her. Flushing, I twisted awkwardly. We bumped temples and I negotiated a dry peck on her cheek, pulling away early.

"Move," I said. "Go on."

She half smiled, blinking and wiping an eye, before turning and jogging back across the cold street. The doorman heaved open the door and she disappeared inside.

I breathed out slowly and climbed back into the cab.

"Yes mate?"

"Brigstock Place," I said, collapsing against the seat. "Thank you."

"So when did you realise?" Andrew asked, stuffing his red book away and gulping his scotch back with a cough.

"Not for a while," I sighed, chewing my cheek. The pub was filling up around us with the chattering Barbours and slingbacks of Theatreland. "Hope, I suppose. I got back to the shop just after eleven. Had a coffee with a guy called Schwartz. He runs a bookshop next door to my place. Reminded him to clear the rubbish from round the back which he'd forgotten to do *again*. I tidied up. Tried to keep my eyes off the clock. Christopher phoned twice, telling me everything was set, everybody was ready. Not to panic. *Nearly there dear boy, nearly there.* I pulled on my wellies and cleaned up my basement for a while. I had a flood. While ago now. That's how all this . . . Anyway, just for something to do, y'know? Poked away at the drain, gunk up to my elbow. But all the time this . . . this gnawing worry in my insides."

"And you didn't even . . . I mean not for a second?"

I looked at Andrew and down at my drink, moving the coins on the table into a smiley face shape.

"Couple of customers came by. Must have been around half past twelve. Sniffed through my posters, did my crossword. We had a couple of rounds of *Connect Four*, or tried to. They both managed to whip me in about three moves. Which . . . now I think about it, means there's a good chance they were cheating."

"You didn't notice?"

"I couldn't concentrate. I kept staring at my Elvis clock. Looking at the phone. Jane called. Reminding me to pick up some dessert for – shit," and I checked my chunky watch with a woozy blink. Ten to three in Bangkok and ten to five in Rio de Janeiro. Which meant it was ten to where-the-hell-have-you-been in Putney.

"Somewhere you have to be, old man?"

I thought about Catherine and Jack. Of dinner drying out on a low heat. Jane at the window. Jane phoning the shop. Jane thinking I was going to miss the fireworks.

Yeah *right*.

"Neil? Are you all – ?"

"Eventually I couldn't stand it any longer. I shut the shop – four o'clock it must have been – and jogged over to the café to see if Laura was back. If she'd heard anything."

I slid two pennies an inch towards me across the table, turning the copper smile into a frown.

It was busy and loud, the hiss of steam, the clatter of thick china, yelling, laughing. Most of the tables were taken, most of the booths likewise.

"Yes my friend?" a handsome Italian called out, wiping his hands on a tea towel. "What I get for you?"

"Is Laura here? Is she back yet?"

"*Laura!*" he called. "Hey, *Laura!* You boyfriend here!"

"No, I'm – it's nothing like –"

The Italian gave me a wink as Laura pushed through the plastic ribbons between the café and the back area and looked about the shop, finally fixing me with a lost, questioning look.

"Hello?" she said.

"Uhm, no. No sorry, I wanted the other one? The other Laura? Taller, dark hair?"

"I only Laura here," the girl smiled.

I don't know how long we stood looking at each other awkwardly. Probably just a second or two.

All I know is that a hell of a lot went through my head as I stared at this stranger.

None of it good.

None of it good at all.

Fifteen panicky minutes later, my mobile began to buzz, but I barely heard it over the thumping of my sweat glands and slam of my heart. Running, hand waving out desperately for a cab, I fumbled inside my jacket and checked the display bouncing in front of me.

Shit.

"H-Hello?"

"*Hi, it's me. Where are you? Are you on your way home? What's that noise?*"

The noise was Oxford Street. The lower end, near Selfridges. Buses, tourists, shoppers. They filled the street, chatting, dawdling, yelling once in a while as the sweaty lunatic pushed past them in a terrified jog.

"Yes . . . yes, just near the station," I panted as calmly as I could. *Cabs?* Where were all the *cabs?*

"*You sound funny. Are you all right?*"

"Fine, f-fine," I squeaked. "How . . . how are you? Everything okay?"

A bike slammed its horn as I dodged, tripping over a side street.

"*Good. Lana's had her nap. I've tidied around for Jack and Catherine. Did you get dessert?*"

Shit shit shit.

"Yes, yes no problem," I said, trying to steady my breathing. I spotted a cab turning out of Portman Street, roof light on. I began to flap frantically. "See you soon."

"*Love you.*"

I waved my arms, pounding across the busy street, slamming against the taxi.

"Awroit pal? Easy there."

"Kensington," I panted, hanging breathlessly on the window. "You know behind the Albert Hall? Something Mansions or other . . ."

My phone was crackling again. A voice.

"H-Hello?"

"*Jack. Hi, it's Jane. Just a quickie. I've spoken to Neil and he's —*"

"Jane?" I said, clambering into the cab. "It's still me. Sorry, I can't have hung up properly."

I thumbed the line closed. I sat and stared at the phone's display. I didn't hang up properly.

An itchy thought trundled through my head, browsed a moment for somewhere to sit down and then trundled off again.

I continued staring at the phone as the cab pulled out into traffic.

It would be fine. It would all be fine, I chanted over and over, breathing deep, head hanging between my knees as the cab swung west. Maybe . . . maybe Laura wasn't actually a *Laura*. People did that, right? Used their middle name as their first name? You find out years later your friend Bob's real name is Tarquin or something like that. Maybe Laura, *my* Laura, was actually a Janet or a Jessica or a Josephine. Something like that.

Maybe.

Maybe that's why they didn't know her in the café. Yes. Yes, that would explain it.

I mean I'd seen her working there, when I'd –

Well, now I come to . . .

Perhaps I didn't see her *actually* ever . . .

My stomach did something wobbly, my knees joining in with back-up on the chorus.

"Hoy, hoy mate?"

I looked up. The cabbie was calling over his shoulder through the gap in the divide.

"I said round here mate is it?"

I slid forward in the seat, peering out at the tall pink mansion blocks, their ironwork, their concrete steps and intercoms. Their purple doors.

"Yes. Yes, here here," I said quickly and the cab rolled to a halt by the kerb. "Wait for me. J-Just wait for me here. Please," I said and clambered out into the cold. The winding street was quiet. Snaking lines of parked cars – Jaguars, BMWs, MGs, curling out of sight. No green Bedford vans.

My heart leapt up, catching fat and full in my throat, as the purple door swung open with a bang and a familiar eight-year old in a Fisher-Price My Little Estate Agent costume emerged.

"Hey. Hey, excuse me," I called. "Excuse me, sorry . . ."

He turned.

"Hi. I'm . . . Sorry to . . . You were sorting out a room for some friends of mine? In Bloomsbury? It fell through? You had a meeting at Brigstock Place?"

"Brigstock – ? *Heroes Incorporated*, right right," he nodded, smiling. "But it wasn't Bloomsbury. It was here," and he threw a thumb behind him. "Flat six, first floor. Short lease. Vacated yesterday. Did you want to see it?"

The world seemed to tip up slightly, woozily, buildings sliding one way, the horizon dipping another. I put my hand out to steady myself, gripping the cold black railing.

"You don't . . . I mean, Bloomsbury?"

"Don't have anything in Bloomsbury. Never have. You all right? Did you want to look upstairs? It comes partly furnished. But sparse. A few starter pieces of Conran basics – couch, sideboard, bed, bin, broom . . ."

"No *way*," Andrew said, tearing open a packet of beef crisps and laying them on the sticky table top. He delved in.

"He let me in. Showed me around," I said. "It still smelled of bleach. But in the corners, somewhere, it was Christopher. Pipe smoke. Tweed."

"But apart from that?"

I shook my head. "Empty. No drip. No linen. Nothing."

"Bloody hell mate," Andrew munched, beefy shrapnel flying from his lips. "And the chap? The agent? He couldn't tell you anything? He didn't have a contact number? A name?"

I smiled weakly.

"He went through his file. Said it had been rented by the owner of one *Heroes Incorporated*. That's where he dropped off the keys. A Mr Neil Martin from Putney."

I took a very long, very slow walk back to the shop because it wasn't home.

I stopped once, just once, to throw up somewhere near Hyde Park and then I was off again.

I don't know what I was expecting to find when I got back to the shop. My head wouldn't focus. Maybe Christopher and Henry and Pete and Julio huddled outside with bags from the off licence. Ready to pop corks and cheer and divide up the money, asking where I'd been.

Maybe Laura. Wrapped in some vintage velvet coat, shoulders hunched, hood up, with a message. A change of rendezvous. Because I guess even then I was still hoping.

No, I don't know what I was expecting.

But I know what I *wasn't*.

"Hello again," I said, hauling up the shutters with a clatter, fussing for keys. "Come in, come in. You are here for me, I take it?"

"If we can step inside sir," the Scottish Sergeant said and he and his Mancunian colleague clumped in behind me.

Their heavy boots and huge frames rustling in their jackets made the place look tiny, just as they had in my sitting room. I pulled out chairs in the back office, snapped on the portable heater and sat down.

They knew most of it, which surprised me. About Christopher (not his real name), Henry (not his real name), Pete (likewise), Julio (nope) and Laura (real name Margaret, which didn't go at all).

Being British coppers, the first thing they wanted was tea. And then my version of events, starting with the car-jacking and Laura/Margaret's arrival at my door ten days ago. Christ, was that all it had been? So I laid it all out for them in broad strokes, the Sergeant nodding, the Manc writing it all down. The Sergeant then proceeded to slide out a manilla envelope and produce some glossy 10×8 black and white photographs, laying them out one by one on my counter like a storyboard for *Sucker – The Movie.*

"Yes," I said with an uncomfortable cough. "That's him. Christopher. At Claridge's."

"And that's you talking to him. Going over your plan?"

"Hn? Er, yes, yes I suppose so."

"You *suppose*?"

"I mean *our* plan sounds, y'know –"

"And this? Your shop?"

"Right where you're sitting."

"And you're letting these men in to . . . ?"

"Well, that was on, what, the Saturday? Yes. The thirty-first. That was all part of it. Like I said. Preparing the shop. Props."

"Oh, so they did this with your consent? You were aware of it *all.*"

"Of course," I said. "They needed help with the wall hanging," and I motioned at the blank space where a box once hung. "Using the till and everything."

Manc made notes.

"And this?" Scot said, sliding another across the desk.

"Shit. When . . . that was *today*. Where were you . . ."

"Can you just confirm that the gentleman in the cab is you, sir?"

"Yes," I said, staring at the frozen kiss, Laura's hand about my neck. "Uhmm, look, I don't know if this is possible or anything." Scot looked at me. "My wife . . ."

"Mrs Martin."

"Spencer-Martin," I corrected. "She's, y'know. Her dad's . . ."

They looked blankly at me.

"Look, anyway, she doesn't know."

"Know?"

"About this. About anything. Laura, Grayson, the money, the airport. Any of it. And y'know —"

"Oh, you'd rather she didn't find out."

I smiled a little.

"If that's at all possible."

The policemen exchanged looks.

"Hmn. Mr Martin, I'm not sure you understand the full extent of the last few days' events," Scot said. He stood slowly and began to wander about the office, lifting up nick-nacks, peering into envelopes, sniffing at the junk. "You knowingly and deliberately conspired to defraud an American citizen to the tune of half a million pounds."

"What?"

"You *say* that you were involved in this *con game* against your will but all our evidence suggests you were not only complicit, but you went out of your way to be as much help —"

"Wait, no *wait*," I said hurriedly. "What are you . . . I mean, *I* was the — they were conning *me*. The *fifty thousand*."

"Fifty — ?" the constable said, flipping back.

"Of course! That's what this was all about! Getting me to trust them. They said, all along, Christopher, whatever his name is. He said it was all about *trust*. Get the mark to trust you."

"Mark?"

"The guy, the target."

"You said he was called Grayson."

"Yes – no. No me, Grayson wasn't . . . there *is* no Grayson."

"Your story is a little twisted here sir," Scot said, picking up a Betty Boop ashtray with distasteful fingertips. "You identified Grayson – the man you now say doesn't exist. There, in the photograph. Constable?" and Manc riffled through the snapshots again, sliding Grayson out.

"I mean," I said, "he's one of *them*."

"One of *them*?" Scot said camply, eyebrows raised. He looked at the ashtray and then at his colleague. "One of *them*, he says. Hmm. And you'd know . . . as it were," and he cleared his throat.

"For Chrissakes don't you start."

"Sir –"

"Look," I said loudly, trying to slow the world down. I took a deep breath. "Grayson, or whoever he really is, this man here," and I jabbed the picture. "He's one of their team. A conman. *Pretending*."

"The man who you say arrived at Heathrow airport on . . . Here, on the first. On Sunday. You're now saying you were sent to follow one of your own team."

"*Yes*. To make me think, y'know . . . And it's not *my* team, they aren't *my team* –"

"But you do admit to being part of a scheme to defraud this Mr Grayson."

"Yes but –"

"Do you have a lawyer Mr Martin?"

"What are you saying? Wait."

"I'm not arresting you at this time, Mr Martin. However, I will ask you not to –"

"*Arresting*?! Wait, no wait. You . . . you *do* have my money, right?" I said shakily, a feeling of desperate hope fluttering in my chest. "Tell me that at least. You did *catch* them? Christopher, Laura, the others?"

"We do not have anyone in custody at this time sir, no. However –"

"Oh God."

Realisation. Fear. Hopelessness. All oozed into my gut like wet concrete. Cold, thick and slow.

Around me, notebooks were being flapped shut, pencils tucked away and empty mugs handed back. Manc was standing with a stretch and a rustle.

"Wait. Wait, you *had* her!" I barked. "In my flat. Sitting there, drinking my tea. You fucking had her!"

"All right sir, let's just calm –"

"You *had* her!"

"There wasn't sufficient evidence," Scot said. "Anything we could have picked her up on –"

"So you let her go."

"C'mon mate, you can explain it all down –"

"Constable, wait," Scot said. "Wait. Leave him . . . just wait outside for a minute."

"Sir –"

"Outside."

The constable backed out noisily.

The Scot was looking at me, head tilted slightly to one side.

"You're pissed off," he said perceptively.

"You *think*?"

"It's what happens. Look Mr, Martin, truth? Off the record? I don't think you had anything to do with this scam. I think you're the victim. I think you've been taken advantage of by a very pretty face and some very clever men."

I looked at him. His face had softened, just a little, smudgier around the edges. He offered me a cigarette. I declined.

"I'm going to have trouble convincing my superiors of course, because at the moment everything points to you being one of the team. Unless . . ."

"*Unless*?"

"Wait. Wait, you . . ." and he picked up the ashtray again. He looked at me, eyes flashing. "You said they left no prints? Wore gloves the *whole time* they were here?"

"The whole damn time," I sighed. "I watched them put them on at the door." Did he need to rub it in? Jesus.

"But you say one of them posed as *you*? As the owner, I mean? And you said . . . he needed help using your till?"

"My – shit. Shit, yes. Yes he did!"

"Constable!" Scot called.

Dizzily, I found a bin bag big enough to cover the till, helped them unplug it and watched as they heaved it carefully off the desk out into the street.

"Said they'd send a receipt over to me," I sighed. "That with any luck there's a couple of decent prints on it."

"Well that's a good sign? Right?" Andrew said over the rim of his glass. He had moved us onto port, or at least what the small pub considered port. It was more like Ribena but we swirled anyway. "Right? Or . . . what? What's − ? Why are you smiling?"

"Give me your mobile number," I said.

"My . . . ?"

"Your number."

With a little shrug, he did so. I took my phone, skipped past my nine unread messages from Jane and entered his eleven digits.

"What's all this − ?" he began, when his phone suddenly gave a diddly-deet. I swirled my ten-year-old, cask-aged Ribena a little and nodded that he should answer it. He looked at me carefully and did so.

"Uhm, hullo?"

"*Heyyy,*" I said in a posh voice. "*Heyyy is Franny there? Francesca? Mike? That you Mike?*"

"Er, no," Andrew said, eyes fixed on mine. "No, I think you have the wrong number dear chap."

I returned my phone to the table. Andrew hung up. We sat in silence for a moment.

"Now call the police," I said.

"The − ?"

"The police. Call the police. Three nines. Imagine . . . oh I don't know, imagine a woman in a cocktail dress has just been car-jacked outside your house. Or is saying she has, anyway. Come on!" I urged, grabbing his phone and thrusting it at him. "She's screaming. Waking the street up."

After a beat, Andrew, weighing up how well he knew me, recalling three distant years of companionship, finally licked his lips and dialled the three nines, placing the phone to his ear.

"Hullo?" he said.

I lifted my phone to my ear.

"*Police emergency,*" I said. "*Can I help you? Car-jacking you say?*

Why, let me send some absolutely genuine officers over. Your address please sir?"

Andrew stopped, looked at his phone, looked over at mine, back at his, mental gears grinding through the drink and cigar smoke.

"You didn't hang . . ."

I looked at him.

"Bloody hell," he said eventually.

"Quite," I shrugged, thumbing my phone off and returning it to the table.

"That's how . . . Bloody hell, so they weren't − ?"

"Christopher had to return for his fingerprints somehow. Who better than two trustworthy boys in blue I already knew?"

"Bloody hell," Andrew said again, falling back into his seat with a shake of his head. "So what . . . I mean, what happens now?"

"Now?" I said. I stared into the remains of my drink, swirling it about the glass. My head hurt. Hurt from the drink, from every-thing.

"Neil?"

"I go to the real police with what happened. No evidence, mind you. No motive, no evidence and no proof. Meanwhile tomorrow morning, Boatman, Beevers and Boatman start legal proceedings. Maurice will end up getting the shop I expect. And that'll be that."

"Blimey," Andrew said. "But Jane? She'll . . . I mean, she'll understand? Help you through it? If she's still as sweet as when I knew her, which I'm *sure* she must be. God, I haven't seen her in *years* . . ." and Andrew got a far-away look in his eye.

I drained my drink and placed the empty glass in front of me. There was another missed message on my phone.

"No. That'll be it for us," I said flatly. "I've been lying for . . . This'll be it. She'll wait until her dad's home from Brighton next Tuesday before telling him what I've done. He'll get their family lawyer warming up on the touchline for a divorce. So that's my wife and family and the house gone too."

"She wouldn't?"

"Don't think badly of her. She's as sweet as you remember. It's just what I deserve."

"Blimey, mate," Andrew said with a sigh, lolling back in his seat with his drink.

We sat quietly for a moment, a decade between us – Andrew in his success, me in my despair. The impromptu reunion hadn't quite gone the way I might have hoped.

"Nothing changes, eh?" Andrew said. I looked up. He had a faint nostalgic smile on his lips.

"What?"

"You and Jane. Always complicated. Us three. You with no damned confidence."

"Not my strong suit, no," I said. "Never was. Dad –" and the words caught in my throat. I swallowed hard, jaw grinding a little. "Well, you remember him. Wasn't a household full of encouragement. Picking on me, knocking me down, telling me I was *wastin' me time*."

"Until he *needed* a few quid, if I recall?"

"You got it. God, you *remember* all that?"

"Not likely to forget am I?"

"Long time ago."

Andrew nodded with another half smile.

"Pouring out your heart to me over the chess board. All that bad wine. Failed mocks . . ."

"In hindsight, perhaps you weren't the best person to –"

"Who else were you going to tell? It's what friends are for."

I shrugged.

"And *that* got fixed. Look at the three of us now. All grown up. Things get sorted out."

"It's not quite the same thing."

"So *you* say."

"This isn't something we're all going to laugh about one day. This isn't a problem you're going to be able to solve for me with a speech drafted ten times in your little red book. This is it."

"True," Andrew said. "Unless . . . ?"

I looked at him. He reached into his khakis. He pulled out his little red book.

He laid it in front of me, along with a pen.

And a small smile.

"*Unless* . . . ?" I said.

fifteen

"Unless . . . well, y'know? Unless I speak to him presumably? Come to some kind of arrangement?"

I turned the envelope in my hand. It felt heavy. Ominously heavy.

"Arrangement?" the gentleman said, sucking the dregs from his can of Red Bull and buckling it feebly. It was the next morning. Friday. Almost nine o'clock. The gentleman on my front step stood, sleepy eyed, the winter wind flirting with his hair a little. He was in a dark suit, a fat, functional briefcase at his feet, from wherein he had produced the envelope. He hadn't actually said "tah-dah" but I could tell he'd thought it.

"Right," I said. I waggled the envelope as casually as its stiff back and my headache would let me. "An arrangement. Talk to Maurice. Sort it out. Come up with some mutually agreeable . . ."

"An arrangement," the gentleman said flatly. He added a slow blink. A blink that somehow said that if he had a pound for every doorstep he'd stood on hearing this, he'd be able to buy a lot of whatever dull solicitor-types like him liked to buy. Chunky briefcases. Red Bull. Something like that. "Sir, you'll discover, I regret, that the time for coming to arrangements has passed. That," and he pointed at the envelope, "is a summons for you to appear at Bow Magistrates Court on Monday the sixteenth of November at three pm. Ten days' time."

I shifted, one foot in a red Spider-Man sock, the other bare on the sticky hall tiles. Some leaves gusted up the steps and had a playful lap about my ankles. I swallowed hard, tasting cheap port and crisps, and gripped the envelope in two hands, which somehow only made it feel heavier.

The gentleman bent down, clicked shut his case and moved away down the steps, his eyes prowling over the front of the house. He licked his lips. Possibly to gather up the last remaining droplets of energy-drink for the exhausting three-feet trek to his car. Possibly because a voice in his head was muttering *ahhh, precious property. T'will be ours soon. Ours. Mmm, heh-heh.*

Not sure which.

I slammed the door on him, breathing close and tight, like my ribs had been taken apart and rebuilt using only half the pieces and the assembly instructions for a small toast-rack. I stuffed the envelope down the back of my boxers, the thin elastic holding it cold against the small of my back, ruffed my baggy T-shirt over it and trudged back up the stairs to where I'd left Jane in a foul mood, baby in her arms, staring at a stained bathroom lino.

I found her, baby still in her arms, still staring at a stained bathroom lino.

Her mood hadn't changed much either.

"Who was that?" she said.

"Nobody," I lied.

"I can still smell it," she said. Not looking at me.

"I know."

"You'll have to go over it again."

"I know."

"How long have we had this floor?"

"I don't know."

"Great. Maybe if you'd just cleaned it properly when you offered the first time?"

"Yes *maybe*," I said, which I shouldn't have done, but the whole morning had been a little like this.

Jane looked at me for a long, irritable moment and then pushed past to fuss with the baby harness. I got back down on my hands and knees, which caused my head to swim and throb, lights dancing in my eyes. With fragile, morning-after hands, I lifted the cloth and squeezy cleaner for a scrub, a yawn and a mutter.

Coat on, Jane appeared a moment later in the doorway.

"You not going in today then?"

"Not yet. I apparently have some urgent cleaning to do that can't *possibly* wait —"

"*Fine*. I'm going to speak to Dad. Shall I tell him you're still all right to pick him up from outside Victoria next week? Or shall we just presume you're going to forget *that* as well?"

"Benno was *just* as much your friend as mine. *Last week* you were claiming *he* was the one who got you and I —"

"Roll in drunk again? Throw up again? Ruin another dinner? Embarrass me some more?"

I concentrated on the perfume stain, giving it another citrus squirt.

Jane left with Lana, loudly, winter coat hissing, winter boots thudding. She slammed the door.

Barefoot and hungover, I continued to scrub.

"*Fine,*" I muttered, as men will. "*Fine. I'll pick your dad up. Sure. Absolutely. Let me shut the shop for two hours. Mustn't let the fat bastard spend a penny of his millions on a cab, must we. Oh no. Ohhh no. Not while Neil can pick him up.*"

My head was throbbing. Under my furry tongue I winced at that burning, vomity acid taste. I coughed some brown stuff into the toilet with an antiseptic echo and resumed my angry scrubbing mutter.

"*In fact, why don't I just let the solicitors run the shop while I'm out? They're going to get it anyway, what difference does a few days make? And maybe you can divorce me, if I'm so drunk and embarrassing? Marry Beevers or one of the Boatman brothers? Marry MY friend Benno who you've conveniently forgotten you had a crush on for half a term ten years ago. I'm sure they're all more daddy's type,*" and on that, I threw the J-cloth with a splat at the tile and tumbled back against the bath, kicking out angrily. Feeling it crumple and pinch behind me, I wrenched out the buckled summons from my pants and balled it up fast in an angry white fist.

Damn it. Damn it all.

The phone began to ring shrilly.

Breathing slow, breathing deep, I hauled myself up by the toilet and dragged my way into the lounge. Streaky watched me, stretched out in his square of winter sunlight on the floor.

It was Andrew. Either on his mobile or having the north circular diverted around his mini-bar.

"*This is your place right? Heroes . . . I can't read it, the sun's in my . . . Heroes Incorporated? That what the sign says?*"

"What? Where are − ?"

"*You not opening up today then? I'm standing here like a hung-over lemon. Get yourself round. I've had an idea. Well, not an idea. But I think an idea about where we could get an idea.*"

"Idea?"

"*About last night. What we discussed?*"

Last night. A memory dragged itself sluggishly behind my eyes. Jack and Catherine. Fireworks. Arguing. I backed up a little further. Andrew. A red notebook. A plan. The memory then promptly dumped out the remains of its nauseating litter-bin onto my tongue. Whisky. Ribena. A kebab.

"*I've got a meeting with O'Shea in a few . . . bloody hell. Taxi? Taxi!*"

"Andrew? What −"

"*I'll meet you at your shop in ninety minutes. Taxi? Bloody h −*"

The line went dead.

An hour later I was climbing up, out of the underground, a zombie from its crypt. I drifted through Soho floating like litter on the wind, in and out of the gutters and kerbs. The air was cold and misty, my breath fogging, surrounding me like a wraith, adding to the ghostly sense.

Around me, London continued, unaffected by my existence. No one met my eye, no one bumped my shoulder, no car slowed as I crossed. Like a dream where everything is out of reach, everything falling, I moved from street to muted street watching the cast take position, exchange their lines and act their scenes. Finally I wandered over frozen cobbles to the deserted quiet of Brigstock Place. I hauled up the shutters with a dumb rattle, toes bitten and cold in my thin black Converses.

I shuffled inside, picking up the post and snapped on the flickering lights, ignoring the dust and debris, head thudding. The cold walls hung with damp, clammy and spored, the rot from bowels beneath furring my tongue. Above the office archway, Elvis said it was just after ten a.m. and I had no reason to doubt him. As I moved through to the office and the kitchen, I tried not to look at the large empty square on my counter − a ground zero of fluff and forgotten biros − where my till had once stood.

I sat out the back for a while, in the dark, in the quiet, just thinking. Breathing deep, trying to sit on the panic, keeping it down, keeping it low. People and places shuffled around the perimeter of my mind. Jane, Edward, Earl's Court, Robert Redford, Superman, Solicitors.

Andrew.

Hauling myself up, I dragged myself to the kitchen and distracted myself with tea, moving to the laptop while the kettle coughed into life. I booted up wearily and dunked a tea-bag while the signal dialled.

My inbox was empty, save yet more spammy drivel. But trying to focus, to keep tears and rage subdued by the motions of normalcy, I sat down, sat up and selected the spammy *friendsreunited* drivel and double clicked my way onto their site. I waded through gurning snapshots and the hundredth permutation of essential eighties hits on CD, until I unearthed my University. My year.

I sipped my tea.

Ahmed, Anderson, Atherton, Barber, *there*.

Andrew Benjamin, like myself, had chosen to avoid the exclamations and emoticons of his dorm-mates, plumping instead for a straightforward where-are-they-now. *Small family, New York, real estate, happy memories*. And like myself, his posting too was worded to actively discourage replies or reminiscence. But then hey, that had been our Uni' years all over.

Andrew and I were on the same corridor and met about a fortnight into the first term, bonding immediately over that which we had in common. Namely pitiful A-level results, wayward fathers, virginity intacto and – most importantly – a mutual desire to rid ourselves of all the weirdos we'd mistakenly befriended in Freshers' Week. This we managed to do more or less successfully with chess, which we played daily on the steps outside his room. Andrew, an intense young bearded lefty with a collection of chunky-knits and whale posters, had made it clear almost immediately he had no interest in the college cliques and the college cliques made it even clearer they had no interest in me so we naturally gravitated together, orbiting uneventfully about each other for a year.

That was until the emotional upheaval and the eventful arrival on the corridor of –

"Yes yes, tip-top. Never better. You?"

I looked up at the sound of the door's jingle, Andrew's voice wafting in on the chilly breeze.

"Will do. Nice to see you old man," he said with a wave and bustled in. "Morning morning. Blimey, stick a tea on old stick. Christ, what's that *smell*?"

"Don't ask," I sighed, hauling myself out into the light. "Who were you . . . ?"

"Chap next door. Lord, he's got a memory on him, hasn't he? Blimey." Andrew dumped his case on the counter among the biros and rolled his shoulders, peering about the walls while he fished out his mobile phone from his usual pocket junk and popped his hands-free into his ear. "Great shop by the way," he nodded. "Looks like your room at Uni? All the . . ." and he motioned at the kitschy crap on the wall.

"Next door? You *know* him?"

"Hm? Yes." He dialled out quickly. "Keatings . . . You remember O'Shea last night? Said he'd had his eye on a development round here a few years – hello? Mr O'Shea please."

I left him to his call and threw a bag into a mug, returning a moment later with his tea. He was pacing, chatting into his hands-free like a schizophrenic, red notebook flapping.

". . . New York is scheduled to complete on Tuesday. There's no . . . Well the Holborn people are looking at the thirteenth, which leaves us plenty of time in case of . . . Friday, that's right . . . Uh-huh? The site visit? Yes yes . . ." Andrew caught my eye and rolled his, giving a mock yawn. "Well I'll see what I can do. Speak to you later sir. Cheerio," and he hung up.

"Big business?"

"*Don't*," he sighed, popping the earpiece out and taking his tea with ouchy-fingers. "We're selling O'Shea's New York place next week to some fund-managers looking for a temporary Manhattan address. One floor, no bathrooms. Five million pounds. Which'll leave O'Shea with six figures to plough into an off-plan artist's impression over here."

"And this is what you do now? No saving the whales?"

"I'm just a simple estate agent. I'll sell you that, buy you this and take a percent for the trouble. Easiest job in the world."

"And a nice tie to go with it."

"Huh? Yes, bugger off," Andrew said, flapping a poorly judged purple paisley number. "Hotel dry-cleaners again. Total waste of space. Anyway, look at you. Look at this," and he gazed over the walls again. "Where's your Robert Redford? Shouldn't that have pride of place somewhere?"

"Sold it," I sighed. "Needs must."

"And after all the trouble we had getting it on your wall."

"Someone else's problem now."

"Well," Andrew shrugged, trying to gee me up a little. He took a tour of the six dusty square feet. "Cracking location anyway. What are you paying, if you don't mind me asking? You want me to talk to some people?" He flapped his red book and clicked open a biro. "Might be able to get you a better deal?"

"I think my problems extend a little further than saving a tenner a month on rent," I said, and I handed him the morning's crumpled, yet legally binding, summons.

Andrew sipped his tea and gave the document his attention.

I watched as he furrowed, taking it in studiously. As a man would. With a man's sombre intelligence and focus. I then began to torture myself, picking at my mood like a fresh scab, and pictured Andrew in my shoes. Finding a burst pipe one morning. I pictured him calmly moving boxes with spade-sized hands, broad shoulders and a gritty determination. Barking at plumbers, haggling with landlords. Getting it sorted. Getting it done. Jane at his side, her slender frame wrapped by Andrew's tree-trunk arm.

Christ, what was I *doing*?

"Bloody hell old man," Andrew said, handing back the paperwork. "I'd better ask around rent-wise pretty sharpish. How did you get on last night by the way? Get home all right?"

"Bit of a scene," I shrugged. "We had friends over for dinner. I was sick, Jane . . . well let's say our friends didn't have to look too far for the fireworks."

"You tell Jane anything about – ?"

I shook my head.

Andrew's eyes wandered about the shop once again. They came

to rest on where the till wasn't standing. He put his hand to the bare formica, almost involuntarily, shaking his head, fists flexing. "This is . . . ?"

"Used to be," I said.

"God," he sighed. The muscles in his jaw ground and bulged restlessly. "How did they . . . I mean, why you? Why did the bastards pick *you*?"

"Because I'm greedy."

"Heyyy, come on, less of that. We both know that's not –"

"They told me. Told me over and over. The mark is *greedy*. The mark is *stupid*. My *character* is one who is happy to make a dishonest buck fleecing fellows out of their heirlooms. I got what I deserved."

"Neil –"

"I rip off the rude. I lunch with the likeable. Christopher and I have that in common."

"Really?" Andrew blustered loudly, shoving his hands in his pockets like a dad. "So you've now got a completely different personality from when I knew you ten years ago, have you? The guy who did all those posters for Film Soc' in his free time? Could have charged them, but didn't? Who did that Fun Run for the Student Union with Jane and me? Who donated those comics to the Cats Protection League charity shop every month? Who –"

"People obviously change," I said, angrily, slamming debt after debt into a pile.

"People don't change."

"What about you?" I said, deflecting the attention. "Look at *you*."

"We're not . . ." and he trailed off. I saw a frown scuttle across his features. "We're not talking about me."

"*Look* at you though. Mr Madison Avenue? Mr Bigshot? *Just over from New York*. What happened to *you*? You were on that Fun Run too, y'know. In a Bob Dylan T-shirt if I remember the photos. You had an acoustic guitar with a CND sticker on it for God's sake."

"That's . . . Look, we're getting off the –"

"Everybody changes. *I* became a greedy, lazy, selfish idiot who clearly got what he deserved and *you* somehow became a capitalist pig riding roughshod over the little man." I fished out a sheet, turning it over.

An unfinished letter.

"No," Andrew said flatly.

"Maybe it's genetic, like they say? Maybe I'm just my father's son," and waggled the letter with a flap. "And maybe it's for the best? Maybe it was a lucky escape for Jane. Finding out at last who she's really —"

"*NO!*" Andrew yelled, making me jump. His eyes blazed. "God! *Listen* to you! Taking *all* the responsibility from . . . These people are *scum*. The fucking scum of the *earth*. What, you think because they use their *cunning* instead of a *baseball bat* this makes them heroes? That it makes the poor souls they rob more complicit? Man oh *man*." Andrew threw his head back, fists tight.

"All right, all right. I know." I lay my father's letter on top of the pile of bills. "I'm just feeling —"

"When they use your weaknesses *against* you? When they twist your dreams, feed your basest, greediest human instincts and then blame *you* for what *you* did to your*self*? You think this makes them what? *Robin Hood*?"

"I didn't say that. That's not what I —"

"Come on Neil, snap *out* of it man," Andrew shook his head. "Shall we release all the drug lords from prison too? I mean while we're absolving blame? If it's not *their* fault? Or a conman's fault? Or an arms manufacturer's? Remove everyone's responsibility? So that it's *us*, our fault for being tempted into their wares. *Our* fault?!"

Andrew was shouting now. Arms out, spinning, railing at the racks and frames. I got the feeling that somehow, in some way, this went deeper than the last ten days.

"Benno, look —"

"Oh they're just trying to *make a living*, they'll say," Andrew sang, thick with sarcasm. "Just trying to . . . There are *other fucking ways to make a living!*" he yelled. "*Other* ways! That don't leave my fucking friends bankrupt. That don't take away people's homes and families. Other . . . other ways," he said, slowing down a little. He breathed deep, blinking, puffing.

"Are you . . . Hey, hey," and I put down my tea. "I appreciate what you're saying, what you're doing here. I do."

Andrew looked up at me, eyes fixed, breathing slow. His fists opened and closed.

"Where's this come from?" I said.

He looked at me a little longer.

"What aren't you telling me? Why are you taking this so personally?"

"Because . . . just because we go back a long way."

"We haven't spoken in a decade," I said. "You didn't even turn up for graduation."

Andrew stared at the floor.

"I wanted you as best man at the wedding, y'know? Tried to track you down? Did the card never arrive, or did you *get* the invite and not *want* to, or . . . ?"

He looked up at me.

"What *happened*? What's this about, why are you so . . . ?"

"Because *look* at me," Andrew spat. Something was simmering deep within my friend, beneath his appalling paisley neckwear. "I used to have . . . Bloody hell, I *did* have an acoustic guitar. I *did* have Billy Bragg badges on my blazer at school. You're *right*, okay? I had the lot. A donkey jacket with a Red Wedge patch. Kinnock. Amnesty benefits. All that. *That* was me. *That*."

"I know. I remember. Poetry too," I said. "Power to the people."

"Right. And now?" he shrugged sadly, picking at his suit.

I blinked. He had a point. If I hadn't been there those years ago, witnessed it, the three of us baking the carrot cake and signing the petitions together, I would never have believed the Hackett poster-boy now propped up in front of me – Jermyn Street cufflinks at his wrists and a multi-million pound city property-deal in his attaché-case – was familiar with any poetry that wasn't the sort to be sung boisterously at a rugby-club night out by thick-necked public-school bankers with beer glasses on their heads.

"So, what happened?" I said.

"It was a long time ago."

"What *happened*?" I pushed. "When I last saw you, you were bloody President of Greenpeace. Andrew? It's *me*. Chess in the halls, hanging my posters. All those talks. All that. What aren't you telling me?"

Andrew sighed. He checked his watch and then looked at me,

seemingly searching my face for traces of the young man he once knew. He shook his head with a dry, sad chuckle.

"You got anything to drink? A bit stronger?"

"Another teabag?" I suggested.

"Forget it," Andrew said. He furrowed his head, scratching his thick public-school thatch crossly. If a smile had been present a moment ago, it had now made excuses and got the fuck out of the way of things. "I had . . ." He moved around the shop slowly. "Everything was set. Planned, y'know?" he said. "I had it all sorted. You remember? Degree in geography, then it was a masters in oceanography."

"Living on a trawler or something? Wasn't that the plan?"

"Right," Andrew nodded. "The big enviro-liberal. Helping. Doing my bit. Because that was what life was *about*. Cooperation. Socialism. Communal . . . I don't know. *Responsibility*."

"Right on," I said, waving the obligatory ironic two fingers.

"I honestly believed then that the country, the world, would be a better place if we could all be a bit nicer to each other. Lend a helping hand. A few less rich p'raps, a few less poor − more of us all mucking in together somewhere in the middle. Everyone's basically *good*. And up until it . . . it happened, I believed it. Truly. In here," and he prodded his chest.

"*Happened*?"

"I was . . . I don't know what you call it. Robbed. Burgled. Turned over."

"*You* were? When was *this*?"

"One Christmas. Years ago. It was clever. I didn't see it coming. They talked their way in. They *talked* like I knew them. There were doubts but . . . I let them in. I don't know what I was thinking. Seeing the good in people I suppose. Didn't think for a minute they'd . . ."

"God. And they took − ?"

"Oh everything. Everything that mattered. Without a second thought. No remorse. No hesitation. Turned, just like that. I pleaded but . . ."

I looked at him as the memory barged about his head. The anger curling his face. Breathing slow and loud.

"Did they . . . ?" I eased carefully. "I mean were you hurt? Did they − ?"

"They pretty much left me for dead."

"Jesus Christ."

"Eventually, that is. While it was going *on*, they . . ." and he swallowed, tasting the memory. "It was violent. Childlike violence. That thoughtless, toddler, *battering*."

"God, Andrew . . ."

"And *prolonged*. So they *told* me, anyway. I don't know how long it *actually* took but it *felt* like months. I was just a wreck. Physically. Mentally. Psychiatrists tried . . ." but he didn't finish, trailing into thought.

"But you're okay *now*?"

Andrew took a silent moment. I saw a bitter, hateful smile dance across his face and then he looked at me. And he laughed.

"*Now?*"

It was nearing midday and Andrew and I were on a second cuppa, camped out in the chilly back office. The portable heater clanked and groaned noisily like a petulant teenager on a family holiday.

"And what, you're saying that was what changed you? Your direction?"

"Changed everything," Andrew said, sipping his mug with a slurp and stretching his back. "How could it not? That was that. When I eventually recovered, was able to think. Sit up. Feed myself. It was still there. The . . ." Andrew searched for the word for his pain. "Anger. I couldn't focus. For weeks. The shock of it. For ages I found myself collapsing. Just sitting down on the floor, wherever I was. On pavements. In roads. Shaking. *Rage*. That people could be so . . . so . . ."

"Bad?" I said.

"*Bad*, right. Just so blatantly, cold-heartedly . . . It opened my eyes, I tell you. Made me grow up. I must have aged a decade. Everything I believed, everything I thought. About human nature, about my so called fellow man. It just fell away. Leaving a . . . a dark hole. A dark hole where liberal, friendly *trust* used to be."

"Because of your attackers."

"Who took my plans to care about the world and beat them to death. Beat everything good in me to death," Andrew said, lip

curled, chin on his chest. A face shadowed and haunted by these
ghosts. He plucked at his shirt sleeves spitefully. "All this? Cufflinks
and . . . Madison bloody Avenue? This is them. This is what they
left me with. Business. Dog-eat-dog. The big deal. Sixty hours a
week screwing the other guy because you know he'd be screwing
you. It was the only thing that made sense after that. *Jesus*," he
spat suddenly, grabbing at his ugly tie, yanking it, pulling it, the
knot tightening. Over his face, over his head, hard, caught, before
throwing it to the dusty floor. I watched him sit, chest heaving
for a moment, eyes hard and glassy.

"I've never forgotten," Andrew said. "They've never let me forget.
And I'll never stop hating them either. Because they turned me
into *this*. They —" and the words caught in his throat for a moment.
He let out a long slow breath, picking up his mug and staring
into it. "Because they took everything. Everything. My trust, my
soul. Tore them right out of my chest and replaced them with
fucking hate."

"But . . ." I began. Andrew looked up. I got the impression from
his face that if there were 'buts' to be considered he'd already given
them a thorough drubbing and seen them off with smarting back-
sides. But hell, *years ago*? It needed saying.

"This was years ago?" I said, shrugging a bit, palms aloft, trying
to suggest forgiving-forgetting-and-moving-on with my eyebrows.
Andrew blinked at me and smiled a small smile.

"*I know*," he said. "I know. A *long time*, right? Time's the great
healer, isn't that what they say? But *one day* Neil. *One day*. Not
soon. But give it a while," and he pointed a finger at me, narrowing
his eyes. "You'll discover what *I've* come to learn about our old
friend Father Time." He spat the words, dribbling a little onto his
shirt. "The *great healer*? Ha. Time is the greatest get-out clause for
any bastard in the fucking *world*."

"Get out – ?"

"You'll see. *Yoooou'll* see. You add enough *time* to any wrong-
doing – a con, an affair, a robbery – and you'll find while you
sleep, all blame just *jumps the fence*. Just like that," and he clicked
his fingers three times. "Jumps. The. Fence. You wake up one day
and suddenly now it's *you*. *You* who's in the wrong. *You* who's the
bad guy. All pity vanishes. Suddenly you're labelled *childish*. Immature.

Obsessive. Hung-up. *Move on, man. What's the matter with you? It was a long-time-ago man. Lighten up, get over it,"* Andrew said. "The bad guys? The *actual crooks?* Hell, no one can remember their names. They're off. Scot free, screwing some other poor blighter. Leaving you to sit alone being pitied by your few remaining friends." Andrew glugged the dregs of his cold tea and slammed down the cup, wiping his mouth with the back of his hand. "Which is why I *won't* let it happen to you."

I looked across at my old friend as he got up, tugging his red book from his back pocket and giving it a waggle.

"Your idea?" I said anxiously.

"To get your money back," Andrew said. "From this guy, this Christopher. I want to be involved. I *need* to be involved," and he began to clear a space on the desk, brushing fluff and pen lids to the side. "First, it's not going to be easy. I mean, we're smart, you and I. Successful. I'm at Keatings, you've got this place. We might have two good brains between us, sure. But compared to this *Christopher?* We're kindergarten level."

He was talking quickly, eyes bright.

"Now I tried to sketch out some thoughts," and he riffled his book feebly. "Last night, in my hotel. But I was a bit drunk and . . . well, I think we have to face it. You and I aren't cut out for this stuff. Swindles and switcheroos? We wouldn't know where to begin."

"Agreed."

"If we're going to come up with some scheme by which we can get back your fifty grand without getting ourselves killed, we're going to need help. Someone with this sort of experience. And if not exactly this con-trick stuff, then at least someone built *that way.* Someone who thinks the way these guys think. Who's lived in the shadows. Who can give us an insight into how these people work. How they *think.*"

"Okay," I said, rather dragged along by all this.

The shop went quiet. Andrew looked at me expectantly like a Labrador with a lead in its mouth.

"What?" I said.

Andrew raised his eyebrows hopefully, nodding at me like a simpleton.

I blinked. I looked about the office. Over my shoulder. Nope, neither Nick Leeson nor Ronnie Biggs had snuck in behind me. I looked back at Andrew and shrugged.

He widened his eyes and nodded a little.

And then the realisation leaked cold into my gut.

"It's perfect. He's still alive, right?"

"No," I said. "I mean, yes yes. He might be still alive but *no*. Not in a million . . . No. Just no."

Undeterred, Andrew scuttled up to the chair next to me, spun it around and mounted it backwards in the New York style, flapping his hands enthusiastically.

At least I think he did. I had my eyes shut in exhausted quiet despair at the time.

"Listen, listen it's perfect," his voice said in my ear, eagerly. "You talked about him all the time at college."

"No. No I didn't."

"You *did*. You said he'd never done a day's work in his life."

"He still hasn't."

"How he would use the system. Benefit fraud, all the loopholes. How old is he now?"

"I don't know. I don't want to think about it. This isn't going to −"

"How old is he? Fifty-five?"

"Now?" I sighed, eyes still shut, counting slowly in the darkness. "He'd be fifty-eight."

"Fifty-eight. Bloody hell, you can't just blag your way through fifty-eight years without having this stuff in your blood. So I think you should call him. You don't have to tell him specifics. Talk . . . talk hypothetically. Just asking his advice. He might −"

"No."

"*C'mon* Neil. Think about it. If we're going to do this − and I don't see what choice we have −"

"We can go to the police," I said, opening my eyes and squinting in the flat shop-light. "Like normal people do. We can go to the police −"

"Yeah? With *what*?" Andrew said.

"I'll tell them . . ."

"Go on? What's the big clue? Where's the big lead?"

I looked around the peeling walls in chilly silence. Fifty years of tatty, comic book crap peered back at me.

"*And why you, sir?*" Andrew said in a pompous, *Dixon of Dock Green* tone. "*Where are they now sir? Any witnesses sir? Anything they might have touched, sir?* I've been there, mate. This is what happens. What can you tell the police?"

My throat closed slowly, tight and panicky.

"We *have* to do this," Andrew said, "and we have to do this *ourselves*. Or we have to *try*."

"But I won't involve . . . We'll try it. You and I. Okay. But I'm not going crawling to −"

"We *need* his help."

"I *don't*. I don't need *anything* from him."

"Neil, listen to me," and Andrew got up, sliding his chair away with a clatter. He tugged up his trousers like a grown-up and squatted down on his haunches. He had black, grown-man's socks. Spider-Man nowhere to be seen. "We need every advantage we can get going up against this man. Did you see this *Christopher* back off from a trick? Go easy on you?"

I grunted.

"Neil? Did you?"

"*No*," I said, hands now over my face. "No but . . ."

"Then what's *your* idea? Try and come up with something ourselves? Some clever double-triple-quadruple cross that Christopher won't spot in the first three seconds? This is what this man *does*, Neil. Neil? What are you saying, take your hands away from your −"

"I said, we discussed it."

"You − ?"

"We discussed it. A long time ago. After he . . . That was *it* for us. I write to him. Once a year. Keep him up to date with things. A lifeline, I suppose. Births, deaths and marriages. To let him know the world goes on. But . . . but that's it. He's my father. I owe him that. But that's all. I don't want any part of that life. That was *his* way, *not* mine. Not me."

The office went silent. I looked up at Andrew. He sighed.

"But you don't get to make that choice now. Whether it's what you wanted or not, part of that life is now your life. Nothing you can do to change that. So you can either become a victim. Become me. Spend the rest of your life with gritted teeth and a hardened heart. Or you can look at him as a gift. Use this one life-line. Get him round."

The office fell into another silence for what felt like an age. Andrew's purple paisley tie drifted back into fashion at one point and then just as quickly back out again. Finally I spoke.

"I can't."

"Oh come on Neil, aren't you *listening*? We —"

"No, I mean even if . . . I mean I can't just call him. I can't *get him round*."

"You don't know where he is?"

"I know exactly where he is. That's the problem."

sixteen

One of the worst aspects of a job in retail management is that one is never at home. Early starts, late closings, stock-takes. It's a twelve- sometimes fourteen-hour day, resulting in a sleepy, blurred home life of reheated dinners and broken promises.

Of course one of the *best* aspects, similarly, is that one is never at home. The early starts, late closings and what-not mean that not one matrimonial eyelid is batted should one, say, disappear out of the house for an entire Saturday. It is just presumed one is slaving over a hot till.

Even when one is actually taking the Nissan Micra for an anxious and fretful drive down the M2, out to the quaint little village of Selmeade in Kent.

"Straight through, follow the yellow line. Sit at the allocated seat. The number is on your card. Keep moving, follow the yellow line."

My card had D12 stamped inkily on it. I wove nervously through the five rows of empty chairs and small tables in the draughty hall until I found my spot. The floor echoed and squeaked like a school gym, the air stale and wet with bleach. Along the fat bricked walls, hospital green with a greasy shine, broad men with clip-on frowns paced, beady eyes darting, watching other pale visitors – mostly tired-looking women – unload carrier bags of fizzy drinks and biscuits. Above us, on iron walkways, more shiny-capped men measured out the hour in plodding, purposeful steps while blank-eyed CCTV cameras whirred and prowled.

Bottom hot and itchy in the plastic seat, I watched as five or six dozen men in tracksuits began to file in past a desk on a raised dais at the front, their names checked, their numbers given. It took a few stomach-tumbling moments before I realised that the grey man in the raspberry tracksuit squeaking towards me was him.

HMP Selmeade's prisoner FF9191.

Or Dad, as I call him.

He eased himself down, waving off my awkward bobbing hand-shake-backslap fumble.

"S'all right son. Probably best we ain't on friendly terms," he said, motioning at the inmate/out-mate couples either side of us who were hugging, groping and kissing noisily. "Best way to getcha'self a strip search is that." He placed a dented tobacco tin on the table between us with a loud *clack*, tapping his hollow cheeks. "Drugs. In the mouth. S'how they get 'em in. Bring me doo-dahs did you?"

I looked at him for a moment. It appeared pleasantries were over. With a sigh I emptied out the canteen carrier bag onto the table. The tobacco, bottles of Coke and the red tub of Brylcreem he'd asked for on the phone. Dad smiled with a *good lad*, hugging the items to his thin chest, rheumy eyes shining.

A longer look. A closer look. He wasn't well, not that the track-suit did him any favours. It was cheap, thin, prison issue. The other men sat around us filled theirs out with gym-buffed shoulders and thick, lifter's necks, but Dad's hung on his frame like a dust-sheet on a xylophone.

"If this is a tickin' off," he began, sliding the cigarettes into his tracksuit shiftily and popping open his tobacco tin with twitchy yellow fingers. "Some *closure* cobblers your therapist is makin' you do then we'll keep it short son. I got a Kaluki game I'm missin' 'ere."

"I'm not . . ." I said. My voice was loud, flat against the swim-ming-pool echo of the cold hall. I took a deep breath, heart heavy. "No-one's ticking anyone off. That's not . . . I just thought I should . . . How are you doing?"

"Whadda you care?" he said.

"I'm your son."

"You been my son for *twenty-five years* –"

"Thirty-one, Dad."

"Thirty – ?" and he stopped. I watched his thin mouth twitch and chew a little.

"I'm not here to tick you off," I said. "I'm well past that. Haven't you been getting my *letters*?"

"Got the first few," he said. He coughed, a wet, old man's cough, shoulders shaking within the thin polyester. "Your *opinion* of me seemed pretty plain. Didn't see much point in puttin' m'self through that every year."

"You haven't – ? You haven't been reading them?"

My father shrugged a weak shrug, popping the lid from his buckled Golden Virginia tobacco tin with skeletal fingers.

"Missed some *big news*, 'ave I? That what's dragged you in 'ere? Get kicked out of University or something, is it? Good thing too. Getcha'self in the *real* world, boy."

"I can't believe you haven't been reading . . ." I trailed off, dizzily. "I . . . I finished University *ten years ago*, Dad. And the real world and I get along fine. Thank you."

"I bet," he said dryly. "You always were a workin' man. Even as a boy. Runnin' errands for fifty pee."

"Not that I ever *got* the fifty pee."

"I was teachin' you a lesson son," he smiled the neat, ordered smile of cheap dentures.

"I'm *married* now," I said.

"Yeah?" Dad said, barely looking up.

"You . . . you have a grand-daughter."

Dad stayed watching the table for a moment. The plastic grain, the peeling edges. He took a deep, quiet breath and then met my look.

"Lana," I said, tugging my unfinished letter from my jacket, opening it up and sliding out a couple of photographs. I slid the lot across the warped formica. "She's just six weeks."

Dad sat in silence, peering at the pictures, while he fussed and dribbled over a fresh roll-up.

"That's Jane there with her. And her father. Edward, the Earl of Somewhere or other Shire."

"A nob, eh?"

"You'd like him," I said. "He hasn't done an honest day's work in his life either."

"Married up. Good lad. Bet he's worth a bob or two, eh?" and he winked, shaky tongue wetting his cigarette paper. "Should'a thought o'that m'self. That would'a suited me. Not that your mum didn't look after me, o'course. But she never got 'the life'."

"No," I said. I gathered the photographs.

"Old fashioned, she was. Up to the end. Day's work for a day's pay, all that. You got that mug's game streak from her."

"Us teacups, eh?" I said.

"The lot of you."

It was extraordinary. Even here. *Here*, among freezing gantries and heavy guards where you'd think reality would finally sink in, he clung to it. Locked behind steel doors behind high concrete walls, nothing had changed. It was still all *us-and-them*. Even though his self-proclaimed savvy friends, with their schemes and know-how were sat around him in thin tracksuits, eking out roll-ups and shuffling in concrete shadows for twenty-three hours a day, years reaching ahead of them, they were still all above us 'mugs' who could up and leave, walk free, taste the air, feel the grass on our feet and the wind in our faces whenever we wished.

"Well?" Dad said, placing his hair-thin cigarette on the table neatly.

"Well," I stumbled, looking down, trying to say everything that needed saying through the usual ineffectual manly gruffness. "I thought I'd come and see you. Just to . . . well. To see you. See how you're keeping."

Dad said nothing, just watched me wriggle.

"The thing *is* though . . ." I said, lowering my voice a little. "See, the thing is I'm in need of . . . This is rather embarrassing . . ."

"It's a bit late for the birds an' bees son."

"I-I suppose you'd say I'm in need of your *expertise*."

The table went quiet. Around us, the couples' chatter continued in a low murmur. Chair scrapes. Muffled tears.

Dad blinked. Then blinked again, before sitting back with a crooked smirk in exactly the way I'd hoped he wouldn't.

"Well well. My *son*. Realised the error of your ways 'ave you? Finally cottoned on that the old man isn't as green as 'e's cabbage looking, eh?"

"No, I'm not −"

"Got it into your college-boy head that you might 'ave something left to learn at last? Bet you wished you'd paid a bit more attention at home now, don'tcha. Breakfast time? 'Stead of 'avin' your nose in a comic? Listened to your old dad? Well, well. I never thought I'd see the −"

"*Dad!*" I hissed, startling him a little. "It's not like that. I'm not . . . Look, what I said in those letters. The *first* letters, I mean. After it happened. That still stands. Your life, your way − it isn't mine. Our values, our . . . look, nothing's changed. That's not what *this* is . . . I didn't want to follow you as a boy and I don't want to follow you as a man, you understand me? Sitting around at breakfast, listening to your little *lessons*? Your *tricks*? Whatever you called them −"

"I was just teachin' you to play the system, lad. System's like a piano. Even in 'ere. Built for −"

"Built for *playing*, I remember. Well I never understood it and neither did Mum. She would have rather you put *her* first, instead of your petty victories. Let the system *win* once or twice and put some food on the −"

"System *win?!*" Dad coughed. "I'll let you mugs bend over and grab your ankles for the system son. Your dad's smarter than that."

"You think it's smarter to go without? Sit around −"

"I'm *smarter* than that!" Dad yelled, slamming a thin fist on the table, tobacco tin jumping. His eyes were wet, flashing like neon in oily puddles. At the far wall, a warder lifted his chin from his starchy collar and peered across at us. We hunkered down a little among the plastic bottles.

"She didn't *care*, Dad," I whispered. "'Cause, y'know, sitting around hungry while you marched about in your vest, talking about how *smart* you were? Lording it about like you were Ronnie Biggs just because you'd wrung another eight quid out of the Social? It might surprise you Dad, but she didn't care. I didn't care. Nobody was impressed."

"Nobody was − ? Listen to 'im. I could'a walked into any pub in that town, any pub, and had a dozen fellahs −"

"Oh well done *you*. No stair carpet. No shoes. Same school blazer for five years, but the darts team all thought you were *the man*. Great."

"So. *This* is what this is about?" Dad said. He looked tired, bony shoulders round and heavy. "What happened to needing my *expertise*? I can get a parenting sermon off Father Pollack at Chapel. I don't need to waste precious association time hearin' it from you. I could be a hundred points up at Kaluki b'now, 'stead of getting' an ear-bashin' from an ungrateful son."

"I'm sorry," I said, breathing deep. My hands were wet and warm. "I just wanted you to know . . . y'know, what was what. But I do need your help. I've got involved . . ." The words were fat in my throat. "Shit, this isn't easy to . . ."

I looked up. Dad had sat back, arms folded, polyester sleeves crackling. The galvanised rubber chair gave a groan. He had his crooked smile wrapped about his roll-up, Bic lighter halfway to his mouth. He chuckled, cigarette bobbing, lit it and let out a stream of smoke from his nostrils.

"What 'ave you done?"

"Done?"

"Sitting there all Mr Straight-and-narrow? Givin' it all the high-and-mighty? Sounds like what the shrink we got in 'ere calls *trans-ference*. You ain't pissed at me. You're pissed at *you*. Look at'cha. Wringing your hands, fidgeting, bags under your eyes. What you got yourself into? Drugs?"

"Drugs? No." I sighed, heart thumping. "Look, Dad, it's a long shot. You're the only person I know who might be able to –"

"Cut to the chase, lad, we're on the clock 'ere," and he motioned to the wall. Behind a rusty grille, hanging on the polished green brick, a large institutional face counted down the hour. Beneath, a wide warder paced, chin up, rolling his shoulders, moving between the mutters, the hand-holding and pain.

"Okay. Right. Well." I focused back on my father. "In short, I need . . . What do you know . . . what do you know about confidence tricks?"

I took the next ten minutes outlining my situation in a hushed voice, us both leaning in over the table like two grandmasters. The warder who'd directed me in wandered past a couple of times, causing us to break apart rather clumsily and remark about the food in loud theatrical voices but he promptly left with a stern, forceful look on his face, humming what sounded suspiciously like a Shania Twain medley.

Dad *I-gotcha-ed* with a nod throughout my story, head cocked to one side slightly like a bird, staring at the table top, taking it all in, until finally he looked up at me.

"That it?" he said.

"That's it," I sighed, chest light, temporarily relieved of its burden.

"*Jesus*," he sighed. "Jesus *Christ*, boy. I can hardly . . . This is a son of *mine* talkin'. At no point did it *dawn* on you . . ."

"Dad, we haven't *time* for −"

"At no point during this farce, did you think, *'ang on, it's all a bit convenient. This American just happens to be short −"

"*Dad!*"

"A son of mine. A son of *mine!*" and he rolled his rheumy eyes, staring up at the iron lights and the high netting above us. "Did you learn *nuffin'* growin' up? Of *course* the dame's in on it. The dame's always *in* on it! Dear God . . ."

"*Please* Dad. The *time*? I'm sorry, okay? I'm sorry. But this is your grand-daughter's future in the balance here."

Dad shook a sad, slow head for a moment and popped his cigarette tin open once again.

"Not so full of yourself *now*, are we, Mr Straight-and-narrow-workin'-man? Mr *System*?"

"Dad, look, I've come here for help. I don't know what else to do. If you're just going to −"

"'Awright 'awright. 'Ow long you got?"

"What? Well that's the thing," I whispered. "Jane's dad is back in three days. I'm meant to be picking him up from outside Victoria Station on Tuesday. He's going to talk to his accountant and that'll be that."

"And the summons? This Maurice bloke?"

"Nine days. And between now and then I'm meant to be running a stall at Earl's Court, which is a whole other set of problems. I don't think I can afford *not* to set up. I've paid my deposit and I've had a van booked for months. But with only half the stock? I-I . . ."

"S'all right, calm down," Dad said. He was thinking. I watched him sit back and go through the production line steps of another thin cigarette. I noticed the pale spots on the backs of his hands as he held the paper to his trembling tongue. Finally, smoothing the edges, he laid down the cigarette neatly on the table as before.

"Dad?" I said, tapping my chunky watch face.

"This Andrew? He that poofy fellah you hung around with at school?"

"It was University. And he's married with twin daughters."

"Well spoken?"

"Fairly I s'pose."

"I remember him. Poofy fellah."

"Dad –"

"Had my doubts about him. All that hippy stuff, weren't it? Ban the bomb, save the whale, all that?"

"I shouldn't have come. *Christ,* what was I –"

"Shush, let me think, let me think." He balanced his cigarette on the edge of his lip and dragged a rough thumb over the lighter, sparking hot and blue. Dad took a tiny puff and sat back. "Now if I know felons – an' there are one or two in 'ere who fit that description – this Christopher fellah will 'ave gone underground."

"Underground?"

"Off the radar. 'E won't risk stickin' his head above the parapet for a long while. Not wiv' you still smartin' from the whippin' 'e gave you. Which I *still* can't believe a son of *mine* . . . I mean, law, didn't you *think*? When this dame –"

"All right Dad," I squirmed. "Point made. Can we stick to the –"

"A'wright a'wright, I'm just sayin'. If 'e's as smart as you give 'im credit for, 'e'll stay out of London and off the grift for six months. My bet is he'll split your fifty K and live the high life for a while."

"Great," I said, a dark shadow rumbling cold over my spirit. "So what do I do? Try and track him down in the home counties next summer? My wife will *leave* me. She'll take my daughter, my house, *everything* I have. Everything I *am*. I can't afford to –"

"Wait," Dad interrupted. He twisted open a bottle of Coke. "Wait," he said again, brain ticking over. He slid his cigarette out of his mouth and slugged a fizzy glugful then wiped his lips with the back of his thin hand. "There's a guy we got in 'ere. Fraud. Seacat o'course, so I don't see 'im much."

"Seacat?"

"Category C. Non-violent repeat offenders. They keep 'em

away from us Bs. They're in G–Block, over the way. Where I should be by rights. But I see him in Chapel once in a while. Always bangin' on about *next time*, 'e is. 'Ow next time'll be perfect. The big one. Payday. End of the rainbow stuff. Like a broken record, on and on. Not that 'e's different to most."

"I don't follow?"

"The pot of gold. S'what gets everybody collared in the end. That belief that somewhere, *somewhere* out there, is the *perfect* job. The one mythical pay-off that'll set 'em up for life. That's what everybody's hopin' for. S'what brings 'em out of retirement for that one last blag. *Everyone.* The guys in hidin'? Guys tryin' to lay-low? Pretty much every lag in stir has jacked it in at some point, gone the high road, until they got a whiff-of-the-myth."

"The pot of gold."

"*Right.* See," and Dad leant in a little, checking over both shoulders shiftily, which to me seemed like the ideal way to get the warders bouldering over with stirrups and rubber gloves, but I was on his turf and had to presume he knew what he was doing so I hunkered down and let him continue. "Crooks are lazy. S'what gets 'em caught. An' why the big one-off retirement payout is so irresistible. Oh they'll make out they put in the hours of prep and rehearsal, but it's all too much like hard work. They're a shiftless and bone-idle lot in the most part."

"Not like you then," I said.

"Hey. Hey 'old yer 'orses there, Sparky," Dad said, pointing a bony finger my way. "What *I* did? How I chose to live? That wasn't idle. I put in the hours, ask anyone. Day in, day out at that bookies. Followin' the tips, checkin' the form. That weren't grift, that was *graft*. I worked at it. Got it down to a fine art."

"Until," I said.

"That was a last resort, son. I've told you that. Tragedy. For everybody. Things just got a little out of hand. Run of bad luck, that's all. I just needed to get m'self clear. Start again."

"I'm sure his widow sees it that way too."

Dad looked at me, lips closed and chewing small angry chews.

"Well that's up to her," he said flatly. "She's out there and she can see it how she wants, lad. That was all a long time ago for us all. Another lifetime."

"Gosh, well that's all right then."

"Time moves on boy. You'll learn that one day. What's done is done. Her grief'll pass. Memory fades. But I'm still 'ere."

I looked at him. This all sounded horribly familiar.

"You're . . . Wait, you're not – ?"

"S'all I'm sayin'," Dad nodded.

"He's right. Jesus, Andrew's . . . son of a bitch is right."

"Right?"

"Yesterday. Andrew."

"The poofy –"

"The *poofy fellah* Dad, yes. *Jesus.* He said . . ." I could hardly believe it. But there it was, in front of me. Smoking thin cigarettes through cheap false teeth. "You actually think it's *you* who we should feel sorry for now. Because you're in here and she's out there. You genuinely feel . . . In your head. In your *thinking.* The blame. It's . . ." and I searched for Andrew's phrase. "It's jumped the fence."

"Fence? What're you talkin' about lad? Who's jumpin' – ?"

"Andrew. He said you add *time* to any wrong-doing and the crook is off scott-free. And you agree with him."

"Scot – ? I look *scot free* to you, lad?"

"Yes," I said, almost shouting. "In your head, you clearly are. Free of guilt, free of blame. Just a poor victim of the system."

"I didn't have any choice. It was me or 'im. I was in trouble."

"*Yes* Dad, but when most men are in trouble, y'know, they put in overtime. Get a second job. Bar-work. Mini-cabbing. They don't . . ." I ground my teeth tight. "They don't get up halfway through a family wedding, bloody *Fools and Horses* ring-tone going, slink out the back and hold up a damned –"

"*Five minutes,*" a voice yelled, echoing about the hall. There was a sudden chatter and rattle of carrier bags.

"*Mini-cabbing?*" Dad spat, wiry eyebrows flustering, not knowing whether to knot in anger or fly upwards to the gantry in surprise. "It would have taken more than a couple of runs to Heathrow and back to raise what I needed, son. No. I'm not proud of what I did, sure. And I'll admit that how it turned out was a tragedy. A *tragedy.* But understand, these men weren't going to wait around for me to scrape the cash together with a bit of evening work.

Mini-cabbing? Tch. A mug's skivvying don't bring in what men like me need."

"But it *does*, Dad," I pressed. I needed him to understand. He *had* to understand. "It does. Week by week, putting a bit aside. Over the years. It's called saving. It's what fathers are meant to teach their sons."

"Teacups, son. How many times 'ave I told you? 'Fink about it. If hard work never killed anybody, who's —"

"— that clogging up the cemetery? I remember," I sighed, shaking my head.

"Your Dad's better'an that. He's got bigger plans."

"*Plans?*" I barked in surprise. Surprise with an unhealthy full-fat spoonful of anger thrown in. Anger at the relationship, that this attitude, this life had kept from me. "What plans? A game of cards then once round the yard before slopping out?"

Dad stopped, sparrow's chest heaving inside his flimsy tracksuit top. He looked me over with his wet, yellowing eyes. I began to shift itchily in my seat. He stubbed out his cigarette slowly and purposefully in the thin foil ashtray. Finally he lifted his Coke bottle and sat back, holding it to his chest. He sat like that for a while, just the wheezy whistle of his breathing and the odd blink before he eventually sniffed, curling a crooked bitter smile.

"*You*," he sneered, shaking his head with tired, cynic's wisdom. "You workin' mugs. Always first in line to dish out the sentence, ain'tcha, eh? Up there, lookin' down on us *real* men. Us who said *no* to the commute, to the grind, to the forty-year slog and the cheap golden fuck-off. Oh, nice wristwatch there son, by the way. Very *bling*."

I scowled, tugging down my sleeve.

"You 'ave to get *pompous* about it, don'tcha eh? Helps you sleep does it? Helps you forget the men like me with balls you wouldn't *dream* of," and he held his hands out like he were judging the two finalists in the *World's Largest Melon* contest. "You've gotta make out you're so much *better*, ain'tcha? Your little *theories*? *Blame jumps a gate* or whatever it is? I'm the *lazy* one. Well if you wanna talk about lazy, son, let's talk about the second job *you* got when you let your basement get flooded, shall we? Let's talk about your mini-cab runs, your bar-work, the night-shifts *you* were pulling down to keep bread on the family table when the plumbing went tits-up."

I began to examine my hands carefully, chewing the inside of my cheek.

"If you're so bloody clean, how did this Christopher get his claws into you, eh? If you're so straight, what was following this Grayson to the airport all —"

An angry buzzer sounded, making everyone jump. I looked up. Women were getting to their feet slowly, hoisting bawling children onto their hips. The prisoners didn't move.

I looked back at Dad and he folded his arms.

"You and me maybe ain't so different lad. Despite what you tell yourself. Maybe you're your father's son. *Juuuust* a little bit . . ."

I trembled, feeling my guts writhe in angry, guilty snakes.

"In yer blood, son," he went on. "*Family.* You know what they say. You can't change what you *are.*"

"No," I ground, teeth tight. "Not me."

"Oh yes. That's what's *got* you here. But, see, that's what'll get you *out.*"

"How?"

"You're gonna have to play by their rules. If you're gonna do this right. And maybe that bit of your father in you you scold so much is gonna be the edge you need. First off, you're gonna getcha'self outta here, sharpish," Dad said, stretching his back with a horrendous dull clicking noise. "Go on, you'll get me in schtook. We 'ave to stay seated 'ere until you're all clear," and he popped the top of his tin and slid out another cigarette paper. "C'mon, you're eatin' into our association time 'ere. Shift yerself."

I sighed and stood up, stomach tumbling when I felt a tight dry grip grab my knuckles hard. Wincing, I looked down. Dad was holding my hand, wet eyes fixed on mine, wide and shaking.

"And second job is getting my grand-daughter's future back, y'hear me? I might not have raised the gambling prodigy I wanted but I didn't raise a sap, neither. You're smart. In a teacuppy sort of way."

I smiled a little.

"You think about what I said. These men? This Christopher? Lazier and greedier than the fattest mark, remember that. So for a *real* payday? A pot of *gold*? They'll come sniffin' around. They won't be able to help 'emselves. Figure out the *details* yourself. You know 'im. Find 'im. However you think you can swing it. But *swing* it. Dangle him a once-in-a-lifetime. Something he can't turn down."

"I will," I said.

The buzzer blared another angry metallic moan.

"Thanks Dad. I . . . I'll see you again," and I turned from the table.

"Lemme know when y'comin' next time son. Gimme a bit more notice," he said behind me, voice dry and low. "*There's a fellah you can pop over an see for me first.*"

I turned, holding a sigh tight in my chest.

"What *fellah*?"

"Heh-heh, never you mind, *nudge nudge,*" and he popped his cigarette in his mouth with a grin.

I turned again and followed the long slow yellow line out of the hall to the car.

seventeen

"Payday?"

"That's what he said. The pot of gold. End of the rainbow, way up high. Anything less and Christopher just won't come out. Your go."

It was four o'clock the same afternoon. Andrew and I were sat, bums cold in the chilly shop, hunched over a game of *Connect Four*. Instead of heading back to Putney to face an awkward *home-a-bit-early-aren't-we* from Jane, I'd slung the Micra in the NCP on Brewer Street, hoping against all experience I might make enough from the remaining hour's trade to be able to afford to pay its extravagant bail at five o'clock. So far, however, it'll come as absolutely no surprise to you to learn, apart from Benno, I'd had only one visitor. A young man, after *anything* (serious face, intense brow, girlfriendless wardrobe) related to Robert De Niro. I'd been more than happy to show him a rarity – the US first advance print one-sheet from *Raging Bull*, illustrated by Kunio Hagio, only to find him less than happy to see me fish it out of a sopping basement bin-bag in six bits. So that was that.

Andrew, in *mostly* his own clothes as per usual, dropped a yellow disc into the blue frame and sipped instant coffee.

"He's probably right. I don't know much about it, but it's not going to be worth Christopher's team risking capture for a couple of hundred pounds. We'll have to think big. Your go by the way old man."

I scanned the red and yellow dots, tapping a disc on my teeth, just as I had done all those years ago in the freezing college halls, among echoing shouts in distant stairwells, the smell of tinny toma-toes and the pop of tinnier speakers crackling early nineties compilation tapes – a lot of *The Wonder Stuff* if memory serves. A hundred evenings had seen us, sat together just like this. Board between us. Chess, *Scrabble*, *Mousetrap*. Sometimes a game for games' sake. More often a coded approach to a tricky topic – idle chat about strategy and manoeuvre before something touchy was tentatively raised: missed lectures, absent fathers. Or famously one cold, third-year morning – where Jane and I had been all night?

Back then I had waited, writhing, for Andrew to ask what needed asking. To say what needed saying.

Here, ten years later, he still hadn't got the hint.

"What?" Andrew said suddenly, which made me jump rather. "*What?* There's that look. What am I meant to be saying?"

"No no, nothing."

"*Neil?*"

"Well, I thought . . . Payday wise . . . maybe O'Shea?"

"O'– ? Oh. Oh no. No no no . . ." and Andrew began to shake his head slowly, sliding away from the desk. I began a bit of verbal scurrying about.

"He's new in town," I said. "Bit smug, bit pompous, got these millions to spend? Can't we . . . I mean, isn't there any kind of property . . ." I floundered a bit. "Not *scam*, exactly –"

"Neil . . ."

"– but a bit of jiggery-pokery you know of? We get O'Shea to meet Christopher . . . *somehow*," I inserted a little limply. "Christopher brings some money in a bag, we . . . I dunno, get O'Shea to swap the bag for . . . uhmm . . ." It was coming apart badly. "*Another* . . . bag . . . thing?"

Another bag thing? Oh excellent Neil. Dazzling.

Andrew shook his head. Or was more than likely just still on the head-shake he'd started five minutes ago. Either way, quite understandably I suppose, he wasn't having any of it.

"I can't," he said. "I'm sorry old chap. I *can't*. Even if there *was* some scheme, I still couldn't risk . . . O'Shea is my way *in*. The brass bloody ring. He's been talking about offloading this Manhattan place for *years*. I think his father gave it to him in his will or some such thing. Anyway it's got that it's kind of an in-joke among New York agents. Every year he puts his toe in the water, makes some inquiries. All the Manhattan agents fall over each other giving him a valuation and then boom – he changes his mind. Cantankerous old bastard. Sits back and waits another bloody year."

"But how's this time any different . . . ?"

"He called *me*. Out of the bloody blue. I think I gave my card to his sister-in-law's neighbour at some party? Anyway, as usual he says he fancies a change of scenery. Getting tired of New York. What will his money get him in London? At first I thought forget it, penny-pinching old git, but Veronica talked me into going after him. But *really* going for it. The hard sell. Keatings said I was wasting my time but I thought hell, why not? This is how senior sales executives become partners. Played golf, took him to lunch, met his wife, all the time pushing the agency. Old bastard signed me up at his kitchen table."

"Congratulations."

"Now all I have to do is bring this one home and I'm *set*. We're talking share options, corner office, executive washroom. We can take the place in Long Island . . ."

"Okay," I said, nodding. "Forget it. I was clutching at straws," and I waved him away, focusing again on the *Connect Four* board, dropping in an idle disc and trying to hide my absolute, crushing, flattening, *steamrollering* disappointment. It had been *all* I could think of all the way back up the M2 that afternoon. I'd mapped it all out in laughably detail-less detail. Some simple switcheroo that Andrew would fortuitously have up his well-tailored sleeves. Bing bang bong, fifty thousand, thank you very much.

"Plus O'Shea's the wrong man anyway," Andrew said. He sat down again and dropped in a yellow disc quickly. "Far too cautious. Oaf insists on having every dime signed for in triplicate by his lawyers. I've almost blown this once by rounding up the Holborn valuation by a penny. You should have seen him bluster away. A *penny*? But . . . but actually that's all moot because you *saying* that has just made me realise. *Whatever* we do, he's got us over a barrel."

"Barrel? Who, *O'Shea*?"

"This Christopher. Hell. It's going to be trickier than we . . ." and Andrew got to his feet quickly, almost upsetting the board. He began to pace urgently among the racks and bin-bags, humming to himself.

"You all right?" I said.

"Look, let's say . . . let's say we did try some real estate oojah. Some contract drawn up for some plot of land. A phoney survey, valuation, I don't know. Five acres on the moon. Whatever." Andrew had reached the far end of the shop, hands in pockets, clicking his tongue. "Our problem is that if your Christopher's an *expert* – done his research for a property scam *before* maybe – he's going to see through us straight away, right?"

"Right," I sighed.

"*But*," Andrew said, almost before I'd answered, face screwed tight in thought. "Flip side is, we dangle some multi-million pound property swindle under his nose and he *isn't* au fait with the ins and outs? Well, we haven't got him *then* either."

"We haven't? But –"

"No. Because we know from your experience he's going to want to find himself a mentor chappie first. Just like he did with *you*. Someone to teach him the jargon, lend him an office, the whole bit. Put up a professional front. It could take *weeks* before he's confident enough to step up to the plate."

"Weeks that I haven't got," I sagged sadly. My head filled with Edward. In three short days I'd be outside Victoria hefting his suitcase into the Micra while he sat bulging in the passenger seat drumming gloved fingers on my dashboard asking about accountants. "So you're saying . . ." I said, brain lagging behind a little. "Shit, sorry, what are you saying?"

"I'm saying old man, if we do what your father says and try to draw Christopher out with the unmissable promise of some big payoff – cards, horses, comics, stamps, property – we've got to be *sure* of how much *he knows* before we –"

"*Wait*," I yelled.

"What?"

"That's it. The pot of gold," I said again, brain flipping ahead fast like a spoilsport with an Agatha Christie. "I might . . . Wait right there," and I got up, sending the *Connect Four* toppling with a cheap plastic clatter. I scurried out into the dark back office, returning with two soggy bin-bags, held high in two fists. I dumped them on the counter with a rustle, tearing at the thin plastic and ripping a wide mouth in the top of the fatter bag. A foul, wet, mouldy stench burped forth, biting the back of my throat. I took a deep breath and began to rummage among the sopping paper filth of mush and mash.

"What? Christ, what have you lost?" Andrew said, creeping forward.

I tore open the second bag quickly. Another green rotten fart guffed from within.

"In there. Get digging."

"What am I – ?"

"A letter," I said, fishing through the grey remains of buckled cardboard and posters, coffee cups and crap. "I *completely* forgot. What with everything . . . I mean half the time I don't even remember I've got it, his lordship insisting it's vacuum-packed and buried in a vault for when his grandchildren . . . C'mon . . . c'mon where are you . . . ?"

"A letter from *who*?" Andrew said. He was picking up on my Christmas morning giddiness and fishing through his bag of sopping waste.

"*A-ha!*" I cried triumphantly, unpeeling the soggy corners, browned from spilt food. "Here, here," and I thrust both halves of the torn-up missive at him.

Andrew looked at me warily before allowing himself a peer at the sopping sheets.

"*Dear Mr Martin,*" he read aloud, laying the furry torn edges together. "*In response to your letter of the fifteenth, without a viewing, we are unable to put an accurate valuation on your . . .* Bloody *hell.*"

"How's that for a pot of gold?" I said, breathless.

"Is this *real*?"

"It's what happens when you marry the daughter of an Earl. Jane never really let it show when you knew her. At college, I mean. What with her purple dreads and stripey leggings. But boy, they don't do things by halves these types you know? You should have seen the wedding reception. Marquee like a bloody aircraft hangar."

"I wish I could have old mate," Andrew said. He looked at me, brow crinkled.

"*Did* you ever get the invite. You didn't . . ."

"I got it."

"You *did*?" I said, which came out louder and squeakier than I'd hoped. "God. We presumed . . . Because we never heard from you –"

"Yeah, yeah I'm sorry about that."

"I mean not even an RSVP? Jane couldn't work out why you didn't get back to us."

"You've never told her about − ?" Andrew shrugged, hauling a wide hand through his waxy public school mop.

"I wasn't sure if that was . . . I mean that was a long time ago."

"A *long* time ago."

"So − ?"

"Work," he shrugged. "We were moving house. The twins," and he sighed. "I'm sorry. I really would have loved to have seen it."

We let that sit there for a moment. I thought I saw something happen behind Andrew's eyes. Regret, was it? I licked my lips, thoughts hanging there like nervous divers.

Andrew moved on, focusing back on the soggy paper in his hand.

"So . . . hold up, you *own* this?"

"Wedding present," I explained. "Well, an heirloom for Edward's grandchild *disguised* as a wedding present I expect. But yes. Presented it on the day. I didn't know where to look. You can't imagine. Jane and I have been snogging out on the lawn . . ."

Andrew looked at me, blinking, all very faked interest.

"Well . . . that's not . . . we were outside. And the MC rings his bell and we're *summoned* in and Jane's dad gets this drum roll from the *sixteen piece band thank-you very much*."

"Bloody nora . . ."

"Everyone hushes up and he presents me with this framed whassit. A certificate of ownership. That and a safety deposit box number at some bank in the city. Big cheer, the band start up the theme. *Dum-da-daaaah, dah-duppity-dahhh*, all that. Jane had given him the idea of course. He'd just written the cheque."

Andrew just stood, looking over at the Sotheby's letter some more.

"He got it from a dealer in Japan I think. Mint condition, or near as," I said, shoving my hands in my pockets. "June, 1938. First appearance. So what do you think? Any better ideas?"

"Does . . . does *Christopher* know you have this?"

"Christopher? No. He never asked, I never said. No reason he'd have a clue."

"Lordy . . ." and Andrew did all but wipe his forehead with a theatrical *phew*. "Well if this valuation is correct −"

"It's correct. Matches the current *Overstreet*, give or take a grand."

"Then, ladies and gentlemen, I think we have ourselves a pot of gold. But are you *sure* about this?" Andrew looked at me sideways on, eyebrows raised in concern. I felt like one of his twins asking to have the stabilisers taken from my bike.

"What? You think he won't go for it?"

"Er, *Superman* number one? Eighty . . . where is it?" and he flipped over the sheet. "Eighty-five *thousand pounds'* worth of comic book? Oh he'll go for it."

"Then we use it. What choice do we have? Like you say, comic books, memorabilia, collectables? That's the one field I *know* I know better than he does."

"But letting it out there, even just as bait. What if . . ."

"What if?"

"I mean he's still the expert," Andrew said. "The swaps and the switcheroos and whatnot. Even letting him *look* at it . . ."

"I can't worry about losing it. I can't. My *family*. Jane. Lana. *That*, I'm not going to lose. Not at any price. Life without them . . . ? With respect to Siegel and Shuster, thirty-six vacuum-sealed, full colour pages of wham-bam cape-pant action aren't going to be much company. Price tag or not. I can't see another way. Dad's right. Pot of gold. It's my only choice and time's running out. We're doing this."

So we did it.

Andrew booted up my laptop and opened up a new email account under a false name while I paced, chewing the inside of my cheek and watching Elvis on the wall backcomb his quiff with the long hand. It was twenty to five. I knew from his black book that Christopher checked eBay for likely marks daily at 5pm and, time being of the essence, every passing day potentially taking Lana's financial future further and further from me, I was keen to get our worm on the hook.

Our phoney seller now born – superfan36@hotmail.com – we scanned in the *Action Comics* photograph Sotheby's had returned to me, downloaded it onto eBay hastily, Andrew typing while I paced, dictating a snappy, no-nonsense, business-like description of this once-in-a-lifetime collectable. To avoid it being snapped up by a genuine buyer, we instructed a three-hour window and added a ludicrous reserve price, thus insuring the comic would stay unbought, on-screen and alluring until 8pm. Hopefully long enough.

Hopefully.

I was just having a final jittery pace, Andrew reading the copy back to me, when we both jumped at the sound of the phone.

"*Heroes Incorporated?*"

"*God, there you are,*" Jane said. "*I've tried you four times.*"

I could hear Lana gurgling in the background.

"Sorry, it's been busy," I said with a throat-clearing, no-honest-really cough. Andrew spun around on the office chair, eyebrows aloft. In my ear, the line went quiet. I knew that quiet.

Jane, it seemed, had decided to fling open a window for apology re: my performance at Thursday's dinner. Last night had offered a small opportunity but between me locking myself in the study to Google *prison visiting hours Selmeade* and Jane consequently locking herself in the bathroom with Lana, I'd missed the window completely.

So I seized the frame and threw myself through it.

"*It's all right,*" she said, interrupting my grovelling. "*I've spoken to Jack and Catherine. They forgive you. I forgive you. Old friends are old friends. So how was Benno after all this time? Still got the big beard and jumper? On shore leave from the SS Activist?*"

"Uhm, not quite, no —"

"*Did he tell you why he didn't come to our wedding?*"

"Er, he's here now as it happens. In the shop." Andrew looked up at me. "He dropped in to see me."

"*You want to invite him over for supper?*"

"Uhm, you sure?" I said, although I wasn't sure why. Niggling thoughts breaking the surface. Andrew's little red notebook of poetry. The three of us then. The three of us now.

"*Why not?*" Jane said. "*You're cooking.*"

"I'll ask him. See you ladies a little later."

"*Love you.*"

I hung up.

"Ask me what?" Andrew said. I extended the offer. "Marvellous," he said, eyes bright. "The old gang," and with a small smile, he spun on the office chair to face the laptop. "Here we go," and he crossed his fingers and jabbed the return key, sending the bait down the line.

We both looked up at the clock. It was four minutes to five.

"That's it," Andrew said. "Nothing to do now but wait."

I nodded, queasily.

"What do we do if he doesn't respond?" I asked, grabbing my keys from the desk.

"I think our big worry old friend is what the hell we're going to do if he *does*."

"Benno? More spaghetti?"

"Huh? N-no, I'm fine old chap," Andrew chomped with a tomatoey chin, mouth full. He waved a fork. "This is grand tuck. A treat. Your skills have improved in the last ten years."

"God *don't*," Jane said, head on one side, smiling. "I can't believe what we used to eat back then. What was your speciality sweetheart?"

"Me? White sliced with marge', wasn't it?" I said.

I scuttled to the kitchen, sliding the large serving bowl onto the cluttered counter top among the spills and onion peel, snapping off the light and returning to the warmth of the lounge. I eased myself to floor level with the others.

"No no, you were always *Bovril* and *Super Noodles*," Andrew was saying with a chuckle. "Often on the same plate. Don't you remember? You bought shelves of the stuff. From Mad Jackie in the *Spar* on Queen Street."

"Christ," I said, my head tumbling through wine-misted recollection, down dusty corridors of forgotten years. "Mad Jackie. How do you *remember* this stuff. We're going back a *decade*."

"Being so far from home," Andrew said. "Makes remembering more . . . I don't know. Important?"

It was getting on for eight o'clock. Tired and smiling, woozy on nostalgia, the three of us were spread, legs out, shoes off, on cushions about the rug in the lounge talking in hushed terrace voices. An 80s *Best Of . . .* CD was playing, succeeding in adding to the reunion atmos'. On shelves and sills, tea-lights cast long dancing figures on the dark walls, light winking on mineral water bottles and smeary wine glasses. Lana slept blissfully throughout in her carry-cot, Jane's left hand set on auto-baby-entertain, bobbing and stroking and wiping and stroking some more, almost of its own accord. In fact, watching it as I scraped a chunk of warm ciabatta about my bowl, I was confident we could have all moved into the kitchen and her hand would have stayed – Addams Family style – amusing Lana beneath her blanket for the rest of the evening.

"New York sounds amazing," Jane gushed. "We should come out and visit. Neil? We should visit?"

"Huh? Yes, yes absolutely."

"Maybe when Dad's accountant has gone through the books next week? We'll see if we can't scrape together a cheap fare, yeah?"

The room went a bit quiet. I could sense Andrew looking at me over his wine glass.

The stereo twiddled Spandau Ballet inappropriately.

"Well . . I guess we'll see," I said. Why hadn't I told her? Why hadn't I told her *everything*? What was I doing? What was I *doing*?

"Well. Old *Benno*," Jane said for the fifteenth time. "Who'd have thought it. I *still* can't get over how much you've changed. You look better without the beard."

Andrew shrugged a manly shrug and smiled a rakish smile. I looked across at Jane who was looking at him. I watched them watch each other, feeling altogether odd about the whole thing. Partly the wine, perhaps. Partly that book of moony romantic poetry I found in Andrew's room at the start of the third year. Partly his New York expense account and his broad manly shoulders.

Partly knowing that somewhere Christopher could be on eBay, bidding on Lana's future.

Mostly the wine though I think.

"I was telling our Neil here," Andrew was saying, "I was sorry I missed the wedding. I bet . . ." and he began to fuss with his bowl, avoiding our look. "I bet you looked beautiful. As always, I mean," and he blushed a little, covering it with a wink at me. "You're a lucky fellow. I always thought –"

"Uhm, y-you having more bread sweetheart?" I said suddenly, getting up with a clatter of bowls and spoons.

"Huh? No, no, not for me," she said.

I moved into the kitchen, stomach tumbling, chewing the inside of my cheek.

What was going on in there? Was Andrew flirting with my wife? Had he spent the last decade thinking about the one that got away? Was all this just —

The cooker clock said *20:04*.

Shit. *eBay*. It would be all over by now. Anything Christopher was going to do, he'd have done.

I splashed a little cold water from the sink onto my face to sober up a bit and, with a deep breath, returned to the lounge making concluding *ah-well* and *right-then* sorts of gestures.

"You trying to break up the party?" Jane said. She looked up at me from her bean bag. Her skin was pale and soft in the candle light, eyes big and shining. Her whole face, her hair, her whole beautiful body reminding me why I loved her so much.

And of course, proportionately, reminding me of what an utter shit I was keeping everything from her.

"Not at all," I fibbed. "It's just, Benno's probably got work, and —"

"C'mon then sweetheart," Jane whispered and slid up, onto her haunches. Andrew and I watched as she gazed lovingly at our baby for a long moment. Leaning forward to kiss the dozing bundle, her violin back bowing, Jane's perfect skin peaked as her shirt rode above her jean tops. She hoisted herself up, lifting the cot.

"Do you want to see the nursery?" Jane asked Andrew. "Not quite your Hamptons summer house I know, but . . ."

"It's getting late maybe?" I said, pulling the plug on the mood quickly. I snapped on the main light, causing everyone to squint and moan.

"Do you not want another drink? There's plenty." Jane said.

"Uhmm . . ." Andrew said, looking at me.

"Er . . ." I countered.

"Maybe a . . . a *coffee*?" Andrew said.

"Yes, yes. Coffee," I said, all too eagerly.

Jane looked at us both.

"Then . . . then I'll show you that thing," I said.

"The thing."

"The *thing*," I said, clearing my throat conspicuously.

"Thing?" Jane said.

"Neil wanted to show me something."

"Right. On the er . . ."

"Computer."

"Web site."

"Right. In fact why don't I put Lana down," I said quickly, lifting the cot from Jane. "And Benno can look at the computer while I get her sorted."

"And I'll do the coffee?" Jane said. She looked a little bewildered by the Abbott & Costello back and forth.

"Great. Perfect. Lovely," I said. I pecked her on the cheek and led Andrew down the hall to the nursery.

"Jane hasn't aged a day," Andrew said as the computer stuttered into life in the study. He pushed the door closed and began to pick through the plush nick-nackery and soft-toy clutter as I gently laid Lana down in her cot. "Not a *day.*"

"God, my heart's going, I tell you," I hushed. Kissing Lana gently on her milky soft skin, I crept whispering to the computer chair and eased myself in, jittery fingers slipping over the keys. I double-clicked and dragged the stubborn mouse from its sticky slumber. "C'mon, c'mon. God, if Edward or Jane had *any* idea what I was doing . . ."

"Seeing her again. It reminds me of the impact she had when she first appeared in halls. How everyone stopped what they were doing, just to stare . . . Long time ago now. And hey, don't worry. Neither Edward nor Jane could trace this to you, even if they happened to see it. Which they won't. So relax."

The homepage tinkled into life.

"What you *do* need to worry about though," and Andrew motioned at the chunky gold on my wrist. "Is that ugly fake monstrosity. Why are you still *wearing* it?"

"I know, I know," I said. I typed in eBay's address and double-clicked *GO* anxiously. "I told Jane it was a freebie from work. I figure if I take it off now, it'll start another conversation about why I'm now *not* wearing it. I figured I'd just let the whole thing . . . ah, here we go," I said, sitting up a bit, nervousness running her long painted fingernail between my shoulder blades. The eBay homepage appeared, winking and flashing in stuttery animation.

"There. Vintage comic books," Andrew whispered, and I felt him scuttle up behind me. I click-drag-double clicked. The page wiped and the blue timer-bar began to fill across the bottom of the screen. 12% . . . 23% . . .

"What if he hasn't seen it?" I said softly, quickly checking that the nursery door was properly closed.

"Every day at five, you said. He'll have seen it."

38% . . . 46% . . .

"He won't. He won't, I just know it. Today will be the one day he won't have checked. He'll be on holiday. Spending my fifty thousand pounds. He'll have taken a year off. A sabbatical. To study pick-pocketing at the Sorbonne."

"He'll have made a bid, don't worry. It's like your father said. Just wait."

78% . . . 86% . . .

"And if he hasn't?" I began to squirm in my cheap office chair, threatening to have it collapse beneath me in a tangle of foam and bolts. "This is *it*. Our *one* idea. If we can't find him with this, then I —"

94% . . . 97%

"He'll be there, he'll be there . . ."

100%

He wasn't there.

My heart sank. Andrew shoved me aside and, rattling off some colourfully well-spoken curses, scrolled hopefully up and down, up and down, but nothing. Not a single bid.

"P'raps we didn't leave enough time," he pondered, biting his lip. "P'raps if we try *again* —"

"That's it. We're done," I sighed, my throat fat and full. "Fifty grand. Lana's whole . . ."

"Wait, wait, wait. Perhaps . . ." Andrew said slowly, hands hovering over the keys, but there was an uneasy desperation in his voice. "Perhaps, er . . ."

"That's it," I said, teeth angry. "That's it," and I reached forward and signed off the internet.

There was a light tap on the door. Jane.

"Coffee's in the lounge."

Andrew and I sat in silence for what felt like an age, illuminated only by the faint glow of the screen. Neither of us wanted to speak because only one thing remained to be said and it didn't need saying.

"It was worth a –"

"No no, absolutely," we both began together awkwardly. "Thanks," I said.

"You never know . . ."

"Right, right," I nodded with a half-hearted shrug, but I knew. Christopher's five o'clock eBay scan was the only thing I could recall from his little black book. A man as elusive as he would find the nano-sized shadowy half-life between winking electrons in space about the only place safe enough to stick his head out.

"Fuck," Andrew spat, shaking his head, his one opportunity for vengeance dashed.

"Coffee?"

"I should go mate," Andrew said. "Pick up a taxi. I've got to be wide awake enough to lose a game of Sunday golf halfway convincingly in the morning."

"O'Shea again?"

"Me, him and the Holborn team are making up an awkward fivesome. But . . . hey we'll talk Monday?"

We moved into the hall where Jane met us. He made his apologies and kissed Jane gently on the cheek, lifting his woollen overcoat from the bulging hall pegs. They swapped must-catch-ups and must-make-plans, leaving me to take in the serenity for a moment – the smell of fresh coffee, the candlelight dancing through the door on the lounge wall, a man and wife, their beautiful daughter dozing contentedly, seeing off an old dear friend after dinner.

I had a small pang, wishing Andrew would stay where he was, making plans, recreating the good old days, to freeze the moment for a little longer. Say, I don't know, the next seventy years or so.

Andrew left.

Mind a million miles away, I followed Jane about the flat for a while as we cleared dishes and blew out candles. She asked about our computer dealings, the details of which I naturally fudged and fumbled with an idle wave.

"Any emails from Dad?" she said, stacking plates in the sink.

"Huh? No, no. You *expecting* something?"

"Just checking he's still on for Tuesday's train."

"Well I'll have another look tomorrow. I've got to . . . *wait*."

"Got to . . . ? *Neil?*"

"Huh?" I'd had a thought. Could it be . . .

"Neil?"

"Uhm, wait. Er, yeah, yeah actually, I'd better do that," I said excitedly, a light feeling growing in my chest, expanding, filling my heart with helium, lifting me like a fairground balloon.

I scurried down the hall quickly.

Maybe, maybe . . .

Door shut behind me, the computer sluggishly woke from its daze and dragged itself to life, ignoring my bouncy urges and clicking fingers. Behind me, in the dark, my daughter slept.

Down the hall, in the bedroom, my wife undressed.

Of *course*? Why didn't I think to check while Andrew was here? I flashed a look at my chunky watch. How long before he was back at his hotel? A cab to the West End? Or wait, his mobile . . .

I crept quickly out of the nursery, down the hall to the coats, flapping through my jacket until I found Andrew's number.

"You all right?" Jane asked, appearing from the bedroom. She was in a big Strontium Dog T-shirt, loose-necked and bare legged. "Is Lana asleep?"

"I'll be in in a second," I said. "I-I mean yes, yes I'm fine. And yes. She's out light like a light. You all right?" but I was back in the study, heart pounding, before Jane could answer.

I closed the door and sat down, opening up the computer. I skidded the mouse about and clicked onto the internet, left hand all fingers and thumbs, putting down the greasy slip of paper with the number on it, and snatching up the telephone extension.

I logged onto Hotmail with one hand, dialling Andrew with the other.

My chest thudded, knee bouncing on the ball of my foot.

"*Hello?*" Andrew crackled.

"Benno, it's me," I said breathlessly. I shoved the phone under my chin and clicked open a link. "What was the email address you gave our phoney seller? I just had a thought."

Andrew spelled out the details.

"And password?" I typed them in hurriedly.

"*What are you thinking?*" he said, his voice thick and muddy inside the cab.

"When you use your email address as your name on eBay," I said, clicking away, mouse skidding and squeaking, "buyers sometimes contact you direct at the end of an unsuccessful auction to see if they can do a deal on the side. I had a couple for my Siegel and Shuster photograph so I thought, if people didn't want to pay top whack, then they might . . . fucking hell."

Inbox. 336 unread items.

"*Neil?*"

"There are . . . Jesus, it seems we've shaken up sleeping geeks all over the place. Hundreds of . . . God, everyone's gone nuts . . ."

I opened a random message. *marvelsux@btyahoo.*

Superfan36 – I saw that no-one bid for your Action Comic. *If you want a quick cash sale, I am willing to offer $500.*

Five hundred? Christ, he was hopeful wasn't he? I clicked another excitedly. *Green.Lantern24@aol.co.uk*

R U genuine?? If so, I want 2 talk. Will pay BIG for this. If fake – how you get?

"*-eil? You there old man?*" Andrew crackled. "*My batt-'s -unning low?*"

"I'm here, I'm here. Christopher has to be one of these, he has to be." My eyes scanned down the sea of senders' addresses, despair elbowing hope aside as I reached the bottom. None of the names were familiar. "God, if he's posing as a geeky collector trying to get my attention with an offer, he's done it too bloody well."

Unoriginal collector's name after unoriginal collector's name scrolled past. Five madbuffyfan@s, four look.whose.tolkien@s, three nerdforwindows@s, both peterparker14@ and peterparker72@ and my particular favourite dickgraysonscodpiece@aol.com.

"I don't know how I'm going to find him . . ."

"*-ou got -em listed alpha . . . ry oing it by –*"

"Hello?" Andrew was breaking up. "Hello?" Nothing. What was he saying? Change the listing? How was that going to help? I looked across the top of the file. A click and they were relisted by title. No good, as they all called themselves *RE: Action Comic.* Another click and they arrived by –

Shit!

"That's it! Benno, that's it!" I yelped as loudly as I dared. Lana stirred behind me with a rustle of cotton and a gurgle. The page had all the enquiries now listed chronologically. I scanned down the times they were sent.

One at 16:58. One at 17:07. Then nothing until 17:44.

I clicked on the 17:07.

From a gregoryfitzgerald@maurandfits.com

Maurandfits?

Gives it that little bit of credibility. Gets one's brogues in the door . . .

Of *course.*

Re: Action Comics #1.

Dear superfan63, here at Maurer & Fitzgerald we have over 45 years' experience in the valuation, insurance and agenting service of a wide range of vintage collectables, from art to autographs, cartoon to costumes. Our web-search service has flagged that you have an item unsold on eBay that we may be able to offer you assistance with. We have worked in the past with the original pieces by among others Stan Lee, Steve Ditko, Bob Kane and Siegel & Shuster and we guarantee a swift and professional valuation, grading, insurance and sales service which will put you in touch with collectors in the Far East and USA . . .

And on it went. Gush gush, fawn fawn, slurpy licky please sir.

There was a link to the Maurer & Fitzgerald website but – oh what a surprise – it was temporarily offline.

"*-eil?*"

"It's all right," I said down the dying line. "Benno, it's all right. He's here. We've got him. I'll call you tomorrow."

"*-eil?*"

"Hello? Andrew?"

He'd gone.

That was fine. News this good could wait until Monday.

I hung up and sat back, heart thumping in the darkness.

"Neil?" Jane called from the bedroom.

"*Be right there,*" I hissed.

Son of a bitch. Gazing at the screen, I felt a fresh, rising venom. Rage, bubbling, building. Somewhere, Christopher was sitting – notebook at his elbow, pocket-watch in his waistcoat, pipe in his gob and my daughter's trust fund in his wallet – thinking he was reeling in another sucker.

I gritted my teeth hard until my gums began to ache.

Another sucker?

Oh not *this* time, buddy.

Not this time.

eighteen

The job of adding conservatories and slapping magnolia about the financial districts of the world was clearly a well-paid one, if the brass and marble of Andrew's London office was anything to go by. And from the rough manner with which Andrew grabbed my elbow and led me stumbling away two days later, it was an image Keatings didn't wish to have tarnished by a nail-bitten man in battered trainers and three-day stubble.

"We'll have to be quick old chap," Andrew said, as the throng of employees hurried past us for ciggies and sarnies. "The golf yesterday paid off."

"O'Shea?"

"Holborn chaps and I spent bloody eighteen holes giving him the schpeil – investment opportunity, developing post-code, all the usual guff. Bugger me if he isn't up there now with the London sales manager going over the plans and plotting his turf. Quick sarnie?"

Hurrying across the beep-beep of taxi traffic, we pushed into a sweaty sandwich shop, bell jingling. The small space was jostled with harried legal secretaries all comparing low fat engagement rings.

"Personally," Andrew went on, "I think it was down to the old fellah's fluky birdie on the fourteenth, but for share options, a Long Island holiday home and a corner office overlooking the park, I'll happily take the credit. So hey, c'mon," his eyes flashed, "what developments with eBay?"

I produced the print-out of Christopher's email from my satchel. Andrew scanned it quickly.

"*Maurer & Fitzgerald*?"

"They're a front. Fake valuations. Just a name on a letterhead to get his foot in the door.

"*Yes ma fren*'?" the burly sandwich maker hollered from behind his counter. Andrew ordered baguettes and teas.

"Jane all right?" Andrew said, wading through the usual mints, matches and lighters before finding his wallet.

"*Daddy* called from Brighton," I said. The usual guilty worms slid about my kidneys.

"Earl whassit?"

"I was in the nursery so I only caught half. Same old thing though. Me not being quite the son-in-law he'd have wished for, does Lana have everything she needs, don't forget to call his damned financial advisors. Dufford, Chandler and whatever."

"*Lebrecht*? Jeepers old man, you're in the big leagues. *Cheers then,*" he nodded to the café owner and, sandwiches bagged, we squeezed back onto the gritty honk of the street, plastic tea lids scalding our fingers. "How long have you got before she calls them?" Andrew said. He tore off a waddy mouthful of bread.

"Jane? Who knows. The whole thing could be out of the fucking bag by now. The *whole thing . . .*" and my mind thudded, spinning and spiralling with confusion and regret.

"Come on then old man," Andrew chewed. "*Focus.* You've worked with these men. What's our next move?"

"Now? Christ. I . . . I guess we've got to make contact. Show him the pot of gold."

"Righty ho, skip," and Andrew rested his cup on the top of a plastic bin, shoved his sandwich under a pinstriped arm and fished his hands-free kit from his suit pocket. "What do I say?"

"God I don't know, I haven't . . ." and I paced a little, popping the top of my tea carefully. "I guess take him . . . take him up on his offer? You have a valuable comic book, he's in insurance and valuation. Suggest you get together to talk."

Andrew began to dial out with his thumb quickly, reading the number from the email.

"Be . . . y'know, be careful though," I said, jittery.

"Hello? Hello Mr Fitzgerald?" Andrew said. He looked up at me.

My palms went cold, breath held tight in my chest. His phone crackled.

"My name is . . ." Andrew suddenly stopped, eyes wide.

Shit. We'd never stopped to give our superfan36 a real name.

"Uhm, sorry. My name is Mr . . . Mayo," he said, catching a

look at the baguette leaking down his suit. "I received an email from you yesterday regarding an item I was auctioning on eBay . . . *Action Comics*, right . . . What *exactly* does your firm do . . . ?"

It was unbearable. I turned and walked away a few steps, chewing the inside of my cheek. Around me, the lunchtime world bustled busily on its way. Newspaper vendors, black cabs, secretaries, all single minded and oblivious, in their own worlds of holiday plans and low-fat meal deals. I lapped at my sweet, watery tea, letting the scalding sip slap some sense into me.

I turned around. Andrew was finishing up it seemed, nodding. It hadn't taken long. He was arranging something.

"Japan? I see . . . Well I suppose . . ." and he waved me over frantically. "Yes, as long as it doesn't put you to any . . . No no, that's splendid. Six o'clock. Excellent, see you then," and he thumbed the line closed.

"Six o'clock?" I skittered.

"My word," Andrew said with a sigh, popping out the earpiece. "He can talk can't he? *Indeedy dumplings*? What the bloody hell's that?"

"That's him," I said. "What's six o'clock?"

"An early dinner," and Andrew tugged out his red spiral notebook, jotting the details. "Our Mr Fitzgerald is apparently flying out to Japan to see a big client of his tonight. A Mr Cheng?"

"*Cheng*?" I spat. "Slimy . . ."

"But he's eager to see me before he goes. Very excited about my item he is, *very* excited. Suggests I meet him at their offices on Aldersgate."

"Right. Except he doesn't *have* offices. It's just a front. To make it sound above board. Y'know, *swing by the office old chap*. Put you at your ease."

"And when I arrive . . . ?"

"He won't let you. My guess is that he'll call you back at the last minute and say it's being painted or fumigated or some such and suggest elsewhere."

"Well either way, that's what he said. Six pm, Aldersgate, with the item in question."

"With – ? No. Ohhh, no no no."

"He wants to take a look at its condition."

"No. No way," I said. "You tell him it's locked away. Vacuum-sealed. I'm not letting it out in the open. I'm certainly not letting him spill soup all over it in some restaurant."

"But Neil, this is the pot of gold. This is the *bait*. The hook, the lure. How else is it going to work?"

Fear writhed and wormed, eating away at my insides. The world was slipping. I was losing grip. The weight taking me over the edge.

Andrew was talking.

"What?" I said, moving from foot to foot with a jitter.

"I said it's only going to work as a trap my old stick, if he thinks he can get his hands on it. And calm down. *Look* at you. It's simple. We wave it under his nose this evening, all innocent, get him drooling —"

"Drool — ? He's not drooling on it. You keep it in the dark, wrapped, sealed in its airtight case the whole time. Christ, and check the lighting. I can't have it exposed to —"

"It'll only be for a second. Relax. Just enough to let him get the old whiff," Andrew said. He checked his watch. "I better be getting back. O'Shea will be climbing the walls. Can you get it by six? Where is it kept? *Neil?*"

"Christ," I sighed, knees loose, tasting bitter nausea and nerves in my mouth. I pictured the fragile, crumbling pages on a table-cloth. Being slid towards Christopher's delicate fingers, his cufflinks twinkling.

I didn't like this.

I didn't like this at all.

An hour later I came to realise that whichever firm of nineteenth-century architects had been behind Andrew's offices in St Paul's, they'd clearly only actually got a surly work-experience girl to doodle something half-heartedly on the back of an envelope while leafing through the latest Dickens. The real drawing-board big-wigs were clearly busy upstairs sharpening their T-Squares and letting loose with polished marble and white stone, working on the blueprints for No. 3 Ravensgate, a grand building in the heart of the financial district. Inside, among the high ceilings, a home was made for hushed staff, leather blotters and fat Mont Blanc fountain pens that didn't need chaining to the counters as it took about three large men to lift the lids off the fucking things.

I sat squirming in a fat, farty Hyde Wing chair in the quiet lobby while the girl on the front desk took my ID and fetched someone who could look after me. My trainers squeaked and echoed loudly, causing aged bankers to peer over their pince-nez at me from time to time. I offered back a small wave limply and tried to stop sweating.

Andrew had scurried back to his office, ramming a baguette into his face, pinstripes flapping in the wind while I'd descended down to the tube to catch the Central Line a few stops east. I had three hours in which to pick up the comic book and get back to Andrew's office for a rehearsal before we headed over to Aldersgate. Plenty of time, as long as I didn't stop to chat. Not that there was any danger of meeting anyone I −"

"Mr *Martin*? It is isn't it? Good lord."

Some polished brogues appeared in my sightline. I looked up, passing the regulation navy pinstripes, pink shirt and old school tie. Above two or three portly chins, a round, ruddy, forty-year-old face greeted me under a thinning bouffant of greying hair.

"Er, yes?" I said.

"Greg Dufford," he boomed, holding out a pink, pudgy hand for pumping. I duly pumped it, standing up slowly. "Thought it was you, and there it is. Recognised you from your photograph. You and Jane are up in Ted's study. Well, look at that."

"Hi," I said. "So you're . . . sorry?"

"Dufford. *Chandler Dufford Lebrecht*. We look after Ted's assets. Offices just round the corner. Funnily enough, I spoke to Ted this morning," and he began to flap in his jacket pocket. "He spoke to your wife and called me to put something in the diary . . ."

Shit.

"Ted was keen to get us all together last week, have a look at your finances, but . . . Here we go." Greg had a slim pocket diary open, busy with times and names in a flourishy blue-black hand. "How's tonight? I'm pretty crammed but your wife said you'd be free in the evening? Around seven? Just to go over a few things. It's the business books I understand? And the trust for your daughter?"

"Tonight? Uhmm . . ."

"Ted's back from the coast tomorrow of course and between you and me I think he was hoping we'd have sorted you out by then." He flipped his diary pages back and forth.

"Well, I-I mean if you wanted to wait until next week?" I said. "Rather than putting you out . . . ?"

"*Ha. Shilly-shallying m'boy?*" Greg boomed in a passable Edward impersonation. "Best not. No, it's fine," and he slapped his dairy closed, tucking it away. "Tonight at seven. I'll tell Ted it's all sorted. I know what he's like. Anyway, I should shoot off." He shook my clammy hand gruffly once again. "What brings you here anyway?"

"Mr Martin?" A young woman in a short suit and glasses appeared at Greg's elbow, handing me back my identification. "Do excuse me. That's all fine. If you'd like to follow me downstairs?"

"Down – ?" Greg said. "Of course! The old wedding gift eh? Having the annual gander? We put Ted in touch with this place for security. *Top drawer* facilities they've got down there. A lot of the big West End galleries use them. Air tight, moisture control, all the biz. Anyway, I'll get out of your way. Until tonight then."

Greg pumped my hand heartily for the third time because he seemed to be that sort of fellow and then he left. I followed the bank clerk across the spacious hall towards the lifts, rubbing some feeling back into my knuckles and calculating the amount of hours I had before my life fell apart.

As clearly wrong as Greg was about shoulder and knuckle maintenance however, he was certainly spot on about the basement facilities.

Popular thinking goes that the primary reason for the escalating value of your *Supermans* and *Batmans* and *suchlike-mans* is the fact that they are – or at least used to be – designed to be disposable. Read once and thrown away. Low-quality ink, cheap paper, flimsy staples, if a grubby fingered urchin back in the thirties could get all the way through the wham-bam story without it falling to pieces, its job was done. They were never meant to last, which is why the ones that *have* are worth the *immoral* sums they are.

A solid enough theory I suppose. But it leads one inevitably, (if one has too much time on one's hands in the afternoon and nothing else to occupy one's mind while one scoops sopping mulch into the tenth leaking bin-bag of the day) to wonder why then aging dishcloths and toilet paper aren't similarly priced. They too are old, mass produced and not built to last.

The *Martin Theory*, named after some handsome comic-collector, is this: comic books are what the aging, white, middle-class multi-millionaires of today grew up on and their collectablity is purely to do with their desire to recapture their youth. If women made up the majority of millionaires, high streets would be full of *Retro-Doll-Marts* and *Rare-Bear-Ariums*.

This is neither there nor here of course. For whatever reason, vintage comic books in pristine condition are big bucks and keeping them that way is a complex and expensive business.

The bank clerk silently led me through a number of double doors and down in an oak-panelled lift. She was silent, I mean. I was whittering on like an idiot, trying too hard to appear relaxed and calm. The doors opened with a soft ding and I was taken down a long, chilly corridor to a basement room. The bank clerk keyed a number into a bleepy entry pad and pushed the heavy doors open with a suck and a hiss of escaping air.

The room was half-lit and hummed with chilly air-conditioning, thermometers and dials running along the wall. We moved quietly, the clerk's heels clicking, her skirt rustling with static. The body of the room was made up of wide open metal shelving, holding heavy picture frames, canvases, boards and portfolios, all wrapped in soft pale sheeting and tagged with labels of ownership. My business, however, was along the furthest side of the room where a couple of hundred cold, dull deposit boxes ran wall to wall.

The clerk handed me a small key and showed me to my box, tugging out a flat sliding tray from beneath the metal door where I could rest the contents. Clammy handed, heart thumping, I slipped in the key, turned it twice and slid out the metal box with a teeth-edging scrape, resting it upon the tray. Opening the lid, I reached in and pulled out an A4-sized black velvet wallet, throwing a quick look above me at the soft humming bulbs.

"It's all right," the clerk said, clearly noting my hesitation.

"Sorry," I said. "It's just . . ."

"Light is our clients' number one concern. Along with air quality of course. The whole room is UV free. Plus you're in a Mylar container there," she said, pointing to the tag on the key. "US National Archives and the Library of Congress use the same system. Mr Spencer was very anxious his investment was protected."

His investment? Figured.

I hurriedly slipped the velvet pouch into the protective darkness of my satchel, feeling the cold solid sealed plastic box through the fabric and handed her back the key.

"That it sir?" she said.

I nodded quickly, heart in my throat.

"I'll need your signature on the release slip. Will you want the box kept here for you?" she asked.

"Yes yes. God, it'll only be away for a few hours I hope."

"Letting an expert take a look?" she smiled.

"Uhm, of sorts," I said.

My phone was deedly-deeting as I emerged back, squinting, on the chilly street.

"*He's -anged the venue,*" Andrew crackled. "*Must be as you said. Throwing -e a dummy to -ake it sound convin –*" The line was breaking up. "*Says he's -ot to get an earlier fligh –. Wants to meet at the restau . . . four.*"

"Four? Meet at *four*? Shit. Where? Which restaurant . . . ? Benno? Hello?"

"*-ello? Oh bloody h –*"

The line fizzed and crackled and died like a damp, pay-as-you-go firework.

I stood, trainers sticky on the pavement, glued by panic and indecision. An hour. Around me, city boys jostled and barged with huge weekend-rugby shoulders. I clutched the satchel hard to my chest.

Think. Think Neil, *think*.

I shut my eyes, buffeted and elbowed by the sea of Hackett elbows and Loake's brogues. Where would Christopher take him?

Somewhere fancy. Somewhere fitting a high-rolling city insurer. *Claridge's* again? No. Not after the jiffy bag and kitten sting. He wouldn't be going back there again. Then where? Somewhere else in his little black note – ?

Wait.

The world lurched forward suddenly. I opened my eyes, the winter sun low and bright.

Wait.

Twirling and spinning, horizon tipping, I stumbled around, eyes scanning the street. Sandwich bars, travel agents, key-cutters, *there*!

Satchel tight, digging into my ribs, I darted across Ravensgate to the blare of taxi horns into a small WHSmith. The shop was humming. Suited men buying *Evening Standard*s, women choosing monthly glossies. I scanned the signage like a lunatic until I stumbled breathlessly past newspapers and greetings cards into the travel guides section. I dumped my satchel to the floor and craned my neck, eyes peeling over the shelves until – a-ha. I took the fattest, most comprehensive London restaurant guide from the shelf and flicked towards the index where the eateries were listed alphabetically.

C'mon, *c'mon* . . .

That afternoon at *Claridge's*. Sat at the table. He'd flipped to the back of his notebook where a list of some sort had been written in his neat blue hand. *The Clarendon I've done*, he'd said and crossed it out.

How else would you do it? If you conned a free dinner out of a different London restaurant every day, what simpler way than this to make sure you didn't accidentally dine at the same place twice?

I scanned down the guide, closing my ankles tight about my bag on the floor. *Clannaught* in Mayfair. *Clarendon* on St James. *Claridge's*, Hanover Square. That had been last Friday. So, Saturday, Sunday, Monday . . .

I began to count down the list. Ten days since then. Ten entries down.

Page 96. I thumbed back quickly. A short entry. Ultra modern, stripped wood, low lighting, international cuisine. Starters from £12.

That could be the one. *Should* be the one.

God *please* let that be the one.

I shoved the book back on the shelf and grabbed up my bag, hurrying from the shop and waving for a cab.

"Soho mate," I said, hauling myself in and falling all over the vinyl.

I slammed the door and with a wide lurch, we were off.

It was creeping up on three twenty-five when my phone began deedly-deeting again. Fumbling fingers, I eased it carefully from the satchel and thumbed it open.

"*It's me,*" Andrew said. The line was clearer. "*My cell's playing silly-buggers. I'm calling from my desk so I've got to be quick. O'Shea's calling a meeting this afternoon at the Holborn site for something or other but I've told him it's an emergency. Did you manage to get you know what?*"

"Right here," I said, running my hands over the hard square shape in my bag.

"*Great. But we've got a problem. The bloody restaurant he's picked is all the way over in Soho.*"

"Lexington Street?"

"*What? Yes.*"

"*The Crib*? Two stars. Terrace at rear?"

"*Jesus, how did you − ?*"

"Lucky guess. I'm halfway there. What's the plan? Outside in fifteen minutes?"

"*You're on. Find a doorway or a phone-box opposite side. I'll see you there.*"

Andrew's cab finally pulled up at ten to four, just as I was re-reading the phone-box's hypnotic, soft porn interior décor for the thirtieth time in an attempt to keep my reeling mind steady.

Breathe *in* . . . eighteen-year-old pre-op transsexual new to area wants discipline . . . and *out*.

"All right?" I said as he heaved open the door to join me, his cab pulling away in a cough of London dust. He clambered in and shuffled up a bit, the heavy door swinging shut slowly.

We breathed warm breaths intimately, our chests pressed together, elbows banging on the glass.

"Fine fine. What time you got? Ten to? Okay." He was as nervous as me but trying harder not to show it. Through the greasy glass panes we had a view of the restaurant opposite. *The Crib* was a large modern place with a brushed chrome and oak façade, its lettering in a squat, lower-case orange that had been cutting-edge for about an hour and a half two years ago. Through its smoked glass we could see stocky gay men laying out linen, horsey blonde waitresses three-day eventing between them.

"Right then," Andrew said, composing himself with a puff and a cough. "Christopher said on the phone he was bringing someone from valuation with him. Any clue as to who that'll be?"

"God," I said, and if there had been room to shrug I would have done. "If he's working with the same team, then it's most likely to be Henry – Australian guy, youngish. Or maybe Pete. Black guy, tall. They seem the tightest with him."

"Righto. I gave the restaurant a bell on the way here to see if I could get you a table for one, but –"

"Me?!" I jumped, banging my arm on the phone painfully. "Ow. *Me*? I can't be seen in there. Are you out of your *mind*?"

"I just thought it would be helpful, y'know? Have you listen in. Round a corner or something. But the maître d' says it's all pretty open plan. We'll have to come up with something else. I thought this might work," and Andrew banged his elbows a bit, tugging out the usual breath mints, matches and a Zippo, laying them on top of the phone before fishing out his phone.

"Do you carry this shit with you everywhere? You don't even smoke."

"True. O'Shea does though. Corny I know, but it never hurts to light a man's cigar."

Unravelling his hands-free cable, he stuffed the tiny earpiece into his inside pocket, letting the wire and mouthpiece dangle just inside the jacket. He slipped the phone into his trouser pocket and let his jacket fall closed, hiding the wires.

"There. An instant bugging device. If you call me on *your* phone, you should be able to hear everything we say at the table."

"You sure your phone's reliable?"

"Hmn. Could be right there old man. Let's try yours," and we swapped them over. Andrew pointed at the phone-box receiver. "You can call from here if mine's clunky. Try it."

I lifted the receiver and shoved my credit card into the slot, dialling my phone. Andrew thumbed open the line and slipped the glowing handset into his jacket. He cleared his throat.

"*Ahem. I'll have the prawn cocktail cocktail, the chicken kievs kievs followed by the black forest gateaux gateaux,*" he said, his voice echoing a second later in my ear. "How's that that?"

"Loud and clear."

"Then that's it. You have the bait?"

I took a deep breath, swallowed twice and handed him my satchel.

"Is it all right in here? Nothing I need to know? Don't get it wet, don't feed it after midnight, anything like that?"

"It's in a velvet pouch and sealed in an Impregnated Mylar-S Sleeve with an Oxy-Sorb inside," I said. "You don't let him take it out of the pouch unless he's wearing gloves and you keep it out of direct light."

Andrew nodded, pushing open the heavy door. The street was quiet. Just the distant sigh of traffic.

"It'll be all right," he said. "We're just going to see what he says. We'll be on the coffee before you know it and you'll have it back in the bank." He waggled his lapel. "Don't forget I'm on Radio Con FM."

He let the door swing shut and checking the street, jogged across to the restaurant whispering into his lapel.

I placed the phone to my ear, stomach rolling, seasick with nerves.

"*Receiving me? Niner niner ten-four come back?*" Andrew crackled. "*Here we go.*"

Crouching down in the little booth, I watched him through the tiny panes as he entered the restaurant. He approached a lectern where a tall blond man waited with a book.

"*Good afternoon. I'm meeting a Mr Fitzgerald here at four o'clock?*" he crackled in my ear.

Andrew's shape was lost among the reflections in the window, just as a large black reflection peeled up to the kerb.

I swallowed hard at the sound of slamming doors and familiar voices, my hands cold around the receiver. I found myself stumbling back, further from the scratched glass, trying to lose myself amongst the Blu-tacked calling cards. Oh to be a fluorescent eighteen-year-old pre-op transsexual, new to area and needing discipline, I thought.

Two figures emerged from the cab.

Christopher. In a sombre suit, the silver attaché case in his hand, pipe in his mouth, shoulders back. Ready for business.

I could feel my teeth grind. My lip curl.

Hot, purple hate raged up inside me.

I wanted to shout. Bang on the glass. Yell, scream, tear at him like an animal.

Trembling, I watched.

Behind him, his valuation expert climbed out of the cab and paid the cab driver.

She then adjusted her stockings, undid a button on her blouse, and followed him in.

nineteen

"*Then, dearie boy, I think we might just have ourselves a deal-ette. Cheers.*"

"*Ch-cheers.*"

"*And . . . mmnm, and how does your wife feel about the possibility of a sale, Mr Mayo?*"

"*I-I'm not married. And please, call me An . . . g-gus. Angus.*"

"*Angus?*"

"*(cough) Right. (clatter) Oops S-sorry, was that your − ?*"

"*It's fine. Really. I quite enjoyed it.*"

I jammed my finger knuckle-deep into my ear and pressed my head against the receiver hard, breath fogging the scratchy glass.

They were on their main courses as far as I could tell. That is to say, I'd heard them all make the same yummy noises, the same two asparagusy chomps and the same unsatisfied sighs as they'd then all pushed their plates away a second later. Introductions had been brief, Christopher ladling on the *righty-hoes* and *indeedy-dooberies* in his usual flowery manner and they'd got down to business immediately. Andrew had brought out the Mylar sleeve to a round of gasps and a *well-bless-my-gracious,* the rest of the wine and starters being been taken up by Christopher's well-rehearsed whittering − scarcity, market value, auctions − all text-book stuff and all lifted verbatim from me and what sounded like half an episode of the *Antiques Roadshow*.

In fact, standing there in the callbox, my only real concern was Laura. Or Margaret. Or whatever the hell she was calling herself.

"*And you were saying, you're not married?*"

"*Huh? No, no, I'm −*"

"*Free and single?*"

"*Well (cough) uhmm, is that your (yelp thud giggle).*"

God, what the hell was she *doing* to the poor man?

This *free and single* line was just the latest in a meal-full of giggles, come-ons, chat-ups and breathy adolescent flirting. From the moment they'd sat down in fact, Christopher had had to crowbar his valuation and insurance waffle between Laura's coquettish compliments and tarty teasing. All *gorgeous tie, Mr Mayo. Can I feel?* and *oooh, it's warm in here.* All these accompanied by sporadic whimpers, yelps and bangs of cutlery, leading me to only imagine at what was going on under the table.

Now you need to understand, it's not that Andrew's a bad-looking bloke. He isn't. At college at least, the Byronic beard, fisherman's jumpers and brooding concern for wildlife, all wrapped up in broad shoulders and Nordic, eco-warrior jawline was quite the catnip to the hall full of moony first years.

But Laura's flirty temptress act? This was out of *all* proportion. Now clearly she was just role-playing her usual part in Christopher's elaborate set-up. The same part she'd performed for me. But as I listened intently within the stuffy callbox, face screwed up, straining for every murmur, I could tell something wasn't right. Her tone, her manner. It was different from before. Dangerous. *Urgent*, even. The pouty coffee-shop girl had been replaced by a more obvious bored-business-woman-looking-for-a-quick-hotel-room-and-a-good-hard –

Deedle-ee-deet deedle-ee-deet deedle-ee-deet dee.

Shit. Shit shit shit.

Deedle-ee-deet deedle-ee-deet deedle-ee-deet dee.

Dropping the handset with a loud plastic crack, I fumbled in my jacket, Andrew's clunky mobile phone trilling out again. O'Shea's name flashed in the display.

Christ.

Deedle-ee-deet deedle-ee-deet deedle-ee-deet dee.

Panicky and cursing, I swallowed hard and thumbed open the line.

Deedle-ee-deet dee –

"H-hello?"

"*– enjamin? That you?*" the line crackled. *Where da – ell are ye?*"

"Er, I'm sorry," I whispered. "Andrew's a bit tied up . . ."

"*Eh? What? Speak up, I -anny hear a ting there. Benjami – ?*"

"Can I give him a message? He's just away from the phone."

"*-essage? Jeezus, you can tell -at greedy eejit that I didn't just -ome*

over on the la . . . erry. Who does he th- . . . dealing with? -ello? I -ant
to see his f- . . . xplain wh- ello? -y half past fi- . . . -ello?"

The line went dead.

Shit.

I thought about Andrew. His share options. His Long Island
holiday home. A corner office overlooking the park.

Biting my lip hard, I retrieved the swinging handset and pressed
it to my ear. It had gone eerily quiet. Oh God. Oh God, had they
heard the ring? Was the game all –

"*Neil?*" a voice hissed down the line. "*Neil? Where are you?*"

"I'm here, I'm here," I jittered. "O'Shea just called. Where are
you – ?"

"*Gents. It's all . . . Just get over here. Get over here now.*"

A moment later I was shuffling in a half crouch, past the brushed
chrome and pale wood, under pin-pricks of halogens, down a short
echoey corridor. Thudding through the door, I fell into the polished
glare of the bathroom.

"Thank God. You all right?" Andrew said quickly. He was at
the wide basins in his shirt sleeves, running a tap noisily. My satchel
leaned up against the wall. He scuttled forward and pulled me
further in with soggy hands.

"You okay?"

"Bloody hell. I'm not cut out for this," and he paced, puffing,
breathing deep.

"What's he . . . I-I mean, have you figured out what his game
is?"

"I've no bloody idea," Andrew said, splashing water on his face,
moving dripping to the blow-dryer. "He's got my signature on
some form."

"Signature – ?"

"Got me to sign with a fountain pen. A *validation*. Saying I've heard
his opinion and am aware of the potential value and so on. Paperwork.
Just covering their backs, nothing more. But Lordy, this *Linda*?"

"Linda?"

"It's what she's calling herself. Linda something. Phew-ee, I see
what you mean old stick. She's all *over* me. Shoes off under the
table, toes in my groin, I don't know where to look."

"All part of the plan, y'think?"

"Possible."

"Only *possible*? You think she *genuinely* . . . ?"

"I don't *know*, do I? All I know is, Christopher's trying to butter me up, lure me in, get me all excited. But all the while the woman's got her shoes off and her toes halfway up my trouser leg. I'm just saying, if they wanted me to concentrate on his *pitch*, she'd be better leaving her toes where they . . . wait," and he stopped suddenly. "Wait, you say O'Shea called? Hell's bells, what did he say?"

I explained the garbled message. Something about not coming over on the last ferry? Who you think you are dealing with? Greedy eejits?

"Bloody hell," Andrew said, spinning and snarling. "He doesn't . . . Shit." He flashed a look at his watch. "They're going to be wondering where I am. There's a meeting at five. Can you . . ." he paced, panicky. "Look, here," and he tugged a fat wedge of folded paperwork from his hip pocket and a couple of twenty pound notes. "Here. This is where O'Shea is. Take this, get a cab back to my office. I'll get someone there to put the paperwork at reception," and he snatched the phone from his inside pocket.

"Wait wait wait. Paperwork? Leave you here?" I checked my watch. "Isn't there some other *wh-EYY!*" I yelped, suddenly stumbling backwards, Andrew shoving me hard in the chest. I slammed into a toilet cubicle loudly, arms flailing, bumping the backs of my knees against the lavatory and found myself suddenly sitting on the loo. Andrew, eyes wide and panicked, put his finger to his lips quickly and swung the door shut.

I sat, dizzy, blinking and bewildered in the small cubicle, rubbing my bruised chest when I got the faint whiff of pipe tobacco and heard what Andrew had obviously heard already.

"Bah! *Here* you are old fruit 'n' nut."

"H-Here I am," Andrew squeaked. Taps were running again. "Just finishing up. Sorry to keep you . . ."

"Not at all dear fellow, not at all," Christopher warbled. "Need a quick pinch-off myself." I heard his brogues clicking across the tiled floor, a shadow passing in the two-inch gap under the door. I held my breath, hands out against the thin wooden walls, heartbeat hammering in my ears. "Heady numbers taken you by surprise I bet, hmmn?"

"No no. I-I mean yes. Yes. I had no idea it was so . . . I mean, like I said, it was my father's . . ."

"Well. It's a mint condition Golden Ager, you see. 1938 to 45. Perennial." I shut my eyes at the sound of a belt buckle, of zip, a pause, and then that familiar masculine sigh as he took a seat in the cubicle next door. "Like anything else, there's an element of fashion to the market," he went on, voice echoey. "If an artist dies it's helpful. Or a fiftieth anniversary," and on he went. "Anyhoo, if all's *Con Brio*?" Christopher said standing, zipping up. "I've ordered coffee." He flushed loudly and moved back out into the bathroom.

"Be one second," Andrew said.

I held my breath as brogues clicked, a tap skooshed and the door swung closed with a clunk.

Oh this wasn't good.

This wasn't good at all.

"He's playing you," I said, pushing out into the bathroom. Andrew was drying his hands. "It's started. Whatever he's doing, it's started. We need to be careful."

"You sure?"

I motioned at the cubicle.

"A pinch off? He didn't make a sound. Not a parp, not a strain, not a plop. In fact . . . " and I slid into his booth. "Look." The lid was down and the loo roll was still folded neatly into a virginal point. "He only came in here to check you were alone. Make sure you weren't calling the cops or changing your tape player. He's up to something. We just don't know what."

"Then I had better find out. You've have that address?"

I waved the paper at him.

"I'll call the office. You pick up the artist's impression from reception and take it over to Holborn. See you back here in an hour."

I nodded and, taking a last longing look at my satchel, crept out of the bathroom.

"Thank you," I said to the maître d' quickly as I slunk past, but nobody paid me any attention. Not him, not the man at his lectern.

An Australian man dressed in a navy suit holding a battered burgundy briefcase.

A familiar man. Very familiar. As familiar, in fact, as his driver.

Sat at the kerb in a shiny Mercedes, smoking a foul cigarette, peaked cap pulled down, hiding his eyes. And, if I wasn't mistaken, an unruly thatch of thick brown hair.

A speedy cab had me climbing Andrew's office steps near St Paul's fifteen squirm-filled minutes later. The security guard gave my attire an inquiring "Awright sir?" which I batted back with a small smile and a purposeful stride, pushing through the glass into the busy lobby where dozens of suited men and women milled about in front of the desk, heels clicking, phones trilling. The envelope was just where Andrew had said it would be so I was back on the street and into the cab, turning a wide circle back towards Holborn moments later, resuming my journey and picking up my paranoia just where I'd left it.

What were Henry and Julio's roles in all this? Where was this going? My mind had played it over and over again, trying every possible permutation of cross, double-cross and triple double-cross with extra cheese. Was Henry about to join their restaurant table? A mysterious Aussie stranger with a case full of money?

A sickening thought arrived in the back of the cab with me. I didn't want to budge up to give it room but it didn't seem to care as it plonked itself on my lap with a horrid grin.

Was Henry swinging by their table at that very moment? Playing the greedy buyer? Would Henry top Christopher's valuation? Offer quick cash?

No. No, it couldn't . . . Andrew . . . He wouldn't. He'd see though that. He'd . . . Christ.

"This it mate? Hoi, mate?"

The cabbie's voice stretched out to me like a lifeline, hauling me from the thick quicksand of worry. I looked up. He'd pulled up at a wide kerb, huge building boards circling the block, the world shaking with pneumatic drills, shouts and clangs, a film of pink brick dust on the air.

I piled out, the cab's motor idling, looking up and down the street quickly.

"Hey! Hey fellah!" O'Shea's voice rang out over the industrial din. He was positioned by a doorway to the site, a fluorescent yellow waistcoat over his fat suit, a dusty hard-hat perched high on his head. "Hey! You lookin' for me, boy?"

I scuttled over, handing him the envelope.

"Sorry!" I hollered over the steel chatter of drills. "Andrew got caught up. Said this was what you wanted. Sends his apologies."

O'Shea's dusty fat fingers scrabbled the lip open.

"Jesus has dat boy gat himself some cheek, that he has." He shook his podgy face, tutting, a curled lip releasing whisky breath and yellow snaily teeth. "I'm not some fetlock-tuggin' farmhand, y'hear me? What does he think? Oim' some charity is it? Some charity? Help The Eejit?"

"I . . ."

"Only 'ting worse than that boy's manners is his golf-swing."

"I . . . Sorry, Mr O'Shea, I have to be getting going . . ."

I was backing away. Try as I might, I couldn't help but picture Andrew sliding a velvet sleeve across a dining table, Laura's toes in his groin, his mind in her cleavage, Henry swapping cases surreptitiously behind his back.

"T'inks missin' a hole or two'll warm me to him does he?" O'Shea stuffed the contents of the envelope back in roughly. "While he pulls a stunt like this? You can tell 'im oi ain't impressed. Tell 'im that from me. Oi ain't impressed at'all, y'hear? Hey, y'hear?"

It was creeping up on five-thirty, as the cab crept up on Soho.

God. Please. *Please* let it be all right. Fear bunched tight like wet rope in my throat, short shallow breaths pumping. Let Andrew be paying attention. Let him . . . Let him talk his way out of it. Feign another appointment, make his excuses. Up and leave. Not suspicious, not shifty. Just . . . just God, let him leave. Get clear. Get safe. Please God.

The cab wheeled round onto Wardour Street. We were a minute away.

Or let them have gone. God yes. Left him to finish his coffee. Let this have been stage one. The long con. Stage one of ten. Just laying the groundwork.

We turned onto Lexington Street.

"Here is it?" the cabbie said, slowing.

"*No!*" I yelped, sliding towards the scratchy partition. "Sorry, can you . . . can you just drive past slowly, I . . . Just, I need to see if someone's . . ."

"You're the boss," he said, and the cab continued its crawl, *The Crib* sliding towards us slowly. Hunched down, I peered out through the side window as we passed the restaurant.

Their table was empty.

Empty.

"All right?" the cabbie said.

"Shit," I murmured. "Shit, no." The cab interior began to swim.

Andrew.

Andrew couldn't have . . .

No. No, don't be . . .

"Stop. Please, stop," a voice said, my voice said, distant, miles away. "Stop the cab."

The cab didn't stop. The cab began to pick up speed.

"*Stop the cab*," I said loudly. Please . . . please no.

"I've gotta turn 'round 'ere. 'Old on . . ."

"*STOP!*" I screamed, slamming my hand against the partition hard. The cab lurched and I slipped from the seat, dizzy, heart pounding. My hands skittered about the latch.

"Oi, easy there −"

The lock caught, the door swinging wide, cold air and traffic loud in my face as I fell forwards onto the crunchy street.

No. No he couldn't.

I slammed down the street, hands shaking, throat burning, mind mad mad mad with fear, crossing side streets with bounding steps until I skidded up to the oak and chrome front.

Pressing myself against the glass, eyes pulled back wide, I scanned the table. Scanned all the tables until I was sure.

They'd gone. Christopher, Laura, Henry, Andrew and my comic book.

They'd all gone.

twenty

"You bastard. You complete . . . Well bastard about covers it."

"You got my note then. Come in, come in."

In was a W1 hotel room and a pretty damned swanky one at that. Fat furniture, fat lamps and a fat sprawling bed, the whole room looked like it had enjoyed something of a Christmas blowout and then posed itself in front of a funhouse mirror.

The *bastard* was Andrew.

"Yes I got your note," I said, sliding in jumpily. It had been something of an anxious journey over. "The blond fellow, the maître d'? He came out and handed it to me on a silver dish. But not until he'd watched me whirl about in a panic on the pavement for five minutes. Christ, I thought you'd . . . I don't know *what* I thought."

"You get to Holborn all right? See O'Shea? Sorry about sending you off like that. S'just I promised him the artist's impression and he —"

"It's fine, fine. Christ, I gotta sit down . . ." I wandered about the huge room, among side tables and regency armchairs, trying to get my breathing back in order, finally sinking into the folds of the fat couch.

"I had to leave. Christopher, Laura, *everyone*. They were all heading out, I couldn't just sit there."

"It's all right," I said, dragging my hands over my tired face. "What happened? I saw Henry arrive and Julio in the car waiting for him. Did they come over to the table?"

Andrew cracked a couple of mini-bar Cokes, perched on the end of the bed and began to explain how the coffee course had panned out. He said something about Laura. Something about Henry. And he might have added something about after dinner mints too, but to tell you the truth, my mind found itself suddenly elsewhere.

Andrew knowing me as he did however, didn't take long to notice.

"It's in the bathroom," he said.

"Hn? What, sorry?" I blinked.

"What you've been sitting there looking about the room for? It's safe. I hid it in the bathroom."

"I wasn't . . ." The game was up. "Sorry, I . . ."

"Go, take a look," he said.

I sat on the couch for an awkward moment, wanting to tell him not to be silly. That if that's where he'd put it, then that's where it was. Hell, I didn't need to check. I trusted him. Weren't we in this together? God, if I couldn't trust Benno, a friend from a decade back, a guy I'd virtually lived in the pocket of for three whole years then what the hell was going on?

Like I said. What I *wanted* to tell him.

But *sorry* is what I said and, hauling myself out of the squashy couch, I scuttled through into the echoey en suite where I found my satchel, wrapped in a robe, under a pile of towels.

"*I don't blame you old man,*" Andrew called through, his voice sad and tired. "*Really. I don't.*"

And I knew he didn't. Because Andrew understood. He understood what men like Christopher did to you. What they'd done to *him* all those years ago. The way they spoiled you. Ruined you. Left you to a life of double-checking your change, double-checking your friends.

I brought the satchel out into the lounge area and busied myself with the clips and clasps, sliding out the firm velvet pouch carefully and peering into its darkness. *Action Comics*. June 1936. The thin, crinkled paper was faded, the bold red ink washed salmony by a lifetime of All-American sunshine. Around the rusty staples, the paper furred and pulled, the corners dog-eared and thumbed behind its plastic Mylar sleeve. All present and correct. I allowed myself a relieved sigh.

"Bastard thought all his Christmases had come at once," Andrew said. "You should have seen him pawing at it, trying to be all blasé? But I swear his eyes were spinning round like a one-armed-bloody-bandit. Ding ding ding! Jackpot."

"He didn't suggest you leave it with him? Nothing shifty like that?"

"Nope. Whole thing was on the level. If I didn't know who they were, I'd have sworn it was legit. Until the Aussie shows up that is."

"Henry?" I tucked the pouch away and slid the satchel behind a plump embroidered cushion.

"Very shifty. Far too shifty to be just shifty, if you know what I mean."

"Right. Absolutely. I mean . . . nope, sorry, what?"

"Henry wasn't some bad grifter blowing his cover," Andrew said, swigging his Coke. "He was *playing* it shifty. All backwards glances and hushed voices. If he'd slunk in on his stomach in a black balaclava with suckers on his hands and a safe-cracking kit on his belt, he would have looked less suspicious."

"And who was he playing? Another insurance man?"

"You tell me. He sidled up, handed Christopher this fat, wad-of-cash-sized envelope and thanked them both for a job well done."

"A job?"

"That was all. *A job well done.* A tap of the nose, a winkity wink and then he slides on out to his Merc."

"Did you ask . . . ?"

"I did. I figured they were waiting for me to."

"And?"

"*Another time perhaps my dear,*" Andrew said in Christopher's oiliest voice.

"That's it?"

"That's it." Andrew drained his can and crumpled it in his fist. "*Another time perhaps.* Then it was all mints and cheque-please and off we went."

I sat down on the fat couch with a sigh. Andrew watched me from the edge of the bed for a quiet moment.

"This is a familiar sight, eh?" he smiled eventually.

He was right. Replace the dull hotel water-colours with a *Blues Brothers* poster and the laminated room service guide with a back issue of *Melody Maker* and we could have been back in our halls of residence. One on the bed, one in a chair. Talking it out. Talking it through. Our fathers, our friends, our future.

"I don't know what the bloody hell they're up to," Andrew said, moving on.

"Laura didn't let up?"

"Boy oh boy, what she can't do with those toes of hers," Andrew said with a shake of the head and a less than discreet adjust-of-the-groin. "It was like she was trying to solve a Rubik's cube down there. Christ I almost tipped the bloody table over. I was trying to listen to Christopher, keep one eye on the satchel and one eye on the Aussie, all the while she's licking butter off the asparagus and making these *mmmmm* noises? I mean steady on. Where I come from, women like that are usually accompanied by a five dollar a minute premium-rate phone bill."

"All part of their plan, y'think?"

"I don't know. It's what I thought to *begin* with," Andrew said, getting up and tugging off his tie. "But it was almost like Christopher didn't approve. He kept shooting her these looks, muttering behind his menu. Like she was his teenage daughter or something. Maybe . . . ? Oh I don't know," he shrugged, moving over to the large mirror over the dressing table. He peered in closely, smoothing his clean chin, pushing his hair from his face.

"What? What's that? *Maybe . . . ?*"

"It *could* be, of course, that she was just . . ." He stood back, checking his reflection again. One profile, then the other. "I mean . . . ?"

"Benno, old chap. You've always been a handsome devil. Even ten years ago when you had plankton growing in your beard. And yes, now you're a New York big shot with the suits and the shoulders, but really . . ."

"Yeah yeah yeah. Shut-up. I'm just *saying*, it didn't seem to be part of the script. It is *possible*, y'know."

"That you're so irresistible she'd put an eighty-grand con at risk?"

"Well I don't know, do I? I'm just telling you what . . . *shit!*"

We both stopped and listened.

A hurried knuckle knocked on his door again. We exchanged glances.

"*Room service?*" I whispered. "Maybe they've sorted out your laundry?"

"Could be. Yes, yes, bound to be. 'Bout time," and Andrew moved over to the door. "It hasn't been adding to O'Shea's confidence in my negotiating skills, having me turn up for meetings in a New York Mets sweatshirt."

"Unless you're right of course and it's Laura," I said, sitting back, allowing myself a small smile. "Unable to keep you from her pants for a moment longer."

Andrew peered through the spyhole.

And then he turned back towards me, face pale and slack.

"No," I said.

"She's outside. She's outside the room. Now."

The next thirty seconds are currently appearing on a seaside summer-season stage near you under the direction of Ray Cooney and the title of "*What Ho, Matron, You're Sitting On My Collectables*" (AKA *Capes, Pants and Boompsie-Daisy!*)

I legged it about the room, elbows akimbo, Andrew hissing hiding-place suggestions at me and trying to get his hair tidy. We shoved the satchel back into the bathroom hurriedly, stacking tumbling towels on top before remembering it was meant to be Andrew's anyway and positioning it as casually as we could on the bed.

"*Underneath,*" Andrew hissed, grabbing my arm.

There was another knock.

"One second!" he shouted. "*Underneath.*"

"*The bed?! I'm not hiding under the bed. For Chrissakes, I'll . . . I'll hide in the bathroom.*"

"*She might need the bathroom. Go, under the bed. Quick.*"

"Fuck it," I said and dropped awkwardly to the carpet in a tangle of unsupple limbs. I began to feed myself in feet first like a letter into a fax machine, pile burning my elbows.

"*What can she want?*"

"*Lord knows,*" Andrew said. "*You under?*"

Chest tight, chin burning on the carpet, head jammed in the dusty darkness beneath the wooden frame, my Adam's apple somewhere behind my eyes, I gulped in the affirmative and watched Andrew's twitching ankles and shoes move to the door in widescreen letterbox format.

A click of the latch and the bottom of the door opened, Laura's shoes and slim ankles waiting politely. Her feet moved in, Andrew's stepping back to let them past but past didn't seem to be their agenda. In fact, they all met in something of a four-shoe pile-up, brogues and heels head on, then on-top of each other, then side to side in a clash of leather, Laura's handbag dropping to the floor.

High above me, out of sight, Andrew's voice was that of a well-spoken man with his mouth full. Full, I could only presume of Laura. Meanwhile, at my level, the four feet stumbled clumsily in urgent circles over towards the wall, into the dark-wood mini-bar with a loud musical crash. Then like some kind of foot-fetish's pinball machine, they rebounded back, spinning, stumbling over towards me and then abruptly all four disappeared.

No. Oh God no.

The mattress slammed down hard, thudding my head into the rough carpet, banging my chin and giving me a jawful of fluff. I shut my eyes as the world squeaked and crushed around me and I got a sudden understanding of what the life of an accordion must be like. With a crackly hiss, one of Laura's heels tumbled to the floor, followed quickly by another, landing inches from my face. In the darkness I could make out the faded label inside. A size five, manufactured by the nice people at Office. Andrew, it turned out two thuds later, favoured Church's size elevens.

And then as hastily as it had started, suddenly it was all over. There was the mumbled sound of apologies, a bouncy-bouncy-squeak as bodies edged quickly from the bed and then Laura's feet returned. They seemed smaller, shier suddenly, toes curling in little steps.

"I-I . . . I'm sorry," she said, far above me. "I . . . I can't do this. I . . . *shit.*"

Squeaky-squeaky and then Andrew's black socks landed flat by my face.

"Is everything all right? What's . . . I don't understand?"

Laura's feet moved away, the handbag lifting out of sight, Andrew continuing to ask woozy, confusey, mid-coital questions. There was the snap of a lighter and the warm smell of cigarette smoke as Laura stumbled away across the carpet to the bathroom.

"Linda?" Andrew called out. The door slammed shut.

I breathed out, shifting uncomfortably in my spring and wool sandwich.

"*Benno?*" I hissed. "*Psssst. Benno? What's going on?*"

"*Buggered if I know,*" his voice whispered back. His socks paced about the room anxiously. "*One minute she's all over me then suddenly she breaks away saying she can't do it. Something about it not being . . . Wait.*"

The bathroom door opened and Laura's stockinged feet emerged. Baby steps, frightened, sticking close to the wall.

"I can't. I'm sorry, I never should have . . . Forget I came. I can't . . ." Her voice was edgy. Tearful.

"Are you okay?" Andrew asked gently. His feet moved over to her, soft on the carpet.

"I'm fine," Laura sniffed. "I'm fine. I mean I'm *screwed*, obviously. But *apart* from that . . . Just *peachy*. Christ . . ."

"Linda, this . . . all this. Is it *me*? I —"

"My name's not Linda. Okay? You can stop calling me that. None of this is what you . . . My name's not Linda."

"I don't understand."

"I'm not Linda. He isn't Fitzgerald. To tell you the truth none of us know *who* he is. There's no valuation company, no offices and we don't know shit about antiques, get it? It's . . . Look, you're a nice guy, okay? But you've just fallen in with the wrong people. It's nothing personal. *Christ*. What am I *doing?*"

I could hear her puffing angrily on her cigarette. What the *hell* was going on?

"Hold on a jiffy. You're saying *what*? Your website . . . ?"

"There's no website," Laura said. "There's nothing. Just a scam."

"*Scam?*"

Laura sighed.

"How do I . . . ? Look, the man you met today? His name is Christopher. Or that's the name he goes by anyway. His team. Me, Henry, Julio, the others. We just go where he tells us to go, wear what he tells us to wear," and she kicked out at her shoes, sending them tumbling across the carpet. "Fuck who he tells us to fuck. It's a scam. A con game. A grift. It's what we do. We get guys off the net. Bait a hook and reel you in. Christopher spins a line, I stick my toes in your crotch, take you to bed, make all the right noises. It's all just prep to keep you on a short leash."

"I don't believe it."

"It's nothing personal."

"And the chap in the restaurant? The Aussie with the cash? Are you telling me he's part of this too?"

"Henry David," Laura sighed. The tears sounded drier now. Replaced with a firmer edge. An anger. "Although that's probably not his real name either. These fucking people."

"That's what the envelope at the table was about? The *job well done?*"

"I need another cigarette." Laura moved softly across the room towards the bed where she must have dumped her bag.

There was a rattle and a click of a lighter. She moved over to an armchair and I watched one foot disappear as she sat down and crossed her legs.

"The envelope's just the lure. To get you asking the right questions."

"What questions? Wait, exactly what have I walked into here?"

"It works like this," Laura sighed. "Christopher and I pose as antiques experts. We find someone on the net with a valuable vase, a book, a painting, a comic."

"I can't believe it . . . I can't . . ."

"Whatever it is. We invite you out, tell you it's worth some outlandish sum. Makes us all best friends. And just as it's sinking in, Henry drops by the table with a nudge and a wink and a fat envelope full of reddies. Naturally, you want to know who this Henry is and how he makes his money. You and I subsequently become lovers and I tell Christopher we can trust you to share our secret."

"Which is?"

"That we have a way of making clients like Henry, clients like *you*, a little extra on the side, no questions asked."

There was a long pause as Laura drew on her cigarette, toes curling in the thick carpet. Andrew's feet remained at the mini-bar. Beneath the bed, crushed and wheezing, my heart slammed in my ears as I tried to take it all in, brain lagging behind breathlessly.

"It's called the Pigeon Drop. Nobody knows how old it is. It's been out of circulation for a while, but you can't keep a good grift down."

"Go on," Andrew said firmly.

"It's very simple. We borrow *your* comic book. We put it in a briefcase and dump it somewhere out of the way – an alley, a car-park, under a bench. Doesn't matter. Christopher then locates a victim. Some greedy son of a bitch. He steers the mark towards the briefcase, all casual like, *my, what have we here*? But just as they find it and are thinking all their Christmasses have come at once, *I* step up and say *I* saw it first. So we have a problem."

"I can't *believe* what I'm hearing," Andrew said with convincing disbelief. "So *nothing* you said today was – ? The valuation? The *website*? I . . ."

"Get over it. Listen, we figure the comic book must be stolen. We can't stand around discussing what to do with it so we retire to a nearby pub for a discussion. Now, we can't split the comic book three . . . are you following this? You said you wanted to know what we were going to –"

"Yes, yes sorry. It's just all a lot to take in . . ."

"We can't divide your comic book up because it's a one-off piece, right? So. Big conundrum. Who gets to keep it? First, *I* offer to hold onto the case for a while – a few weeks say – just so we know it doesn't appear on *Crimewatch UK,* agreeing that if enough time goes by and nobody asks questions, we meet up to arrange an equal split."

"And why would they trust you to do that?"

"Well they *don't* trust me, that's the point. Christopher starts saying how shifty I seem and before you know it, our greedy mark is the one offering to play babysitter with your comic book."

"And why do you trust *him*?"

"Because *he* can afford to put up a bond. Like a . . . a good faith kind of thing. A few thousand pounds each to Christopher and myself. That way, should he renege on the deal and run off with the comic, nobody's out of pocket."

"Unbelievable. This . . . this is *unbelievable*."

"So the mark pays out to us, sticks the case under his arm and we all walk out of the pub."

"I'm guessing it's not that simple?"

"Nothing in life is simple. Because who should then appear but the comic-book thief himself? One of our team again of course.

He wants his case back. There's a big struggle, a gun goes off – I go down screaming in a pool of blood. The thief grabs the bags and he's off in a cloud of smoke. Leaving Christopher shouting and screaming for the cops, covered in splattered blood, me lying '*dead*', and our mark with no choice but to leg it before the cops show up and start asking questions about stolen goods. And that's that."

The room went quiet as Andrew mulled this over.

"And so I fit into this *how*?" he said eventually. "You were going to ask me for *my* comic book to use as bait for one of these drops, right? To catch some *mark*?"

"*Ask* you? No need. A tumble in the sack with me plus a sneaky peek into Henry's envelope and I wouldn't have had to ask. You'd have been *begging* to be allowed in."

"And you keep the mark's money? The bond, I mean. It works?"

There was a pause. The mood in the room, even at floor level, seemed to shift.

"*Works*?" Laura laughed. "Ha. You could say that."

"I don't follow," Andrew said.

But under the bed, teeth gritted, angry fists tight, *I* followed.

I followed only too well.

twenty-one

"So . . . I'm not with you," Andrew said a few thoughtful minutes later. "If this is all true. If this is what you do, shouldn't we be cavorting on the old bedstead? Isn't that your plan? Shouldn't you be . . . I don't know. Leaving envelopes full of cash next to my bedside hoping I'll stumble over them on my hunt for a Gideon?"

Laura gave a long sad sigh.

And I would have tried one myself if my ribcage hadn't seized up with cramp and the pins & needles in my face numbed me from the nose down. Still beneath the bed, hands buzzing and dead, I tried to edge over an inch silently, get the blood up and running again but there was no room to even shift an opinion. I don't know how long I'd been cramped-out but I wasn't going to last much longer. Mouth full of fluff and dust, I tried to content myself with slow, shallow breathing, head-thudding concentration and keeping a lid on a simmering rage.

I could only see her feet as she talked, but I *hated* her feet. I hated her little feet curling in the carpet and I hated her slim ankles. I loathed her long legs, her hips and waist and curves and shoulders and her greedy-grabbing hands and that mouth that kissed and lied and lied and lied. I tensed all over, trying to hold in the bursting fury. I wanted to yell. I wanted to scramble out like a commando under assault-course netting, leap up and grab her by the throat. Scream. Roar with hot spit and hatred. Because of what she had done. What she had taken from me.

But instead, I listened.

"I should be, yes," Laura said. "And as far as Christopher's concerned, I am."

"But?"

"But I'm not. Not today. In fact not any day. Not any more." Laura's legs uncrossed with a crackle of stocking and she wandered over to the mini-bar and opened it. "I'm done."

"You're done."

"You have any idea what it's like, this life? What we do? I mean hell, people say that our *marks* end up ruined, but at least the sad bastards get the luxury of mourning. They can at least face themselves in the mirror, look themselves in the eye, take a deep breath and try to get on with their lives. *Me*? Where can *I* look? How do *I* 'put it behind me'?" She bent and I caught her slim hand sliding out a half-bottle of white wine. "When it's there, in front of me, stretching on for years. A lifetime more of lies, deceit and betrayal. Watching poor gullible soul after poor gullible soul have their dreams plucked from their hands and taken to the cashiers. I can't do it. Not any more."

"You're retiring?"

"While I still have a soul to be redeemed."

"And you decided this . . . what, just now on the bed? Bloody hell, I'm a better kisser than I thought."

"Don't flatter yourself. You want the truth?" There was the distant tinkle of tumblers, a screw-top lid bouncing on glass. "I made up my mind at eleven o'clock last Thursday morning. November the fifth. Outside the Waldorf Hotel."

Under the bed, I held my breath. My pins & needles gave a tingle. *Hello*, I thought.

"We were playing a mark. Some Zorba the Geek who needed a quick buck to get himself out of a hole. Cheers." There was a beat and a sigh as she swigged her wine.

"Nerd made flesh. God you should have seen his flat. Superman here, Superman there. Anyway. Everything had gone like clockwork. Just another con trick. I was standing waiting when he arrived with the score. Fifty thousand pounds."

"Fifty *grand*?"

"I never said it didn't pay. Not bad for five days' flirting, eh? But . . ." and Laura thought for a moment. "It was the look on his face. It was wrong. It wasn't greed. He wasn't licking his lips or rubbing his hands. It was this look of hope. This pathetic look of *hope*. The sad bastard. Because he wasn't doing it for himself. He was doing it for his wife and daughter. This wasn't some fat tourist we were fleecing. This guy was that rarest of mythical beasts – the good husband." She chuckled dryly and lit another cigarette.

"Even when I'd try it on with him in his crappy little shop, he'd always pull back. He was just a pitiable, desperate man terrified of losing his family. How exactly did he *deserve* to get fleeced?"

I listened as the room went quiet. Laura smoked her cigarette and sipped her wine, easing herself back into her chair. Andrew said nothing, just curling and flexing his toes in his black socks.

"Which is," Andrew coughed after a moment, "well, a heart-warming story Linda . . ."

"Laura."

"Laura. Sorry, I'm having difficulty keeping up. All this has come as something of a surprise."

"Just think yourself lucky you didn't meet me a week ago."

"But I'm not a priest. You still haven't quite explained why you're unloading all this on me."

"Why? *Friends*," she said. "Now, Christopher says that there's no such *thing* as friends. '*Friends*' to Christopher is an American sitcom. Nothing more. He believes that anyone you get on with in life is merely someone who hasn't found you out yet."

"Charming."

"The team? Pete, Henry, Julio? They're the same. We aren't *pals*. We don't hang out because we *get on*. There's no trust. Any of us, if caught, would squeal on the others like *that*. We're *Get Out Of Jail Free* cards. Nothing more. That's what Christopher has always taught us."

"And you're going to cash them in. Right? Is that what you're saying? As part of your retirement? A big golden fuck-off."

"They're going to offer me immunity. Full immunity."

"*They?*"

"Fraud Squad. I've spoken to a barrister. Off the record, of course. He's cutting me a deal. My freedom in exchange for the team, caught red-handed in a last final scam."

"The *scam* in question being . . ." and Andrew followed this thought to its inevitable conclusion. "Oh. I see."

I lay there and listened as the whole point of Laura's visit, the purpose of her confessional, finally settled in quietly between them. They sat and looked at it for a while in a silence heavier than . . . well, heavier than the double mattress I had balanced on my head.

Laura excused herself and I held my breath as I watched her pad across to the bathroom.

"It's up to you," she said and the door slid shut with a hiss and a slam.

"*Neil?*"

"*Christ,*" I gasped, breathing out with a dusty cough, my crushed lungs like two hoover bags. I edged out a few inches into the glare of the room, gulping a few dry lung-fulls, wincing at my cricked neck. Andrew scuttled over hunched low.

"*What do we do?*" he hissed. "*Do you believe any of this?*"

"*I don't know,*" I whispered, rolling sore shoulders in the tiny space. "*She's either wiping her slate clean or just trying to make you think she's wiping it clean.*"

"*Having her on side would make it easier to get your money back though. There's no denying that.*"

"*True,*" I said, my head weary with worry. "*But this is the third character I've seen this woman play in five days. And there's something not quite —*"

"What's going on?" Laura said flatly.

"*Shit —*"

"I heard . . what are you — ?"

"Er, Laura, j-just hold on . . ."

"Who's there? What the hell's — ?"

Laura moved around the bed, around Andrew's crouching frame and caught sight of me, half in, half out. It shook her all about.

"Shit," she said, stumbling backwards.

"Wait, it's all right, Laura," I said, puffing and heaving myself free but Laura was panicked, skittering like a bird trapped in a strawberry net. She grabbed up her bag and a shoe, holding it out like a weapon, stumbling about the room.

"What *is* this?" she said loudly, eyes wide and fiery. "What's . . . Is this some kind of set-up? Who else is here?" She stabbed out with her stiletto, moving fast across the room, flinging open the empty wardrobe, Andrew backing away, hands raised.

"Laura," I said, getting cautiously to my feet, brushing the fluff from my chest "Laura, *relax*. It's not a set-up."

"I'm leaving," she said, face dark and angry, taking trembling steps towards the door. "I'm leaving and you're staying, you hear me? Your money's gone. Gone, understand? Don't even think about following me . . ."

"Laura," I said carefully, and bent and retrieved her other shoe, holding it out as a high-street peace offering. "It's all right. We just want to talk to you."

Her eyes flicked back and forth between us warily.

"I mean it," I said, raising my own hands in submission. "Please. Andrew?"

"Right right. We just want to talk. We . . . we can help you."

Laura narrowed her eyes.

"Look, you say you want to go straight?" I said. "Quit the life? Turn Christopher in? You think what, we're going to *stop* you?"

Laura lowered her heel a tiny bit, almost imperceptibly.

"Benno here's a friend of mine."

"*Benno?*"

"Sorry, that's me. Andrew Benjamin," Andrew said, offering a hand. Laura looked at it. Andrew put it back in the air.

"*We* set this up," I said. "eBay. To try to get Christopher out of the woodwork. I . . . I just want my money back. You can help us. And we can help you."

"The comic's *yours?*"

"Who else? Zorba the Geek?"

Laura took a deep breath, licked her lips and looked at us both, back and forth. Deciding something. Weighing it up.

We stood watching, breath held, hands aloft. The air conditioning hummed quietly. On the street far below, West End traffic sighed and hissed. Somewhere a siren called out.

"You'd help *me?*" she said, voice edgy and firm.

"I just want my money back," I said. "Whatever it takes. You want to bring the team down into the bargain, that suits me fine."

Laura narrowed her eyes, looking at me. Then at Andrew. Then me again. Then, after a long, heart-thudding minute, she finally tossed her shoe to the bed with a sigh, shoulders limp.

"Jesus," Laura sighed. "Look at you. Martin & Lewis. Either of you comedians got a cigarette?"

It was almost six o'clock. Outside, November had brought a cold darkness to London's night.

Inside, Laura was on her second glass of wine, lit by the glow of one of the fatter table lamps. Room service had sent up a greasy teenager with a packet of *Lucky Strikes* on a silver dish, hotel match-book placed just-so on the doily – it was probably going to cost Keatings about nineteen quid plus tip. Laura curled up in a Regency armchair and smoked them. Meanwhile Andrew and I sat opposite, either side of her, which we imagined made us look like a couple of grizzled undercover cops instead of the two nerdy, totally-out-of-their-depth losers that we really were.

As she talked, I tried to continue hating her. Really, I did. Brow furrowed, focused, I churned up my stomach, my bile, turning up the heat, adding a sprig of venom and two heaped tablespoons of rage. Got the whole dark, loathsome mixture bubbling away.

But the mixture wouldn't set. I stirred and folded and whisked but nothing. Was it her newly acquired vulnerability? Pale hair loose, dwarfed by the armchair, sipping wine like an air-sea rescue victim with a warming hot-chocolate?

Or was it perhaps her desire to make amends? To join, if not quite the side of the angels, then at least warm up on their reserves' bench.

Maybe it was the fact that *I'd* had something to do with it. That it was the hope in *my* face that day outside the hotel. That it was my actions as a *good husband* that finally sold her on taking a different role in life.

Either way, I could only bring myself to sit and listen.

"It wasn't what I dreamed of," she said, exhaling a long slow mouthful of blue smoke. "As a girl. All *this*. Believe me, it's not what I wanted. Not what I wanted at all."

"So now you've changed?" Andrew said. "You want out?"

The three of us exchanged looks.

"Because you felt sorry for my friend here? Finally, after all these years of hate and deceit, you feel . . . what? Remorse?"

"I can't feel this way any longer," Laura said. She tipped her head back and exhaled a long sad cloud of smoke. "Call it a character flaw. Maybe his Superman fetish appealed to me? Maybe I needed some truth, justice and the American way?"

Heart thundering, I looked at her curled in the chair, helpless and apologetic.

"No," I said.

"Neil, listen to what she's —"

"No," I said again. "I don't buy it. I don't buy it for a second. This isn't to do with *me*. This is something else. Why now? Something's happened, right? Money drying up maybe?"

"Money — ? Er, fifty *grand* you gave us, wasn't it?"

"Fifty grand I gave your boss," I said firmly. "How much did *you* see of that? Ten? Five? Minus expenses? Those new dresses. Shopping trips."

Laura's eyes flickered.

"He didn't give you a penny, did he?"

Laura sucked hard on her cigarette, sloshing back the smoke with a mouthful of white wine.

"He's a conman," she said, placing the glass on a fat side table. "What should I expect? For him to stick to his promises? Fair's fair? Ha. Everything . . ." she fixed her jaw. "*Everything* that comes out of that man's mouth is a lie. *I've invested the take on a new mark, money's tied up in a stocks scheme, trust me, your cut's safe. Just transferring some funds dearie-dumpling, fret ye not.* Meanwhile he's glinting away in new diamond cufflinks."

"So *that's* it," I said. I almost laughed. "It's nothing to do with me or any other hapless, hope-faced husband. It's revenge. You're just out for *revenge*. And *you* want *us* to help you?"

"*Listen,*" Andrew whispered appearing at my side, hand on my shoulder. I glanced over. Laura hadn't moved. "Listen old man. What choice do we *have*? The game's up. She *knows* you and I are in this together now. What else *can* we do but trust her? *Let her go*? Let her tell Christopher about our cosy little meeting? We *have* to trust her. Hell, maybe she *does* want out. Why else would she let on about the Sparrow Plop trick or whatever it is?"

I turned and looked deep into Andrew's anxious face. The same kind face I'd looked at across a chess-board a decade ago.

"Trust. Right," I said and looked over at the liar in the chair. "Laura. My *dear*. You want to tell Andrew here about trust?"

Laura shifted a little, hands loose, reaching for her wine glass.

"The scam you revealed. What was it? *The Pigeon Drop?*"

She held the glass in her hand, turning it slowly, the lamp light playing on the grease of her lipstick. She looked up at me. She said nothing

"Explain the details *again* if you would." I began to pace a bit, trying to keep a lid on my jumpy, twitchy anger. "Andrew here would just be providing the *bait*, right? That's what you told him? And *together* you'd all con this wealthy mark Christopher has found. Tell me, this wealthy mark. He wouldn't be a rather rotund, rather *portly* gentleman would he? With perhaps, oh I don't know, perhaps a blue baseball cap? Leather handbag? Suite at the Waldorf? Am I warm?"

Laura looked at me. Then over at Andrew. Back to me.

I took this look and tossed it over to Andrew. Andrew threw it back to Laura. We did this for a while like three five-year-olds with a tennis ball. "Do you want to tell him?" I said finally.

"After you," Laura sighed.

"Will *somebody* tell me?" Andrew spat, exasperated.

So I told him.

"*Me?*" he said a few moments later as I rounded off what I'd spent my cramped minute under the bed putting together. It was pretty much what I'd expected him to say. "*I'm* the target?"

"Just like I was." I spun around and faced Laura. "This is how they do it. Con you into thinking you're helping them play *another* swindle. I'm guessing the Pigeon Drop goes according to plan, but at the last minute it all happens to go terribly wrong?" I said. Laura flicked a little ash and blinked a slow, tired blink. "And that *valuation agreement* you had Andrew sign at the restaurant a few hours ago with the big fat fountain pen?"

"An insurance policy," Laura said, beaten. "Accidental loss. So when you realise you've been swindled and try to report it, the police find *that* and presume you must have been in on it for the insurance."

"Jesus . . ." Andrew whistled.

"Okay okay, I didn't give you the *whole* plan. But I'm telling you," Laura pushed. "It doesn't matter either way. Because the Fraud Squad will pounce and the whole thing will –"

"And this. *This* is who you want to trust to help us?" I spat.

"God. What the hell are we doing here?" I felt sick. Physically, deep down in my gut.

"But *Neil*. Neil, *think* man," Andrew said, trying to slow the whole world down. "What else do you suggest? You want to walk *away*?"

"What do I *suggest*?" I yelled. "What do I – ?" My mouth flapped loose for a moment, my elbows and wrists deciding it looked like fun and joining in wildly. "I *suggest* she just gives me back my fifty thousand pounds. She gives me my fifty thousand pounds or we turn her in." I marched across to the bed and snatched up the brown hotel phone. "How's that for an off-beat fucking idea?"

"There is no fifty thousand pounds," Laura said.

"Oh really? *Really*? What a fucking surprise. All gone has it? In four fucking days?"

"It was in that envelope. The one Henry was waving at the table. Now? Who knows. It's probably luring some other sap into some other scheme somewhere."

"Then you get it," I hissed.

"Just like that. For old time's sake?"

"*No*," I writhed. "No, because it's that or the *police*," and I waved the handset awkwardly.

"The *police*? Who are going to be involved *anyway*? I told you, I've got a barrister negotiating a –"

"Then . . . then because *otherwise* . . ." and I stumbled a little bit here, losing my momentum rather. I gathered my thoughts up quickly, aware that stuff like this was all in the delivery. "Otherwise I go to Christopher and tell him you're selling him out."

"Do that," Laura shrugged. "You still won't have your money back. But, if it'll make you feel better while you're living in your one-ring bedsit visiting your daughter every other weekend."

The retort caught in my throat, fat and thick. I stood, glued to the carpet, phone receiver in hand. I swallowed hard, blinking.

Edward. Edward coming home on Tuesday. Talking to Jane. The accountants.

Fifty thousand withdrawn?

Divorce. Custody.

"See, divorce lawyers tend to look more favourably on the

parent who *hasn't* lost the child's trust fund in a confidence game, Neil. They're kind of old-fashioned like that."

Andrew and I stood fuming, teeth grinding, our combined frustration threatening to set off the smoke alarms.

"I *can* get you your money back," Laura said finally. "But only if *you* can help me get Christopher. Working with me, double-crossing the Pigeon Drop."

"You're already double-crossing the Pigeon Drop."

"All right, all right, *triple*-crossing it then. Setting up this play and leading Christopher and the others to the police. It's the only way you'll *ever* see that money again."

Andrew and I exchanged sad, spent looks. The world turned beneath us for a while.

Eventually our shoulders slumped and we sighed shruggy sighs.

"So . . . how would it work?"

twenty-two

"God, there you are," Jane scowled at the top of the stairs, Lana hoisted to her hip. "Where have you *been*? It's almost nine o'clock."

I clambered upward making my apologies and checking my stupid watch. She was right. I gave Jane and Lana a minty kiss, courtesy of Andrew's hotel gift-shop Polos, and peeled off my jacket hurriedly, my heart thumping like a marching-band bass drum.

"Sorry, sorry. Mondays, y'know. It was . . ." I shook my head in an attempt to imply a frankly unlikely non-stop twelve-hour day of poster tubes and ringing tills and scuttled into the kitchen to glug a chin-full of tap water.

"Mr Dufford's been through what I could find, but we needed you here for the shop stuff."

I wiped sweaty hands on my jeans and shut off the tap.

"Mr . . . ?"

"You *forgot*?" Jane withered.

"Forgot? No, no no, don't be silly. I-I was just held up, that's all," and I smiled a thoroughly unconvincing smile. Jane turned and left and I followed, head thudding and spinning.

Forgot? Forgot what? Dufford? Why does that name mean something?
I pushed into the sitting room.

What was − ?

Oh. *Shit.*

Mr Dufford was perched on the edge of our couch. Fountain pen in hand, glass of wine by his feet and parting professionally centred, he had an irritated, *in-your-own-time-mate* scowl buried behind a professional banker's smile. He stood, hand out.

"Mr Martin," he boomed. "Nice to see you again. Busy afternoon?"

"Uhm, y-yes," I gulped.

"You know each other?" Jane queried, the world tipping over a little.

"We bumped into each other this mor –

"Mor . . . e fool me for forgetting. Ha. Right. Good good. That long ago eh? Crikey. Ahem," I interrupted, wrestling the words from him, easing him back into his seat boisterously. "Good to er . . . good to . . . uhm . . . crikey, you have been busy . . ."

Christ. The sitting room floor was an assault course of files and papers, stapled and paper-clipped, fanned and folded, stacked and strewn. On the couch, among box files and bank statements, Dufford's laptop glowed in the sitting-room light, a bright Excel spreadsheet filled with black and red columns.

"Anyway, sorry I missed you," I jollied, picking my way across the paperwork checkerboard floor to the stereo. "Perhaps we could reschedule for later in the month? Is there more wine sweetheart?" I quickly slung on disc two of *Now That's What I Call the Best Amadeus Hits Album in the World Ever*, which Jane had sworn worked in soothing soon-to-be-born Lana. I was hoping it would prove to be just as soothing to soon-to-be livid wives and soon-to-be-aghast financial advisors.

"Actually," Dufford coughed, "we haven't much more to look at. Your wife has given me most of what I need. It's just the shop's books. Do you have them to hand?"

Fountain pen poised, the sitting room went quiet.

"Might you have that to hand? At all? Mr Martin?"

Oh Christ.

"Neil? *Hello?*"

"Did you . . . sorry? Did you say there *was* more wine?"

"Neil, the books?" Jane pushed, jigging a gurgly Lana up and down.

"Oh. Uhm sorry, I think . . . God, actually I think I left them at work," I said, face collapsing in contrition.

"Oh *Neil.*"

"Sorry. Sorry Mr Dufford. I . . . I remember now, I took all the paperwork in to work to sort out. Y'know, t–to make this evening easier."

"When was this?" Jane pressed.

"When? Oh, Saturday."

"*Saturday*? Oh that's all right, I've seen a file of yours in the study . . ."

"What?!" I squeaked. "I-I mean, what? Which . . . er, where?" but Jane had wandered off to search the study. "*Shit*," I hissed, leaping after her. "Jane, Jane wait, don't – Sorry Mr Dufford, uhmm, sorry, one second."

God. Don't let her have found anything. *Please*.

I found her rootling through the files by the computer.

"It was here . . ."

"Let me, let me," I busied, flapping around her. "Go and see to our guest."

Jane sighed, turning to look at me, head tilted, beautiful face lit by the soft green glow of the night-light. She slid the nursery door ajar silently.

"*I can't believe you were two hours late and still forgot to bring the paperwork?*" she hissed, embarrassed. "*I've had to keep him talking all evening. Dad's going to go beserk.*"

"I'm *sorry*," I said, brow furrowed. "I-I mean, yes. Er . . ." realising just too late how guilty all this uhmming and shrugging appeared, so I began to quickly fuss about the baby, slipping a hand around Jane's waist, totally over-doing that too much instead. "Busy that's all. Just busy."

"Always busy," Jane said in an odd tone, peeling out of my arms and pulling open the door again, heading back to our guest.

Quickly, I scrabbled about the cheap shelving, sliding the file of business account statements out and shoving it under Lana's cot, pushing it to the back among dust and lost toys. I hurried out to where Mozart wafted down the hall and Jane was coming back the other way with Dufford's wine glass.

"Find it?" she said hopefully.

"Hn? Uhmm no. It er, it was an empty one. I'd taken everything out."

Jane looked at me, cocking her head to one side slightly. Something was going on behind her eyes. Something she didn't like. Something I didn't like much either. I crossed my fingers that Wolfgang had a particularly stringy, soothy bit coming up in the next five seconds.

"*Are you all right?*" Jane whispered softly, edging me away from the lounge.

"*All right? Fine. Fine, I'm . . . fine.*"

Jane continued her look. I began to panic discreetly.

God. What had Dufford shown her? What had she seen? How much did she know? And why was Jane looking at me like that?

"*Neil?* Are you listening?"

"Huh, sorry what? I was . . ."

"I said you don't *seem* fine. You're all jumpy and nervy. Coming in late, fussing about. What's the matter?"

"I'm *not*," I said, guiltily. "Just busy. Earl's Court, y'know."

"And you've forgotten tomorrow I expect? Being so *busy*?"

"Tomorrow?"

Shit shit shit. What the *hell* was tomorrow? November tenth? Lana's birthday? My birthday? Clark fucking Kent's birthday?

"Any joy?" Dufford called through. He was closing up his laptop. "It's getting on. Don't worry too much if you haven't, I'll leave my fax number . . ."

Jane gave me the empty wine glass, sighed and turned, carrying our daughter off to the lounge. Stomach tumbling, I made mumbling noises and scuttled back to the nursery, pushing the door closed behind me.

Christ.

I leant against the rickety cot and closed my eyes, head hanging loose. The fat, familiar urge to tell Jane everything stirred in my stomach, waking up, rolling its shoulders, threatening to burst out and run roaring around the office chair, over the night-light and dance wildly on the mouse-mat.

I swallowed hard instead, forcing it down like bile.

God, how did our marriage come to this? Hiding under hotel beds? Hurrying home drunk and late, full of excuses and lies? What happened to the sharing? The trust? That wasn't so long ago was it? The swapping midnight secrets? How had I allowed that to wear away? Our marriage still had romance, still had the flirting, the weekly massage, the sex. Didn't all the magazines and manuals say *they* all disappeared first? God, wasn't *trust* supposed to be the one, solid, immoveable constant that *remained*.

God. *Trust.* What had I done?

★ ★ ★

An hour ago, Andrew and I had been bickering about that very thing, batting it back and forth, examining it from all sides in his hotel room.

First we'd decided we couldn't trust Laura. Simple as that. Laura worked for Christopher and Christopher was the man who'd taken my milk of kindness and left it on a radiator all summer. Either they were playing us together or somehow she was playing us all – toes in our pants, hair mussed just-so – planning to ride off with the money, the comic and our hope.

Andrew and I promptly drank some more and looked it over some more, at one point diagramming it all out in Andrew's red notebook, trying to second-guess the whole thing. What if he was playing her? What if she was playing him? God, what if they're both playing each other?

By the time two wine bottles were upside down in a bin littered with torn-up pages, we'd reached only one woozy conclusion. I'd thought about this as I hauled on my jacket and stumbled through the hotel lobby into the clear November night.

If Laura had been lying – making it up, spinning a line, telling us *anything* to buy her way out of the room – then that would be that. She'd disappear. We'd never see her, Christopher or the money again.

"Bet you thought you'd never see me again?"

"*Nyyeahhyy,*" I blurted, stumbling with a shallow splash, heart and larynx enjoying a quick tango. "Christ, you scared the . . . *Christ.* You came back then?"

"I called out upstairs but you didn't hear me. Figured you were down here. Clean up not going so well, huh?"

It was eleven o'clock the next morning. Tuesday. Laura stood, weight on one sassy hip, halfway down my cellar steps. She was in large Ray-Bans, loose denim jeans, hung low revealing a strip of tanned flat stomach and the hint of lace knicker elastic. On top she wore a short, sharp white tee, pulled tight across her chest. A green hooded military-style coat hung over her shoulders, a fat leather bag over an arm, a newspaper under an elbow, filling the low room with the obligatory blue cigarette smoke. I, by contrast, stood ankle deep in thick black water surrounded by filthy plastic buckets, washing-up bowls, bin-bags stacked against Schwartz's rusted iron door, holding the pulpy sopping remains of a highly prized *Wizard of Oz* lobby stand.

"I've had better days," I said, splashing over to the iron shelving, cardboard dripping. "Although damp Munchkins are the least of my worries at the moment."

"I imagine."

"Even if you manage to get Christopher arrested –"

"*We* manage," Laura said, sucking on her cigarette.

"Either way, there's still the matter of my court appearance." I waded back across the room to gather the dripping cardboard remains of the stand. "Where a judge will decide exactly how much of my soul I'm going to have to fork over to Maurice as compensation for ruining all his –" and at that, the sopping cardboard gave up hope and collapsed, folding into the water, leaving me holding Judy Garland's severed head in one hand, the Tin Man's in the other. " – stock." I laid their faces on the shelf and peeled off my pink marigolds and followed Laura back up the greasy steps to an empty shop that seemed to brood with unease. However this turned out to be principally due to Bernard Herrman who I'd left slicing his way through a *Best of Hitchcock* cassette on the stereo. I snapped it off, hoping the resultant quiet would be more settling.

It wasn't.

"What about you?" I said anxiously. "You speak to Christopher last night? You tell him Andrew's on board? Did he buy it?"

"I spoke to him. Relax, it's all –"

"*Relax*? Right, right. *Relax*, she says. Sure. I've got a court appearance in six days, minus fifty grand in the bank, a basement full of soggy Munchkins and a wanted criminal standing in my shop. All this on November the tenth of all days."

"What's November the tenth?"

"I have absolutely *no fucking idea*. But my *wife*, whom I *love*, who is about to *leave me* because of my suspicious jittering, is going to have forty fits if I forget November tenth. Which I *have*. So, y'know, I'll relax another time if that's all right?"

"That's all right."

"What did Christopher say? Is he's going to phone Andrew about borrowing the comic for his scam? The . . . what was it? *Pigeon Drop*?"

Laura checked Elvis above me.

"Is probably doing so as we speak. Think your friend will agree to the meet?"

"He'll agree. A little thing called *trust*. When's the meeting scheduled?"

"Noon."

"*Today?!*"

"No sense in wasting time. Christopher's going to tell him that we've a big score in place. He's using this fair of yours on Friday in fact," and she reached into her newspaper and peeled out the faded, crumpled Earl's Court flyer I'd given her in my sitting room sixteen long days ago. "Adds a little credibility don't you think? Dealers? Collectors? He'll tell Andrew that we have a mark ready to bite but Henry's dropped out at the last minute and we need an emergency bait."

"Which is when Andrew's supposed to offer the use of my −"

The phone jangled on the counter suddenly. Hands twitchy, I licked my lips and picked up the handset.

"*Heroes Incorporated?*"

"*It's me,*" Andrew said. "*Were you trying to call old fellow? I've been in with my bosses. It's all bloody gone knackers up. O'Shea's threatening . . . Oh I don't know what his bloody problem is. You'd think an agent had never . . . He's an idiot. I never should have got involved.*"

"Andrew −"

"*Plus I'm standing here trying to reassure everyone of the firm's professionalism in a shirt three sizes too small because the bloody hotel screwed up my dry cleaning again.*"

"That him?" Laura asked. "Has Christopher called?"

"*Who's that?*"

"Huh? It's Laura. She's here with me. Have you spoken to Christopher?"

"Put him on speaker," Laura said. I jabbed the button and replaced the receiver. Andrew crackled, tinny and distant.

"*Just now. He wants to meet me at noon. Embankment station, rear carriage, westbound District line of all places. And you were right. Said he wants to discuss something discreet.*"

"Get there early. Eleven forty-five. I'll meet you on the platform,"

Laura said. "I've got a microphone you can wear. I'll listen in from the next carriage and get it all on tape."

"*I've got to go. O'Shea is demanding my personal assurance that . . . Actually, in truth I don't know what he wants. Forget it. Eleven forty-five. Embankment. Westbound District line.*"

"Tape?" I said, hanging up. "For the police?"

"Barrister says the more evidence I've got the better. Plus I'm not leaving this Andrew of yours alone with Christopher without knowing *exactly* what's being said. Right now I don't trust anybody." Laura stubbed out her cigarette in my Betty Boop ashtray. "It's just possible *Christopher's* spoken to a barrister. Or Henry has. Or Julio. Or any of them. Could be the cops are setting *me* up. Plus, how do I know Christopher didn't swing by Andrew's hotel room last night after I left? Offer you a sweeter package?"

"He didn't."

"Right. So *you* say."

"God. Quite a life you've carved out for yourself here," I said. "You trust *anybody*?"

"Just me. Which can get lonely for a girl."

"Which is why you want out."

Laura hoisted her bag to her shoulder.

"You'll be here when we're done?" she asked, flicking her hair from her sunglasses.

"*Done* – ? Are you joking? I'm coming with you."

"With – ? No you're not."

"I am."

"Oh no you're not."

"And as much as I hate to turn this into a panto –"

"You're not. You stay here and dry your Munchkins. It's too dangerous. What if Christopher sees you?"

"What if he sees *you*?"

"He won't see me, honey. I've done this sort of thing before."

"Good. Then as long as I stand behind you, I'll be fine."

"*Neil* –"

"No. I'm not letting you out of my *sight* until Christopher and the rest are in custody and I have my daughter's future and the trust of my wife back." I grabbed my jacket from my chair and snatched up my keys. "Let's go."

By twenty to twelve I was paying the cab driver and scuttling after Laura, weaving through the tourists, through the thud-hiss of the barriers and down to Embankment's westbound platform.

It was busy. Under sickly yellow light, loud gaggles of Europeans in rustling anoraks clustered about tiny maps, laughs echoing off the clean white tiles. The dot matrix board rolled around announcing arrivals, every three minutes another grimy train sighing in and out. Doors rolled and thudded, slicks of hassled commuters spilling among us.

I followed Laura to the far end of the platform where the crowd thinned to a couple of lone men.

"Here," she said, dumping her bag. She began to rummage, leaving me to pace and skitter and twitch like one of the many pigeons on the platform opposite.

"*Could it be this one?*" I whispered, reading the indicator board. "*Going to Richmond. One minute?*"

"He won't be here until precisely noon."

"*Might he be early?*"

"He won't be early."

"*What if he's early?*"

"Neil?"

"Sorry." I shoved my hands in my pockets and shuffled over to Laura. She was perched on the bench, unrolling the broadsheet paper on her lap, revealing a small sandwich of that bobbly camera-case foam. Lifting off the top half, the sandwich filling turned out to be an *iPod*-sized black box, a tangle of thin black wire, a fresh pack of batteries and a big fat fountain pen chunky enough to have been stolen from my bank by three men with a flat-bed truck.

Behind me, a train burst into the station with a loud blare making me give a startled jibber.

"Make yourself useful," and Laura handed me the batteries and the black box. "Careful."

"What's this?" The box was plastic, edged with flat black switches, a headphone socket and the head of a telescopic radio-antenna.

"The receiver. Change the batteries."

Heart thumping, I fumbled with the plastic packaging, throwing the batteries all over the floor.

"Stop mucking about," Laura scowled as I scurried about in a crouch. "Now how much do you know about this Andrew?"

"Know?"

"Where did you meet?"

"University," I said, gathering up the final battery and slipping them one by one into the casing. The platform clock read eleven forty-nine. No Andrew.

"He said in the restaurant he did something with property?" Laura was carefully, with nimble fingers, unspooling the thin black wire.

"He does," I said, one eye on the clock. It was eleven minutes to. "Works for some New York firm. Glorified estate agents. He's over here trying to get a promotion. God where *is* he?"

Laura took the receiver from me, plugging in the earphone wire and extending the antenna. She checked her watch.

"He misses this appointment, we're screwed. Christopher doesn't trust a mark who won't do as he's told."

"He'll be here, he'll be here," I said. Eight minutes to noon. "Do *you* know why today's important by the way? Yom Kippur? Ramadan? Jane thinks I've forgotten."

"You have forgotten."

"Thank you. That's very helpful."

A train rolled in. A train rolled out. Christ, *c'mon*.

I paced, eyes flipping from the matrix board to the platform steps, back and forth.

Six minutes to.

"I've been through my diary," I whittered. "No birthdays, no anniversaries . . ."

"Here we go, this could be him."

A train rolled in, a train rolled out.

Four minutes.

"C'mon old pal. *C'mon.*"

Three minutes.

A train rolled in, Andrew fell out.

"*Jesus Christ,*" Laura hissed. "*In your own time.*"

"Sorry, sorry," Andrew panted. He was breathing fast, face pink, not helped by his ill-fitting shirt. "O'Shea's accused Keatings of embezzling."

"*Embezzling?*"

"I *know*. Because we're holding on to his New York profit for three days before his London purchase goes through on Friday."

"Isn't that standard practice?"

"*Exactly!* That's what we said. Standard practice. But no. He's back there now flapping about loss of interest. What does he think we're going to do with it in *three days*? Take it to the bloody dog track?" He shook a hassled head. "How much time we got here?"

The indicator board showed a District Line train due in three minutes.

"Stick this in your top pocket," Laura said hurriedly, handing Andrew the fountain pen. He took it, giving it the once over.

"This looks familiar," he hummed. "Didn't I sign that validation yesterday with this?"

"Very observant," Laura said, double checking the receiver. "It has a miniature condenser mic in the lid. For all your covert surveillance needs. Sends a signal to me in the next carriage," and she waggled the black box. "Twist the cap until it clicks."

Andrew did so, a tiny red LED snapping into life on the receiver.

"That's it. Radio Free Europe."

The next train on platform four will be your westbound District Line train via Earl's Court.

"*Hello?*" Andrew spoke into the pen. "*Hello hello?*"

"Gotcha," Laura said, pressing the earpiece in tight with a finger.

"Where's Superman?" I asked quickly.

"It's okay. The hotel has it in the safe. Don't worry old man, I explained how fragile it was. They've got plenty of facilities and insurance. It's safe."

"Right," Laura said, tucking the receiver into the folds of her broadsheet and closing it gently. "I'll move down a couple of carriages —"

"*We*," I interjected. They both looked at me. "*We'll* move down a couple of carriages." I felt a little like they were playing a playground James Bond and I was being sidelined into the Moneypenny role somewhat.

"Fine. *We'll* be just down here. Keep that on, in your top

pocket. Get him to sit on your left if you can, but don't make it obvious."

The train burst into the station.

"*The train on platform four . . .*" the tannoy squelched. "*Is your westbound District Line train . . .*"

"Don't forget. Be greedy, be eager. In fact *insist* he lets *you* play a part in the drop," Laura hissed quickly, shoving me away with her up the platform. "But y'know, not *too* greedy or *too* eager or *too* insistent."

We stumbled up a carriage or two, leaving Andrew wide eyed and alone on the platform, blinking like a lost child, lips mumbling as he mentally prepared a tone that suggested a non-greedy greediness and an un-insistent insistency.

Laura gripped my arm, head bowed into her chest and finger in her ear as the train slowed to a stop. After a sickening second, the doors hissed, rolling open with a thud. Laura hauled me on and I turned quickly, giving Andrew a last quick thumbs-up before he climbed aboard.

The doors shut behind us, Laura pulling me down low into a corner seat.

"Well?"

Finger pressed in her ear, a small smile slid across Laura's face. "Got them," she said. "Hold tight."

The train rolled out of the station.

twenty-three

"What's he saying? What's he *saying?*"

"*Shhhh*, for God's sake, I can't . . . He's giving Andrew the *Marmeladov* bit. *Experience tells me you are a man of education, unhabituated to the beverage.* All that."

"He did that to me, what *is* that?"

"*Crime & Punishment.* He knows it by heart."

"The whole *book?*"

"The whole, *shhh*, wait . . ."

The lunchtime train rocked and rattled through the darkness, grey pipes shimmying past, tunnel lights whisping by like ghosts. Around us, passengers stood, passengers sat, lost in their own worlds. Slapping tabloids, wrestling with broadsheets, texting, eating, sleeping.

Crammed in a corner like socks in a suitcase, Laura and I sat low, chins in our chests. She had one finger pressed tight in her ear, the other over her earphone leaving me to squirm, fidgety and apprehensive.

The train burst into St James' Park station, a few suits dotted amongst its stark, prison-toilet tile.

"We're onto his *'vating is that of the motor driven variety dear chap'*," Laura whispered. "*We can choose to be lions or we can choose to be antelopes. Everyone makes that decision for them* . . . shh, here we go. Christopher's laying out the . . . A greedy collector called Grayson."

We stopped, the train doors rumbling open. A few suits clambered on board, a harried-looking middle-manager among them, dropping into the seat opposite. He tugged a file from under a sweaty arm, flicking a look at the pair of us. I coughed a bit and sat up awkwardly, trying to look less peculiar.

The doors rumbled closed and we began to heave westward once again.

"*Earl's Court*," Laura hissed, jabbing me in the ribs. "He's telling him about your fair . . ."

The man opposite looked at her. Then back at me.

I smiled a bit, attempting to suggest we weren't a couple of schizophrenic weirdos, remembering only after he'd quickly looked away that people who smile on the tube are mostly schizophrenic weirdos.

"*A staged robbery at one of the stalls . . . a scuffle . . . valuable comic gets nicked . . .*" Laura muttered. "Andrew's showing an interest . . ."

Around us, a couple more people sat up, deciding that the whispered play-by-play going on in the corner was considerably more interesting than the *Evening Standard* Quick Crossword and Nokia *Snakes*.

"*Christopher will be in the Earl's Court car park with Grayson . . . They'll find the thief's bag . . . argue over the split in the car-park . . .*"

The train burst into Victoria station. A few commuters took their leave of us and began to get up. I hunkered down and leaned in to Laura.

"What's going on?"

"*Shhh . . . Pub . . . Decide on the split . . .* Andrew's getting it . . ."

The tube doors rumbled open, passengers filing off. The wide platform was busy, thick with travellers returning from all over the –

Wait.

Victoria?

Wait. I sat up a bit. A sick feeling began to abseil from the back of my head, lodging itself tight in my throat for a moment.

Wait. What was today? The tenth. *Tuesday?*

No. I checked my chunky Faux-lex timepiece.

The sick feeling worked its way loose from my throat and slid greasily down into my stomach.

And you've forgotten tomorrow I expect? Being so busy?

Tuesday.

Victoria.

The platform crowds thronged and jostled with suitcases, beginning to pile on board one by one.

Oh shit.

Ted's back from the coast tomorrow of course and between you and me I think he was hoping we'd have sorted you out by then.

Oh shit *no.*

I'm going to speak to dad. Shall I tell him you're still all right to pick him up from outside Victoria next week?

No. Shit, no.

— or shall we just presume you're going to forget that as well?

Shit no shit no shit.

The carriage was filling up. Panicky, I half stood. Shit. Damn fuck and —

"Well well *well!*"

Bollocks.

"Edward," I gaped and gasped. "God, what are . . . I-I mean, I'm so . . . I totally —"

Edward loomed over me, anger spilt across his puffy cheeks like red wine on a couch. Back from Brighton, sweating in a fitted tweed jacket, he hauled a bulky, expensive looking suitcase in his little pudgy fist, barking and barging the shins of everyone around him.

"Half an *hour* I've been standing out there! Half a *bloody* hour! Jane said *eleven-thirty*. Eleven-thirty, by the newsstand."

"I'm sorry, really. I . . ." and I reached out for the suitcase. "Let me —"

"Get your hands off that," Edward barked, barging through to tuts and scowls. The suited man opposite looked up and grabbed his briefcase, sliding over to make room. Edward puffed and whinnied, squeezing his fat frame onto the seat, suitcase blocking everyone's passageway.

"Half a *bloody* hour," he boomed, fishing out a spotted silk hanky and wiping great sheets of upper-class sweat from his face. "Had Jane on the phone. She's been trying you at the shop. What are you *playing* at?"

I felt a sharp stab in the ribs. I turned.

"*Andrew's in,*" Laura whispered, oblivious. "Christopher's told him Henry's dropped out and we need a —"

"*Ahem!*" I coughed loudly, sending a rib-stab back Laura's way. She looked up, lost in her own world.

"And who's *this?*" Edward harrumphed, shooting a sly look at me.

"Uhh, this is . . . a friend of mine," I squeezed slowly, testing and tasting each word one by one. "Uhmm, Laura. Er, can I introduce my father-in-law."

"Uhm, a-a pleasure," she said awkwardly, popping the earphone from her ear.

The three of us went quiet as the train rattled west. Quiet, save the soft hum of Edward perusing this cosy, lunchtime tête-à-tête and scrabbling to his own suspicious conclusions.

"And who's looking after the shop, hnn?" he said finally, hauling an eyebrow up towards the hang-straps. "While you are busy. . . *entertaining*?"

"It's er . . . I've got uhmm, Ted. You remember Ted? From the other Sunday? He's lending a hand while I . . . while Laura and I . . . view some . . . see some . . ."

"My collection," Laura interrupted, rescuing me rather. "Neil has kindly offered to sell some items for me."

The train rolled into Earl's Court station with a clanking sigh. Around us, passengers stumbled to their feet.

"I *see*," Edward juddered in the low-high, *dum*-daaah not-seeing-at-all manner. "And what of young Dufford? Sat down with him yet?"

"Last night sir, yes."

"Hmn. About time too. I can't say I'm altogether happy with you young man. Can't say I'm happy at −"

"*Shit!*" Laura screamed, leaping to her feet and everyone else's. Edward, the businessman and I all jumped, yelping in a tangle of shoes. "*There they are!*"

Outside on the platform, I watched as Christopher, dressed in a generous dark green tweed suit and cap like he were walking Labradors across his fields, led Andrew hurriedly past the window, hand on his shoulder towards the station exit.

"Move, *move!*" Laura yelled, bag flying, hands grabbing, ear-piece dangling as she pulled her way through the crowds.

"*Neil?!*" Edward flustered. "What is the meaning of − ?"

"I-I . . ." I stammered, Laura grabbing my sleeve. "S-Sorry. It's our stop. Nice − *ow! Sorry* − nice to see yoouuuahh −" and I fell stumbling to the platform, the doors thundering shut behind me with a bang.

I sat, puffing on the filthy platform floor, rubbing my knee as the train hissed, clanked and began to grind westward, Edward's accusing face sliding away from mine.

Sliding towards Putney. Towards Jane.

"I'm screwed. I'm totally screwed."

"*Shhhh*. And slow *down*, we've got to keep our −"

"*Screwed.*"

"*Neil*. For heaven's *sake*," and Laura grabbed my denim sleeve, dragging me to a halt halfway up the tired steel stairs. "Keep back."

"*Back*? You know who that *was*?" I writhed, pulling free and spinning around. I gazed out across the grey light of Earl's Court station. A cavernous, echoing hangar under a pigeon stained roof. "That was my father-in-law."

"So you said. Look, calm −"

"And you know where he's *going*?"

"Neil, just calm down," Laura said, twisting her earpiece back in place, breathing fast and flushed. She tugged out the receiver and began to adjust the frequency. "Let me find out where Christopher and Andrew are before you go rushing . . ."

"He's off to see his daughter and his grand-daughter. To tell them tales of his travels. Tales of how his useless working-class dick of a son-in-law failed to pick him up. And why? Because he was taking the day off to ride around the District Line with a mysterious woman."

"Yes, and haring off after Christopher and getting spotted and blowing the whole thing isn't going to help. Slow *down*. Take a breath."

"Letting him *get away* isn't going to help much either. Come on!" I yelled. "In half an hour Edward's going to try to break my wife's heart just to spite me. Break Jane's *heart*. Now *move*!"

We reached the large tiled foyer moments later, Laura leaning panting against a map and adjusting her earphone against the rumble of traffic. I paced up and down, clapping my hands, teeth tight.

"*Andrew's saying he has doubts . . . he doesn't trust him fully . . .*"

"Where are they? Are they far?"

"*Shhhh.*"

A few feet away, London buses coughed and whined, vans honked and bubbled, the world grumbling north up the Warwick Road to the West End.

"*Thinks it's dangerous. Lending him his comic book . . . how does he know Christopher's on the level?*" Laura shook her head. "It's quietened down where they are. They must be somewhere fairly enclosed."

"Then let's find them," I said.

We scuttled out to the roar of the street, scanning the pavements for any sign. Traffic slid past slowly, drum 'n' bass thudding from speakers, the air dusty and loud. Across the road, Earl's Court Exhibition Centre sat, fat and imposing, mouth wide, a great tongue of red tarmac sprawling out front. Flags fluttered, vans drew up, the yellow gates lifting and dropping.

My heart gave an ache as I clocked the two building-high banners hung on the left and right of the entrance, advertising the coming weekend's convention – Spider-Man, Frankenstein, Bogart and Darth Vader making unlikely banner-fellows as they spun, lurched, shrugged and wheezed in garish colour.

"Wait," Laura said, grabbing my arm. Her mouth hung loose, listening attentively to the faint voices in her ear. "Wait . . . Christopher's . . . He's saying it's quite safe . . . *we'll drop it here . . . loading bay . . . Loading Bay C . . .* Where's Loading Bay C?"

"Shit. They're in the Centre," I said. "Loading Bay C. It's where the stall-holders unpack. C'mon. C'mon!"

"*Hey!*"

But I was off, weaving in and out of the honking traffic.

"Wait," she hissed. "*Wait!*"

Through the wide blue gate and past the guard kiosks, she finally caught up with me as we neared the front steps.

"There's not a lot of cover. It's all wide doorways and parking zones," I said, heart hammering and thinking back to previous years packing and unpacking with Maurice among the ramps and fire escapes. I scanned the wide front, the smoky glass doors, the twin ticket booths on the left and right, mind racing. "Here, quick," and I led Laura up the steps to the doors, pushing our way in.

The huge lobby was echoey and quiet like an airport terminal on Christmas day. Cold and still with just a wide empty floor ringed with steel turnstiles and shuttered kiosks.

"We can watch from here. They'll have to come back out this way," I said and we huddled up to the smoky glass, peering out the front. Laura fished the receiver from her bag and adjusted the volume, head cocked to one side.

"Andrew's . . . Good man, Andrew's insisting on playing a role. My part . . . *doesn't want to let the comic out of his sight . . . Willing to wear a cacklebladder . . .*"

"A what?"

"Cacklebladder. It's a . . . *wait* . . . Christopher's telling Andrew it"ll mean taking a dive. Bursting the bladder, dropping to the floor, playing –"

"Christ . . ."

"But . . . That's it, Andrew's insisting . . . He'll wear the bag and take a dive. *It's that or he walks . . .*"

"Is that good?" I squirmed.

"The con only *works* if Andrew's involved," Laura nodded. "It's how the double-cross – *wait*. Sounds like they're moving."

Shoulder to shoulder, we huddled by the door, fingertips squeaky on the glass. Breathing deep, nervous breaths, I could smell Laura's familiar woozy warm perfume.

We watched as Christopher and Andrew appeared outside, moving away from the rear loading bays and back out down the wide red tarmac towards the station. Christopher had his pipe in his mouth and his arm over Andrew's shoulder, all pally, and I could hear his voice hissing away in Laura's ear.

"Where now?"

"They're . . . Quick, he's showing Andrew where they'll do the split. C'mon."

We followed Christopher and Andrew for a while, keeping a good distance back, over wet leaves and past the orange-bricked flats of Warwick Road. Around us, the traffic hissed and honked, the air at turns wet with rain and dry with fumes. Laura had her finger in her ear, muttering snatched staccato non-sequiturs of bugged conversation – *Andrew wears chest-bag, Pete fires a blank, Andrew goes down, Grayson panics and runs* – while I walked ahead a little, stomach churning, weaving in and out of school-boys and bob-haired Brompton Road mums.

"Where – *whoopsie*, sorry, where does Christopher think *you* are by the way?"

"What? Oh, right about now I'm meant to be with Pete. He's driving the route between his place, Earl's Court and the pub, making sure the timing's – *quick*, down here," Laura hissed and took a sudden left, scurrying ahead down a leafy terrace. I followed.

"Won't you be missed?" I said. "Won't Pete wonder where you are?"

"Hardly," Laura whispered. "Pete's at the bookies. Asked *me* to cover for *him*. Here," and she jinked right.

"Can you still hear them? Where are we going?"

But Laura didn't answer, just hurried, head down, along a quieter, narrower road, the traffic now just a distant sigh. Past large, expensive cars parked in even larger, even more expensive residents' parking bays until we finally turned into a narrow, cobbled mews. Past a couple of BMWs slung casually about, at the far end there was a black ironwork gate buried in a thick hedge.

Laura slowed to almost a creep as we approached.

"*What is this?*" I whispered.

"Shhh," she said. "They're ordering."

"*Ordering?*"

"Sounds like they're staying inside. C'mon," and she heaved open the heavy gate.

Inside, surrounded on three sides by thick, high hedges, sat a quiet pub garden. Smallish, with room for but two *Fosters* umbrellas, two wet benches and a humming aluminium garden-heater, it was understandably deserted on this, a chilly November afternoon. The pub itself, a crumbling red brick affair, mumbled and clinked behind wobbly glass.

We took a seat, sliding into a clammy bench, huddling under the blue brolly.

"They're going over Andrew's part one more time," Laura whispered, pulling down her hood, finger pressed to her ear. "*Agreeing to the split, following Grayson onto the street, how to burst the bag. Dropping dead for beginners.*"

I gazed about the garden. Secluded, the hedges working well at deadening the noise, it was eerily quiet.

"You've been here before I take it?"

"We use it all the time," Laura said. "Out of the way. We can get away with murder."

She looked up at me.

"Theatrically speaking of course."

"Of course," I said.

Laura adjusted her earpiece, head cocked to one side. A small smile drifted past her lips.

"*What?*" I asked.

"He does it every time but it never fails to impress . . ."

"Who? Who does what?"

Laura waited a beat, checking the voices in her ear had settled in for their drinks before lifting out the receiver and rolling down the volume with her thumb.

"Do you remember the first *three* things Christopher said to you? The *very first* things? At Claridge's this would have been?"

"God," I shrugged. It seemed an awfully long time ago. "Well he gave me all that Marmelade stuff. And called the wine list the *pop* list if I recall. Why that didn't have me getting my coat and walking out immediately, to this day I couldn't −"

"Immediately after that," Laura smiled. "He would have asked you three questions. Probably something like, as you say, *is that the pop list?* Then *neato li'l diner they got here, huh?*"

"Right, right," I nodded.

"And then asked if it was the first time you'd eaten there. Three questions, right off the bat."

"He did."

Laura smirked, rolling up the volume control on her receiver, gazing off for a moment, and then rolling it down once more.

"Notice anything unusual about those questions? Or rather something repetitive about your responses?"

"I would have said yes. Every time. Three yeses"

"*Three* yeses. You don't know the man, you have no idea what the meeting's about but there you are, nodding, agreeing, nodding some more, complying, yes yes yes, sending little positive yes vibes, little affirmative signals. Three short positive responses in a row, in quick succession like that at the top of a conversation, your brain's already pretty much given up making negative choices. You're going to agree to virtually everything you're asked. You can't help it."

"Dale Carnegie," I was about to say, it all sounding all too familiar, when we were suddenly interrupted by the chirp of Laura's mobile. I held my breath as she thumbed it open.

"Yes it's me, go ahead . . . Did the mark buy it? . . . You certain, where are you . . . ?"

On the other side of the hedge, the sound of the pub faded up suddenly as a door swung open. Footsteps on the pavement. Christopher's voice. Close.

"*Leaving now,*" he said. "*Drooling dopelet was practically begging to play your part. This could be the simplest one yet. How were the timings in old Bedford? You and Pete all set?*"

"Fine," Laura whispered, hunching over the phone, pulling up her hood. "He's just parking."

"*I'll see you back at the flat animato! Cheerie-pip!*"

We made out Christopher hollering for a cab as we huddled under our umbrella. A cab engine bubbled, a door clunked and they wheeled off, fading into the hum of traffic.

"So far so good," Laura said. "C'mon. Let's go see how your man's holding up, shall we?"

A few moments later, Andrew, Laura and myself were sat in the warm pub around a dark sticky table finishing our drinks. Andrew seemed a little worse for wear.

"Bloody *hell,*" he said, taking a throaty pull on his fresh lager and wiping his mouth. "That was, without doubt, the longest bloody ninety minutes of my life. I'm shaking, look *look,*" and he held out a tremulous hand. "And I thought handling O'Shea's money was a nervy business. Look at that. Bloody hell. Did you get it all? Could you hear? Where were you?"

"Had you the whole time. Loud and clear," Laura said. "You did good, soldier." Andrew unclipped the pen from his pocket and Laura tucked it away. She also tucked away her reassuring eyes and replaced them with some face-the-front-and-listen-to-me ones.

"Now look," she said, sliding the newspaper package into her bag carefully. "I've got to be back at Christopher's by three o'clock otherwise he'll be asking questions so pay attention. The team can't have *any idea* they're walking into a double-cross. Up until the very last *second,* they have to still believe we're all screwing Andrew here out of his heirloom. They get even the *faintest* whiff that the play isn't going like clockwork, they'll drop everything and walk away."

Laura was talking quickly, nervously. Making sure we understood.

"I've been planning this for a while and I've come up with how to do it, but I'll be straight with you. It's tricky. "It'll need precise timing and a faultless performance from the pair of you. Especially you Andrew. You did good today," and Andrew took an embarrassed swig of lager and tugged out his red notebook. "But Friday will be the real —"

"Wait," I said, voice oddly high, stomach oddly low. "Sorry. Wait, what are you . . . the *pair* of us?"

"It needs three," Laura said flatly.

"*Three*? But . . . *I* can't . . . I mean, they *know* me. Christopher, Grayson, everyone. They *know* me."

"My plan keeps you out of sight for the play. You're just behind the scenes. Plus they'll be focused on Andrew here. Put on a baseball cap, let your beard go for the next few —"

"Wait. Wait, hold on a second." I swallowed hard, eyes flicking between the pale, apprehensive come-down of my oldest friend and the hard edges of . . . whoever the hell Laura really was. "I'm all for this. And Andrew?" I fixed him with a solemn look. "God bless you for helping out. But if any of them catch even a glimpse of me —"

"Look *pal*, it's all or nothing, understand?" Laura was facing me, thunder rumbling across her brow. "The plan won't fly with just us. Andrew and I need to work the inside, keep it all bubbling along. I told you, if Christopher or the others get *any* idea we're fixing to turn this —"

"But isn't there . . . God, isn't there *another* way?"

"Another way? Yes. Yes of course there is," Laura said fishing out a cigarette and getting to her feet. "We forget the whole thing. You lose your wife, your daughter, your home and your business, I go to prison forever and your best friend here can get on a plane back to New York knowing he's leaving his oldest mucker truly in the shit." She looked at me. "We can do that."

"Christ," I writhed, thoughts scurrying around my head like lab rats in a maze, U-turning at every wall.

"Neil, *Neil*," Andrew said, shushing me, soothing me, calming me down. "The whassit, the Sparrow Plop thing . . ."

"The Pigeon Drop," Laura said.

"Right. Christopher said the whole thing takes two hours." He put a large hand on my shoulder. "By midday Friday you'll have your money back and be back in your shop having lunch like nothing ever happened. Right? Laura?"

"Right."

I breathed deep, the world slowing down a little.

"Hell, *I've* gotta see O'Shea around noon to complete contracts and my plane's at eight," Andrew smiled, slapping my upper arm. "Christopher assured me it'd be long over with by then. We're both doing the most important deals of our lives and we won't let anything stop us."

"Whole thing, done and dusted by twelve," Laura said, hoisting her bag to her shoulder. "Latest."

"Okay," I said. "Okay. So what's this plan? How do we turn this thing on it's head."

"Drink up," she said, zipping her coat. "And I'll show you."

twenty-four

Much like the ugly drummer in a teenage rock band who is kept in only because he's got access to a van, the district known as Earl's Court is a dull, functional piece of London acting as the glue holding the more groovy Fulham, Chelsea and Kensington together. Full of grotty bed & breakfasts, warehouses, industrial estates and of course the Exhibition Centre, its residents – mostly backpacking homosexual Australians – pour from the doorways at night and hurry off somewhere else more appealing, cabbing it back only once the hours are small and the streets are too dark to see clearly. Meanwhile the real residents – batty old dears with wigs like small dogs and vice versa – avoid the place by staying in, mostly to count up the rent they're earning from all the homo-sexual Australians in their back bedrooms.

All of which goes some way to explain why, as we made our way through the wide, quiet avenues that Tuesday afternoon, we were pretty much the only souls about.

Andrew hung back a little, jabbering anxious business into his mobile phone. I only caught every fifth word or so, busy as I was jabbering telephone business of my own.

"No, I'm not *at* the shop. I–I'm finishing prep. You know, for the fair?"

"*But you remembered to pick Dad up at lunchtime?*"

"You haven't . . . ? I–I mean, you haven't spoken to him? He hasn't called you? He's not there now?"

"*Dad? No. No, why? Did you meet him all right?*"

"Uhmm . . . hello? Hello? Jane? Are you still there?"

"*I'm here, I can hear you fine. Did you pick him up?*"

"Hello? I'm losing you I think? It must be the conference centre. I don't think the signal's very –"

I thumbed the line closed.

Shit.

"Everything okay at home?" Laura smirked, fishing out a fresh cigarette, November leaves crackling underfoot. She jinked left and we followed, down Lillie Road, another wide, leafy avenue. Around us, traffic hissed along wet streets.

"Just *promise* me this is going to work."

"As long as your friend keeps his nerve, it'll be fine."

I looked back at Andrew, flagging a few metres behind. He had his hand knotted in his thick hair, fear etched in his eyebrows and phone to his ear.

"Yes yes I understand that sir, but I *did*, I made that *clear* to him," he bluffed, shuffling and dodging in the splashy kerb. "Standard business practice for periods under five working days, but he insisted . . . No, quite the *opposite* sir, it was Keatings' reputation I was endeavouring to . . . No no, it's done . . . and he's happy sir yes . . . Noon on Friday . . . I understand the penalties sir, yes, but noon is firmly . . . will do. Th-thank you sir. Thank you so much . . ."

He snapped the phone closed angrily and stuffed it, muttering, into his jacket.

"You all right?" I said.

"How much further *is* this?" he spat, not looking at me.

We trudged along in guilty silence for a couple of streets, stumbling about the bases of trees, each ringed with aging Pekinese turds.

I was asking a lot of him. I was asking too much. He'd been back in my life after a decade and *this* was what I had him doing? Wasn't what I'd asked of him at University enough? What was wrong with just a game of darts and a curry?

"Sorry old man," he said finally, shrugging off his mood. "Just the office. O'Shea and what have you. Chin up. Soon be over," and he cuffed me on the shoulder with a small smile.

Where did Andrew fit in Christopher's twisted Circle of Life speech? Where was his type's mirror in nature? Nowhere, that's where. There was no species of antelope offering to put their necks into lions' mouths *for old time's sake*. No genus of fly, diving kamikaze-style, into webs to signal spider-danger to other flies because *they all went back a few days*. And yet here was Andrew Benjamin, in a bad mood, a grotty part of town and an ill-fitting shirt, doing just that.

"Not much further," Laura said, swinging us around a tree, turning right into Herne Road, another quiet side street lined with orange-bricked mansion flats, criss-crossed with scaffolding, skips and flapping polythene.

See what Christopher and his smug, rationalised, Nietzschean, right-wing, psycho-babble, lion-antelope cobblers theory failed to take into account is what people like that *always* fail to take into account. Goodness. Kindness. Call it what you like-ness. Thankfully in this grim old world, some people, for whatever reason, genuinely *do* put others first. Take time out of their day. Lend a helping hand. Let you play the white pieces in chess for a whole term while you learn the rules. Listen to you unload your family worries as your father's birthday passes. Help you plot the seduction of a close friend even though it will ruin the dynamic and cause months of awkwardness and difficult moods. Even when it means –

"O'Shea's insisted the profit he cleared be *removed* from Keatings' holding account," Andrew muttered, interrupting my thoughts. "Why should *we* be the ones making the interest? So I've got to go back this afternoon and set up bloody passwords and bloody clearance codes for a new, non-interest, high-security, barbed-wire, keep-out, *achtung* account he can keep his precious cash in for three bloody days. Had to get Keating himself on the phone to calm O'Shea down. Three days. What a waste of bloody time."

Laura stopped walking. Andrew and I came to a slow halt around her.

"We're here," she said, stopping beneath a resident's parking sign.

"*Here?*"

Here was Redcliffe Gardens. Another in a long line of wide, terraced streets. No different to the half dozen she'd already led us through. The BMWs parked in this one might have been a touch more obnoxious, the 4×4s a smidge more smug, but apart from that, identical.

"Where it's all going to happen. Now listen."

Andrew flipped out his red book and we huddled up a little.

"Whatever happens, keep one thing in mind," Laura said. She tugged out a fresh cigarette. "Christopher is trying a double-cross of his own. He spent the train journey telling you how you're lending him your comic book on Friday? To help him play the drop on this Grayson? The supposed *mark*?"

"He did," Andrew nodded.

"Well that's what he wants you to think. And that's how it's going to look. Everything he said about the plan? The car park, the pub, the split? Taking Grayson's money, giving him the comic book to look after?"

"And Julio turning up, stealing it all back, guns blazing? Grayson running for the hills?" Andrew nodded, flipping back a few pages and sucking the end of his pen.

"Right. In three days' time, in the doorway of The Atlas public house, all that's going to happen. Just as he told you."

"Just as he told me."

"Right. Up until Grayson, whoops, pulls out a '*surprise*' gun of his own," and Laura popped her cigarette in her mouth to waggle some inverted-comma fingers. "It all, ahem, *goes wrong*," – waggle waggle – "everyone flees and *you* Andrew, are left with nothing."

"Grayson . . . surprise gun . . ." Andrew jotted.

"Now Neil, to you." Laura snapped a match from a buckled book and the flame sparked and hissed. She lit her cigarette and flicked the match away. "What do you drive?"

"Drive?"

"What car do you have? Something big? Because come Friday morning, at eight minutes past ten, you'll be blocking this street."

"With a Nissan Micra?"

Laura stepped off the kerb into the quiet centre of Redcliffe Gardens, hands on hips, eyes prowling the logistics.

"Hmn. I don't think a Micra's going to do it. Can you get hold of something bigger by then? You can't leave room for a car to pass on either side."

"Bigger? I . . . Wait. Wait, Friday? I'll have a van. I've hired one for the trade fair. Back when I had enough stock for a trade fair. And to fill a van. A Transit. I'm still scheduled to pick it up tomorrow afternoon. I was going to cancel, but . . ."

"Perfect. Get the longest wheelbase you can. Nothing can get down this street. Oh, and make sure it comes with a Haynes manual too. You're going to need some under-the-bonnet –"

"*Hold it*," Andrew said suddenly. We both looked up at him. He was standing on the kerb, flicking back through his notebook. The November wind played with his hair a little. He looked up at me, expressionlessly. Then he looked over at Laura.

"It's all right," she soothed. "I'll go over it all again. I know it's a lot to take in. Oh and before I forget, one of you will need a passport."

"Passport?" I said. "Where the hell are we *going*?"

"We're not going anywhere. I'll need to exchange it for a —"

"*HOLD IT!*" Andrew hissed, eyes blazing. "Just . . . just hold *everything*. Aren't you *forgetting* something my dear?" he said flatly.

The mood had shifted. The silent street somehow went even more quiet, as if the tarmac and trees were holding their breath.

"The police? Your precious bloody Fraud Squad?" and he waved the red book like a football referee. "*Immunity?*"

Christ he was right. It had completely slipped my mind. Where *were* they? Shouldn't they have a part in all this? I looked across the street to where Laura was standing. She hadn't moved.

"*Your freedom in exchange for the team,* you said. *Caught red-handed in a last final scam.* Well?" and Andrew threw his arms open wide. "Coo-ee? Mr Policeman? Don't you want to know the plan? Coo-ee? You can come out now?"

All was still.

In the middle of the street, Laura sucked on her cigarette, exhaling the warm blue smoke into the afternoon.

"I thought you were going to turn me in," she said, shifting her weight to one hip.

"*What?*" Andrew scowled. "When?"

"That night. In the hotel. When Neil appeared from under the bed. I'd taken fifty grand of his daughter's money. I thought you guys were going to call the cops."

"Wait. So you *lied*?" I said.

"It's what I'm good at."

"And the cops? *Immunity?*"

Laura smiled, shaking her head a little.

"I figured it was the only way to keep you quiet. Telling you I'd turned myself in already. It meant you wouldn't bother to."

"Oh *bloody* hell," Andrew spat. "Bloody buggering *hell!*" and he walked away a few steps, head thrown back in disbelief. Finally he spun around. "You're a real piece of work, you know that? So the whole thing? This whole *bloody* thing? You don't want *out*. You don't want out at *all*. So what is this? Some kind of double, triple . . . double . . . quadruple-cross?"

"No! No no *no*! I *do* want out," Laura said quickly, taking short, scared tugs on her cigarette. "I *do*. Okay, the cop thing was a line, fine, I admit it, you got me. But I just thought you'd be more likely to help me if you thought it was all Home Office approved. I *do need* your help. This plan? All this?" and she gestured at the quiet street. "This is *going to work*. Neil?" She looked at me, wide eyed. "This is going to get your money back. This is going to repair the damage. Save your wife. Save your marriage. And it's going to get me out. Free. Once and for all."

"And how," I snapped, "is it going to do *that* exactly?"

Laura stopped, breathing deep, like she was trying to slow the world down a little. She looked at me. Then at Andrew. Her arms were crossed about her body, curled tight and scared, pulling her military jacket around her slim frame.

"Because . . ."

Somewhere a dog barked.

"Go on?" I pushed angrily. "I'm all ears. How exactly is this magical *plan* of yours going to get you free of Christopher and Grayson and the others?"

"Because . . ." Laura chewed her lip. "Because once they're loaded, blank bullets and real bullets are almost impossible to tell apart."

part three

twenty-five

"Are you still on hold there, old man?" Andrew said, appearing in the doorway clapping the dust from his hands and wiping basement grime on his Abercrombie T-shirt.

"Yep," I sighed. "But my call is important to them so I should please stay on the line. Oh, and this you'll like. Am I also aware, as a member of their mailing list, that tomorrow they're hosting the nineteenth annual London Collectibles Convention and I'm eligible for two discounted tickets?"

"How generous. What's next? All these?"

It was Thursday afternoon. A quiff past a collar by the shop clock. The stereo crackled some MGM greats and two take-out hot chocolates sat on the counter where, long ago, a till once stood. A large tatty London *A-Z* lay flapped open, red marker pen wobbling across tomorrow's route. On the narrow cobbles of Brigstock Place, the blue rented Transit that would follow those wobbles was hunched, back doors open, hazards blinking pink in the winter gloom.

"Those tubes there," I said. "Plus the box they're sitting on and that's it."

"That's *it*? You're barely a third full out there."

"That's all I could salvage. So until Wembley Arena holds its first annual Soggy Papier Mâché Convention, I —"

"*Hello, exhibitions?*"

"Sorry, h-hello," I said. Andrew heaved up an armful of poster tubes and moved out to the chilly street, sliding them into the back of the van. "My name's Mr Martin. I've a stall booked for the convention tomorrow? *Heroes Incorporated*?"

"*Stand 116?*"

"Th-that's right. I was just explaining to your colleague, I'm not going to be able to make it. Something's . . . something's come up. I'm sorry. I was wondering about the deposit though?"

"*If you look you'll see your contract stipulates that exhibitor cancellation notice is ten working –*"

"I–I'm aware of that. It's just . . ." I looked up. Over Chewbacca's hairy head, I could see Andrew, poster tubes under his arm, chatting to Schwartz from the bookshop next-door, apologising for his blocked entrance. "It's just that I . . ." My stomach rolled over queasily. "Well there's something I need to do. But I can't afford to just write off –"

"*Your co-exhibitor will be in attendance though? Maurice Bennett . . . Will he be –*"

"No. No, Maurice and I . . . No. It's just me. Is there nothing you can do to help me out? Nothing at all?"

There was, it appeared, nothing she could do.

I hung up and breathed out slowly, eyes closed, face in my hands. Somewhere distantly, Judy Garland was urging me to not only *come on*, but to *forget my troubles* and *get happy*. Easy for her to say.

The slam–slam of the van doors snapped me back to earth. Andrew moved back into the shop, shutting the door with a jingle and retrieving his hot chocolate while I showered him with thanks.

"What are old college pals for? Besides, I'm keeping my head down. Nobody at the office is very keen on what I've done with O'Shea's capital. His short-term instant access account I told you about? Turns out the old bastard was *right*. Keatings had *every intention* of getting as much interest from his millions in the three days as we could. Best I keep out of their way, so I thought I'd drop by. Any joy with Earl's Court?"

I explained the lack of joy.

"God. This whole thing really couldn't have come at a worse time, could it?"

"Not really," I sighed. "I should move that van anyway. I'm blocking Schwartz's door," and I swept up the keys from the desk, getting to my feet.

"I suppose . . . Hell, I suppose no one would blame you, y'know, if you just . . ."

"If I just . . . ?"

Andrew looked at me.

"With everything else? The summons, the exhibition, the Maurice fellow? Plus Jane? Your family? I'm just *saying* old man, no one could blame you for maybe just telling Laura . . ."

The shop went quiet. Judy told us that if we felt like singing, we should sing.

Neither of us did, much.

"Well . . ." and Andrew shrugged, popping the top off his cup and taking a sudden interest in its contents.

"What are you suggesting?"

"Hmn? No no, nothing. Mmm, this is good," and he wiped a finger about the lid.

"Benno?"

"I just mean if you called it off. Told her you'd changed your mind. That you'd had second thoughts. *I* for one would totally understand. That's all I'm saying."

"You want to call it off?"

"*Me*? No no, God no. I'm just *saying*. If *you* did, I'd understand. If you thought it had all got a little out of hand."

"You want to call it off, don't you?"

"No, no no," Andrew stressed. "God no. Absolutely not." He sipped his drink and perched himself on the edge of the desk.

"Okay. Let me move the van," I said and shuffled up the shop.

"Yes," a small voice said behind me as I reached for the door. "Yes I do."

I turned. Andrew sat there, chewing the inside of his cheek. Something about the look was familiar. A distant memory stumbled past like an Autumn wasp.

"I want out."

"Benno . . ."

"It's getting . . . I mean bloody hell. Bullets? Blood bags in our shirts? Phoney road-blocks? The crazy woman is fixing to engineer a *bloodbath*."

"She said we wouldn't be involved. Couldn't be implicated. They'll be wiping each *other* –"

"Wiping each other out, right. Like that makes it okay. It's a gangland slaying. A gangland bloody slaying on the streets of Earl's Court."

The years had fallen away and the Andrew writhing in front of me was an angsty, socially responsible, beardy eco-warrior, with a Greenpeace sticker on his guitar and an oil-soaked guillemot in his arms. The New York swagger was gone. The big-cocked, big-business big-shot had been substituted at the eleventh hour for his own ghost of lectures past. A good man. An honourable man. A man of principle.

"I can't do this. Be part of this. I can't."

"Benno —"

"Performing lines? *Hold your horses old stick, I saw this first. I just . . .*"

"Benno —"

". . . *That's eighty grand's worth of comic book. Why should we trust you with it?* I can't do it. I won't. Knowing she's going to . . ." Andrew shook his head. "You might be comfortable with all this, old man, but that's you. I can't —"

"*What?* What does *that* mean?" I interrupted. "Comfortable?"

"You. Hurting people. Harming people. Leaving them . . . leaving them for dead at the side of the road."

"Wha-? What are you *talking* about?" I said.

"I mean with your father and everything. It's something you've been around."

"Wait, you think I'm *comfortable* with what my father did? Holding up a bookmaker's? Shooting that woman? What is it, killing's in my family's *blood*? I'm *more up for this* plan because it's in my *nature*?! Jesus . . ."

"No," Andrew said, confused, angry. "I'm sorry, old man, I didn't mean —"

"I'm doing this for *one* reason. One reason. My family. Lana. Jane. When I think about losing them, when I think about going on without them? Me? Alone. Just . . ." The words caught fat in my throat. "Screw them. After everything they did, what should I do? Walk away? No. No way. Let them wipe each other out. *Lions versus lions is at least a fair fight.* Well he's got a fair fight now."

"I know, I know, but . . . God, it's so . . . I mean, *road blocks?* What do *you* know about road blocks? Do you know how you're going to disable the van?"

"No, but I've got the manual. It can't be *too* tricky. Bonnet up. Unscrew the . . . the whassit. Disconnect the spark . . . burettor . . . cable. Thing," I coughed.

"Great. That's confidence inspiring."

"I'll manage it."

"But she's *nuts*," Andrew implored. "This plan of hers? You swap this, I swap that? Giving her your *passport* for heaven's sake?"

"She said she needed it. The guy —"

"She *said*?" Andrew threw his hands in the air like a Jewish mother. "Well, if she *said* . . ."

"Her plan needs a gun and that's what the gun-getter wants. What do you want her to do? Offer him roller-boots and an Etch-A-Sketch instead? He isn't Noel fucking Edmonds."

"I know, I know. But —"

"The man sells handguns for passports and Laura traded hers years ago. There's no *way* you're handing over yours. You've got a wife and family expecting you home. I'm not going to be the one standing in the way of that. You've . . ." I looked at him. "You've done *enough* for me over the years. We never talk about . . . *it*, but —"

"Forget that. That's not . . ." Andrew gnashed and writhed. "I just —"

"*What?*" I pushed. He wasn't looking at me. "Yesterday you were *fine* with this. When we went through the plan? You said he had it coming. *Live by the sword*, all that. What aren't you telling me?"

Andrew sighed, chin in his chest and reached behind him, tugging a buckled piece of heavy stationery from his hip pocket, tossing it across to me. I caught it. Crackled it open carefully.

"When I said the office weren't keen on my initiative," Andrew said. "I mean they *really* aren't keen."

When sitting down with the nice people at Pront-A-print, the marketing bods at Keatings had plumped for a classy, well-spaced letterhead. A rich navy colour on a weighty cream paper. Formal, classic, dependable. Just the sort of impression you'd want to create in fact if you were in the business of persuading wealthy investors to buy and sell expensive office complexes in the major financial capitals of the world. Everything about the letter in my hand said a long tradition of i's dotted with creaking oak and t's crossed in hand-tooled leather. Even the language employed had a whiff of brandy and cigar. There was none of that chummy, open-door, dress-down Friday *nu-bizniss* speak. Nothing was being run up a ballpark, no hot-buttons were being pushed nor was anyone blue-skying a platformed networking solution.

No. Andrew simply was being asked to appreciate that (clear throat) *these are not the negotiations of a future partner.*

"This O'Shea thing. Me moving his money. The private account. It's caused . . . doubts."

"Doubts?"

"My making partner at Keatings, my whole *future* in this business, is dependent on closing the O'Shea deal."

"Which you're about to do?"

"Right," Andrew said. "*I'm* about to do. *Me*. I pulled this out of the fire. Going the extra mile like this? Opening this private account for him? It's turned O'Shea around on the whole firm. Keatings' greed was about to blow the whole shebang. O'Shea was in my office shouting, yelling – *I ain't some fetlock-tugging farmhand.* So I come up with this account move idea and bang – he's all smiles. I've not only saved *this* deal, but when he comes to unload the Holborn site in a year he'll come to *me*. His millionaire golfing chums will come to *me*."

I looked over the letter again.

"It doesn't sound like New York know that?"

"No but they *will*. They will when I walk into the New York office on Monday morning with the O'Shea deal – the *legendary* O'Shea deal – done. When I show them his letter of recommendation. When I show them my red notebook full of all of O'Shea's friends and contacts."

The shop fell silent, the *MGM Greats* having shut off. There was just the grind of the wheezy fan-heater and the chilly sigh of early evening traffic.

"What I'm saying is . . . the deal. The whole thing? It completes Friday. It's a big day. I can't screw this up. I can't let a single hiccup blow this deal. This deal is my future. My family's future. Partner? Corner office? The Long Island house?"

My heart sank, leaden and dull.

"I know . . . I know what this means old stick, I do. But I just don't know if I can risk it. There are escalating penalties for every hour past noon the money isn't transferred. And you need me to spend all morning dressed up like a geek, running around with a comic book in a briefcase and a bag of corn syrup under my shirt . . . ?"

"But . . ." I began, chewing my lip. "But y-you said Christopher was planning the con for the *morning*?" I eased gingerly. "Ten o'clock wasn't it?" I was pushing it, I know. Andrew wanted out and had good reason to.

But I had a wife, a daughter, a business and fifty thousand other pretty good reasons myself.

"Your deal with O'Shea isn't until *noon* . . ." I added. I was building a case with delicate, fragile fingers like it were a flimsy house of cards. "Even if Laura's plan over-runs, which she said it *can't*, mightn't you still not be able . . . I-I mean, I understand what you're saying old friend . . ."

"I know," Andrew nodded. He looked up at me. "I know."

"And . . . hell," I grinned, trying to both lighten the mood and somehow get Andrew back on side. "What happened to my chess partner? The oceanographer with the Arran sweater and the saving the whales? What would *he* say if he heard you banging on about corner offices and partnerships?"

Andrew shifted a little uncomfortably, his demons waking, yawning, scratching, searching for their pitchforks and to-do lists.

"And God, what about *revenge*? Revenge on those bastards who forced you to grow up and turned you into this corporate machine in the first place? This is your chance to hit back at *them*. How long have you been waiting for that?"

Andrew writhed some more.

"This is your one *chance*. For the years of self-loathing. God, for the eco-warrior you never became. The people who ruined *your* life, ruined *my* life. Tomorrow they're going to get what's coming to them and you're being offered a ringside –"

"And then what? Huh? Then what?"

"What do you mean? Then *I* get my money back, my *life* back, and *you* close your deal and –"

"And everything's put right again?"

"Well . . ."

"This? All this?" and he plucked at his shirt with contemp-tuous fingertips. "*This*. This is what I am now. This is what they *made* me. Being the man who helped the man who helped the woman who helped the man get a crook *killed* isn't going to change that. *This* is what I am now. Revenge isn't going to change that."

"Well," I said, letting that thought settle. "If that's what you *want*."

"It's what I *am*."

"So Christopher wins. The bad guys win. All of them."

Andrew stared at the floor, shoulders jumpy. I could see the muscles in his jaw bulge and tighten as he wrestled with it all. He looked up, eyes fixed, mouth tight.

"Revenge," he said softly, clearing his throat a little.

"I know," I said, nodding. "I know. It's a dirty word. Not what good boys are taught. We're meant to be . . . meant to be *above* it. *Superior*. But you think when a crook gets away with ripping someone off, he gives them a second thought?"

"That's not the point," Andrew said.

"*Mugs*," I said. "That's what they think. That's what my father thought. *Saps*."

I let him think about this. Let it sting a little.

"*You're* why they get away with it," I said flatly. Andrew lifted his chin, mouth tightening. He wasn't happy with that. Not happy at all. "You," I pushed. "People who say nothing. Who do nothing. Who *let it go*. You're the reason all this . . . all this *crap* is called escapism," and I threw my hands in the air, at the peeling posters and portraits. "Why stories where good men triumph and bad guys are punished are called *fantasy*. Because it doesn't happen. Because good guys don't take *revenge*. We don't *fight back*. We don't *punish*. We turn the other cheek and get fucked all over again."

Andrew said nothing. He just stared at the dusty lino.

"*Geeks*, they call us. *Weirdos*. Ha. Us who like to be inspired, like to be lifted by simple stories in which good men stand up and fight. *Weirdos*."

Andrew looked at me, then around at the costumed characters on the walls.

"Revenge is what they deserve. Justice. I dunno, call it . . . call it the law of the street. Eye for eye. Whatever. Tomorrow we're gonna let them do to each other what they'd do to us without blinking. And we leave them for dead."

"Dead," Andrew swallowed.

"It's the life he's chosen."

Andrew looked at me, eyes narrowing a little. He was deciding something.

"Say that again," he croaked. He breathed deep, chest filling.

"It's what he *deserves*," I said.

Andrew stood quietly for a moment. Then slowly, he sat up a bit, took a long glug from his paper cup and wiped smudgy chocolate fingerprints on his T-shirt.

"It's *not*, you know?" he said flatly. "It's not what he deserves. Him and his *type*."

"Benno –"

"It's too *good* for him."

"Too – ? Being shot in the chest by his accomplice?"

"He deserves to *live*," Andrew said. He was breathing deep. He took a last draining suck and dumped his empty cup in the bin. "A long, long life of misery and regret. Live with what he's done."

"He's living with it now," I said sadly. "Doesn't seem to bother him overly."

"Oh we'd have to do it properly. *Painfully.* Plan it out. Make him suffer." Andrew's eyes got distant, lost in the black thoughts of revenge. Revenge on the world that stole his soul.

"We've only got twenty-four hours, old mate. It's this or he walks."

"You're right," Andrew shrugged, shaking off the darkness. "I was just . . ."

"Tomorrow morning. We go in, we get out and we're done. You off to your promotion, your corner office, your New York partnership," and I gestured at the heavy letter. "Me back to my family. All over. Like nothing ever happened. They won't know what's hit 'em."

Andrew looked down at his letter once again. He looked up at me. Cleared his throat.

"*No. No, that's it. I don't need this bloody shit.*"

I grinned.

"*I'm not doing it. I'll walk. I'll go out there, tell him to keep his money, take my bloody comic book and walk. I only came to you for insurance. All this tricky stuff was your idea. Forget it.*"

"*And it's* . . . ?" I prompted.

"Right, right. *And it's Mr Mayo, to you pal,*" Andrew smiled.

twenty-six

"Bloody hell old man, that was quick. Have you got the phone in bed with you or something?"

"Something like that." I blinked hard, rubbing my eyes and peering about the chill blue stillness of the sitting room. Streaky stirred, waking on my lap and choosing that moment for a quick three-sixty and a ten-thousand mile claws-check. I shoo-ed him *ow-bugger*-ing from my bare legs onto the floor with a wince.

"Hello – ?"

"It's just the cat. What's wrong? You all right?" I got up, creeping with sticky bare feet to the sitting room door, listening for Jane. Down the hall, the mattress gave a heart-gripping creak . . . then all was still.

"Glad I caught you. I need a favour. This corn syrup stuff Christopher left for me to practise with?"

"In the chest-bag?"

"It's stickier than I thought and I've gone and got it all over the clothes you lent me. The bloody dry-cleaners have left me with just my suits until lunchtime . . ."

"You need some more gear?"

"Would you mind old man? Sorry to be an arse. Today's going to be complicated enough as it is, I know."

"No problem," I whispered. "I'll stick some in the van. How you feeling? Ready for this?"

"Pretty good, pretty good. Can't sleep though."

"Me neither," I said, moving back to the window, peering out at the rented Transit parked in the November darkness. "Been up since four. What the hell are we doing, old friend?"

"Our bit. Like you said. Lions versus lions. Bringing a little justice to the world. Talking of which, I've had a thought. Made a decision about our conversation yesterday."

"Go on?"

"*I've . . . No, I'll tell you when I see you. And don't forget the clothes. I don't think stripy jim-jams really say professional memorabilia expert somehow.*"

"You'd be surprised."

Andrew hung up. Breathing deep and slow, I crept out of the sitting room, down the dark hall, under the suspicious gaze of Luthors Hackman and Spacey to the bedroom. Easing open the door with a carpety hiss, I held my breath and slid inside. With one eye on the soft rising and falling of the duvet, I pulled on my jeans silently, tugging a shirt over my head and sliding sticky feet into my canvas baseball boots. Teeth clenched, I then eased open the wardrobe and picked out an armful of my baggier, Andrew-shaped clothes: jeans, T-shirts, jumpers, the wire hangers tinkling like wind-chimes. I crept back out, sliding the door shut behind me.

I breathed out. Moving quickly to the kitchen, I fetched a bin-bag from under the sink and, in the dim light of the cooker-clock, shovelled most of the clothes inside, knotting the top tight. I hefted the bag onto my shoulder and slid out, down the stairs silently like Santa Claus.

In the darkness of the freezing street, toes cold in my thin All-Stars, I unlocked the van and pushed the bag in among the boxes and poster tubes. Easing the metal doors shut with a wince, I took a quick look up at the warm windows of my home before climbing into the driver's seat.

The next time I saw my home, all would be well. All would be back to normal.

Please.

I started the engine, revs bouncing loud off the quiet houses, ground the gears and slid out onto the morning street.

It was Friday. It was ten past six.

It was time.

"Jesus *Christ*," I said as Andrew greeted me in his hotel-room doorway. He was in just his pants, a taped-up blood-bag and an anxious mood.

"I know, I know," he said, taking the bulging bin-bag from me and sliding me inside. "This the Geek-Couture?"

"Morning gorgeous," Laura said, appearing in the bathroom doorway and leaning against the jamb with a coffee cup. "Ready for a little payback?" She was dressed for battle. Boots, combats and a black vest, hair tied back under a New York baseball cap. Face pale, she was without make-up for once, save, naturally, the trademark vibrant stripe of red lipstick.

"Ready? No. Not really no," I jittered. "I'll be glad when this is all over. More of that coffee about?"

"You sure you brought enough kit?" Andrew said, upending the bag and tumbling armfuls of clothes onto the bed. "It's just me we're outfitting, old man. Not the whole cast of *Revenge of the Nerds*."

"I wasn't sure what would fit you. How's the chest-bag?"

"Heavy," Andrew said, holding my blue Superman shirt up over it, tossing it aside instead for a baggier Incredible Hulk number. "Feels like I'm six months' pregnant. And this damned syrup stinks. Plus the tape's taken half the hair off my shoulders."

"Yowzers," I said.

"And the bloody drawing pin on my wedding ring keeps – ouch, *bugger* – keeps catching on things." He waggled his hand with a scowl.

"Put the gear on," Laura said, sliding into the fat hotel couch, pushing aside Andrew's syrup-stained polo-shirts. "Let's see how you look."

Andrew hopped about, tugging on one of my old pairs of black jeans, turn-ups grimy with basement sewage, before sliding the Incredible Hulk over his head, pulling it down.

"Loose," I said, pouring a coffee. "Nobody tucks them in."

Andrew stood in front of us, arms out for inspection.

"Not bad," Laura nodded.

"Not *bad*? They don't fit," Andrew said with a squirm. "Under the arms? And this waist is a bit –" He puffed, breathing in a little.

"You're a geek," I said. "You're not meant to care. Your mind is on higher things. *Star Trek Voyager*. *Battlestar Galactica*. What Wonder Woman looks like naked."

"Blood-bag all right under there?" Laura asked. "Comfortable?"

Andrew adjusted it a little bit under the Hulk before miming a gunshot, bringing his hand up sharply to his stomach.

"Hey hey, easy there cowboy," Laura said. "We've got three hours yet. We don't want a puncture at this stage."

"What news of O'Shea?" I asked. "All ready for lunchtime?"

"Huh? Oh, account's all set. No thanks to Keatings. But it's just a matter of completing and a telegraphic transfer of funds, making him the new proud owner of a hundred-thousand square feet of prime City office space."

"And you, by extension, a proud partner with corner share-options overlooking Long Island. I guess congratulations are in order?"

"Thank you. But no." Andrew was climbing into his denim jacket gingerly, standing in front of the wardrobe mirror. "I spoke to Veronica. About what you said yesterday? Had a long talk."

"Everything all right?"

"I asked her how she fancied a new permanent houseguest. An aging, eco-idealist with a Jack Kerouac novel in his bag, a Bob Dylan album on his iPod and a Range Rover full of sick sealions. I think he's someone Veronica and the twins would like to have around, don't you?" He smiled the smile I hadn't seen in a long time.

"Are you serious? How – ?"

"When this deal goes through this afternoon, Keatings are going to make me a partner. And with a partnership comes a healthy bonus."

"How healthy?"

"*Healthy*," Andrew said. I watched his grinning face in the wardrobe's reflection. "Enough to get us out of Manhattan and onto a boat. Well, a ship, really. Artic circle. Six months."

"My God. Won't . . . won't Keatings mind?"

"Let them mind," Andrew said. "Once I'm partner and their cheque's cleared, there's nothing they can do. Funny thing is of course, I'd never have been able to afford to do it if I hadn't made such a killing in real estate. And I wouldn't be in this bloody business if it wasn't for people like this Christopher. In a strange way, on this – the last sorry day of the bastard's life – he's actually doing some good."

The last day of his life. The words hung heavy in the hotel room for a moment, stale and sickening, like old cigar smoke. We all sat and inhaled them in silence for a moment.

"Well good for you, pal," I said loudly, opening a metaphorical window and squirting a metaphorical air-freshener. "Really. Good for *you*."

"Couldn't have done it without you, old stick," Andrew said and he turned to face me. I got up. Andrew extended a hand.

"Yeah yeah yeah," Laura interrupted from the couch. "As much as I hate to break up the shaving-cream ad' here fellahs, it's quarter past seven."

"Hn? Oh, right," I said and Andrew and I examined our shoes for a moment, coughing self-consciously.

"Now, you handled one of these before?" Laura asked.

I looked up and saw that she had an oily chamois leather in her lap which she was peeling back, unwrapping corner by corner like a picnic.

Christ.

"Er, no. No I haven't."

"Here," she said. She had her palm held out, the cloth draped over it. In the centre lay apparently as much handgun as a modern passport will buy.

"Bloody hell," Andrew whistled. "Bit flashy?"

Licking my lips and swallowing hard, I reached out and took it.

It was heavy. Much heavier than movies had taught me. Like a brick. It had a shiny, oily finish and smelled like dead batteries. I bounced it a little in my grip, fingers flexing over the wooden handle.

"It's a good thing your passport was new," Laura said. "The nickel finish comes at a price."

"It had to be nickel?"

"Nickel is what Julio's got."

"And it looks like this?"

"A year or so older but otherwise identical," Laura said.

"Explain again why Neil can't just swap the bullets?" Andrew asked, perching on the end of the bed cautiously, fussing with the sticky-tape under his shirt.

"Time," Laura said. "To remove all six blanks and replace them with six live rounds would take a good minute, even for an expert. He's not going to have that long. Back of the van, glovebox open, swap, glovebox closed, out again. This is the only way."

I looked the ugly gun over again. The six gold circles in the six barrels behind the hammer.

Soon to be just five.

I swallowed hard.

"Andrew, you have the receiver there?" Laura said.

Andrew reached into his denim jacket and plucked out a tangle of wire, unspooling his fountain-pen and handing me the little black box.

I wrapped the gun in the chamois and placed it carefully on the bed, taking the receiver and unwrapping the earpiece.

"Batteries are fresh and will go for six full hours," Laura said. "So don't worry. Keep it on, keep the earpiece in and keep calm."

"Easy for you to say."

"*Check, check?*" a voice crackled close by, making me jump a little. It took me a moment to follow the words out of my head, through my ear, down the wire to the blinking light on the receiver. I looked over and saw Andrew whispering into his pen with a smirk.

In fact, considering what we were about to do, the mood in the room was surprisingly upbeat. Energetic, bouncy, jokey even. As if we were preparing for a beach-volleyball game. Rather than bloody revenge.

But then, I suppose, we were all of us on the verge of something. Something better. Laura – final freedom from a life of lies, tricks and extortion. Andrew – a chance to begin a new life, the life he wanted, at last.

And me. In three hours I would be walking away with Lana's money back. Home to Jane. To explain. To explain everything.

We charged ourselves up with a fresh pot of coffee and went over the play one more time, double-checking we each knew each other's roles before Laura straightened her baseball cap and told us it was eight forty-five. We packed our gear quietly, solemnly, moving out into the hotel corridor.

Around us, guests were appearing from rooms, exchanging nods, hellos, rolling newspapers under their arms and heading down for breakfast. My heart thumping, Andrew shut his door and we shuffled down the corridor silently, climbing into the lift.

"I-I need the bathroom," Andrew said, eyebrows bouncing.

"Bathroom?"

"I-I need the *bathroom*. I can't *do* it. The *blood*, the *shooting*. This *chest-bag*," and he shifted a little in his awkward clothes, smoothing the Incredible Hulk over the broad pouch underneath like an anxious expectant mother and shooting me a nervous look.

"You can't do it?"

"It's a job for *professionals*. You should have let the *girl* do it. You should have let *Laura* do it."

"*Linda*," I corrected. "Should have let –"

"Shit, sorry. I had it. *Linda*. Right, right. It'll be fine."

The lift gave a *ding* and opened out to the cool lobby. Watery November sunlight washed through the glass, over the oak and marble, the place bustling.

Laura and I hung back by the rubber plants while Andrew tripped quickly across the polished floor to the front desk, muttering his lines to himself again. We watched in silence as he signed a form, gave a nod and waited.

"It's going to be fine," Laura said softly.

"You know what you're doing?" I said.

Laura nodded.

I turned to her.

"I mean you know what you're *doing*?"

"Lions hunting lions is at least a fair fight."

"Got it," Andrew said, appearing beside us. He had my brown satchel in his hand, knuckles tight and white about the handle.

"Then let's go," Laura said.

We marched across the bustling lobby, through the doorman entrance, pushing out to the traffic blare of the busy street.

"Fetch your car sir?" a young man in a bright waistcoat bobbed on the steps.

He hesitated a moment, looking over the three of us. Laura in her GI Jane utility gear, Andrew in soggy-bottomed, ill-fitting jeans, brogues and a strangely lumpy Hulk T-shirt. And me, jittering and twitching between the pair of them. I handed him the van keys and he slid off the steps slowly before scuttling off to the parking bay.

"Taxi!" Laura hollered, a cab shutting off its yellow light and peeling out from the rank to stop at our feet. Laura cranked open the back door.

"Keep in touch," Andrew said, waggling the fountain pen.

I tapped my earpiece.

"Good luck," I said, my voice oddly squeaky. They piled in. I shut the door behind them, Andrew pumping down the window.

"It'll be all right, old man. Two hours from now it'll be all over. No more Christopher. No more lies. No more worries."

"I know," I said. "I know. Look, thanks for this mate," I said. "I . . ."

Andrew winked.

"See you soon."

"Earl's Court Exhibition Centre," Laura said, the cab wheeling away, round in a tight circle and sliding into the morning traffic. In its space, my rented blue Transit peeled up to the kerb. The bellboy climbed out, handing me back the keys.

I thanked him and clambered in, slamming the door shut with a dull clang.

The bell-boy stood, bobbing expectantly at the window.

"Sorry," I said. "You want a tip?"

"Thank you sir," he nodded. I started the engine.

"Never ignore a dripping basement pipe," I told him and pulled out into the traffic.

twenty-seven

"Julio? May I introduce Angus Mayo. Kindly supplying our valuables for this morning's play."

"Linda here talked you through it? Good man, good man. Our matey with the baitey, yes? In your satchel there?"

Adjusting the earpiece, I swallowed hard at the thought. A few streets away, in Earl's Court's underground carpark, among vans, Volvos and vintage Volkswagens – most if not all slapped with peeling bumper-stickers announcing that *My Other Car Is KITT* and *Comic-Book Fans Do It Fairly Infrequently* – my best friend was handing over a leather satchel to one of Christopher's team. My leather satchel. With what remained of my world within.

"Look good. Should work like charm."

I shifted in my seat, a sick, dull cramp gripping my kidneys. I breathed deep and checked the clock on the van dashboard. *09:32.*

"You know what you doing?" Julio's voice crackled. *"Got the bag taped on good? Practised your fall? Must burst bag first time and go down loud and hard, understand?"*

"G-Got it," my best friend said. His voice was shaky.

"And ready for meet-up?"

"Absolutely. T-Ten o'clock sharp, I come round that corner and spot the satchel among those bin-bags."

"But not before you see the boss-man and mark come down ramp. Remember, you have to catch sight of it together. All three of you. Simultaneous, or the story not hold up."

"Ramp. Got you. No problem."

A sharp car-horn jolted me from the voices in my ear. I looked up and saw the light was green, the road ahead clearing. Crunching the gears, I slid forward, following the morning traffic west along Cromwell Road.

"And where is the mark now?" Laura's voice. Clear. Close. Standing

very near Andrew. Or at least very near his fountain pen. "*Christopher got him?*"

"*They're finishing breakfast. He's going to wheel Grayson round here, keep him chatting and they'll be entering the Exhibition Centre through bay C, which brings 'em down the ramp.*"

I blinked hard, trying to focus on the traffic, poster tubes rolling and clanging about behind me as I took a left down Earl's Court Road. I put my hand out to steady the bag next to me, feeling slightly sick at the thought of the cold, solid shape inside.

It was about seven minutes to ten by the time I wheeled round onto Redcliffe Gardens. The street was quiet, Tuesday night's BMWs now clogging up the City, the 4×4s off blocking up the kerbs of King's Road and Knightsbridge, their hazards blinking while nannies scoured grocery shelves for obscure olive oils.

In my ear, I could make out Andrew's echoey mumbling as he lurked anxiously behind a concrete car-park pillar. Watching. Waiting.

"*Come on. Come on. Five minutes. Where are they? Where are they?*"

I pummelled the van north up the quiet, leafy street. All was still, the traffic just a distant sigh. Or that might have just been Andrew in my ear. I couldn't be sure.

"*Nine fifty-six. Come on. Come on.*"

I slowed as the van slid towards the chosen spot, finally coming to a squeaky halt at the side of the road under the residents' parking notice. I sat in the silence of the cab for a moment, heart hammering. Breathing deep, checking the empty wing-mirrors, I ground the gears into reverse and heaved the wheel right, sliding the van around so it was at ninety degrees to the road, blocking the traffic. I then slid it forward slowly, slowly –

"*Nine fifty-eight. Cutting it fine, cutting it fine . . .*"

– until the front bumper was almost touching the parking sign on the pavement. I shut off the engine, taking a deep breath in the silence, licking my lips before unlocking the door and jumping out to inspect my rudimentary road –

Shit. I clambered back in quickly.

There was a good fifteen feet between the back of the van and the far kerb. More than enough to let Julio past. Grinding the gears, I slid the van backwards a few feet. Shutting it off, I climbed out once again. Better. There was no way he'd slide past behind me. And in front, he couldn't possibly squeeze –

Oh for Chrissakes. There was now about nine feet of road in front.

"*Ten o'clock. It's ten o'clock. And where . . . Bloody hell, that's . . . that's them. Shit. Here we go. If you can hear me, Neil old chap, this is it. This is it.*"

I mean what the *hell* – ? I jittered about the van, brain crunching, squeezing, panicking, trying to fill the empty space like it were some Krypton Factor puzzle. No way. I couldn't do it. Not without a trailer or a welding torch. Had the council been busy in the last forty-eight hours with some kind of emergency road-widening work? It had *fitted*. I was sure of it. Before, with Laura, that evening. She'd stood right *here*. Unless – ?

Taking off up the street, feet pounding, my eyes peeled over the identical mansion blocks. Was it further up? Further down? I spun and twirled. Did the road narrow at some point?

"*Er, bloody . . . bloody hell, what's this? Hey, hey look there's something buried in here . . .*"

"*Damn right, boy. Lemme see that.*"

"*Well bless my goodness, so there is. Well-spotted Mr Grayson.*"

"*Hold your horses old stick, I saw this first . . .*"

Shit shit shit. I was panicking now, head thudding with voices. I checked my watch. Ten o'clock.

I scanned up and down the wide, empty street. What the hell was going on? Was I in Redcliffe *Road* by mistake? Redcliffe *Crescent*? Redcliffe *Drive*?

My heart thundered, a deadening bass-beat blocking out the voices in my ear.

"*Is . . . fastened . . . try . . . here . . . me . . . Holy . . !*"

I spun around crazily. This was definitely the place. I remembered the tree. The Pekinese poop underneath. The street lamp. The residents' parking sign. And all the residents' BM –

No. No, oh no.

Cursing spitty curses over and over, I slammed over to the van, hauling open the door, rummaging in the carrier bag, pushing the leaden chamois leather parcel aside and pulling out my mobile

phone. I scrolled down and thumbed Laura's number quickly, my
earpiece crackling.

"*Is this . . . ? Mah gawd, you know what we got here boy?*"

"*By jove, what a haul! What the bally bum-burps is it doing buried
here do you think?*"

"*Stolen maybe? Someone stashing it?*"

"*Mah gawd . . .*"

"*Hello?*"

"Laura. Laura shit, it's me." I paced and flapped and flustered.
"The parking. It's all . . . Shit, I can't block the street. I'm not wide
enough. I'm not fucking *wide enough!*"

"*What are you talking about? Redcliffe Gardens? You're definitely at
Redcliffe Gardens?*"

"Yes I'm at Redcliffe fucking Gardens! There's nobody parked
here! They're all out screwing the third world and chivvying little
Lottie to cello lessons. Christ, you could park Edward's three fucking
Bentleys across the middle of the street and you'd still have room
for him to stroll about between them with his belt off. We need
to rethink this. We need to rethink this *now.* Can you persuade
Julio to come another route? I can't block him here."

"*Too late. He's headed your way now.*"

"Now?"

"*They've found the satchel. They're arguing over it as we speak. Aren't
you listening? Julio's headed across to the pub to set up. He'll be passing
you in . . . in about six minutes.*"

"Six – ?!"

"*Come up with something,*" and the line went dead.

Holy crap. I tossed the mobile onto the van seat and tried to
keep calm, pacing quickly, mind thudding. There was nothing else
for it. I grabbed the keys from the steering column and hurried
around to the back of the van. Throwing open the doors, I began
to grab armfuls of memorabilia. Poster tubes, postcards, books,
photographs, stills, display material, dumping it all to the wet
tarmac. C-3PO, Bogart, Allen, Dorothy, cardboard rolled, cardboard
stuck, paper fluttered and flew, photos splashed in great stripes of
colour all over the road. Boxes brimming with junk, stacked one
on top of the –

Blaaaaaaaaaaaaare

I jumped, heart in my throat, dropping a box of black and white stills, sending them spilling out at my feet. I turned. A small Citroën 2CV was trying to pass.

Shit. Kicking boxes, kicking tubes, I scrabbled about with gritty fingernails, apologising, gathering the fluttering debris, clearing a narrow path.

"Jesus, man. Who the fuckin' 'ell died an' made you a Lollipop Lady?" the driver yelled.

I stopped. I turned.

In the windscreen, sat low, a ruddy, goateed face scowled, hairy hands waving. The driver pumped down the side window.

"What tha fuck is all —"

It was then his turn to stop. He blinked, hairily.

No. No, not now. Why now? Why *now*?

His rusty door cracked, swinging open and he clambered out, expanding, filling the street with his wide pyjamas and fat boots. Christ knows how he fitted in the car. Citroën must have taken on some of the engineers from the TARDIS.

"You?!" he bellowed.

"Maurice," I squeaked, chasing a wind-snatched *Fantastic Four*. "Maurice, God, how . . . er how are you? Sorry, you want to get through?" and I grabbed up a couple of stray tubes and stood to one side, boxes stacked about me, waving him past.

"What in fuck's name do ye think you're doin', man?" he barked, peering at the mess. "Settin' up a little off-shoot street stall here, eh? Settin' up a little Earl's Court annexe?"

"Look, look Maurice, I'm sorry, I haven't time to —"

"You know you're due in court on Monday, right? Three o'clock? You are *aware* of . . ." and he stopped, staring at the barricade of boxes at my feet. "Is this all your shit?"

"It . . . it is," I said.

"You told *me* it was all *lost in flooding*?"

"It is. I-I mean it *was*. This is literally *everything* I have left. Six boxes. I lost as much as you did. I'm down to my last postcard. The shop is empty."

He seemed to think about this for an agonising moment, before stepping forward and hefting up the top box in his thick arms. He turned and staggered back to his car with it.

"Maurice?!" I yelped. "What are you − ? Christ, no, Maurice, *please!*" I checked my watch.

10.02.

Opening his boot, he dumped the box inside and clomped back towards me.

"Thirty-six thousand pounds," Maurice growled. He hefted up another box. "Thirty-six thousand pounds you took from me." Again he lumbered to his car and dumped a box in his boot. "I guess the court will decide how best for you to repay it. But this'll do for starters."

"Maurice. Maurice not now. Please. Not *now* . . ."

"I trusted you with that stuff. *Trusted* you. Couldn't be arsed to send off a little cheque though, could ye eh? Couldn't be arsed to call a plumber. Too much fuckin' trouble. That was my *livelihood*. That was every fuckin' thing I had. You know what it's like to lose every fuckin' thing you had?"

"*Yes!*" I bellowed, feet almost leaving the floor. "Yes I do! Please, Maurice, you've got to −"

10.03.

"Christ, please Maurice, listen to me." I danced about in a jive of panic. "I know how you feel, okay? *I* trusted someone too and now I'm about to lose everything *I* have, okay? *Everything*. I trusted someone but they screwed me and now I'm about to lose more than just money. My daughter, my wife, my home, my business, *everything*."

"So now you know how it feels."

"I *do!*" I yelled. "I do. Yes. Yes I know *exactly* how it feels. And I know . . . shit, I know it's easier to get angry. Give up. Sell real estate for fat Irishmen when you should be saving the whale. I understand that."

"*Saving the whale?*"

"I'm sorry, I'm babbling. And that's because a green Bedford van is going to turn that corner in the next three minutes and I have to disable this Transit so I can get in the Bedford and do something unspeakable in the glovebox and I really am babbling now −"

"You really *are* babbling now."

"I am, Maurice. But that's because it's important. I *will* come to the court on Monday. I *will* stand up at three o'clock and swear on a Bible and pay you back what I owe you. I *will*. But *only* if I do this thing *first*. If I don't do this, then you won't see me at three because I'll have lost everything and nothing else will matter. I *have* to do this one thing. And this one thing means blocking this street which means you giving me those boxes back, right now, getting in your car and driving away very quickly and not asking any questions."

Breathless, panting, I checked my watch. Four minutes past.

"Please." I gripped his arms hard. "Learn to trust again. Start now. Get a job on a trawler in the Arctic. Write your dad a letter. Trust me on *this*."

"Trawlers? Write my what a − ? And trust *you*?"

"I don't lie, Maurice. I fuck up. Oh I fuck up big. But I don't lie. I *used* to. Lied to my *wife*. To my *daughter*. My *father-in-law*. But a few weeks ago I lied to a smelly man in a woollen hat about what a photograph was worth and I am *never lying again*."

Maurice looked me in the eyes. Looked at the floor. At the grey November sky, finally turning and trudging back to his car, hefting up both boxes and returning them to my feet.

"If you're conning me . . . ?"

I had to smile. I couldn't help it. The smile of the helpless.

"Maurice, the last thing I have time for is conning *you*."

"Then I'll see you in court on Monday," he said.

"Three o'clock," I said, heart hammering. "I promise."

He gave me a sideways look and turned, taking a slow walk to his car. Clambering in, he wheeled around the debris and sped off with a *honk-honk*.

10.05.

In a desperate flurry, I began to scatter the poster tubes about again, spreading out the heavy boxes, until I heard, distantly, amongst the sigh of traffic, a rev. Then a gear change. Louder.

Then louder still.

Leaping over the debris to the van, I heaved open the bonnet and stared dumbly at the filthy mess of boxes and pipes.

The revs were louder.

Shit. I bustled around to the cab, shoved the keys back in the steering column, grabbed the carrier bag and dived off the street, tumbling behind a low scrabby wall, clattering into some bins.

I lay there, heart hammering, chin in my chest, not daring to move.

My earpiece, loose, gave a crackle. People were talking. Three voices in urgent discussion.

The revs got louder. Louder still, blurring into the roar of a heavy engine.

The engine slowed. A horn hollered. And hollered again, loud and long like a wounded cat.

I shut my eyes.

Another horn. Longer. Louder.

Engine off.

The scrape of a van door. Angry footsteps, scuffing. Mumbling. Quickly.

Then the clang of a box being heaved into an empty van. And another.

Teeth tight, I rolled over onto my knees and peered over the brick.

Julio. Muttering, spitting, cursing, hurling my litter out of the road, checking his watch.

Head thundering, I lifted myself to my toes and fingertips and, sliding the heavy chamois from the bag, scuttled, low, out into the wide street. Quickly, feet flying fast, until I dropped again to the floor behind his van.

Licking dry lips, I reached into my pocket and pulled out the second set of keys Laura had provided. I swivelled on the ball of my feet with a wet squeak, raised up and slid the key into the lock.

Turning, it clicked and I felt the old doors sigh out of their frame.

With a wince, I eased open the back and stepped inside, keeping low, closing the doors behind me.

In the cool darkness, through the windscreen I could see Julio, still trying to clear the street of the bulging boxes of stills and 10×8s, checking his watch.

I pressed the earpiece in properly as I reached the front. An American voice was crackling.

"*Take a seat, take a seat. Let me get some drinks and we'll talk about how to split this.*"

Squeezing through the gap in the front seats I reached out and flipped the catch on the glovebox, easing it open, praying that Julio –

Shit!

Glovebox crap began to spill out of the sides. A mobile phone, an *A-Z*, a tin of cough sweets all clattering to the metal floor of the cab. Panicking, I pushed through the seats, ribs crushing, scrabbling them all together, stuffing them back inside. The map, the sweets, the –

Fuck. Fuck fuck *fuck*.

The jolt had knocked the mobile's battery cover loose. I tried to click it back on, but it wouldn't take. It . . . shit, it wouldn't take.

No time. Dammit, no *time*.

Shoving it all back in, I reached into the glovebox and slid out a blue J-cloth, wrapped tight, holding something. About the weight of a brick. With the dull smell of dead batteries.

Quickly, laying it out on the seat, I unwrapped the gun, swapped it for the one in my cloth and wrapped it again, stuffing the blue parcel back into the glovebox and Julio's blank revolver into my belt. I stole a quick low look through the windscreen to where Julio had been clearing the remains of the street to pass.

Had been.

Not any longer.

Panic rising, building, I felt my gut tense, hard and tight.

Footsteps. Near.

Outside. *Approaching.*

Heart leaping, I jolted back, tiptoeing panicked footsteps back, breathless, into the dark body of the van, hands out against the cool walls.

A crunch and a clang as the driver's side door was wrenched, metal scraping metal.

"*Now here we go genner'men. Let's juss see if we can't come to some kind'a agreement shall we?*"

I ducked, low, almost double, edging backwards quietly against the metal shell.

Julio clambered into the van, muttering to himself.

"Jesus Christ, just have your booty-car sale wherever you like! Do not mind me! Christ, eight minutes past . . ." He buckled himself in and craned forward to the glovebox.

Breath held, crouched in a tight ball at the van's rear, I waited, heart banging wildly in my ears over the crackle of distant voices.

"Awww fack!" Julio spat, the glovebox contents clattering to the floor. The back of his head disappeared as he bent to retrieve his phone and I stepped backwards quickly, falling against the door.

It held fast.

Crouched low, heart thundering, I flew my hands over the doors in the darkness, pushing, easing my weight against them silently.

Locked.

I started, spasming as the enging gunned into life beneath me. The shell rumbled, grumbled, vibrated. Mouth dry, head thudding, I began to panic. The van lurched forward with a crunch of gears.

No. No no no.

"Hello?" Julio barked from up the front. "Hello? Laura it me. I run late, get word to bossman, some arsehole park his . . . Hello? This fack battery. Hello . . . ? Hello?"

The van gunned and revved, squealing off, through the few remaining posters, buckling tubes and sending photos fluttering past the windscreen.

Throat tight, I lowered myself down, blank revolver pressed in the small of my back, hard against the cold metal of the rear doors, bouncing and bumping. Oblivious, Julio lurched the van left sharply, sending me toppling, hands out, clanging against the metal.

"Laura, can you hear . . . ? This damned thing . . ."

"*He's coming back,*" Andrew was whispering in my ear. "*He's got drinks and he's coming back. I-I'm not . . . I'm not sure about this . . .*" I pushed the earpiece in harder, engine noise revving and echoing about me.

"*Take it easy. Just take it easy.*" Christopher. "*Let the mark do the talking. Bag still secure under the Hulk there?*"

I threw my hands out against the filthy aluminium, steadying myself, acceleration pushing me back, hard against the doors, skull banging and thumping with the jolts.

"Fuck it," Julio spat, and in the silhouette of the windscreen ahead, he tossed his knackered phone among the faded dashboard crap of maps and cups. He churned the gears again and put his foot down with a blare of horn.

Crouched low, terrified, head full of noise, oil and rust, I closed my eyes and thought of Jane. Of Lana.

We headed west. Towards the pub. Towards Christopher. Towards Grayson. Towards Andrew.

Towards who the hell knew what.

twenty-eight

"*And what? Yur suggestin' we just trust you? Ah got no idea who you are, boy. Where the hell you get off —*"

"*That's eighty grand's worth of comic book — who should hold on to it? You?*"

"*Why the hell not me?*"

In the rolling tombola darkness of the freezing van, my watch said 10.14, my earpiece said the negotiations were going as planned and my bowels said they very, very much wanted to go home now, thank you very much.

I had managed to prop myself in the back corner, jammed low. Scruffy Converses against the peeling plastic of the rear wheel arch, my back hard against the door hinges, hilt of Julio's gun gnawing my spine, I buried my chin in my chest, feeling the panicked heartbeat pound my skull. Bumping and bouncing, engine roaring in my head, Julio wheeled the Bedford left, my teeth tight against every pothole.

"*A bond? What are you talking about, a bond?*"

"*To show you fellahs faith.*"

"*And how much faith did you have in mind?*"

Swallowing hard in the half light, trying to keep a lid on the panic, I fumbled in my greasy jeans, tight pockets biting the skin on my cold hand, and I slid my mobile phone free. Hunching down even lower amongst the filthy black ridged floor and the snagging rusty edges, I tilted the phone at an awkward, wrist-aching crick to keep the dim screen light hidden and selected: Create Message. I jabbed away a predictive plea.

H . . . E . . . L . . .

HELLO

Delete, delete, delete.

Screw it.

Messaging off, I scrolled down the address book and thumbed

the number, lowering my ear to the handset, joints screaming and pinching.

One ring.

Two rings.

God where the hell – ?

"*You done? All swapped?*" Laura crackled. "*Where are you?*"

"Shh, it's all gone wrong," I hissed, hunching low against the metal.

"*I can't hear you? Where?*"

"Shhh! I'm in his *van*! I'm trapped in the back of the *van*!"

"*Fifty thousand?*"

"What? Fifty – ?"

"*Cash. Divided between the pair of you guys, naturally.*"

"I said can he see you?"

"What?"

"*And you have the money now?*"

"*Neil?*"

"Wait, wait, wait," I twittered, popping the hissy earpiece from my head, focusing back on the phone. "I've got six fucking voices going on at once here. Grayson, Christopher and Andrew nego- tiating in one ear, you in the other, Julio cursing up the front and my survival instinct telling me to put up my hands and call the whole thing off. You've got to get me *out of here*!"

"*Stay low, stay low, he must be almost here. Just keep out of sight.*"

"Out of sight?! He turns around and I'm *dead*! I've given him a gun full of live ammo! He sees me he'll unload the *lot*."

"*You'll be all right, just for Chrissakes stay hidden.*"

"Shit, *no*?! *Really*?!" I spat.

"*Listen to me, first things first. You said you did it? The swap? Did you find the blue J-cloth with his –*"

"I did it, I did it," I said. Swallowing hard, my eyes darted to Julio, hunched over the wheel in the front of the cab, sliding in and out of traffic. "It was right where you said. In the glovebox, along with everything else he's ever owned." I shifted a little against the doors, the cold oily metal of the blank revolver massaging the base of my spine.

"*And you're certain he didn't –*"

"He has no idea. You spoken to him?"

"*In a manner of speaking. His phone keeps cutting out. Battery problems. I'm only getting every fifth word.*"

"Shit. Look, I uhm —"

"*But the plan holds. He'll be out front, cocked and ready at ten twenty-five sharp as planned. Right now your boy should be making his excuses. Can you hear them?*"

"Hold on, hold on," and I lowered the phone and fumbled the tiny earpiece back in.

"*. . . until we know there's no heat. Comic book of this value? Who the goddamn hell knows who's out looking for it.*"

"*I think he's right. It sounds safest. Angus? What do you say?*"

"*Hn? Oh. Uhm . . .*"

"*Are you in? Angus? What do you say?*"

"*Uhm, let me . . . I-I need the bathroom.*"

I popped out the headphone and leaned back into the mobile phone.

"That's it. Toilet break. Right on schedule. Christ, he better pull this off."

"*He'll be fine,*" Laura crackled. "*Keep your ears open and for Chrissakes stay out of sight,*" and the line went dead.

I slid the phone away awkwardly, hunching lower, shoulders biting the freezing metal. I thumbed the earpiece back inside. Andrew and Christopher were arguing, voices echoey from the toilet tile.

I held my breath. C'mon old friend. This is it.

This is *it*.

"*Mr Mayo, what the hell's going on?*" Christopher. Angry. "*Toilet breaks? He's out there with his fifty thousand, while you're —*"

"*In here with Superman,*" Andrew hissed. "*He's not going anywhere.*"

"*Oh and you're the big expert on mark behaviour now? Shake your snake and let's get out there.*"

"*I . . . I can't.*"

"*What are you talking about? Keep your nerve. We're almost there. Fifty thousand —*"

"*I mean I can't do it. The blood. The shooting. This . . . this chest bag.*"

"*Careful!*"

The van motored on. Folded and crumpled, breath held in my

buckled chest, I tensed further, eyes tight shut. In my ears, my heart thundered.

C'mon Benno old chap.

"*You were right,*" Andrew said, worried voice wobbling off the tile. "*Okay? You were right. It's a job for a professional. You should have let the girl do it. Linda. You should have let Linda do it. Look at me, I'm shaking. Look at me? I can't do this.*"

"*But you — ?! Jesus H Christ!*" Christopher was losing it. Losing it bad. His voice was fading in and out. He was pacing. I shut my eyes, picturing them both in the acrid pong of the chipped toilets, his brogues shuffling on the puddled floor. "*You insisted you wanted to get involved.*"

"*How . . . how does this come off?*"

"*What are you doing?! What in the name of frolicking fuckbusters are you doing?!*"

"*I can't do it. I won't. I'm sorry. Burst the bag? Fall down screaming? I can't do it. I can't play dead. I can't. I'll screw it up. Here. Here you —*"

"*Leave that there! Put your shirt —*"

"*You have to do it. I — ow, this tape — I can't. I won't. Here. You wear it.*"

"*Are you insane?! Julio's on his way over! He's in the van, on his way over, right now with the gun. How's it going to look? He fires a blank at you but I'm the one who goes down?! Grayson'll smell a —*"

"*Then call this Julio. Phone him. Tell him to fire at you. Tell him you're doing it. I can't.*"

The van was slowing down.

Oh God. Oh God we were *here*.

The indicator ticked, the van grumbled and bubbled idly, revving hard. I tumbled sideways as Julio swung a wide arc, my hand out against the cold metal floor. He dragged the van forward, engine coughing. Five yards, ten yards, shadows falling across the windscreen.

An alley. A narrow alley. Slowly. Slower.

We stopped.

Petrified, gripped with terror in the freezing darkness, I didn't allow myself even to breathe. Julio shut off the engine and the van descended promptly into a gaunt, heavy quiet. A fart of vinyl as he leaned forward.

My heart slammed slammed slammed.

A scuffle. He sat back, cigarette in his mouth. A rasp and flare of matches and the shell of the van filled with sick blue smoke.

Not daring to move, pins and needles beginning to crawl and numb, I shut my eyes and concentrated back on the crackling voices in my head.

"*. . . and I said we're not altering anything at this stage.*"

"*Then I quit.*"

"*You —*"

"*No. No, that's it. I don't need this bloody shit.*"

"*Angus —*"

"*I'm not doing it. I'll walk. I'll go out there, tell him to keep his money, take my bloody comic book and walk. I only came to you for insurance. All this tricky stuff was your idea. Forget it. And it's Mr Mayo, to you pal.*"

"*But . . . ! You . . . !*" Christopher spat. "*Fine! Fine, give it here then. Jesus, I've never — careful of the ring! You'll puncture the fucking . . . Easy there, easy . . .*"

Breath held tight, I listened to the distant soft sticky ripping of tape, Christopher fussing, snapping.

"*Let me . . . Give it here, hold my jacket . . . where's the damned mirror . . .*"

Among the thick cigarette smoke, Julio sat back, checking his watch, stretching his arm across the back of the passenger seat, flexing a fist. He pumped down the driver's side window, distant traffic noises hissing, honking and sighing. He leaned forward. I saw him fuss with his mobile phone, slapping and clicking the broken battery cover. He slid it back to the dashboard.

"*That's it,*" Christopher was saying in my ear. "*That's it. Now give me the damned phone. I have to call Julio. Quickly . . .*"

Silence.

Nothing in my ear. Nothing in the van. Nothing in the world. Just the throb of my heart, the sticky tack of a dry tongue and the bite of cramp in my feet and —

I jolted suddenly, the metal popping and buckling beneath.

Julio's phone was ringing. Distorted. Crackly.

Oblivious to me, Julio flicked the cigarette from the window and scuffled up the phone from among the dashboard debris. The ring was cutting in and out a little, fading and sweeping like a radio in a tunnel.

Pins and needles biting and tingling, I allowed myself to shift a half inch, teeth tight against the thick pop of metal.

"Go ahead," Julio barked.

"*Julio? Julio it's me,*" Christopher crackled distantly in my earphone. He was echoey. Still in the toilet. Andrew had to be standing near. "*Change of bloody plan. Angus has – hello? Julio, you there?*"

"Hello? Hello Christopher? This facking phone . . ."

"*Julio? I'm losing you . . . Angus has lost his nerve. He and I have switched places. Julio? Can you . . . Julio?*"

"Hello? I can't hear you? Say again. Plan change? Say again?!" Up the front, Julio was flustered, slapping the broken battery cover, banging it loud – one two – on the plastic dash. "Fack it. Hello? Hello?"

"*Julio? I repeat: fire the blank at me, understand? Me. I have the blood-bag. Not Angus.*"

"I can't hear you. I'm losing you. You're *also* target? You *both* have bags? Repeat, the battery won't stay in the . . . shit. Are we still on? I've got T-minus three minutes. Hello? Christopher? Three minutes."

"*I've got the blood-bag. Not Angus. Julio? Can you hear me?*"

"Got it, got it. You've got one too. Hello – ?"

No.

Oh God.

Oh God *no*.

I began to shake. A hard, angry hand slid fat fingers about my stomach. They closed, wormy and tight, slowly, slowly.

No no *no*.

Pins and needles biting, numb, banging and pinching my toes, my fingers, my elbows, I began to slide. Slide, out, out of position, up, rolling, out, into the body of the van. Driven by fear. Driven by terror. Breath short, shallow, panic closed my throat, terrified tears swelling, welling.

"I can't *hear* you," Julio was shouting. "Hello? *Hello?* Facking battery, piece of – and he hurled the phone to the dashboard with a loud plastic *CRACK*.

"*Julio? You there?*"

"*Everything a-all right?*"

"*I think he's got it. He'll be waiting for us. Ninety seconds. Move, get back out there, Grayson will be panicking.*"

Christ, *no*. No, you *idiot*, I writhed. You fucking . . . *NO!*

Moving fast, sweating, heart thundering, I rummaged my phone from my jeans in the puffing silence.

C'mon c'mon c'mon c'mon c'mon –

"*Laura.*"

"*Call it off!*" I hissed, swallowing a cue ball of sweaty panic. "*Call it off!*"

Julio was bending forward. The click of glovebox lock.

"*Relax! It's going to plan,*" Laura soothed. "*They've swapped the chest-bags . . .*"

"*Listen to me!*"

"*They're out of the bathroom.*" She sounded excited. Exhilarated. "*I can see the three –*"

"*Julio hasn't got the message! Julio doesn't know about the swap!*"

"*It's fine, Christopher's called him. They're both back at the table . . . Christopher's talking . . . Andrew's sitting . . . Just wait where you –*"

I didn't catch the rest, thrown tumbling backwards as I was, Julio lurching the van forward. The boxes and bundles toppled over, smothering my pitiful yelp. He was steering with one hand, bouncing the van down the alley.

His other hand rested on the back of the passenger seats.

The greasy nickel gun held tight.

"*Then if tha's everythin' gennermen?*" Grayson crackled in my earpiece.

"*That's everything. Angus?*"

"*Uhm. Right. I-I guess we're all set.*"

In my ear the three men were moving out. A scrape of barstool on parquet, coats zipping, the wet clink of drinks downed.

Through the front windscreen, the van burst out into the main street with a blare of horn, watery winter sunshine blinding us. Julio yanked down the sun visor and hurtled the van forward.

Crouched low at the base of the doors, I couldn't move. Hands out to steady myself, eyes peeled wide like grapes, heart pounding with panic.

I couldn't *move*.

In my ear, a burst of traffic as a pub door swung open.

"*Then here's where we say our goodbyes, gennermen? You have the money, ah gat Mr Superman. We'll rendezvous as agreed.*"

The van lurched left, bumping and bouncing. Julio leaned over, pumping down the passenger window.

Through the jolts, I craned up a little.

Oh Jesus God.

Over Julio's shoulder, accelerating fast, I saw the pub far ahead. The Atlas. Silent and still. Hanging baskets glistened. An A-board on the pavement, scrawled with lunch offers.

Three distant figures circling each other on the quiet pavement. Briefcases in hand.

"*As agreed,*" Christopher crackled in my ear.

I could see Christopher, far up ahead. Holding a hand out to shake. His other hand played nervously across his now slightly pudgier-than-I-remembered stomach.

"*Here we go,*" a voice said.

Not Grayson. Not Christopher. Not Benno.

"*Here we the fack go,*" Julio said again.

The van exploded with a deafening blare as Julio slammed the horn and hurled the van forward with a whoop. I fell back, hitting my head a dizzying *CRACK* on the inside door.

Julio's left hand steadied himself on the dash, low trees slapping and whipping the windscreen.

On the pavement, Andrew turned, face white with horror.

Christopher and Grayson steadied themselves, ready for action.

Julio cocked the revolver.

I screamed.

The van swerved, sending me tumbling like a mannequin against the side of the shell with a dull *clanggg*. In the rearview, Julio's eyes widened, his jaw slack with shock.

The van continued to pummel forward.

"Who's *back there*?! What the fack going *on*!"

The van scraped the kerb loudly, hubcaps grinding.

We lurched right with a swoop, sending me toppling the other way. Loose limbed, balance lost, I threw myself forward with a roar, clanging, banging, head scraping the filthy ceiling.

There was a scream of brakes. Three faces in wide-mouthed horror filled the windscreen.

I lost my footing, falling forward towards the peeling vinyl seats and buckled metal frame.

A click of something. Seatbelt? Julio spun in his seat, turning to me as I fell.

Right hand off the wheel. Coming round. Swinging. A flash of nickel.

I shouted. Not a word. Just madman terror.

The butt of the gun smashed me, broke me. Bang. A wet crunch, nose exploding hot coppery blood, pain shooting into my eyes. I gasped, winded and whimpering. Dizzy. My feet left the ribbed rubber beneath and I fell backwards. The world dipped and tipped, knees bending, buckling beneath me.

I screamed and hit the floor with a planet-shaking *clanggg*, like a dull gong being hit with a wet sandbag.

I clutched my screaming nose, blood on my hands, blood in my mouth, metal and blunt. Teary eyes flooding the world like dimpled glass, the roof of the van swam and splashed.

Voices. Shouts.

The sudden soothing blast of cold November air. Slamming doors.

More shouting. In my ear. Outside.

Everywhere.

Drop it. That's mine. What is this? Step away.

I swallowed, brown, battery acid tang, coughing chewy blood into my hands.

Easy now. Listen to me. Hand it over.

I tried to sit up, tongue checking my teeth, mind flooding. *Andrew.*

Please.

Please Andrew.

Don't make me. Jesus they've both got one. Mr Grayson! Mr Grayson no!

Silence.

A long, woozy, sickly silence.

I closed exhausted eyes.

Then a bang. Loud and flat.

A bang louder than I ever dreamed. Shaking the floor, shaking the world.

And then another.

Oh God. Oh *God.*

I heaved myself up to a sitting position, the cold shell bucking and swooning, my head screaming with pain. I put my hands out to steady myself.

My head continued to scream. Loud. Andrew's name. Raw and thrashing and screaming.

It took a moment to focus.

Andrew's name again.

But it wasn't my head that was screaming.

twenty-nine

"Benno? *Benno?!*" I whimpered, palms cold, tasting bitter panic. "Jesus, *Benno no*. No no *no*." It was everywhere.

He was everywhere.

Head pounding, nose throbbing, I fell to the morning's freezing pavement, kneeling in the oily blood and grit.

"Oh God, Benno. Benno, can you hear me? Oh God. *Oh God*."

Around me there was a bang as Julio exploded back out of the pub, wooden doors crashing around him.

"Where *is* it?" he bellowed. "*Where the fack IS IT?!*"

But no one was in a position to answer. The small band of people about him had other things on their minds. Other things on their hands. All over their hands.

"It's okay . . ." Andrew winced, angry and hurt. "It's ohh-kaayyyoow! Shit, ahh, shit." He sighed, licking his pale lips, head lolling back in Laura's lap.

She was cradling him, holding him as he writhed and gasped on the pavement, one bloodied hand pressed to the bubbling wound under his sopping shirt, the other scrabbling with her phone.

"Help him!" she gnashed at me desperately, eyes wide and white. "*Help him!*"

I stumbled to my feet, mind thudding, trying to take it all in.

Somewhere a phone was ringing. The green Bedford was half on the pavement, driver's door open, engine running, one back door hanging loose where I had thrown myself dizzily against it.

Julio was in the kerb, clawing at his boss, who lay there, eyes tight, gasping in the gutter, a mess of tweed and guts.

"I'm *sorry*. Chris I'm *sorry*. It all facked. I *knew*. I fack *knew*. It's all facked up."

"Leave him!" Grayson hollered. He stood, pale and transfixed by the bewildering tableau, his fake gun still held out, mouth slack and pale. He looked at Andrew, writhing and bloody. He looked at Laura. He looked at his boss in the kerbside, dying and gurgling in a thick pool of blood and syrup. He looked at me, a face from the past, brain trying desperately to fill in the gaps. "Leave . . . Just . . . shit we've got to go. We've got to *GO!*"

I meanwhile jittered like a marionette, spinning and toppling, the world whirling about me. A thousand things to do.

Somewhere a phone was still ringing.

"*Neil!*" Andrew rasped, legs kicking spastically.

"*Don't talk,*" Laura soothed, hand over the sopping wad that was once an Incredible Hulk. "*Shhh, don't talk, don't –* hello?" she broke away into her phone. "Hello, emergency? Please. I need an ambulance. Now, right now. A man's been shot."

"Where the comic? Where the money? Where our facking *haul*?!" Julio was yelling, whirling about the street. "What *HE* doing here?! What the fack going *ON*?!"

"We gotta go! Julio. *Julio!* We gotta *go!*" Grayson was at the van door, all traces of his accent gone.

"But –"

"*NOW!*" Grayson bellowed. "Look *around* you! Focus. *FOCUS!* We have to *go!*"

"The Atlas pub," Laura was saying quickly, pacing. "Seagrove Road. Earl's Court. It's just . . . it's just a wound I think but I can't stop the bleeding. Hurry. Please *hurry.*"

"We have to *go!*" Grayson bellowed again.

Julio spun, taking in the bloody scene, sticky footprints leaving panicky circles on the pavement like macabre dance instructions.

"*Neil –*" Andrew gasped, grabbing my leg and my attention tight. I knelt down quickly, eyes on his. This was bad. Oh this was very bad. "*Neil I'm sorry –*"

"Don't talk. Benno, don't talk," I said, sniffing, wiping stinging eyes, throat tight. "It's going to be all right. We've got an ambulance coming." I looked up with panic at Laura. She nodded, face torn with grief. "It's fine. You did great, old friend. Hang in there."

In the gutter, Christopher gave a moan, head rolling against the brick, bloody bubbles popping on his lips.

A phone was still ringing somewhere.

"We can't leave Christopher," Julio said, hurrying to the kerb side. "Laura? Laura, leave him. Help me get Christopher into van. *Help* me."

"Fuck you," Laura scowled. "Fuck you *all*."

"Are you out of your –"

"*Forget her!*" Grayson screamed. He clambered into the van, slamming the door with a rusty bang. "We've got to *go!* Keys! Give me the *keys! Move!* Fucking *MOVE!*"

"I . . . I did great old friend . . ." Andrew said woozily in her lap, eyes rolling.

Julio roared, spinning, tossing the keys to Grayson and leaping over Christopher's still body. He clambered into the van's passenger seat. Half inside, Grayson threw it forward with a squeal, whirling around in a wide circle, scraping parked cars with a teeth-grinding shriek before gunning off fast down the quiet street and away.

"Andrew," I said in the quiet, breathing deep, holding his cold hands tight. "Andrew listen to me. It's all right. Shhhh, it's all right."

"I . . . oww, *ahh, shit*, I screwed it up . . ."

"No," I pleaded, squeezing his hand. "No. You did good. It's *me*, I . . ."

"The bags . . . *arrghh Jesus!*" and he screwed up his face, eyes tight, teeth bared, the pain knifing his sides. "It all happened . . . lost the *bags* . . ."

"Shhhh, we got the bags, we got the bags . . ." Laura hushed, stroking Andrew's sweat-sopped fringe from his pale face.

A phone still called out, over and over.

"*Bags?*" I said, head spinning. In all the horror, I hadn't even *dreamed* that –

Laura knelt up a little, Andrew's head bouncing and wincing in her lap. She soothed an apology, sliding from beneath her a battered satchel and a sliver attaché case.

"First thing I grabbed," she said, a timid smile playing over her frightened face. "You did great."

"What's . . ." I said, ear cocked, trying to focus. "What's that *ringing?*"

"*That's . . . that's for me . . . I've got . . .*" Andrew began to mumble, trying to twist around.

"*Jesus!* Jesus no, *no!*" Laura yelped, wet red lines seeping between her fingers. "He's tearing it. He's tearing the *wound. Andrew!*"

"*The phone . . .*" he croaked dreamily.

"I-I've got it, I've got it," I said, reaching under his sweat-soaked jeans and tearing at his pockets, pulling out everything I could find – cigarettes, a Zippo, matches, penknife, fountain pen, breath mints, an old Bic and finally at last the handset, his red notebook stuck to the plastic with blood.

"That . . . that son of a *bitch*," Laura was spitting. "Stupid son of a bitch Julio didn't understand the change of plan. Thought Christopher was trying to tell him to *add* a target."

I smeared the blood from the screen. *O'Shea.*

Oh God.

"*Phone keeps cutting out?* His fucking brain keeps cutting out. Neil? *Shhh, it's all right. Ambulance is on its way. Five minutes. You're all right.* Neil?"

"It's O'Shea," I said, panic rising. "Benno's got this deal. He's meant to be completing some big deal . . ."

"*Tell O'Shea –*" Andrew gasped, face pale and scared.

"Neil, I need you to hold this. He's losing a lot of blood . . ."

The phone still ringing in my hand, I knelt slowly to my best friend's side, a cold claw of horror gripping my gut.

"*Old . . . Old stick,*" Andrew croaked, grabbing my sleeve hard, hauling himself up an inch. He had blood on his lips and teeth.

"Benno. Oh God, mate I –"

"*They . . . they can't know . . .*" Andrew winced, eyes tight, grabbing at the phone.

"*Shhhh,*" Laura soothed. "*The ambulance is coming. Shhh. It's all right. Neil will take care of it. Business can wait . . .*"

But kneeling there in Andrew's blood, the phone calling out, calling out, I knew on this day of all days, business couldn't wait. The phone kept ringing. Somewhere, Andrew's future – his wife's future, the future of the Artic Circle – drummed its fingers, twiddled its thumbs, refilled its coffee and checked its watch with a tut.

"Shit," I said. "I've got . . . I've got to take this."

"*They can't . . .*" Andrew hissed, breathing short and tight, reaching out to me.

"Shit," I said again. "Don't . . . don't worry old friend, I've got it covered. I've . . . I've got it covered," and I swallowed hard, stood up and thumbed open the line.

Fifteen minutes later, I sat bouncing, scared and tearful in the back of a black cab, hemmed in by King's Road traffic. On the seat next to me lay a silver attaché case full of my daughter's money. On top of that, within a tired, blood-caked satchel, behind its protective sleeve, a fading seventy-year-old *Superman* held a car aloft above his head. In my trembling, bloodied fingers was a scrap of paper. Torn moments ago from Andrew's sodden red notebook, it was scrawled with numbers and names. Clamped under my chin, I had Andrew's lifeline.

"*I'm sorry, who is this?*" the phone crackled.

"A friend. I-I'm a friend of Mr Benjamin's. An old friend. Please —"

"*And you say he can't come to the phone?*"

"He's told me . . ." My mind thudded. "He's doing a deal for a man named O'Shea? An important deal? Something in Holborn?"

"*Where is Mr Benjamin now?*"

Up ahead, the traffic began to clear and the cab moved forward a few feet, which was more than I could say for the situation on the telephone.

"He's . . . Look please, I just need to know how I can complete this deal for him. It's very important. He's wiring across some money or something? From a new account?"

"*One moment please,*" the voice said and the on-hold music came back.

Teeth gritted, I checked my chunky watch, as the cab slid forward another few feet.

It was five past eleven. The ambulance would be there by now. Paramedics tending to him.

Please God, I prayed silently. *Save him.*

"*Hello? To whom am I speaking?*"

"What? Sorry. My name is Neil Martin. I was telling your colleague —"

"*Did you say Mr Benjamin is unable to complete the telegraphic transfer as stipulated? When did you speak with him?*"

"He . . ."

I jumped at the blare of siren behind me, rearview mirror flashing with blue light. In front, the gridlocked traffic began to shuffle, edging, inching apart, sliding sideways.

"Hold on," I said to the phone, the cabbie heaving left all the inches he could spare.

"*Hello? Hello?*" the phone squawked. "*Hello?*"

"Sorry, there was . . . it doesn't matter. Look, Mr Benjamin is aware of how important it is that this deal goes ahead and I need to make sure it does. He's given me some figures. Hello?" I shoved my finger in my ear as the ambulance weaved slowly through the traffic past me, siren screaming, edging between Chelsea's vans and 4×4s. I flapped the sheet of notepaper. "Eighteen, twenty, fifteen, then what looks like forty . . . forty million, a hundred and −"

"*What you have isn't . . . Look, we need to speak to Mr Benjamin. When is he likely to be free Mr . . . ?*"

"Martin," I said, watching the ambulance disappear among the throng of traffic up ahead.

"*Mr Martin, I'm not certain you understand the complexity of this situation. Without Mr Benjamin's written authorisation, clearance codes and password, the money simply can't move from the account.*"

"But . . ."

"*Until Mr Benjamin calls into the office, the deal is suspended and the relevant contractual penalties will be incurred by Mr O'Shea. I strongly urge Mr Benjamin to contact this office immediately.*"

I snapped my phone closed and hurled it bouncing to the vinyl beside me.

"Here," I called to the cabbie. "Left here. Please, as fast as you can."

The cab circled, sending me sliding across the bench, and we accelerated, gunning down Chelsea Park Gardens. It was down here.

Andrew's only hope was down here somewhere.

My ugly watch said eleven minutes past eleven.

By twenty-five to twelve, Andrew's only hope was juddering beneath an oiled ancestor in his first floor study, fat hand clamped about that favourite peaty scotch of his. Trembling, knees bouncing, I sat on the edge of a huge leather armchair, dabbing my punctured nose tentatively with a heavy, monogrammed handkerchief, trying not to get blood on the rug.

"Well," Edward sighed, looking into his glass. I blinked back silently. "Well," he said again.

"Yes," I squeaked, swallowing hard.

Somewhere down the hall, a grandfather clock tutted.

"Well well," he said again. "Quite a *story.*"

Hot-cheeked and shamed, I opted for silence.

"And where is he now?"

"Andrew or Christopher?"

"Both."

"Christopher, I don't know. Shot in the chest. He looked . . . well he wasn't moving when I left. There was blood . . ." My throat dried, lips sticking to my teeth. "I don't know. Guess the police'll have it all fenced off. Laura was waiting for the ambulance with Andrew," I said. "She thinks it's just a wound but he's in a bad way."

"Laura being who I caught you with that day on the Underground, I assume? Who did you say she was then?"

"I can't remember," I said.

"A collector, I believe you said," Edward harrumphed. "A *collector.* Which is what I informed my daughter."

"Jane *knows?*"

"I gave her enough information for her to make her own mind up. She covered for you of course. Said you met a lot of collectors. Not many *leggy female* ones though. *That* surprised her."

"I didn't know what else to *tell* you. I was trying to clear everything up. Put it right. I hoped —"

"What you *hoped* is that you'd get away with this insulting, *criminal* charade, lad. That's what you *hoped.* That you could weasel your way out of your *infantile* mess and that no one would be any the wiser. Treated *me*, treated *my family*, like *fools.*"

"I was just trying —"

"Oh *save it.* Save it for the *judge.* You're no liar, young man. You're no liar, just as you are no businessman."

I sat in silence.

"I mean . . ." Edward spluttered. "I mean good *God* boy, what were you *thinking*? *Bar-rooms* and *blood-bags*? This isn't the movies! This is *my family!*"

I looked up into a fat face of ruddy loathing.

"What were you *thinking*, boy, *hmm*?"

Lovely boy, Mowgli, lovely boy, a-hnn hnn hnn.

"If it's *any* – sorry," I croaked, "If it's any consolation, that's what *my* father wanted to know too."

"Your fa – ? *Well*," and Edward rocked back in his little brogues, shaking his head. "I might have known he'd be involved some-where." He placed his tumbler on his desk. "What is it with your family, eh? Eh?"

I took a deep breath.

"Edward," I said. "Edward, my oldest friend is –" and I stumbled, voice cracking, words thick in my throat. I scowled, angry, trying to frighten them out. "My oldest friend has been shot and it's my fault. My fault. I dropped Julio's phone and broke the battery, which meant Julio didn't get the –"

Edward just stared at me, fat, wet eyes glassy and cold. Plump lip curled just so.

"Christ, look, look I've . . . God, look, what do you want from me? Huh? I've tried to be a good man. Yes, even with my upbringing. Be a *good husband* to your daughter. A *good father* to your grand-child . . ."

Edward shifted a little in his tight tweed, topping up his glass.

"I have *tried* doing it your way. Truly I have. Jane will tell you. *Shrewwwd*. Killer instinct, *dog eat dog*, all that. But it's not me. It's not my way. I just . . . I'm never going to be the millionaire polo player you want for a son-in-law, Edward. And I don't *want* to be. I just want . . ." I took a big breath, grinding my jaw against tears. "I just want to be a good husband. A good father. That's it. And yes," I looked down at the worn study rug. "Yes, I took stupid pride too far. I tried to manage too much by myself. I should have come clean about my screw-ups, instead of taking these insane measures to correct them alone . . ."

"Indeed," Edward murmured. "You're due in court *when*?"

"Monday. Three o'clock," I said. "But it's all, *all this*, it's only *ever* been to be the husband your daughter deserves. The father your grand-daughter deserves. And in trying to put things right, yes, *again*, I've screwed up. Screwed up *huge*."

"Putting it mildly."

"But this time," I looked up at him. "I've come to you for help. Because it's more than just your idiot son-in-law now. *Andrew . . .*" but I had nothing more to say. I hung my head.

"Where's Lana's trust fund now? The comic book? Tell me you've at *least* −"

"They're all there," I sighed, waving a hand at the case and satchel on his desk. Edward put down his heavy tumbler and moved to the blotter. He clicked on the green lamp, peering at the locks before snapping them open. He lifted the lid, perusing the contents.

A long thoughtful while passed.

"So you've everything back that you lost? Something, at least."

"Everything of *mine's* back, yes."

"Meaning − ?"

"Andrew's family. They might be minus a . . ." and the world began to collapse about me. Throat closing, hard and tight, a fat wave of guilt and grief rolling, growing, crashing like the sea against my heart. I swallowed, once, twice, nauseous, breathing deep, head low.

"C'mon lad. Enough of that. You're being depended on. What's this friend, this Andrew, what's he given you? Numbers, you said?"

Limp and wrecked, I handed him the crumpled paper, blood-stained and sweaty.

"They said something about a telegraph . . . something?"

"Hmn. Telegraphic transfer. These look like account details. How much are these developers expecting to agree completion?"

"I don't know," I said. "But it's that or it doesn't go through and −"

"And if I know firms like this, that'll be your friend out on his ear. This character?"

"O'Shea."

"O'Shea. He'll see to that. Hmn. They'll be stung with a hefty penalty for every hour after the deadline that passes too. A cost your friend will be expected to pick up." Edward sighed. "You trust this chap?"

"Andrew? With my life. With . . . with more than my life. I owe him . . ."

I looked up at Edward.

He may as well hear it. He may as well hear it *all*.

"We met at University," I said. I had a small glass of Edward's scotch, and I swum it around idly, watching the light play in the amber. "Same halls. Didn't have much in common really but . . . I dunno, we gravitated together. Same outlook, attitude I guess. Same . . . well, turns out the same taste in First Years."

"Jane?"

"Jane." I was breathing deep and slow, trying to steady my heart. "We both . . . *noticed*? Is *that* the word? Doesn't seem . . . Well, we noticed your daughter. But we didn't mention her. Not to each other. Talked about everything *else*, but not . . . Says a lot I suppose. It was how Andrew was when she was *around*. When we were out as *three*. See, we got chatting in halls. Over chess. Three of us. We kind of all buddied up, but . . . Fact is, I fell for her immediately. Didn't say much to Andrew. Didn't want to make it awkward. Make him feel like a *gooseberry*, y'know? But Jane and I started seeing each other when Andrew wasn't around."

I swallowed hard, head flooding with memories in the little study.

"He was a good-looking guy, though. Andrew. I never understood why he wasn't snapped up by someone else. But the three of us still hung out, all through the second year, all through the third year, Jane and I seeing each other . . . not *on the sly*, because we were both single. Andrew wasn't . . . But it was *awkward*."

"Awkward?"

"I'd found *poems* he'd written about her, hidden away. It was pretty clear. Put me in a difficult position."

"To do the right thing by a friend."

"Right, right," I nodded. "Anyway . . . Christmas. Third year. Night of the ball. We're all in tuxedos and smoking cigars and swapping hip flasks. All the girls showing shoulders and wearing heels and the whole bit. I've had a little mulled wine and I decide I'm going to propose to your daughter."

"*Drunk?*" Edward harrumphed.

"Dutch courage," I said. "But I know what that's going to do to the three of us. No keeping *that* secret. So I drop by Andrew's room and he's got candles lit. Listening to Jona Lewie and fixing his cufflinks. Little CND signs I think. From a velvet box on his desk. And I tell him I have something I need to get off my chest. And he says he does too."

"Go on?"

"Well I can't hold it in. So I tell him. Jane and I . . . I'm going to propose. I apologised for sneaking around and I hope he understood and that we could all stay friends. And he just looks at me. Blank. I'll never . . . Just stares at me. I'm waiting for a bear-hug or a handshake or a punch in the mouth. *Something*. Which is when . . ." and the words tighten in my throat a little. "On his desk. A velvet box."

"*Andrew* was going to –"

"Yes."

"Jane. Are you *sure*?"

"He told me. Said he'd bought it a month ago and was going to wait until Christmas Eve. Said he'd never felt that way about anyone before. Wasn't sure he ever could again. Had had a sick ache in his stomach the day she'd arrived and it had never gone away. Then he sat on the end of the bed."

"You told Jane?"

"No. Never have. But *that* isn't . . . this is why . . . he went to the bathroom, washed his face. Came back out and asked me what I was going to say. To Jane. How I was going to do it. Like he wanted to hear the proposal."

"A little *morbid* . . . ?"

"I don't know. But he was my friend. We talked about everything else. So I told him. Gave him my little speech."

"His reaction?"

"He got out his red notebook, turned to a fresh page and we spent the most extraordinary hour. Drinking wine, watching the snow, Andrew helping me write a poem. A proposal. He wanted her to accept. He wanted us to be happy. If he couldn't have her, he wanted to make sure *I* did. He put all his feelings aside and . . . and he brought us together. He's an extraordinary man."

The study went quiet for a while, just the slow ticking of the heavy hall clock.

"Did he come to the wedding?"

"No. No, we invited him but . . . working. Family commitments."

"*Keatings*, you said, wasn't it? His firm? I'm not familiar with them . . ."

"Well they're about to *fire* him, if . . . He needs my help. It would be just for an hour. A couple of hours. Just until Andrew can get to a phone. Just to keep his job . . ."

"And the deadline?"

"Noon."

Edward peered at the carriage clock on the mantle.

"I'll make a call or two. As he's a friend of *Jane's*. I'll speak to Greg. Check out this story. No promises mind. Go. Wait for me downstairs."

Limp and aching, I pushed out of Edward's study, taking the wide wooden staircase slowly to the ground floor, passing under heavy oils and chandeliers. I tugged out my phone, scrolling down to Laura's number. Would she be in the ambulance with him still? Could you use mobile phones in hospitals these days?

I needed to know where they'd taken him. To know he was okay.

The phone began the bleep of dialling out.

Began ringing.

I reached the bottom of the staircase. There was a muffled slam of a car door in the quiet street, a cab sliding past the large hall window.

The front door-lock clicked, Jane struggling inside with our daughter.

Our beautiful daughter. My beautiful, *beautiful* Jane.

"Hey," I said.

She looked at me, pale and horrified.

"What are you doing here?" she said. "And *Jesus*, what have you – ?"

"It's all right," I said, dabbing at my throbbing nose. I leant in a little to the ornate, heavy mirror in the hall. There was purple swelling along the bridge and dry coppery crusts about the nostrils. I dabbed some more, uselessly. "This isn't as painful as it looks and *this*," I plucked at my blood-stained shirt with what I hoped was a reassuring smile. "Isn't my blood. *However*," and I took a deep, solemn breath. "Well . . . I don't know how to begin . . ." and I reached out for her hand.

Jane didn't move. Just stared at me in silence.

"Your dad's upstairs in his study. I'm making tea. Then you and I need to −"

"Who are you calling?"

"Calling? Oh," and I remembered the phone at my ear. It had cut off. No signal. "Well . . . That's kind of . . . I've a lot to explain."

"*Have* you now?"

"Right. Something's . . ."

"*Explain*," Jane said again under her breath. Adjusting Lana on her hip, she pushed past me, not looking at me, moving down the hall to the sitting room.

"Jane?" I said. I followed her. Warily. "Jane? Is everything . . . ?"

When I got to the sitting room, Jane had laid Lana out on a floor rug.

"Jane?"

After a moment, Jane got up, turning to me blankly, folding her arms.

"Always *busy*," she said calmly.

"Look I'll . . . I'll make that cup of tea shall I?" I said, backing away, trying a small smile.

"Then you'll *explain*?" Jane said.

"R-Right," I said.

"Had better be a *pot*, then. Don't you think?"

thirty

Over the next hour, Edward spoke to Keatings about a transfer of funds.

Downstairs, Jane didn't say much.

No, scratch that. Jane didn't say a word. Not to me anyway. Once in a while she would look away, break the flat, blank eye contact she was holding and glance down at Lana on the rug, wriggling and contented in her bunny baby-gro to let out a soothing "*shhh*," or an "*ooze a good girl den*?", a small tender smile on her lips. But the smile would vanish abruptly when she looked back up at me.

And she said nothing.

Not a word as I sugared our teas and cautiously began a story of mistakes. The parts she knew: burst plumbing and forgotten insurance cheques. The parts she didn't: elaborate traps, of car-jacking and burly policemen. Silence as we sipped our tea and I spoke slowly, calmly of an opportunity to put things right. A Claridge's lunch, an Australian waiter and red cotton underpants.

I think she may have cleared her throat a little at one point, when I pushed a plate of McVities Boasters across the embroidered rug towards her, draining my cup and clarifying the purpose of the bank withdrawal. The purpose of *everything* I had done.

Love. Love for her. Love for our daughter. A frightened husband, a frightened father, trying to make good.

I tried to reach out and take her hand at this point, but she sat back a little, licking her lips pensively and crossing her legs. Settling in for the end of the story. A story of airports. Of tube trains. Of old friends, hotel rooms and the back of a green Bedford van.

But as I finally collected the cups and stacked saucers, a delicate clatter in the plush quiet of her father's Chelsea sitting room, and told her Christopher was dead – that dear Andrew was in hospital, Julio and Grayson were gone and Christopher at last was dead – Jane just looked at me.

I placed the crockery to one side and sat back down on the edge of the plump couch.

We sat in sick silence like that for a moment.

"I was trying to put things right," I said with a tired sigh, a wave of exhaustion sweeping over me. "For us."

"And what did Dad say?" Jane asked suddenly, her voice jarring, out of place.

"Your dad?"

"When you told this . . . this story to *him*?"

I sighed again, shrugging a little bit loosely, underarms prickling. The room seemed oddly warm all of a sudden.

"He . . . Well, he understood. Friendship, I mean. *Trust*. He wanted to help," I said.

Jane arched a single plucked eyebrow.

"I-I mean, he understood how I felt. That it was my fault. Julio's phone. The gun. That I wanted to see him right. Andrew, I mean. Friendship. So . . ." and it was my turn to raise eyebrows.

"He . . . he *believed* you?" Jane said.

I nodded dumbly. What did that mean? Believed me?

"But he's not . . ." and Jane's face went a little slack. She half stood quickly. "He's not . . . ?"

"Upstairs," I said quizzically, eyebrows knotted now. My eyebrows certainly had their work cut out this afternoon. Especially as they then leapt ceiling-wards, Jane jumping up with a scream and thudding past me, taking the stairs two at a time.

Lana began to cry.

"Jane? Jane, I . . . ?" I stood up, lost, bewilderment spinning me like a top. "Jane?" I called out after her. "*Shhh, Lana Lana*," and I knelt, scooping up my tiny daughter, head swimming in that cottony milk smell. I jigged her on my shoulder a little, shushing and soothing. Over the tears, I could hear voices, footsteps thudding above and a car honking outside on the street. Lana was doing her best to drown these out. "*Shhh shhh shhh*," I said, jigging her into the hall where I met Jane thudding back down the stairs, face tearful, jaw set.

"Jane?"

The car honked again.

"Nice try," Jane said defiantly.

"Try – ?"

"Give her to me," she hissed, reaching for Lana. "Give her to *me*!"

Bewildered, lost, I let Jane take our daughter.

Upstairs, I could hear Edward. Slamming drawers. Thudding about.

"Jane, what's –"

"Don't *speak* to me," Jane hissed, cradling Lana and barging past me hard, catching me with her shoulder, sending me back against the door-frame. Murmuring, mumbling she thudded into the sitting room, bending to her bag.

"Jane – ?"

"Nice try. *Niiice* try," she muttered, tugging out a handful of envelopes.

"Jane, I –"

Spinning around, she held them out at arms' length for me, all her weight on one hip.

"Yours, I believe?" she snapped. Her eyes were shining with tears.

I could only shrug, so she hurled them at me, a half dozen or so, hitting me in the chest, the lip.

"Hey – !"

"Take them. They're yours after all."

I bent gingerly to the floor and retrieved one of the envelopes. It was pink and heavy. Addressed to me via the shop in a graceful hand. Torn open across the top and post-dated three weeks ago.

"What . . . what is this?" I said, but as I held it up, I got it. Suddenly. Rushing. Filling the pulp of my nose. My head. My mind.

Chanel.

"Did you *want* me to find them?" Jane snarled, holding Lana to her shoulder, cradling her head, covering her from the blast. "Was that the plan? A stupid cowardly boy's plan?"

"I . . . I don't know *what* you think . . ." I stuttered, suddenly cross, anger caught tight in my throat. "What *are* these?" and I scrabbled out the letter from within. Another woozy waft of Chanel hit me like a cold breaker on Brighton beach. I unfolded it, getting bloody fingerprints on the edges.

The handwriting was the same. Leaning, graceful, flowery. Dated October 29ᵗʰ. *To my dearest Neil.*

"I've . . . I've never *seen* this before," I said, head thudding, eyes drifting over the lines.

. . . and the more I think about your words Neil, the more I feel the same . . .

"What . . . what *are* these? Where did you *get* them? Jane?"

"Which one have you got there?" Jane said firmly. She was pacing. Pacing, soothing Lana, head cradled gently. "Is she telling you that, what was it, just thinking of you gives her a sick ache inside? A . . . oh yes, a painful teenage ache? Because that's how it feels when you're together?"

"Jane. Jane wait," I said, trying to stop her, the world tipping up slowly. Slowly. "I don't know what you think you've −"

"Painful because she imagines you with me and knows she'll have to wait *so* long until she can see you again? *Pathetic.*"

"I . . ." my mouth dried up. "I don't know what these are. Honestly, I swear . . ." and I bent, picking them one by one from the carpet, room tipping, twisting. The handwriting was the same. The addresses the same. Only the postmarks differed. Four months ago. Six months ago.

Outside, a car honked again. Twice.

Edward was thumping down the stairs, muttering.

"You thought I was *asleep* I suppose?" Jane said, face like thunder.

"Where is he? Where *is* he?" Edward barked. He pushed himself into the front room, red-faced and juddering. His eyes blazed. "I *knew* it," he sneered. "I knew it the day I *met* you. Your *kind.*"

"My − ? Edward, wait. Jane, Jane what are you saying. Everyone, *please,*" I pleaded, head spinning, hands out trying to keep the world level. My kind? *Asleep?* What was − ?

"This morning?" Jane spat. "When you sneaked in and got your clothes? Thought I wouldn't hear you?"

"My *clothes?*"

A car honked once again, engine bubbling.

"Don't say another word, Jane," Edward said. "Not another word. We'll let the police take it from here," and he waddled over to an antique occasional table, grabbing up the handset. "Let the *police* hear the rest of his lies. Let them decide . . . Oh for heaven's sake, what's that racket?" and he puffed red-faced across the room to the window, cars honking on the street.

"I see you took mostly T-shirts," Jane said. "Taking you somewhere *hot* is she?"

"Wait, just *wait* –"

"It's a taxi," Edward muttered, peering out through the window. "Someone's . . ."

"Ha, I mean I say *taking you*," Jane laughed darkly. "She'll only be paying until the shop's sold I'm guessing? Not a bad valuation you got."

"Valuation?!" I said. I wanted someone to yell cut. Anyone. To stop the sound effects, the lighting, the extras. Make everything stop. "This is all . . . All this is insane! These letters? And what valuation? I never had any –"

"Came this morning," Jane said, scrabbling in her bag. "*After* you'd sneaked out of the house with your clothes. Didn't plan *that* very well did we? I took the liberty of opening it."

"Someone's . . . . someone's getting out of the taxi," Edward hummed, still at the window twitching the nets, handset in his fat fist. "A girl . . ."

"Here we are," Jane said, sniffing, blinking. She held it out to me. "Valuation of site for sublease agreement. Estimate based on letting period, week ending November thirteenth."

I didn't need to read it. The letterhead was enough.

A classy, well-spaced letterhead. Rich navy colour on a weighty cream paper.

"Not a bad price. Nice to have friends in the trade. Shame he couldn't help you unload your *Superman*. No. No you had to . . ." and Jane was at her bag again. "You had to – here – had to get some *other* experts to help you there, didn't you. Dad? Dad, have you seen this?"

Even from across the room, even sellotaped down the middle and crinkled at the edges, I recognised the Sotheby's letter. The Polaroid stapled to the top.

"Hn? Whassat?" Edward turned, attention still half on the street.

"That . . . I-I can explain *that*," I said, palms cold and shaky. "But I swear I don't know . . ." Adrenaline flooded my mouth, bitter and coppery, room spinning. "I don't know what *any* of this other stuff is, I-I swear to you. Jane, please, I *swear* to you."

"It's her," Jane said.

But then I realised it wasn't Jane talking.

It was Edward, turning from the window, turning to me, puffing out his chest, eyes wide.

"*Her –* ?"

"And she's got suitcases. Oh you foolish, *foolish* boy," Edward snarled, stepping away from the window, fat thumbs jabbing the telephone.

Nine.

Nine.

There was a sharp *rat-a-tat* on the door.

The room went quiet, just the faint bubble of a waiting cab outside.

We looked about each other. Jane, red-eyed, thin-lipped, on the edge of tears. Edward, whispy brows knitted, jowls a-judder.

Rat-a-tat-*tat*.

"I'll go," Jane said, clutching Lana tight and moving towards me, towards the door.

"Wait," I said. "Wait, Jane –"

"Let *me*," Edward harrumphed, bustling past. "Let's see if she remembers *me*."

"How long?"

"How *long* – ?"

"How long have you been seeing this . . ." and she gestured, disgusted, to the letters in my hand. "This *Laura* woman? Long before Dad caught you with her on the train, that I know."

"Please, Jane, I'm not *seeing* –"

"The letters go back six months. That's *before* Lana was born. While I was still pregnant. Was that when it started?"

"Jesus . . . Jesus Christ, *no!*"

"I can't believe I said it. We sat in that restaurant. Not ten days ago. And I *asked* you."

"Jane, for Chrissakes, you have to believe me . . ."

"*Are you having second thoughts about us? Why are you so withdrawn? Not involved with Lana?*"

"I swear —"

"Don't be silly, you said. *I'm fulfilling my promise. Looking after you*, you said."

Voices. Voices in the hall.

"Coming home to the smell of someone else's perfume? Hidden bank statements? Mysterious phone calls at all hours? Does she think I'm an *idiot*?" A silent tear spilled over, splashing Jane's cheek. She rubbed it away hard.

"Neil?" a thin voice said from the hall. A horribly familiar voice. "Neil, have . . . have you told her? Are you coming? The cab's waiting . . ."

Jane's eyes widened, twitching, mouth falling open.

"Neil?"

Laura looked very different to how I'd last left her.

The cap was gone. The boots and vest and combats likewise. She was in trainers and expensive-looking jeans, a bulging, mumsy handbag under her arm. Her hair was tumbling, shiny and set about her shoulders. Shoulders covered, much like the rest of her body in, regretfully for me, one of the baggy, dark blue Superman T-shirts I'd brought Andrew that morning.

"So. You . . . you must be Laura?" Jane said, the tiniest wobble in her voice. She cleared her throat, pulling back her shoulders a little and sniffing. "Sorry. I'm normally in bed or in the bath when you and Neil talk."

"Neil?" Laura said cautiously in the doorway.

"What have you done?" I said flatly, swallowing hard.

"The cab's waiting," Laura said, rummaging in her bag. "I have your passport. You left it by the bed . . ."

She held it out. We all stared at it.

"Your *passport*?" Jane said. "Oh this gets better."

"Your bag's in the cab. Are you coming?" Laura blinked timidly. God she was good at this.

"Laura? Just — Tell . . . tell my wife. Tell her who you are. Cut this shit out right now."

"I don't —"

"Right *NOW!*" I screamed.

Lana began to wail.

"Tell her? I . . . I don't understand. Has it worked? Did the plan work? Do we have his money?"

"Not a penny," Edward said, coming in from the hall, thumbing off the phone with a portly reptilian sneer. "Not an effing *penny*. My daughter caught me *just in time*. No *emergency* transfers, no *money*. Whatever you were pulling, you pair, you arsed it up. But you'll *pay* for this. The police are *on their way*."

"*Bastard . . .*" Jane sniffed softly, voice cracking like a child. "*You bloody . . . How could . . .*" but the word was swallowed. Swallowed by a gulping wave of tears.

"Jane. No Jane, wait," I flustered, the world bending away, buckling, bucking me like a Rodeo. I reached for my family.

"Let . . . *go* of me! *Let go of me!*" Jane bellowed, face collapsing, fingers tight and white about Lana, barging past me, thundering up the stairs.

"Jane *wait!*"

"Sweetheart," Edward hollered. "Sweetheart, don't let him . . ." and he turned to me, face torn with fury. "Oh you'll *pay* for this. It's been a long time coming, but you'll *pay for this.*" Spittle popped and glistened on his ruddy chin. He turned with a waddle and began to puff up the stairs after his daughter. "Sweetheart, Daddy's here . . ."

"*'Afternoon*," Laura smirked softly, leaning in. "*How are ya?*"

I just stared at her blankly.

"You want to say hello to the guys?" she whispered. "They're all in the cab −"

"*Don't −!*" I hissed, spinning, spitting, eyes flashing, nose to nose. "Whatever you're doing. Whatever this is? I . . . I want you to stop. I want you to stop now. This is my *family.*"

"You ever worship someone? Adore them and not be adored back? It's destroying."

"*What?*"

"Your whole world. For three aching, lonely years?"

"I don't . . . what are you − ?"

"C'mon, we did *tell* you, Neil. Portly chief executives, rolling chins in cashmere cardies," Laura whispered. "Laying down wine and laying down nannies? You can't be *surprised*?"

"Oh God . . ."

"That's where the *real* juice is. Never had a problem they couldn't solve with the flick of a Duofold and a wave of a secretary? Christopher did *tell* you."

"This whole . . ." The room began to swim again. I tasted coppery adrenaline, woozy and wet. "But . . . but wait," my heart hammered and hammered. I felt my throat tighten. But not with fear. With excitement. Hope.

With realisation.

"Ha," I barked. "Yes, *ha*! He never *did* it!"

"Whom?"

"Edward! HA! *Nothing's been lost!* No transfer took place! Nothing's been taken!"

"Are you *sure*?"

"Jane caught him in time. You've taken *nothing*!"

"*Money*, you mean? Oh *Neil* . . ." Laura pouted, head cocked. She reached up and stroked my cheek tenderly, soothing, like a nurse. "Sweet thing, you really haven't thought about this at *all* have you? Poor dear. Poor −"

A distant muted thud from upstairs.

Voices.

"*Oops*," Laura whispered, pinching my bottom. "*Showtime.*"

"Get your fucking −"

"*Neil*," Laura whined suddenly, loudly, grabbing my sleeve. "Did it work? Did he do it? The *money*?"

"Pity you never used any of this cunning at your real job, lad eh?" Edward boomed, appearing at the top of the stairs red-faced and wobbling, a scrap of paper in his hand, his daughter tucked safely behind. "Might have made something of yourself? Like *father*, like *son* though, eh?"

Like father, like son.

Of course the dame's in on it. The dame's always in on it . . .

"Oh, I'll *have* you for this. I'll *have* you . . ."

"*Dad*," Jane sobbed as Edward began to judder down the stairs.

"You'll want this back will you? For your next trick? Your *notes*?" and he read aloud from the other side of Andrew's tatty paper. "*They were at least agonisingly* . . . what's this, *agonisingly aware of the easy money in the vicinity, and convinced it was theirs for a few words in the right key. EBAY 5pm Less sleep. Less sleep. O'Shea. Breath mints. Matches. Zippo. Bic,"* Edward growled, balling up the note. "I knew it. I knew it *all* along . . ."

"*Edward,*" I protested. "Edward *please,* I . . . *Jane.* Jane I *love* you. *I love you,* please you have to believe me! I didn't know *anything* about this. *Any* of this!"

"Neil, Neil leave it," Laura whined, tugging my sleeve again. "Let's just *go.*"

"*Hoy!*" Edward yelled, appearing at the bottom step, jabbing me hard with an aristocratic digit. "You stay *away* from my family, you hear?" Edward turned to face Laura. He looked her up and down, lip curled and loathing. "Told you he could make you rich, did he?"

Laura looked at me. Then up the stairs where Jane sat, clutching the banisters, sobbing.

"It was . . . it was all *his* plan," Laura said with contempt. "He's wanted out of the marriage for months but knew you'd cut him off without a penny. Said you'd bring the family lawyers in, take everything he had."

"*Don't,*" I begged. "Don't listen, Jane —"

"So he said he'd come up with a scam. That I was to meet him here with his bags and the plane tickets."

"God. Oh *God,*" I screamed, world falling away from me, knees buckling, refusing to lock. I grabbed the banisters. "Please." A hard, dry ache writhed about my insides, gripping them hard, leaning on my heart, my guts.

"I'm sure you can tell the police *all* about it."

"Neil?" Laura said, touching my shoulder.

"Get off me!" I bellowed. "Jane. *Jane!*"

"*Neil!*" Laura shouted. "What's . . . what's going on? The *plane.* Forget the money. We'll survive. We have each *other* . . ."

"*Jane* —"

"Neil!"

"Jane please . . . I *love you!*" I said, throat fat and tight. "Jane. Jane please you *have* to believe me."

Laura was at the door, talking. Shouting.

"Jane *please.* For Lana's sake —"

"What?" Jane sniffed, looking up. But not at me. Over my shoulder. Past me. She was looking at Laura. "What did you say?"

"I said he can *keep* the watch. He can keep the watch but I'm going. I'm going now," and Laura turned on her heel, wrenching open the door and marching down the steps into the November afternoon.

"What watch?" Jane said, rubbing her tears with her sleeve.

"I . . . I don't know!" I said. "I don't know what she's talking about. I don't know what *anybody* is —"

"Give it to me," Jane said, swallowing hard and standing, moving down the stairs.

"Poppet, leave him," Edward soothed. "Leave him, it's all over now. *Shhh.*"

But Jane kept coming. Towards me.

Towards *me.*

I hauled myself up, holding out my arms.

"Jane. Jane please . . ."

She pushed past her father, reaching out to me.

"Oh God Jane," I said, tears coming, tears brimming. But no. Jane grabbed my wrist, hard, twisting it, teeth bared.

"Aghh! Jesus!" I yelped, knees buckling as Jane wrestled with the clasps on my chunky wristwatch. "Aghh!"

She tore it from me, spinning away tearfully.

"It's . . . it's just a fake," I said, slumped, wrist stinging. "Christopher . . . It was part of a *trick* . . ."

"A fake?" Jane sniffed. She turned and looked at me, holding the watch out. "Fake? This is . . ."

"Poppet, easy now —"

"This is about five grand's worth of watch. She *give* this to you, did she?"

"No. No, I swear on Lana's life, *no.*"

"On *La* —" and Jane's jaw dropped, winded, stumbling backwards. "You . . . you . . ."

Jane stared at me. She looked back at the watch I'd had on my wrist for two weeks. Warm and sweaty, dotted with blood. She turned it over, twisting it in the hall light to look at it more clearly.

"What?" I said. "*What?*"

"On Lana's *life*, you said," and Jane let go of the watch. It fell, almost in slow motion, tumbling like a gold ribbon, hitting the block wooden floor with a crack.

Jane and her father turned from me, climbing the stairs.

A siren pined somewhere in the distance.

Swallowing hard, weak and shaking, I lifted the watch in trembling fingers, peering at the cracked, syrup-spattered face. Twelve diamonds glinted in the surface.

I turned it over. To where an inscription was.

Where one had always been.

To Neil, it read. *To count down the hours until we are together. Lx.*

I closed my eyes. Tight. Wanting more than I ever wanted anything, to awake somewhere else. At my desk, listening to Dionne Warwick. In my shop, John Williams rumpety-pumping on the stereo.

Next to Jane and Lana in the chill blue cold of our Putney bedroom.

I opened my eyes.

Alone in a Chelsea hall.

In the street I heard the bubbling rev of an engine.

Eyes wet, vision dimpled with tears, I staggered up, turning, toppling out into the cold afternoon.

The cab sat at the kerb, the back window crowded with shadows.

You want to say hello to the guys?

I fell down the front tiled steps and slapped across the pavement.

You ever worship someone? Adore them and not be adored back?

I stumbled towards the black doors.

Your whole world. For three aching, lonely years. It's destroying.

I fell against the metal door. Angry. Angry, confused and tired. So very tired.

"What ho old fruit," Christopher beamed, pumping down the window releasing a sweet plume of pipe smoke. "Hoped you'd come to see us off. No hard feelings."

"What's interesting about the whole procedure of course," the smartly dressed gentleman at Christopher's side piped up, gaily. "What your *Watchdog* and your *Daily Mail*s don't realise is that *innocent* parties are never involved. Oh they like to *suggest* those we catch out are poor *victims*. Poor *me,* they beat their breasts. Why *me*? But it's drivel, of course. I mean imagine the logistics of picking marks at random. Poppycock."

He was a very smartly dressed gentleman.

What my father would call, *well spoken*.

A poofy fellah.

"It'll come out of your shirt by the way," Andrew added. "The syrup. I did always love your shirts. Loved everything about you in fact. Long time ago, of course."

Andrew still had a little syrup on his lips. Some, for some reason, in his hair. I looked down. He had some on his hands too, but then that could have come from Christopher.

What with them holding hands as tight as they were.

"I *told* him," Christopher cooed. "He's a good-looking fellow. His wife? Jane? Buys him lotions and moisturisers. What with that and the gargantuan superhero groins and biceps on his walls. Well, it's no *wonder* Andrew here spent three years hoping you'd . . ."

"Oh don't *embarrass* him," Andrew said.

"Wh . . ." I mouthed, lips dry, head thudding. "Wh . . ."

"Why?" Andrew said. "*Justice, dear boy.* Man's to mete out and man's alone. Who else will even the eternal score? *God?*" and he smiled.

I stepped away from the window, winded. Breathing tight and short.

"Posit *this*. I love you and you don't love me back," Andrew said. "My whole world. For three aching, lonely years. It's destroying. Agreed? Observe the sentencing though. *I* am destroyed, *you* are not. *I* am dejected, *you* are not. Is that fair? Is that *justice?*"

"I . . . I didn't —"

"*My* act was to see beauty in another. To forgive faults and foibles and worship unconditionally. *Yours* to reject this worship. To ignore, to pity and to condescend. But it is *I* who is sentenced to spend the rest of my days alone. Outcast, a hole where my stomach used to be . . ."

"*Hole where your* — ? Oh you do make a *scene*," Christopher sighed, but Andrew pushed on.

"In a world *this* crazy, *someone* must even out the score, don't you think Neil? What was it you said? *Revenge?*"

"Revenge?"

"On he who forced me to grow up? Who stole everything, who turned me into this *corporate machine*."

"Me? You said you were . . . two people . . . Robbed. Two –"

"They *talked* like I knew them. And they took everything. Everything that mattered."

"Shit. Shit no, Andrew please –"

"One Christmas. No remorse. No hesitation."

As he spoke, Andrew reached into his jacket. One by one he removed his notebook, penknife, matches, Zippo, fountain pen and notebook, stacking them on the vinyl seat next to him.

"Turned, just like that. Stripped me. Inside and out. Childlike, thoughtless and selfish. I was just a wreck. Physically. Mentally."

"Please Andrew, you never . . ."

"Changed everything. How could it not? Just so *angry*. Found myself collapsing. Just sitting down on the floor, wherever I was. Shaking. That people could be so . . ."

"Don't," I said. I blinked hot, frightened tears. "Please *don't*. You have to come inside. Explain. Tell Jane . . ."

"Ah, here we go," and he produced a small box. He held it in his hand, turning it slowly. "I've never forgotten," Andrew said. "They've never let me forget. And I'll never stop hating them either."

A siren grew louder over the high Chelsea rooftops.

"That was . . . that was a *lifetime* ago. How can you – ?"

"Yes. *Time*. The greatest get-out clause in the *world*. Now it's me who's in the wrong. Me who's the bad guy. All pity vanished. Suddenly I'm *childish*. Immature. Obsessive. Hung-up. *Move on, man. It was a long-time-ago. Lighten-up, get over it.* You're off. Scot-free, screwing some other poor blighter. Leaving me to sit alone being pitied by my few remaining friends," and he gave Christopher's hand a tight squeeze.

"It's all . . . all been just revenge?"

"Like *you* said, it's a dirty word. But it's what you deserve. The law of the street. Eye for an eye. You have to do it properly though, like I told you."

"Pr-properly?"

"*Painfully.* A long, long life of misery and regret. Live with it. Make them *suffer*."

They both grinned. The engine revved, a tubby Irishman at the wheel. Bullish, stocky.

A whisky barrel in a suit.

I turned back to the house. Up the three tiled steps, at the wide front door, Edward stood, stubby arms folded across his chest. One of his chins up. Defensive. Protective.

I would never see his daughter again.

I would never see my daughter again.

The siren was louder now.

A long, long life of misery and regret.

"Neil, sweetheart?" a voice said, the cab door sliding squeakily from my hands, engine revving again. "Neil? Before we go?"

I turned back. Andrew was looking at me.

Leaning forward.

His hand was swathed in a tight, talcy surgeon's glove.

He held out a small velvet box.

Live with it. Make them suffer.

"Ten years late darling, but you might as well have this now," and Andrew tossed it to me through the small window.

I caught it in cold, shaking hands as the cab pulled away down the wide, quiet street.

Quiet, but for Edward.

Shouting my name.

Over the sound of an approaching siren.

now

"Cheng? Cheng, it's me again . . . No, no I'm still at The Atlas. Been telling my new friend here about the last . . . Has your buyer . . . ? Shit. He's *there* . . . !? But I *asked* you, I *begged you*!? A few hours! I said, hold it for . . ."

Hey, how long have you and I been . . . ? Right, right exactly.

"Cheng? My friend here says it's *only* been . . . but you *promised*! . . . Yes, yes I know, but I need it *back!* I *told* you, Edward and the police are talking about charging me with . . . I understand but I'm *begging* you. Please try and appreciate . . . it's *my* one chance at . . . Then whatever they offer, I'll beat it . . . Yes I know what I said a few hours ago, but why don't you let *me* worry about the how . . . ? Okay. Okay ask him and call me back."

God.
    Sorry, sorry I'm getting . . . It's just he has my one – *barman?* Another drink. And hey – one for my new best friend here?
    Sorry. I didn't mean to . . . I've taken up enough of your –"
    Huh? Happened *when*?
    Well.
    They made me go back inside. The *police*, I mean. To Edward's sitting room. Sat me down. Listened to *Edward's* version of events.
    Jane stayed upstairs with Lana. Away from me.
    Christ, *Jane.*
    Where's the phone, I should . . . Notebook, breath mints . . . I put it down –
    A-*ha*. I should try her again. Try and explain . . .
    Jane Jane Jane . . .
    It's ringing.

Listen, thanks for . . . well, for listening. I didn't mean to –

"Hello, hello Jane, I – ? Edward *please*. Don't hang up. Let me talk to . . . I wouldn't, I didn't, I *love* her! It was all . . . I can *prove* it, please, just tell her to *hold on*. I'm waiting for . . . hello? Edward, are you – ? Edward?"

Shit.

I don't know what I'm going to do if Cheng doesn't –

Ahh, drinks. Drinks, thanks so much. Cheers.

S-Sorry, let me clear some . . . put all this stuff . . . letters . . . matches, my Zippo . . . there we go.

God. Now I only hope I can trust Cheng. I mean who'd . . . who'd have *thought* it? That *first day* in halls. Unpacking. Putting up posters.

When Benno helped me tack it to the wall.

God, maybe that was it? How it started? Maybe he thought *that* was something it wasn't? First day and everything. And then the chess? The chats?

The Christmas ball . . .

It's here somewhere, the velvet . . . let me –

God, this syrup's dried on all the . . . Urgh, my cigarettes, fountain pen, it's all . . . *here*. Here you go.

See? A little velvet box. Take a look. Go on, it's . . .

Pretty huh? Eternity ring, I think they're called. He's engraved our names on it, There.

Andrew and Neil.

Proof? Of – ?

Not according to the police, no.

Not compared to Edward's: the watch, the letters, my passport, the shop valuation, the Sotheby's letters, the bank transfer numbers. And the police are all, *yes your dukeness* and *absolutely your worshipful highness*.

Whereas *my* version of events? Well, they wanted *that* at the station.

So that's where I've been. *Explaining*. Or *trying* to. Showed them the *ring*, but no. No good. No proof. No *evidence*. Nothing to back up my story.

They didn't *take* anything, see? Andrew, Christopher? Didn't take a *thing*.

Apart from my whole life, that is.

But anyway, the police have got nothing they can detain me for, so they've let me go. Held on to my passport of course. *Pending further enquiries*.

Came here? No no no, not straight away. I went over to the shop first.

I-I don't *know*, really. One last look? Before it's . . .

Sorry, sorry I'm just . . .

Tell you what, though. At the shop? Just now? Bumped into Schwartz.

Schwartz? The guy − ?

Right. Next door. *Brigstock Books.* Your memory's better than his, I tell you.

Which . . . which is why it never *sat right*. Last week. That he would have remembered Andrew from years ago. Some property development.

Well, answer is he *didn't* of course.

No, I asked him. He remembered Andrew from when he actually met him. *Six weeks ago.* A young, corporate estate agent with a smart blue letterhead offering free valuations. Well, you would, wouldn't you?

A free valuation plus, naturally, a structural survey.

Especially if it included basements, adjoining doors and −

Right. Plumbing work.

I *know.*

So what I'm *hoping*, what my whole family's future is *banking* on is testimony from Schwartz plus . . .

Well, this is awkward.

I know you and I don't really . . .

No. No, forget it. I can't. Forget it. I've chewed your ear off enough, I'm sorry, I'm sorry.

Cheers. Here's to −

Sorry, this syrup is still a bit . . .

Here's to you. One of the good guys. Let's pray that *you* never meet some tall-tale-telling grifter. With some story. Asking you his three *yes* questions. Whatever they are. Look out for *that*.

That the pop list? I'm going to take my jacket off if that's all right with you? Neato diner huh?

Needing help. Giving you an opportunity. Promising repayment. And then −

Shit, that's . . .

"Hello? Hello Cheng? Have you still . . . ? Oh thank the lord. Thank the *Lord*! You don't know how much this . . . And it's still in bubble wrap? It's *very important* you haven't . . . Okay. And how much is your buyer . . . *What*? No. No *way*? I can't . . . Please, be reasonable, there's no way I can . . . Wait, wh-what about a deposit? I could scrape together a small . . . Well, I . . . I don't know, hold on −

Sorry, sorry, shit I need to add up what I've −

Whoopsie, what have we got . . . Here we go, breath mints, matches, Zippo, Bic, pen knife, cigarettes, notebook . . . Here, ten, twenty, twenty-five, twenty-five fifty, twenty-five seventy . . .

Fuck.

"Mr Cheng, look, I-I'm a little . . . I mean I just can't . . . Jesus, Mr Cheng, please. This is my only hope! My wife, my *family*! You have to − Mr Cheng? I . . ."

Oh *God*.

God I . . . That was my one . . .

See, they . . . they *touched* it, remember?

They −

You remember the fake policemen? In my shop? Manc and Scot? They took away my till? You remember? I −

Right. And they took away my till because I told them it was the *only* fingerprints I had of the team? It never even . . . I mean it didn't *dawn* on me until . . . well, until later. A few hours ago. Outside Edward's house. Before the police arrived. When I saw Andrew and Christopher in the cab together. Off into the sunset. Like Redford and Newman.

Redford and Newman.

See I'd made them all *touch* it . . .

The poster. *The Sting*. During my *lecture*. Made them all take off their gloves and feel the ink. The autographs.

Touch it. Prints. Fingerprints. Identification. *All* of them. The poster Andrew helped me put on my wall all those years ago. His prints too.

Preserved on linen-backed paper behind glass.

Every fucking *one* of them.

But Cheng . . .

Well, you heard. A buyer.

So that's . . . I guess that's that.

That's that.

Cheers. Cheers, old friend.

Huh? How much? What, to get the poster back?

Too much.

Too, too much.

Unless . . .

No. No forget it.

I mean I wouldn't dream of *asking*, you know. Especially here.

I mean personally, I don't know about you, I do find public places more private, but hell, we just met, right?

I mean, don't get me wrong. I feel that we're *friends* now.

Don't y*ou*? We're close, you and I.

And that's unusual for me, I can tell you. *Friends,* I've always said, is just an American televisual programme. Merely enemies who haven't found you out yet. In life, as in diarrhoea, we are alone. But you and I . . . ?

And see I wouldn't normally ask but –

But see, if I can get the poster from Cheng and over to the police, then they can lift the prints and that'd clear my name. With them. With Edward. With Jane.

Call it the persuasive power of print. Talk is one thing of course, but I'd be giving them something solid. Proof. That they can hold, they can smell and touch. There in black and white. Ask yourself why Catholics travel thousands of miles to glimpse the Shroud of Turin?

I'm going to be straight with you, this . . . this is my *only* chance.

To get back my *wife*. My beautiful wife. Get back my daughter. My *family*. Get everything back to normal.

Once *that's* done I'd be in a position to, y'know, repay anyone who . . .

No. No, forget it. I can see you're –

From your *expression*. How did the great man put it?

'Oh God, how loathsome this is! Could I really? No, it's nonsensical! It's absurd. Could I really ever have contemplated such a monstrous act? It shows what filth my head is capable of though. Filthy. Mean. Vile. VILE!'

I understand, I do.

But it's just . . .

See I don't know much, but I know something about *people*. People like you.

I know that people with thriving businesses, savings tucked away and a bank manager they play golf with, tend not, by and large, to share drinks with peculiar behaving men in Earl's Court pubs. That's more the behaviour of the desperate, wouldn't you say? More the behaviour of someone in need of a quick fix. A one-off, chance of a lifetime deal, that'll get them out of any unfortunate hole they've stumbled into.

So all I'm saying is, I'd make it worth your while. Pay you back double. Triple.

Anything you might be able to –

I mean, just for a deposit. A few quid. Whatever you've . . .

Or a few *hundred* quid even? Whatever you can get your hands on. Why don't we take a walk to your bank now? You get the money, I do the deal. And then once I'm all square, I'll pay you back triple.

Easy money.

It'd . . . it'd really be helping me out.

C'mon, you can *trust* me.

What do you say, hmm? What do you say? You onboard?

What do you say?